PRAISE FOR *BRIDGE TO HAVEN*

"This is another compelling and moving story by one of the genre's most honored and talented writers."

LIBRARY JOURNAL, STARRED REVIEW

"Rivers returns with a page-turning recasting of the story of the prodigal son, here a prodigal daughter. . . . This story arc will be particularly resonant for Christian readers, but Rivers has the writing ability to reel in others who enjoy a well-told tale of redemption."

PUBLISHERS WEEKLY

"In Rivers's exquisite style, she takes the biblical story of Ezekiel 16 and translates it into a character-driven tale. . . . Richly detailed, at times disturbing, but completely real and dynamic, this is a book to savor."

ROMANTIC TIMES

"Longtime fans of Francine Rivers will not be disappointed in this painful, moving, and triumphant tale of redemption. For those who have not yet given this bestselling legend-of-an-author a try, I highly recommend *Bridge to Haven*."

SERENA CHASE, *USA TODAY*

"*Bridge to Haven* is a wonderful and real coming-of-age story from the 1950s, when Hollywood was the dream and life could be a harsh reality."

CBA RETAILERS+RESOURCES

"It is obvious why [Rivers] is a bestselling author, as she knows her craft so well. . . . Even though the book was set in 1950s America, the themes are universal and timeless."

CHRISTIAN TODAY

"*Bridge to Haven* is a beautifully breathtaking and instantly captivating journey filled with heartbreak, despair, hope, and love. . . . What an amazing story!"
RADIANT LIT

"Rivers's work is always dramatic and holds an underlying thread of redemption throughout. *Bridge to Haven* is replete with this theme of unconditional love meets temptation, trial, and failure. The story speaks volumes about the difficulties of life and how faith, hope, and love can indeed win out."
BOOKREPORTER.COM

"Francine Rivers is perhaps the best novelist of our time. In *Bridge to Haven*, she quickly captured me with her characters and pulled me into the story of this prodigal daughter. It's a story you can't forget."
NOVEL ROCKET

"Francine Rivers shows once again why she is a must-read author in Christian fiction."
FRESH FICTION

"With exceptional characters and fantastic storytelling, *Bridge to Haven* is a gorgeous story of unfailing love and redemption."
THE CHRISTIAN MANIFESTO

BRIDGE
TO HAVEN

FRANCINE
RIVERS

Tyndale House Publishers, Inc., Carol Stream, Illinois

Visit Tyndale online at www.tyndale.com.

Check out the latest about Francine Rivers at www.francinerivers.com.

TYNDALE and Tyndale's quill logo are registered trademarks of Tyndale House Publishers, Inc.

Bridge to Haven

Designed by Jennifer Ghionzoli

Edited by Kathryn S. Olson

Published in association with the literary agency of Browne & Miller Literary Associates, LLC, 410 Michigan Avenue, Suite 460, Chicago, IL 60605.

Unless otherwise indicated, all Scripture quotations are taken from the *Holy Bible*, New Living Translation, copyright © 1996, 2004, 2007, 2013 by Tyndale House Foundation. Used by permission of Tyndale House Publishers, Inc., Carol Stream, Illinois 60188. All rights reserved.

Scripture quotations in chapters 3, 5, 11, and 16 are taken from the *Holy Bible*, King James Version.

Library of Congress Cataloging-in-Publication Data

Rivers, Francine, date.
  Bridge to haven / Francine Rivers.
    pages cm.
  ISBN 978-1-4143-6818-4 (hc)
1. Abandoned children—Fiction. 2. Actresses—Fiction. 3. Alienation (Philosophy)—Fiction.
I. Title.
  PS3568.I83165B75 2014
  813'.54—dc23   2013040115

ISBN 978-1-4143-9139-7 (International Trade Paper Edition)
ISBN 978-1-4143-6819-1 (sc)

Printed in the United States of America

22
8

TO MY SONS & GRANDSONS

Trevor, Travis, Rich, Brendan, William & Logan

ACKNOWLEDGMENTS

OVER THE YEARS, many people have supported and influenced my writing. My husband, Rick, has always been at the top of the list. He encouraged me to start writing in the first place and then insisted I take that manuscript off the closet shelf and submit it. He urged me to quit working, be a stay-at-home mom, and pursue a writing career. Our children, all now adults with children of their own, also encourage me. Our daughter, Shannon, posts my blogs, sends me reminders on what's needed, and keeps an eye on the website mail.

My agent, Danielle Egan-Miller, and her associate, Joanna MacKenzie, take care of the business side of my career, freeing me to concentrate on whatever project I've started. I trust them implicitly and am thankful for the time they spend pursuing new arenas of publication: foreign, domestic, cyberspace. Whatever success I have is largely due to their hard work.

I have been blessed to work with the same publisher, Tyndale House, for over twenty years. Getting a book out has always been a team effort from executives to editors, cover designers to marketing experts and Facebook maven, and all the warehousemen. I am thankful to each who takes part in moving my book from flash drive (or e-mail files) to the printed page and out to stores in our hometowns or online. I want to especially thank Mark Taylor and Ron Beers, who have been strong supporters and good friends from the beginning of my launch into the world of Christian publishing. They've been there from the get-go, cheering me on. Another special friend is Karen Watson, who has always asked the right questions to get me thinking deeper and sometimes send me in a new direction. My editor, Kathy Olson, is a blessing. She knows what to cut and when to add. She sees the big picture as well as the small details. I always look forward to working with her. Thanks also to Stephanie Broene for her input, particularly on the discussion questions, and to Erin Smith for checking my historical facts and helping me with my Facebook author page.

Numerous friends have come alongside me and prayed me through the writing process, especially during dark times when I wonder why I ever thought I could write anything that would make sense to anyone. Colleen Phillips is my kindred spirit in Chile. Our Tuesday evening Bible study family members are mighty prayer warriors. When I need help, I put out the call to my brilliant Coeur d'Alene brainstorming buddies, who love the Lord wholeheartedly, sing like angels, write like prophets, and crack jokes like class-act comediennes. I can't wait for our pray, plot, and play retreat each year.

Those I've named here and so many more unmentioned have all enriched my life beyond measure. May the Lord continue to pour blessings upon each and every one.

CHAPTER I

Yes, you have been with me from birth;
from my mother's womb you have cared for me.

PSALM 71:6

1936

Filling his lungs with cool October air, Pastor Ezekiel Freeman started his morning vigil. He had laid out the route on a map when he first came to town. Each building brought people to mind, and he upheld them before the Lord, giving thanks for trials they had come through, praying over trials they now faced, and asking God what part he might play in helping them.

He headed for Thomas Jefferson High School. He passed by Eddie's Diner, the students' favorite hangout place. The lights were on inside. Eddie came to the front door. "Mornin', Zeke. How about a cup of coffee?"

Zeke sat at the counter while Eddie made stacks of hamburger patties. They talked high school football, and who might win a scholarship. Zeke thanked Eddie for the coffee and conversation and headed out into the dark again.

He crossed Main Street and walked down to the railroad tracks toward Hobo Junction. He could see a campfire and approached the men sitting around it, asking if they minded if he joined them. Several had been around town long enough to have met Zeke before. Others were strangers, men who looked tired and worn from crisscrossing the country, picking up odd jobs along the way, living hand to mouth. One young man said he liked the feel of the town and hoped to stay. Zeke told him the lumberyard north of town was looking for a loader. He gave the young man a card with his name and the church's address and phone number. "Stop by anytime. I'd like to hear how you're doing."

The crickets in the tall grass and the hoot owl in a towering pine fell silent as a car pulled into Riverfront Park, stopping near the restrooms. A young woman got out of the driver's seat. The full moon gave her enough light to see where she was going.

Groaning in pain, she bent and put her hand over her swollen belly. The contractions were coming swiftly now, not even a minute between. She needed shelter, some hidden place to give birth. She stumbled through the darkness to the ladies' room, but the door wouldn't budge. Uttering a strangled sob, she turned away, searching.

Why had she driven so far? Why hadn't she checked into a motel? Now it was too late.

The town square was next on Zeke's route. He prayed for each of the shopkeepers, the council members who had a meeting in the afternoon at the town hall, and the travelers staying at the Haven Hotel. It was still dark when he walked along Second Street and spotted Leland Dutcher's produce truck turning at the mouth of the alley alongside Gruening's Market. Everyone called him Dutch, including his wife, who was in the hospital, suffering through the last stages of cancer. Zeke had sat with her several times and knew she grieved more about her husband's lack of faith than her approaching death. "I know where I'm going. I'm more worried about where Dutch will end up." The man worked six days a week and saw no need to spend the seventh in church. In truth, he was mad at God and didn't want to give Him the time of day.

The truck's brakes squealed briefly as it stopped. Dutch rolled down his window. "Cold morning to be gadding about the streets, Pastor. Have a girlfriend tucked away somewhere?"

Ignoring the sarcasm, Zeke pushed his cold hands into his pockets. "This is the best time to pray."

"Well, hellfire and hallelujah, don't let me stop you from doing your business." He barked a hard laugh.

Zeke came closer. "I saw Sharon yesterday."

Dutch let out his breath. "Then you know she's not doing too well."

"No. She's not." Unless there was a miracle, she didn't have much time left. She would rest easier if she weren't so worried about her husband, but saying so right now would only make Dutch more belligerent.

"Go ahead, Pastor. Invite me to church."

"You already know the invitation is always open."

Dutch wilted slightly. "She's been after me for years. Right now, all I feel like doing is spitting in God's face. She's a good woman, the best I've ever known. If anyone deserves a miracle, Sharon does. Tell me what help God is giving her?"

"Her body will die, Dutch, but Sharon won't." He saw the flicker of pain and knew the man wasn't ready to listen to more. "Want help unloading the truck?"

"Thanks, but I think I can manage on my own." Dutch ground the gears, uttered a vile word, and drove down the alley.

―――――

The child came in a rush of slick warmth, spilling from her body, and the young woman gasped in relief. The iron, clawing embrace was gone, leaving her time to catch her breath. Panting in the shadows beneath the bridge, she looked up between the steel supports to the star-studded sky.

The baby lay pale and perfect in the moonlight, on a dark blanket of earth. It was too dark to see whether it was a boy or girl, but then, what did that matter?

Body feverish, the young woman struggled out of her thin sweater and laid it over the infant.

―――――

A cold breeze was blowing in. Zeke pulled up the collar of his jacket. He walked along Mason, across First and down McMurray, back up Second, toward Good Samaritan Hospital. The bridge came to mind, but it was in the other direction. During summer months, he often crossed over to Riverfront Park, especially when the camp was full of visitors living in pitched tents at the small adjacent campground.

No one would be in the campground this time of year, with temperatures dropping and leaves falling.

The darkness was loosening, though it would still be a while before the sun rose. He should be turning for home, but the bridge loomed in his mind. Zeke changed direction and headed for the bridge and Riverfront Park.

He blew into his hands. He should have worn gloves this morning. He stopped at the corner, debating whether to go to the bridge or make his way home. He always showered and shaved before sitting down to breakfast with Marianne and Joshua. Going to the bridge now would mean he'd get home late.

He felt a sense of urgency. Someone needed help. It would only take ten minutes to walk to the bridge, less if he quickened his pace. He wouldn't have any peace unless he did.

———————

Shivering violently, the young woman rolled up her car window, knowing she would never be free of guilt and regret. Her hand shook as she turned the key she had left in the ignition. She just wanted to get away from this place. She wanted to cover her head and forget everything that had happened, everything she had done wrong.

Turning the steering wheel, she pressed down too hard on the gas. The car skidded to one side, sending a rush of adrenaline through her. She corrected quickly, as the wheels shot pebbles like bullets into the park. Slowing, she turned right, toward the main road, staring ahead through tear-blurred eyes. She'd go north and find a cheap motel. Then she'd decide how to kill herself.

The breeze moved down over the sandy beach and beneath the bridge. No longer in the protected warmth of a mother's womb, the abandoned baby felt the stinging cold of the world. A soft cry came, then a plaintive wail. The sound carried across the water, but no lights went on in the houses above the river.

———————

The steel Pratt trusses rose above the trees. Zeke crossed the old river road and took the walkway over the bridge. He stopped halfway across and leaned on the railing. The river rippled beneath him. It had rained a few days ago, leaving the beach smooth and packed. The place was deserted.

Why am I here, Lord?

Zeke straightened, still troubled. He waited another moment and then turned away. Time to head home.

A soft mewling mingled with the sounds of the river. What was it? Holding the rail, he leaned over, peering into the shadows of the abutment. The sound came again. He walked quickly across the bridge and cut across the grassy knoll to the parking lot. Was it a kitten? People often dumped unwanted litters along the road.

He heard the sound again, and this time he recognized it. Joshua had sounded like that when he was an infant. *A baby, here?* He searched the shadows, heart pounding. He spotted footprints. He went down to the riverbank and followed them across the sand to the gravel beneath the bridge. Pebbles crunched under his feet.

He heard it again, weaker this time, but so close he looked carefully before he stepped. Frowning, he hunkered down and picked up what looked like a discarded sweater. "Oh, Lord . . ." A baby lay so still, so small, so white, he wondered if he was too late. A girl. He slipped his hands beneath her. She weighed next to nothing. As he lifted her into the curve of his arm, her arms spread like a tiny bird attempting flight, and she let out a tremulous cry.

Surging to his feet, Zeke yanked open his jacket, popping shirt buttons so he could tuck the baby against his skin. He breathed on her face to warm her up. "Scream, sweetheart; scream as loud as you can. You hold on to life, now. You hear?"

Zeke knew every shortcut and was at Good Samaritan Hospital before the sun came up.

Zeke came back to the hospital in the middle of the day to see Sharon. Dutch was with her, looking grim and worn. He held his wife's frail hand between his and didn't speak. Zeke spoke to both of them. When Sharon held out her hand, he took it and prayed for her and for Dutch.

He couldn't leave without going back to the nursery. He shouldn't have been surprised to see Marianne standing outside the window, her arm around five-year-old Joshua. He felt tenderness and pride well up inside him. Their son was all gangly arms, long skinny legs with knobby knees and big feet.

Joshua put his hands on the glass. "She's so little, Daddy. Was I that little?" The tiny baby girl slept soundly in a small hospital bassinet.

"No, Son. You were a whopping nine pounds." The look on Marianne's face concerned him. He took her hand. "We should head home, honey."

"Thank God you found her, Zeke. What would have happened to her if you hadn't?" Marianne looked at him. "We should adopt her."

"You know we can't. They'll find someone to take her." He tried to lead her away.

Marianne wouldn't budge. "Who better than us?"

Joshua joined in. "You found her, Daddy. Finders, keepers."

"She's not a penny I found on a sidewalk, Son. She needs a family."

"We're a family."

"You know what I mean." He cupped Marianne's cheek. "You've forgotten what it was like to take care of a new baby."

"I'm up to it, Zeke. I know I am. Why shouldn't she be ours?" She drew back. "Please don't look at me like that. I'm stronger than you think." Her eyes filled before she turned. "Just look at her. Doesn't she break your heart?"

He did look, and his heart softened. But he had to be practical. "We should go."

Marianne squeezed his hand. "Pure, genuine religion in the sight of God is shown by caring for widows *and orphans*."

"Don't use Scripture against me when it's you I'm trying to protect."

Joshua looked up. "Protect from what, Daddy?"

"Nothing." Marianne gave Zeke a quelling glance. "It's just an idea your daddy got into his head a long time ago. He'll get over it. God put her in your arms, Zeke. Don't tell me He didn't." Marianne looked at him with doe eyes. "We have our boy. A little girl would make everything perfect. Haven't I said so?"

She had. Marianne had always yearned for more children, but the doctor had warned them that her heart, damaged by childhood rheumatic fever, wasn't strong enough to survive another pregnancy.

Zeke felt his resolve dissolving. "Marianne. Please. Stop." It had taken months for her to recover after Joshua's birth. Caring for another newborn would be far too taxing for her.

"We can be foster parents. Let's bring her home as soon as we can. If it's too much, then . . ." Her eyes grew moist. "Please, Zeke."

Ten days later, Dr. Rubenstein signed the release forms for little Jane Doe and placed her in Marianne's arms. "You'll make fine foster parents."

After the first three nights, Zeke started to worry. Marianne was up every two hours, feeding the baby. How long before her health suffered? Though she looked exhausted, she couldn't have been happier. Sitting in a rocking chair, Marianne cradled the baby in her arms and fed her a bottle of warm milk. "She needs a real name, Zeke. A name full of promise and hope."

"Abra means 'mother of nations.'" He said it before he could stop himself.

Marianne laughed. "You wanted her all along, didn't you? Don't pretend you didn't."

How could he not? Still, he felt a jab of fear. "We're foster parents, Marianne. Don't forget that. If things become too much for you, we'll call the caseworker. We'll have to give Abra back."

"Give her back to whom? The caseworker wants this to work. And I don't think there's anyone in town who'd take Abra away from us now. Do you?" Peter Matthews, a teacher at the local elementary school, and his wife, Priscilla, had expressed interest early on, but with an infant of their own, they had agreed Abra should stay with the Freemans if they were able to handle it.

Marianne set the empty bottle aside and raised the baby to her shoulder. "We'll need to save money so we can add another bedroom. Abra won't be a baby for long. She'll be in a crib, then a regular bed. She'll need a room of her own."

There was no reasoning with her. All of Marianne's motherly instincts had kicked in, but each day wore her down a little more. Catnapping throughout the day helped, but catching a few minutes of sleep here and there wouldn't be enough to keep her healthy. She was already tousle-haired and ashen, with dark circles under her eyes. "You sleep in tomorrow morning. I'll take her with me."

"In the dark?"

"Plenty of streetlights, and I know the town like the back of my hand."

"She'll be cold."

"I'll bundle her up." He folded a blanket into a triangle, plucked Abra from Marianne's arms, tied it around his waist and neck, and straightened. "See? She's snug as a bug in a rug." And right next to his heart, where she'd been from the first moment he laid eyes on her.

Sometimes Abra fussed when he took her out for his early morning walks, and he would sing hymns to her. "'I come to the garden alone, while the dew is still on the roses . . .'" She'd sleep for a while, and stir when Zeke stopped in at Eddie's Diner or paused to talk with Dutch.

"Good of you to take on that little one. Isn't she a cutie, with all that red hair." Eddie ran a fingertip over Abra's cheek.

Even hard-hearted Dutch smiled as he leaned out the window of his truck to peer at her. "Looks like a little angel." He drew back. "Sharon and I always wanted kids." He said it like it was another black mark against God. Sharon had passed away, and Zeke knew the man was grieving. When Abra's tiny fingers grasped Dutch's pinkie, he looked ready to cry. "Who'd leave a baby under a bridge, for heaven's sake? Good thing you happened by."

"It was no accident, me going there that morning."

"How so?" Dutch's engine rumbled in neutral.

"I felt impelled to go. God does that sometimes."

Dutch looked pained. "Well, I won't speculate. No question that little girl needed someone that morning or she'd be dead and buried by now." Like Sharon, his eyes said.

"If you ever want to talk, Dutch, just call."

"Better just give up on me."

"Sharon didn't. Why should I?"

As Abra grew, she slept longer between feedings, and Marianne got more sleep. Even so, Zeke didn't give up carrying Abra on his walks. "I'll keep at it until she sleeps through the night." Getting up every morning before the alarm, he'd dress and peek into the children's bedroom and find Abra wide-awake, waiting for him.

———

1941

Even the demands of an easy child could wear on someone, and Zeke saw the toll on Marianne.

When he came home one afternoon in June and found Marianne asleep on the couch while Abra, now four years old, dunked her doll up and down in the toilet bowl, he knew things were going to have to change. "You're exhausted."

"Abra can get into something faster than I can say, 'Jack Sprat could eat no fat.'"

"You can't go on like this, Marianne."

Others in the congregation noticed how tired Marianne looked and voiced concern. Priscilla Matthews spoke to them one Sunday after services. Her husband had put up gates so their four-year-old, Penny, couldn't escape the living room. "The whole room is one big playpen right now, Marianne. I gave up and packed away everything breakable. Why don't you have Zeke bring Abra over a couple afternoons a week? You can rest without worry or interruptions for a few hours."

Marianne resisted, but Zeke insisted it was a perfect solution.

———

Zeke bought lumber, nails, tar paper, and shingles and started work on a bedroom off the back of the house. Nine-year-old Joshua sat on the boards, holding them steady while Zeke sawed. One of the parishioners added wiring for electricity. Another built a platform bed with pullout drawers and helped Zeke put in windows overlooking the backyard.

Though Zeke was less than enthusiastic about his son moving into a narrow, converted-back-porch bedroom, Joshua loved his "fort." His best buddy, Davy Upton, came over to spend the night, but the quarters were so tight, Zeke ended up pitching a tent for them on the back lawn. When he came back inside, he slumped into his easy chair. "The fort is too small."

Marianne smiled, Abra tucked close beside her in the easy chair, a book of Bible stories open. "I don't hear Joshua complaining. Those boys sound happy as crows in a cornfield, Zeke."

"For now." If Joshua took after his father, and his uncles back in Iowa, he would outgrow the space before he reached high school.

Zeke turned on the radio and went through the mail. The radio had nothing but bad news. Hitler grew ever more ambitious. The insatiable führer continued sending planes west across the English Channel to bomb England while his troops stormed Russia's borders to the east. Charles Lydickson, the town banker, said it was only a matter of time before America got involved. The Atlantic Ocean wasn't any protection with all those roaming German U-boats eager to sink ships.

Zeke thanked God Joshua was only nine years old, and then felt guilty, knowing how many other fathers had sons who might soon be going off to war.

When Marianne finished reading the story of David and Goliath, she pressed Abra closer. The child was half-asleep, and Marianne looked too weary to rise. When she tried, Zeke came out of his seat. "Let me tuck her in tonight." He lifted Abra away from Marianne's side. The child melted against him, her head on his shoulder, her thumb in her mouth.

Pulling the covers up and snuggling them around her, he bowed his head. She made prayer hands, and he put his around hers. "Our Father, who art in heaven . . ." When they finished, he leaned down and kissed her. "Sleep tight."

Before he could raise his head, she wrapped her arms around his neck. "I love you, Daddy." He said he loved her, too. He kissed each cheek and her forehead before he left the room.

Marianne looked wilted. He frowned. She shook her head, smiling faintly. "I'm fine, Zeke. Just tired. There's nothing wrong with me that a good night's sleep won't cure."

Zeke knew that wasn't true when she started to rise and swayed slightly. He caught her up in his arms and carried her into their bedroom, then sat on the bed with her in his lap. "I'm calling the doctor."

"You know what he'll say." She started to cry.

"We need to start making other plans." He didn't have the heart to say it any other way, but she knew what he meant.

"I'm not giving up Abra."

"Marianne . . ."

"She needs me."

"*I* need you."

"You love her as much as I do, Zeke. How can you even think about giving her away?"

"We should never have brought her home."

Zeke rocked his wife for a moment, then helped her remove her chenille robe and settled her in bed. He kissed her and turned out the light before closing the door.

He almost tripped over Abra, sitting cross-legged in the hallway, her teddy bear clutched against her chest, thumb in her mouth. He felt a jolt of misgiving. How much had she overheard?

He lifted her into his arms. "You're supposed to be in bed, little one." Tucking her in again, Zeke tapped her on the nose. "Stay under the covers this time." He kissed her. "Go to sleep."

Sinking into his chair in the living room, he put his head in his hands. *Did I misunderstand, Lord? Did I allow Marianne to sway me when You had another plan for Abra? You know how much I love them both. What do I do now, Lord? God, what do I do now?*

Abra sat shivering in the front pew while Mommy practiced hymns at the piano, even though Daddy had turned on the furnace so the sanctuary would be warm for tomorrow's service. Miss Mitzi said without the heater up and running properly, "the church smelled damp and moldy as a graveyard." Abra told her she didn't know what a graveyard smelled like, and Miss Mitzi said, "Well, don't look at me like that, missy. Only way I'll go is if I'm carried there in a pine box."

Rain pelted the roof and windows. Daddy was going over sermon notes in the small office off the narthex. Joshua had gone off in his Boy Scouts uniform to sell Christmas trees on the town square. Christmas was less than three weeks away. Mommy had let Abra help make gingerbread cookies for shut-ins and set up the crèche on the mantel. Daddy and Joshua put up lights around the outside of the house. Abra liked going out the front gate after dinner and looking at the house all lit up.

Mommy closed the hymnal, set it aside, and stood. "All right, honey. Your turn to practice." Abra hopped off the pew and flew up the steps to the piano bench. Mommy half lifted her and then let go, stepping aside to rest her hand heavily on the piano, the other hand against her chest. She panted a moment, then smiled encouragement and set a beginners book on the stand. "Play your scales first and then 'Silent Night.' Can you do that?"

Usually Mommy stood right next to her. Except when she didn't feel good.

Abra loved to play the piano. It was her favorite thing to do. She played scales and chords, though it was hard to reach all the notes at once. She practiced "Silent Night," "O Little Town of Bethlehem," and "Away in a Manger." Every time she finished one, Mommy said she was doing so well and Abra felt warm inside.

Daddy came into the sanctuary. "I think it's time to go home." He put an arm around Mommy and drew her to her feet. Disappointed, Abra closed the lid on the piano and followed them out to the car. Mommy apologized for being so tired, and Daddy said she'd be fine, just fine, with a few hours' rest.

Mommy protested when Daddy carried her into the house. He sat with her in their bedroom for a few minutes. Then he came out to the living room. "Play quietly, Abra, and let Marianne sleep awhile." As soon as Daddy went back out to the car, Abra went into Mommy and Daddy's bedroom and climbed up on the bed.

"That's my girl," Mommy said and snuggled her close.

"Are you sick again?"

"Shhh. I'm not sick. Just tired is all." She fell asleep, and Abra stayed with her until she heard the car out front. She slipped off the bed and ran into the living room to peer out the front window. Daddy was untying a Christmas tree from the top of the old gray Plymouth.

Squealing with excitement, Abra threw open the front door and ran down the steps. Hopping up and down, she clapped her hands. "It's so big."

Joshua came in the back door, his cheeks flushed from the cold, but eyes bright. Christmas tree sales had gone well. If the troop raised enough money this year, everyone could go to Camp Dimond-O near Yosemite. If not, Joshua had already talked to the Weirs and McKennas, neighbors down the street, about hiring him to mow their lawns. "They agreed to pay me fifty cents a week. Times two, that's four dollars a month!" It sounded like a lot of money. "I'll have enough saved to pay for camp myself."

After dinner, Mommy insisted on doing the dishes and told Daddy to go ahead and open the box of ornaments and get started on the tree. Daddy untangled and strung the lights on the tree. He turned them on before he started unwrapping ornaments and handing them over one by one for Joshua and Abra to hang. "You take care of the top branches, Son, and leave the bottom half to Abra."

Something crashed in the kitchen. Startled, Abra dropped a glass ornament as Daddy surged to his feet and bolted for the kitchen. "Marianne? Are you all right?"

Shaking, Abra stooped to pick up the pieces of the ornament she'd broken, but Joshua moved her aside. "Careful. Let me do it. You might cut yourself." When she burst into tears, he pulled her close. "It's okay. Don't cry."

Abra clung to him, her heart thumping fast and hard as she listened to Mommy and Daddy arguing. They were trying to talk quietly, but Abra could still hear them. She heard sweeping and something being dumped in the trash under the sink. The door swung open and Mommy appeared, her smile dying. "What's the matter?"

"She broke an ornament."

Daddy picked Abra up. "Did you cut yourself?" She shook her head. Daddy patted her bottom. "Then there's no reason to be upset." He gave her a quick hug and set her on her feet again. "You two finish decorating the tree while I get a fire going."

Mommy turned on the radio and found a music program. Settling into her easy chair, she pulled some knitting from her basket. Abra climbed into the chair with her. Mommy kissed the top of her head. "Don't you want to put some more ornaments on the tree?"

"I want to sit with you."

Daddy glanced over his shoulder as he arranged kindling. His expression was grim.

———

Sunday was cold, but the rains had stopped. Couples gathered inside the fellowship hall with their children, herding them off to Sunday school classes before going over to the sanctuary for "big church." Abra spotted Penny Matthews and ran ahead of Mommy. When Abra reached her, they held hands and went off to their class.

After Sunday school, Mrs. Matthews came and got Penny. Mommy helped Miss Mitzi wash and dry cookie plates. Daddy talked with the last stragglers. After everyone left, the family went into the sanctuary. Mommy straightened up the hymnals, gathered discarded bulletins. Daddy put away the shiny brass candlesticks and offering plates. Abra sat on the piano bench, swinging her legs and playing chords.

The church door banged open, and a man ran in. Mommy straightened, a hand pressed against her chest. "Clyde Eisenhower, what on earth? You scared me half to death."

The man looked flushed and upset. "The Japanese bombed one of our Naval bases in Hawaii!"

As soon as they got home, Daddy turned on the radio. He took off his suit jacket and hung it on the back of a kitchen chair rather than put it away in the bedroom closet the way he usually did. *". . . the Japanese have attacked Pearl Harbor, Hawaii, by air, President Roosevelt has just announced. The attack also was made on all Naval and military activities on the principal island of Oahu. . . ."* The voice on the radio sounded upset.

Mommy sank onto a kitchen chair. Daddy closed his eyes and bowed his head. "I knew it was coming."

Mommy helped Abra onto her lap and sat silent, listening to the voice that just kept talking and talking about bombings and sinking ships and men burning to death. Mommy started to cry, and that made Abra cry. Mommy held her closer and rocked her in her arms. "It's all right, honey. It's all right."

But Abra knew it wasn't.

Miss Mitzi opened the door with a flourish. "Well, if it isn't my favorite little girl!" She whipped her shawl over her shoulder and held her arms wide. Giggling, Abra hugged her. "How long do I get to keep you this time?"

"As long as you like," Mommy said, following them into the living room.

Abra liked spending time with Miss Mitzi. She had knickknacks all over the living room and didn't mind if Abra picked them up and looked at them. Sometimes, she made coffee and even filled a teacup for Abra, letting her pour in cream and as much sugar as she wanted.

Mitzi looked concerned. "You look awfully tired, Marianne."

"I'm going to go home and take a nice long nap."

"You do that, dear." Mitzi kissed her cheek. "Don't push yourself so hard."

Mommy leaned down and gave Abra a hug. She kissed her on each cheek and ran her hand over her head as she straightened. "Be good for Mitzi, honey."

Mitzi lifted her chin. "Go hunting," she told Abra. Mitzi escorted Mommy to the front door, where they talked for a few minutes while Abra wandered the living room, searching for her favorite figurine— a shiny porcelain swan with an ugly duckling by its side. She found it on a corner table under a feather boa.

Mitzi came back into the living room. "Found it so soon." She set it on the mantel. "I'll have to find a better place to hide it next time." Rubbing her hands together, she wove her fingers and cracked her knuckles. "How about a little honky-tonk?" She plunked down at the old upright piano and banged out a happy tune. "After you learn how to play Bach and Beethoven and Chopin and Mozart, I'll teach you how to play the fun stuff." Her hands flashed up and down. She stood, nudging the stool aside, and kept playing, putting one foot out and then the other, in a clumsy hop-kick, hop-kick. Abra laughed and imitated her.

Mitzi straightened. "That was just a little teaser." She swung the end of the shawl around her neck again and lifted her chin, her face grim. "Now, we must be serious." She stepped aside and waved her hand airily for Abra to sit on the stool. Giggling, Abra took her position as Mitzi put some sheet music on the stand. "A little simplified Beethoven is the order of the day."

Abra played until the mantel clock struck four. Mitzi glanced at her watch. "Why don't you play dress up for a while? I'm going to make a call."

Abra slid from the stool. "Can I look at your jewelry?"

"Sure you can, honey." Mitzi waved toward the bedroom. "Look in the closet; check through the drawers, too. Try on whatever you like."

Abra found a treasure trove of sparkly baubles and beads. She put on a pair of rhinestone earrings, and a looped necklace of red glass beads. She added one of pearls and another necklace with jet-black beads. She liked the weight of flash and glory around her neck. Spying Mitzi's rouge pot, she rubbed a bit on each cheek, then used Mitzi's eyebrow pencil. She chose the darkest red lipstick from Mitzi's horde of small tubes. Opening her mouth wide, she imitated one of the women she'd seen in the church ladies' room and smeared on the lipstick. She dug through more makeup and powdered her cheeks, coughing as a sweet-scented cloud engulfed her.

"Are you all right in there?" Mitzi called from the other room.

Waving her hands around her face, Abra said she was fine and dandy, and headed for Mitzi's closet. She put on a wide-brimmed hat with a big red bow and found a black shawl with embroidered flowers and a long fringe. Mitzi sure had a lot of shoes. Abra sat and untied her oxfords, then slipped her feet into a pair of red high heels.

"Oh, my!" Mitzi hurried over and grabbed her hand. "Pastor Zeke is coming to pick you up. I've got to get you cleaned up before he gets here." She laughed as she whipped off the big hat and sent it sailing into the closet. She unwound the shawl. "An admirer gave me this when I was singing in a cabaret in Paris a hundred and fifty years ago."

"What's a cabaret?"

"Oh, forget I mentioned it." Mitzi flung the shawl on the pink chenille bedspread. "And these old necklaces! Good grief. How many do you have on? I'm surprised you're still standing under all this weight. Come on, now. Into the bathroom." Mitzi smeared on cold cream and wiped it away again. She giggled. "Don't you look like a little clown with those black brows and red lips." She giggled again, scrubbing Abra's cheeks until they tingled.

The doorbell rang.

"Well, that's the best we can do." She tossed the washcloth aside, straightened Abra's dress, fingered her hair here and there, and patted her cheek. "You look just dandy, sweetie pie." She took her hand and went back into the living room. "Wait right here." She went to the door and opened it quietly. "Come on in, Pastor Zeke."

Daddy took one look at Abra and his brows shot up. His mouth twitched as he gave a sideways look at Mitzi. "Hmmmm."

Mitzi put her hands behind her back and smiled, all innocence. "Put the blame on my account, Zeke." She grinned. "I told her to have at anything she wanted in my room while I called Marianne. I forgot all the temptations. Marianne sounded so tired, I said I'd call you. I didn't think you'd be here until after five."

Daddy held out his hand. "Time to go, Abra."

Mommy was asleep on the couch. She roused, but Daddy told her to rest; he'd fix dinner. He told Abra to play quietly. Joshua came in the back door and talked with Daddy. The telephone rang. For the first time Abra could remember, Daddy ignored it.

Mommy seemed better when they all sat down to dinner. Daddy prayed the blessing. They all talked about their day. Joshua cleared and washed the dishes. Abra tried to help, but he shooed her away. "It'll be faster if I do it myself."

Mommy went to bed early. As soon as Daddy tucked Abra in, he followed. Abra lay awake, listening to the low sound of their voices. It was a long time before she went to sleep.

Abra awakened in the dark and heard the front door close. Daddy had gone out for his early morning prayer time. She could remember him carrying her on those walks and wished he still did.

The house felt cold and dark when he was gone, even with Mommy in the next room and Joshua out in his fort. She pushed the covers off and tiptoed into Mommy and Daddy's bedroom. Mommy shifted and raised her head. "What is it, honey?"

"I'm scared."

Mommy lifted the covers. Abra climbed up and shimmied under. Mommy put an arm around her, covered them both, and held her close. Abra soaked in the warmth and felt drowsy. She awakened when Mommy made an odd sound, a low groan, and muttered, "Not now, Lord. Please. Not now." She moaned again, her body stiffening. She rolled onto her back.

Abra turned over. "Mommy?"

"Go to sleep, baby. Just go back to sleep." She spoke in a strained voice, as though talking through her teeth. She made a sobbing sound, and then she let out a long breath and relaxed.

"Mommy?" When she didn't answer, Abra snuggled close, curling up beside her.

Awakening abruptly, Abra felt cold, strong hands lift her out of bed. "Back to your own bed, Abra," Daddy whispered. The cold air made her shiver. Wrapping her arms around herself, she looked back over her shoulder as she headed for the door.

Daddy went around the bed. "Sleeping in this morning?" He spoke in a soft, loving voice as he leaned down and kissed Mommy. "Marianne?" Straightening, he turned on the light. Her name came out then in a hoarse cry as he flipped away the covers and lifted her.

Mommy hung in Daddy's arms like a limp rag doll, her mouth and eyes open.

Daddy sat on the bed, rocking her back and forth as he sobbed. "Oh, God, no . . . no . . . *no.*"

CHAPTER 2

The Lord gave me what I had,
and the Lord has taken it away.
Praise the name of the Lord!

JOB 1:21

JOSHUA SAT IN THE FRONT PEW of the church, looking up at his father through eyes blurred with tears. Abra sat beside him, body rigid, tears running down her pale cheeks. When he took her hand, icy fingers gripped his. The pews behind them were packed with mourners, some crying softly. Dad's voice broke and Joshua flinched, his own tears spilling over. Dad stood for a moment, head bowed, silent. Someone sobbed and Joshua didn't know if he'd made the sound or Abra.

Mr. and Mrs. Matthews moved from the row just behind them and sat on either side of Joshua and Abra. Penny squeezed in between her mother and Abra, and took Abra's hand. Mr. Matthews put his arm around Joshua.

Dad raised his head slowly and looked at them. "It's very difficult to say good-bye to someone you cherish, even when we know we will see her again. Marianne was a wonderful wife and mother." He talked about how they had known each other from childhood, back to the farm days in Iowa. He talked about how young they had been when they married, how poor, how happy. He talked about family Joshua had never met because they lived so far away. They had sent a wreath of flowers. Dad's voice grew quieter and more strained. "If there is anyone who would like to say a word or share a story about Marianne, please do so."

One after another, people stood. Mom had many friends, and they all had nice things to say. One lady said Marianne was a prayer warrior. Another said she was a saint. Several older parishioners said she'd come by more than once with casseroles and homemade pies. "She brought the little girl with her, too. Sure did cheer me up." A young mother stood with her baby in her arms and said Marianne always found a way to bring the Lord into their conversation.

The congregation fell silent. No one moved. Miss Mitzi stood. Her son, Hodge Martin, said something, but she squeezed past him into the side aisle and headed for the front of the church. She blew her nose as she walked, tucking her hankie in the sleeve of her sweater. She marched up the three steps and sat at the piano. She smiled at Dad, still standing at the pulpit. "My turn, Zeke."

Dad nodded.

Mitzi looked at Joshua and then fixed her eyes on Abra. "The first time Marianne brought Abra over for a piano lesson, I wondered why she didn't just teach Abra herself. We all know how well she played. She said she never learned to play anything but hymns, and she wanted Abra to learn all kinds of music. I asked what she liked best, and she surprised me." Positioning her hands over the keys, she looked up. "This is for you, honey. I hope you're dancing up there."

Stamping her foot a few times, Mitzi set a rhythm, then launched into the "Maple Leaf Rag." Hodge Martin sank in his pew and covered his face. Some looked shocked, but Dad laughed. Joshua laughed, too, wiping tears from his face. When Mitzi finished, she looked at Dad, her face softening, and started playing one of Mom's favorite hymns. Dad closed his eyes and sang.

"'Jesus lives, and so shall I: Death, thy sting is gone forever . . .'"

People joined in one by one until the entire congregation sang. "'He for me hath deigned to die, lives the bands of death to sever.'"

Dad came down the steps, and Peter Matthews, dressed in a black suit, rose, squeezed Joshua's shoulder, and joined the other pallbearers. The entire congregation stood and continued singing. "'He shall raise me from the dust: Jesus is my hope and trust.'" Joshua took Abra's hand, and they followed Dad and the men carrying Mom in the casket out to the hearse parked at the curb.

Three weeks after Mommy's funeral, the car died with a loud clunk and shudder in the driveway. Daddy got out and looked under the hood while Abra sat in the front seat, waiting. After a few minutes, Daddy slammed the hood, his face tight. He opened the car door. "Come on, Abra. We'll have to walk to school."

It was cold, and her breath steamed, but she grew warm quickly keeping up with Daddy's long strides. She wished she didn't have to go to school. She hadn't gone back for a week after Mommy died, and when she did, one of the boys teased her about being a crybaby until Penny told him to shut up, you'd cry too if your mommy died and you were right next to her when it happened, and she knew because her mommy said so. The next day another girl on the playground said Abra never had a mother. Pastor Zeke found her under a bridge where people dump kittens they don't want.

Abra stumbled and almost fell, but Daddy caught her hand. "Can I come to church with you?"

"You have to go to school."

Her legs ached and they still had blocks to go. "Will we have to walk home?"

"Probably. When you're too tired to walk, I'll carry you."

"Can you carry me now?"

He swung her up on his hip. "Just for a block. Enough time to rest."

She put her head against his shoulder. "I miss Mommy."

"So do I."

Daddy didn't put her down until they were a block from the school. Hunkering down, he held her by the shoulders. "Mrs. Matthews is going to take you home with Penny this afternoon. I'll come over and get you at five fifteen."

Her lip trembled. "I want to go home."

"Don't argue, Abra." He kissed her cheek. "I have to do what's best for you, whether we like it or not." When she started to cry, he held her close. "Please don't cry." His voice sounded tear-choked. "Things are hard enough as it is without you crying all the time." He ran a finger down her nose and lifted her chin. "Go on to class now."

When school was over, Mrs. Matthews was right outside the classroom door, talking with Robbie Austin's mother. She looked sad and serious until she spotted them. "There are my girls!" She kissed Penny's cheek first and then Abra's. "How was your day?" Penny talked on and on while they walked to the car. "In you go, you two." Mrs. Matthews let them both sit in front, Abra in the middle. Penny talked around her.

The house smelled of fresh-baked cookies. Mrs. Matthews had set the kitchen nook table for a tea party. They sipped apple juice and ate cookies. Abra started to feel better.

Penny had a canopy bed with a pink chenille bedspread, a white dresser, and walls covered with pink-and-white dogwood blossoms. The dormer window had a cushioned seat that overlooked the front yard. While Penny rummaged through her toy box, Abra sat in the window seat and looked out at the lawn and white picket fence. She remembered how red roses covered the arbor in summer. Mommy loved roses. Abra felt a hard lump growing in her throat.

"Let's color!" Penny tossed coloring books on the flowery carpet and opened a shoe box full of crayons. Abra joined her. Penny talked and talked while Abra listened for the downstairs grandfather clock to bong five times. Then she waited for the doorbell to ring. Finally, it did. Daddy had come for her, just like he promised.

Penny let out a loud groan. "I don't want you to go! We're having so much fun!" She followed Abra down the hall. "I wish you were my sister. Then we could play together all the time." Daddy and Mrs. Matthews stood in the entry, talking in low voices. "Mommy?" Penny said in a whining voice. "Can Abra spend the night? *Pleeeease?*"

"Of course she can, but it's up to Pastor Zeke."

Penny turned eagerly to Abra. "We can play Chinese checkers and listen to *One Man's Family*."

Daddy stood below, hat in hand, looking up at Abra. He looked tired. "She doesn't have pajamas or a change of clothes for school tomorrow."

"Oh. That's no problem at all. She and Penny wear the same size. We even have extra toothbrushes."

"Oh, goody!" Penny hopped up and down. "Come on, Abra. Let's play!"

Abra rushed to Daddy, clutching his hand and hugging his side. She wanted to go home. Daddy pried her away and leaned down. "It's a long walk home, Abra. I think it's a good idea for you to spend the night here." When she started to protest, he put a finger over her lips. "You'll be fine."

———————————

Zeke checked on Joshua before going out for his morning walk. Abra had spent the last three nights with the Matthews family. He locked the door, put the key in the flowerpot, and headed for Main Street. He followed it north past the end of town and kept going until he reached the Haven cemetery. He'd been to Marianne's grave so many times in the last few weeks, he could've found his way even if the moon hadn't been full. The white marble headstone glowed.

His heart ached for her presence. They used to talk every morning in the kitchen before the children got up. And he needed to talk now.

He shoved his hands in his pockets. "Mrs. Welch came by the church yesterday." The caseworker had offered her condolences before she started asking questions. He swallowed hard, fighting tears.

"I'm sorry I was so selfish, Marianne. I'm sorry I let you talk me into taking Abra home, even when we knew adoption was out of the question because of your health. I gave in because I knew how much you wanted another child." He closed his eyes and shook his head. "No. That's not true. I gave in because I loved her, too." He couldn't speak for a moment.

"I work all day, every day, Marianne. You know the demands of ministry. And I'm failing on all sides. I failed to protect you. I'm failing as a father. I'm failing as a pastor. I'm so caught up in my own grief, I feel crushed beneath the burdens of others." He gave a bleak laugh. "I know I've said it a hundred times to those going through crises, but if one more person tells me all things work together for good, I'll . . ."

His throat felt tight. "Abra's only five. She needs a mother. She needs a father who doesn't get called out in the middle of the night when someone has a crisis."

There was no easy way around it. Zeke put his hand on the mound of earth. "I'm going to talk to Peter and Priscilla today about adopting Abra. You know they wanted her right from the start, and ever since you've been gone, they have offered to help in any way they can. I know they would love to welcome her into their family."

Zeke blinked back tears, looking off into the distance. "Mrs. Welch isn't sure it's going to work. She thinks Abra would have an easier time adjusting in a new place. Maybe it's selfish, but I want her close, not off somewhere in another town with complete strangers."

Was he making another decision he would regret? Not that he would ever regret the five years they'd had Abra. Marianne had been so happy. "Oh, Marianne, you know how much I love her. It's killing me to give her up. I hope I'm doing the right thing." He sat, his whole body convulsed in sobs. "She won't understand." He wiped his face. He let the tears flow. "Forgive me. Please. Forgive me."

If Mrs. Welch changed her mind, Abra would be taken from him in a less gentle manner and placed elsewhere. He wouldn't know where she was. He wouldn't be able to see her grow up.

Zeke walked down to the main road. A Gruening's Market truck pulled over and idled at the entrance. Dutch lowered his window and waited for him. "How you doing, Pastor?"

"Holding on." Barely.

"I know what you mean. Get in. I'll give you a ride back into town."

Zeke stepped up and climbed into the passenger seat. "Thanks."

Dutch put the truck in gear and his foot on the gas. "I used to sit by Sharon's grave and talk to her—every day for a couple of weeks, then every couple of days, then once a week. Now, I go on her birthday and our anniversary. She would've wanted me to go on living." He cast a glance at Zeke. "Took me a while to realize she's not there. Well, she is. But she isn't. You told me. I didn't believe it." He muttered a low curse. "I'm trying to make you feel better and doing a pathetic job of it."

"Don't worry about it."

Dutch smiled slightly. "You told me once there are no tears in heaven." He stared straight ahead at the road. "Well, we have plenty down here, don't we? I know it hurts like the dickens right now." He downshifted and slowed. "You'll wade through the pain and climb out the other side." Pulling over, he stopped at the corner. "Just like I did."

Zeke held out his hand. "Thanks, Dutch." The man had a firm grip.

Zeke slid out of the cab of the truck.

"What do you say to a cup of coffee sometime?"

Zeke looked back at Dutch. After all these years, was the door finally opening?

Dutch looked sheepish. "I've got a lot of questions. Sharon probably told me the answers, but whenever she started talking religion, I closed my ears."

"How about Bessie's Corner Café tomorrow morning when you finish work? Around seven fifteen?"

"Yep. See you there." Dutch raised his hand, put the truck in gear, and turned right.

Zeke smiled slightly as the truck disappeared around the corner.

The sun was coming up. Zeke closed his eyes for a moment, trying not to think about the days ahead. *Lord, just get me through this day. Wade with me through all this pain and help me climb up on the other side.*

Abra cried all afternoon. Daddy didn't want her anymore because it was her fault Mommy had died. She had heard Daddy saying she made too much work for Mommy.

Mrs. Matthews sat with her in Penny's bedroom, stroking her back and telling her how much they loved her and how they hoped she'd learn to love them, too. Abra couldn't keep her eyes open.

She awakened when Penny came home and bounded up the stairs. Her father called her back down before she reached the door. Abra got up and sat in the window seat.

The door opened a few minutes later, and the whole family came in. They came over to Abra, and Penny sat beside her. "Mommy and Daddy said you're going to be my sister." When tears poured down Abra's cheeks, Penny looked uncertain. "Don't you want to be my sister?"

Abra's lip trembled. "I want to be your friend."

Mrs. Matthews put a hand on each of their heads and smoothed their hair. "Now you can be both."

Penny hugged Abra. "I told Mommy I wanted you to be my sister. She said to pray about it, and I did. I prayed and prayed, and now I have exactly what I've always wanted."

Abra wondered what would happen when Penny changed her mind. Like Daddy.

———

After dinner, *One Man's Family* on the radio, and story time, Abra was tucked into bed with Penny. Mrs. Matthews kissed each of them, turned out the light, and closed the door. Penny chattered away until she fell asleep in midsentence.

Wide-awake, Abra stared up at the lace canopy.

Mommy said she would love her forever, and Mommy died. Mommy said God wouldn't take her away, but He did. Daddy said he loved her, but then he said she couldn't live with him anymore. She had to stay here and live with the Matthews family. He said Mr. and Mrs. Matthews wanted to be her daddy and mommy.

Why didn't it matter what Abra wanted?

Rain pattered on the roof, a few drops that quickened to a steady drumming. Penny turned over, talking in her sleep. Pushing the covers off, Abra got up and sat in the window seat. Wrapping her arms around her legs, she rested her chin on her knees. The streetlights looked blurry in the rain. The front gate banged. The wind chimes jingled.

A man came around the corner a block down and continued up the sidewalk. Daddy! Maybe he'd changed his mind and wanted her back!

She rose to her knees, hands on the window.

He glanced up once and slowed as he walked along the white picket fence.

Had he seen her? She tapped on the window. The wind whipped

the branches of the three birch trees in the corner of the front yard. He stood below her at the gate. As she tapped again, harder, Abra's heart thumped.

He didn't look up or come through the gate. He stood motionless, head bowed, the way he did whenever he prayed. When he did that, Mommy always said to wait because he was talking to God.

Abra sat back on her heels, bowing her own head, hands clasped tightly. "Please, God, please, please, make my daddy take me home. Please. I'll be good. I promise. I won't make anybody too tired or sick." She dashed tears away. "I wanna go home."

Full of hope, she rose and looked out the window.

Daddy had walked to the end of the block. She stared as he disappeared around the corner.

Peter and Priscilla talked in whispers. Sometimes they looked upset. Then they'd put bright smiles on their faces and pretend everything was fine. Penny's eagerness to have a sister disappeared. It came to a head when Priscilla made a new play outfit for Abra, and didn't make one for Penny. "I thought it was for me!" Penny wailed.

"You already have several play outfits and Abra doesn't."

Penny cried louder. "I want her to *go home*!"

Peter came around the corner from the kitchen nook, where he'd been grading papers. "That's enough, Penny. Go to your room!" She went, but not before she stuck her tongue out at Abra. Peter told Priscilla they needed to have another talk with Penny, and he and Priscilla went upstairs. They closed Penny's bedroom door and were in there for so long, Abra didn't know what to do. Finally, she went out to the backyard and sat on the swing. Should she go home? Where would Daddy take her then? To another family?

She turned around on the swing until the chains were twisted, then lifted her feet, spinning around and around. *Penny will always come first, come first, come first. Penny is their real daughter, real daughter, real daughter.* Dizzy, she did it again. *I'd better be nice, be nice, be nice.*

Abra had overheard Peter talking to Priscilla in the kitchen that morning. "I haven't seen her smile once in the past three months, Priss. She used to be such a happy little girl."

Priscilla spoke in a hushed voice. "Marianne adored her. She'd probably still be alive if they'd let us take Abra to begin with, and we wouldn't be having all these problems now."

Peter poured himself a cup of coffee. "I hope things get better soon, or I don't know what we're going to do."

Fear had gripped Abra. They were talking about getting rid of her.

"Abra!" Peter sounded upset. He came rushing out the back door. She got off the swing and he let out a relieved breath. "There you are. Come on back inside, honey. We all want to talk with you."

Abra's palms felt wet. Her heart kept pounding faster as she followed Peter into the living room. Were they going to send her away to live with strangers? Priscilla and Penny sat on the couch. Peter put his hand on Abra's shoulder. "Penny has something to say to you."

"I'm sorry, Abra." Penny's face was puffy from crying. "I like having you for my sister." Her voice was dull; her eyes told the truth.

"Good girl!" Priscilla squeezed her closer and kissed the top of her head.

Abra didn't trust any of them.

Priscilla pulled Abra down beside her and wrapped an arm around her shoulders, hugging Penny close on one side and Abra on the other. "You're both our little girls now. We love having two daughters."

Daddy still came over every few days. Joshua never came with him. They only got to see one another after Sunday school each week, and then they'd just stand and look at each other and not know what to say.

Whenever Abra heard Daddy's voice, she flew down the stairs, hoping he'd come to take her home this time. Priscilla would take her hand and lean down. "Don't call him Daddy, Abra. You're to call him Reverend Freeman like all the other children do. When you get older, you can call him Pastor Zeke. Peter is your daddy now."

She cried herself to sleep on those nights and sometimes had nightmares. She'd cry out to Daddy, but he couldn't hear her. She'd try to run after him, but hands held her back. She'd scream, *"Daddy, Daddy!"* but he didn't turn around.

Priscilla woke her up and held her. "Everything is going to be all right, Abra. Mommy's here." But Mommy wasn't. Mommy was in a box underground.

No matter how many times they said it, Abra didn't believe Peter and Priscilla loved her. She knew they'd only adopted her because Penny wanted a sister. If Penny changed her mind, Peter and Priscilla would give her away. Where would she go then? To whom?

The next time Daddy came, Peter talked to him on the front porch for a long time, then came back inside alone. Abra tried to get around him, but Peter hunkered down and held her by the shoulders. "You won't see Pastor Zeke for a while, Abra." She thought that meant she wouldn't see him until church on Sunday, but then Peter drove a different way Sunday morning. When Penny asked where they were going, Peter said they would be attending a different church. While Penny whined and fussed about not seeing her friends, Peter said change would be good for them. Abra knew it was her fault they weren't going to Reverend Freeman's church anymore, and her last hope died. She wouldn't even get to see Joshua now. Penny crossed her arms and sulked. Priscilla gave her a sad smile and said they'd just have to wait and see how things went.

═══════

1950

Mitzi opened her door and peered around it. She wasn't wearing any makeup and her hair hadn't been brushed. "Is it Wednesday?" She waved Abra inside and closed the door. She was wearing a red lounging robe and worn blue satin slippers with a feathery trim.

Abra stared. "You said I could practice here."

"Well, a promise is a promise." The slippers slapped her heels as she went into the living room. "I'm glad you're here, sweetie pie. Just don't tell anyone I wasn't dressed at three in the afternoon. And don't tell anyone I've been smoking." She crushed a cigarette in a small cut-crystal ashtray. "Hodge thinks it's bad for my health." She grabbed the ashtray and took it into the kitchen, where she dumped the evidence of her misdeeds into the garbage. "How about a cup of Ovaltine before you attack that piece of Beethoven I gave you?"

Abra sank into a kitchen chair overlooking the side yard. Mitzi's son, Hodge, lived next door. Abra could see his wife, Carla, busy in the kitchen.

"Pull down that shade." Mitzi waved her fingers as she stayed out of view. "No, wait. Better not. Carla will think something's amiss and Hodge will be over here wanting to know why I'm still in my robe in the middle of the afternoon."

Abra giggled at Mitzi's air of defiance and then wondered, "Why *are* you still in your robe in the middle of the afternoon?"

"Because I am old and tired and sometimes I just don't feel like fussing with makeup and hair and figuring out what to wear. Lookin' good is a major project that requires a trowel and a bucket of foundation. Ah! Finally! A smile!" She spooned Ovaltine into the milk warming on the stove. "How's life treating you, sweetie pie?"

"Penny hates it when I play piano."

"Because she has no ear nor talent for music." Mitzi's expression changed. "And you will forget I ever said that as of right this minute." She held out her hand, little finger extended. "Pinkie promise." Abra complied.

Carla Martin had noticed Abra and waved from her kitchen window. Abra forced a wide smile and wiggled her fingers back.

"You could practice on that sweet baby grand at the church anytime, you know. Pastor Zeke wouldn't mind."

"Why would I want to go there?" Abra looked out the window again.

"I was just thinking . . ." Mitzi turned off the gas and poured steaming Ovaltine into two mugs. "Let's go into the living room." She handed a mug to Abra and pretended to slink out the door. "No point in flying the red flag in front of Carla's face."

Holding the hot mug between both hands, Abra slouched into an overstuffed chair and slung her legs over the arm. "Thanks, Mitzi." If she sat like this at Peter and Priscilla's house, Priscilla would tell her to sit up like a lady. "I like being here better than anywhere else."

Mitzi's smile turned tender. "I like having you here." She settled onto the sofa, kicked off her slippers, and put her bare feet up on the coffee table. Her toenails were painted bright red. "So they're all ganging up on you, is that it? They're trying to nip the bud of your blooming talent?"

Sometimes Mitzi could be annoying. Abra sipped her cocoa and decided to be honest. "They get tired of hearing me play the same piece over and over, and I can't get it right if I don't. Priscilla gets a headache, Peter wants to listen to the news on the radio, and Penny shrieks like a banshee."

"You know," Mitzi drawled, "the real trouble is two thirteen-year-old girls living under the same roof. One day you're bosom buddies; the next you're at each other's throats."

"So you're saying Peter and Priscilla would be better off if they only had one daughter."

Mitzi looked shocked. "That's not what I'm saying at all. I'm saying you both will grow up and grow out of being obnoxious."

"One would hope so."

"Well, you're welcome to use my piano as often as you like. I might howl when you hit a wrong note, but I won't make you quit."

"The three *P*'s-in-the-pod will cheer and do flips around the living room." Abra swung her legs around and put her feet on the coffee table. She liked being with Mitzi. She didn't have to bite her tongue every time she wanted to say what she really thought. Not that Mitzi let her get away with gossip or whining. She had no patience for either. But here, Abra felt more at home than she did at "home."

"Not so fast, missy." Mitzi looked at Abra over the rim of her cup. "I have one condition. You play for Sunday services."

"What?" Abra felt all the pleasure and warmth seep out of her. "No!" She put her mug on the coffee table. Just thinking about it made her stomach flip over.

"Yes. And I want you to start—"

"I said no."

"Give me one good reason why not."

She looked for any excuse. "Because I don't want to do anything for Reverend Freeman. That's why. He gave me away. Remember?"

Dark eyes flashing, Mitzi planted her feet on the floor. "That's a lot of hogwash. And besides that, do you hear Pastor Zeke asking you? You're not doing it for him. You're doing it for me. It would be even better if you were doing it for God."

Fat chance. What had God ever done for her? But knowing how Mitzi felt about Him, she knew better than to say it. "You play a lot better than I ever will."

"You're almost as good as I am, and you know it. I'm running out of things to teach you. And yes, yes, I'll get around to ragtime. But not yet."

"Why are you asking me to play for church?"

"Because I'm getting old and tired and want a Sunday off. That's why. And Marianne always dreamed you'd play for church someday. Do it for her, if not for me."

Tears sprang to Abra's eyes. The old pain rose up, gripping her by the throat.

Mitzi softened. "I'm sorry, sweetie pie. Oh, honey, you're so filled up with fear and there's no need." She smiled bleakly. "Pastor Zeke loves you, and you won't even speak to the man. I'm so glad your family brought you back to our church. Those two years he hardly got to see you were hard on him."

Abra rolled her eyes.

"The man saved your life and gave you a home for five years."

"He should've left me where he found me."

"Wah-wah-wah. You can cry a river, but can you build a bridge? You don't even show him the respect he deserves as your pastor."

Shaking and fighting tears, Abra stood. "I thought you liked me."

"I love you, you idiot! Why do you think I keep you around? For your sunny disposition?" Mitzi let out an impatient breath. "I'm going to say this once and never again. *Get over it!* Abra, sweetie, Zeke gave you away because he loves you, not because he wanted to get rid of you. He did it for your own good. And don't give me that glassy-eyed stare. I've never lied to you, and I never will." She huffed. "I know it's your choice to believe me or not, but you'd better understand this: what you believe sets the course of your life. And don't tell me you haven't been happy with the Matthews family."

"I've been pretending."

"Really?" Mitzi gave an indelicate snort. "Well, if that's true, you're a better actress than I ever was." She still sat on the edge of the sofa. "Will you sit down now? You're making my neck ache."

Abra sat.

Mitzi settled back and put her feet up again. She eyed Abra. "So? What do you say, Miss Matthews? Are you going to climb down off that high horse you're riding and saddle up the piano bench? Or are you going to practice at home and drive your family nuts?"

"How soon do I have to play at church?"

"This week."

"This week?"

"I'll pick some easy hymns. 'Fairest Lord Jesus' is a good one." Mitzi picked up Abra's cup of cocoa and waved her hand. "Enough lollygagging. Warm up with some scales."

Abra spotted sheet music to Dinah Shore's "Buttons and Bows." Mitzi came back from the kitchen and put "Baby Face" in front of her. Abra happily picked through the music without too many mistakes.

"Okay. Enough playtime." Mitzi opened the hymnal to "Fairest Lord Jesus." Mitzi wasn't satisfied until Abra had played it through three times without a mistake. Then she flipped through the hymnal again. "Next one is 'Immortal, Invisible, God Only Wise.'" She paced while Abra played. "Pick up the tempo. It's not a dirge." Mitzi swung her arms in the air and sang loudly, in perfect pitch. When she was finally satisfied, she found "Beneath the Cross of Jesus."

Abra glared. She wanted to slam the piano lid. Instead, she gave "Beneath the Cross of Jesus" a whole new rhythm.

"It's not a waltz. What do you think? People should be dancing in the aisles?"

"Better than sleeping in the pews!"

Mitzi laughed until she had to sit down. She put her feet out, her arms dangling over the sides of the chair. "Two more and you can practice whatever you want. Find 'All Hail the Power of Jesus' Name' and make it sound like a march. This will be the postlude. Play it with passion!"

Fuming, Abra did.

"All we need now is a processional to get them into the pews, and an offertory to soften their hearts enough to open their wallets." Mitzi patted Abra's shoulders. "An hour a day on these and anything you want to learn after. Deal?"

"Do I have a choice?"

"Oh, such enthusiasm." She made prayer hands. "Forgive her, Lord. She doesn't know any better. Yet." Reaching around Abra, she flipped the pages to "Trust and Obey."

"Play that one."

A memory flashed of riding on Reverend Freeman's back through a misty morning as he sang that hymn. She'd loved the sound of his voice. She knew every word by heart. But trust? She didn't trust anyone anymore, least of all Jesus. She pulled the lid over the keys. "I have to go home."

Mitzi's hands gripped her shoulders. "I won't push so hard tomorrow."

"I'm not sure I'm coming back."

Mitzi kissed the top of her head. "Well, that's up to you."

There was no point in pretending with Mitzi. They both knew she'd come. When Abra got up, Mitzi stepped in her way and cupped her face. "I have faith in you. You'll do us all proud." She let her go and leaned over to get the hymnal. "Take it with you. Just read through the words so you'll know how to play. I'll bet if you tell Priscilla and Peter you're going to be playing for church, they'll let you practice." Her eyes glowed with mischief. "That way, when you come over here, we can work on ragtime."

Abra's spirits lifted. She kissed Mitzi's soft cheek. "I love you, Mitzi."

"I love you, too, sweetie pie." Mitzi walked her to the door. "I give you a year and you'll be able to play every hymn in that book. Don't just memorize the music. Memorize the words. Go on now, before Priscilla calls in a missing person's report and Jim Helgerson shows up in his squad car." She hugged her red robe around her as she stood in the doorway. "Toodle-ooo."

Zeke removed his St. Louis Cardinals cap as he entered Bessie's. The bell above the door jangled, and the new waitress glanced over before returning her attention to half a dozen male customers sitting on stools at the counter. She had brown hair in a neat French twist, revealing a lovely, if somewhat remote, face. The blue apron tied at the waist over a plain white blouse and black skirt hinted at a nicely curved figure. The men cajoled, but she served each with a cool, business-only smile and a reserved demeanor.

The swinging doors from the kitchen bumped open, and Bessie came out with three breakfast plates stacked up one arm and another in her hand. "Good mornin', Zeke! You're a little late today. Your booth is waiting for you. Make yourself comfortable, and I'll be right with you." She served four men dressed in work clothes sitting near the front windows.

Before sliding into his usual spot near the back, Zeke poked his head into the kitchen to say hello to Oliver, harried but keeping pace with the morning crowd. "I see Bessie found a new girl."

"She's a good worker. Started last night. Kept up without a problem. Bessie has her fingers crossed."

Zeke left him to his work and took his seat. He liked sitting in back, facing front. That way he could see everyone who came in. Dutch often stopped by, and they'd have a cup of coffee and talk for a while. He'd finally come to church, where Zeke introduced him to Marjorie Baxter. It took a few months of casual conversation before Dutch asked Marjorie to dinner. "We talked about you all evening," Dutch told him with a grin. "Now that we've exhausted that boring subject, we can get on to other things." Zeke couldn't have been more delighted when they started seeing each other on a regular basis.

The new waitress looked his way again. He smiled and gave her a nod of silent greeting. Usually he could guess people's ages, but this woman perplexed him. Thirty-five? She moved quickly, as though accustomed to this kind of work. She looked tired around the eyes, not physically tired, but world-weary, worn down. When she returned his smile, it didn't touch her eyes.

Plates delivered, Bessie snatched a mug off the shelf and headed for him. "You usually beat the crowd." She set the mug on the table and poured a steaming cup of black coffee without spilling a drop.

Zeke thanked her and wrapped his cold hands around the warm porcelain. "I took a longer walk this morning."

"Beats me why you walk at all when you have that sweet Packard 740 to drive around."

Mitzi Martin had shocked him a few months after Marianne's death when she insisted on giving him the 1930 Packard 740 Roadster that had been parked in her garage for who knew how many years. "You need a car, and I have one that's sitting in a garage collecting dust. I want you to have it." She had her mind made up, and all Zeke could do was gratefully accept the offer.

Even after several years, though, he still felt conspicuous behind the wheel of Mitzi's car, and he only used it when he had to be somewhere in a hurry or had to go farther than his legs could carry him in a reasonable amount of time. He'd only taken it out once last week, and that was to give Mitzi a ride in the countryside. They talked about Abra. She'd been playing every Sunday for church, though under protest. "She's nervous about playing in front of everyone, but she'll get used to it. It takes time."

Abra still didn't have much to say to Zeke. She called him Pastor Zeke now, instead of Reverend Freeman, which was an improvement. He told her once how proud Marianne would be to see her playing piano for services. She said Mitzi told her the same thing and that's why she'd agreed to play, in memory of Marianne. She'd said it in a perfectly polite tone, but he'd felt the stab just the same. Mitzi said she was looking at things through a child's hurt. "Whatever happens, she's going to know every hymn in the book, and something might come back to her when she needs it."

Zeke gave Bessie a rueful grin. "I don't want to put too many miles on the car."

"Or you're embarrassed to have a car that's nicer than most of your parishioners'."

There was some truth to that. In fact, Charles Lydickson was somewhat peeved whenever he saw Zeke in the Packard.

He nodded toward the new waitress. "I see you found someone to help you out."

Bessie looked pleased. "Her name is Susan Wells. She came in yesterday, new to town, and said she was looking for work. She said she had experience waiting tables, and after watching her work last night and this morning, I'd say she sure does." She beckoned. "Susan! Come on over here and meet one of my best customers."

Susan dried her hands and came out from behind the counter.

"Zeke, I want you to meet Susan Wells, newcomer to Haven. Susan, this here is Reverend Ezekiel Freeman of Haven Community Church."

Her eyes had flickered at *reverend*. He'd seen that *uh-oh* look on others' faces. "Reverend Freeman." She gave a reserved nod.

"Call him Pastor Zeke," Bessie told her. "*Reverend* sounds stodgy, don't you think? Like some old man." She winked at Zeke.

Zeke extended his hand to Susan. "It's a pleasure to meet you, Miss Wells."

After the briefest hesitation, she shook his hand. One firm shake and she let go. "It's Mrs. Wells." She spoke stiffly. Her gaze flicked away and then back. "My husband was killed in the war."

He recognized a lie. "I'm sorry to hear that."

"Hey, Bessie! How about some service over here?" A customer held up his mug.

"Hold your horses, Barney! What are you doing, anyway? Pouring it in a thermos before you get off your sorry backside and go to work?" Bessie excused herself and headed for the booth.

Susan had stood staring at the exchange in appalled silence. Zeke chuckled. "Don't worry. Barney is Bessie's little brother."

"Oh." She closed her lips.

Bessie and Barney were laughing now. She grabbed a handful of his curly dark hair and yanked it before heading for another booth.

"It's a morning ritual." Zeke smiled. "Welcome to Haven, Mrs. Wells." He met her gaze.

Her expression altered, as though a veil had been pulled over her face, hiding her from his scrutiny. "Thanks. I'd better get back to work."

———————

Joshua found himself trapped on the front porch swing with Abra leaning against the railing while Penny sat beside him chatting about the upcoming eighth-grade graduation and the party her parents were giving. Abra leaned against the porch railing, not saying a word.

Penny scooted closer to Joshua. "Are you going to your senior prom? Isn't it next weekend?"

Priscilla stepped out the front door. "Penny, come inside and set the table."

"It's not even close to dinnertime."

"Now, Penny."

"Okay. Okay." Angry, she left the swing. "Can Joshua stay for dinner?"

Priscilla looked at him in question. "You know you're more than welcome."

A little more welcome than he wanted. "Thanks, but I can't."

As soon as the door closed behind them, Joshua stood. "What do you say we go for a walk?"

Abra's head came up and her face brightened. "Sure."

He opened the front gate for her. She walked with eyes straight forward. He wondered what she was thinking about. "I was trying to bring you into the conversation."

She shrugged. "Penny has a crush on you."

Again, Joshua had that feeling that something was churning inside Abra. The last thing he wanted to do was cause a rift between two sisters. "She'll have a crush on someone else next week."

"*Are* you going to prom?" She cast him a look he couldn't decipher. "You never did answer Penny's question."

"Yep. I'm going." Paul Davenport wanted to take Janet Fulsom, but her father wouldn't allow her to go unless another couple went with them. Joshua would have asked Janet's best friend, Sally Pruitt, but he knew Brady Studebaker had already asked her. So he had called Lacey Glover, who said she'd love to go.

Abra abruptly changed the subject and asked if he was still working on the Woodings' kitchen cabinets.

"Nope. Jack and I finished that project last week. Now he's talking about replacing the balusters on his staircase. He taught me how to use the router and put me to work making balusters from a template. They're for the new bungalows he's building. He wants me to come up with a template of my own—'a baluster with details,' as he puts it." He laughed. "Mr. Wooding has more confidence in me than I have. I've made six so far, and he's broken every one of them in half and tossed them in the firewood box."

"He sounds mean."

"No, he's not mean. He just pushes me to do better. I've learned a lot from him."

"Don't you want to go to college?"

"Someday. Maybe. I don't have enough money saved right now."

"Are you still in Scouts?"

"Not anymore." Jack Wooding had encouraged him to go all the way to Eagle Scout. Joshua had made it last year when he wrote a proposal for a ramp into the public library, designed it, and found financial backing and a crew to make the project happen. "Between school and working with Mr. Wooding, I'm pretty busy."

"You still have time to go out with girls." She glanced at him. "You didn't say who you're taking to prom."

Was she still thinking about that? "Lacey Glover. Her family goes to our church." He watched Abra frown and figured she probably didn't know her. "Tall, brunette, sits in the sixth row on the right side of church with her folks, has a younger brother a year older than you. Brian. Do you know him?"

She shrugged. "I know who he is. I don't know him." She kept walking. "Penny was hoping you'd ask her to prom."

"I doubt that. She's only thirteen and not even in high school."

"We will be next fall."

Joshua tried to tease her out of her low mood. "Any idea who you'd like to have take you to prom someday?"

She gave a short laugh. "I doubt I'll be invited."

"Why wouldn't you be? You're a pretty girl." He wrapped an arm around her shoulders and hugged her against his side. "You will. You'll have guys lined up wanting to take you out. In the unlikely event you don't have a date, I'll take you." He kissed her cheek and let her go as the downtown clock bonged in the tower. "I'd better get you home."

Her mood had changed and she challenged him to a race back. Breathless, they reached the front gate, both gasping for air. "You run pretty well for a girl." He'd barely beaten her. He dug in his pocket for keys. The truck's door screeched when he opened it.

Abra leaned into the open passenger window. "This thing is still a piece of junk, Joshua."

"Hey! This is a work in progress." He patted the steering wheel. "She runs pretty well." He turned the key and the engine choked.

Abra giggled. "Are you taking Lacey Glover to prom in this old rust bucket?"

He grinned. "Dad's loaning me the Packard."

"I've never even had a ride in Mitzi's car!"

"That's your fault. All you have to do is ask him." He turned the key in the ignition again, and the truck shook itself to life.

Abra stepped off the running board and yelled over the noise. "Are you coming to our graduation?"

"I wouldn't miss it! You'd better come to mine." He waved as he pulled away from the curb. He looked back as he went around the corner. Abra was still standing outside the gate, watching him. He felt an odd lift in his chest at the sight of her, a hint of something to come, but he didn't know what.

The George Washington Elementary School auditorium was packed for the eighth-grade graduation ceremony. A *Class of 1950* banner hung over the platform where the students sat.

"Isn't this exciting?" Penny squeezed Abra's hand. Abra squeezed back and looked out at the mass of people. There was Mitzi, beaming, and Joshua, both sitting with Peter and Priscilla. Abra knew Pastor Zeke was standing on the platform a few feet away, but tears were too close to the surface for her to chance a peek at him. Was he proud of her? Was he sorry now he'd given her away?

After the ceremony, everyone surged to their feet and clapped and cheered. Abra saw Joshua put his fingers to his lips and give a piercing whistle. She laughed, returning Penny's exuberant hug.

Priscilla and Peter met up with them outside the auditorium, where pandemonium reigned. Abra saw Mitzi and went for her as toward a beacon. "I'm so glad you came."

Mitzi pulled her close and kissed her temple. "I wouldn't have missed it for the world." She held her at arm's length. "This is just the beginning, sweetie pie."

Peter called out and snapped his fingers. "Penny! Abra! Come on. You have to return your robes and mortarboards so we can get home. I've got to get the charcoal going."

People had already arrived and were milling about the backyard. Pastor Zeke and Joshua stood talking with Peter as he turned hamburgers on the grill. Penny was laughing and hopping up and down with Pamela and Charlotte, probably planning cheers for junior varsity cheerleading tryouts in September.

Abra saw Joshua weaving his way over. His gaze swept her up and down. "You look all grown up, except for your bare feet."

Her spirits lifted. "I am grown up, even with bare feet."

"That dress makes your eyes look almost emerald."

She blushed.

Pastor Zeke joined them, but Priscilla interrupted his congratulations. "Stand together. I want to get a picture." Abra stood sandwiched between Pastor Zeke and Joshua. "Say *cheese!*" Priscilla snapped the picture and then beamed at them before heading off to get more pictures of Penny and guests.

"Marianne would have been very proud of you, Abra." Pastor Zeke took a small box from his pocket and handed it to her. "She would have wanted you to have this."

The last thing Abra expected from him was a gift. She received it with confusion.

"Go ahead," Joshua said, watching with an eager smile. "Open it."

Marianne's gold cross necklace was nestled inside the small blue velvet box. A hard lump formed in Abra's throat and she couldn't speak. Pastor Zeke took the necklace from the box and stepped behind her. She felt his fingers brush against her neck. "There. It's right where it belongs." He spoke softly, a faint rasp in his tone. He put his hands on her shoulders and squeezed gently before letting her go.

Abra touched the cross and fought tears. She couldn't manage a simple thank-you when she looked at him.

Pastor Zeke's expression softened. "Her mother gave it to her." He smiled gently. "I hope you'll wear it in remembrance of her."

She nodded, unable to utter a word.

"Well, don't you look the cat's meow!" Mitzi joined them and put an arm around Abra's waist. "All dressed up and no place to go. You're getting so pretty Peter is going to have to use a baseball bat to keep the boys away."

Abra giggled, her eyes blurred. When she looked toward Pastor Zeke again, she saw someone had already drawn him away. Mitzi noticed where she was looking. "Poor man never gets any time off, does he?"

"Just part of the job," Joshua said, and Abra realized he'd been watching her all along. She felt the heat surge into her face.

"Well—" Mitzi had a twinkle in her eye—"it's something to consider if you're ever thinking about going into his line of work."

Joshua laughed. "I think God's calling me in another direction."

"You never know what God has in mind until He's finished with you." Mitzi looked between the two of them, an odd smile playing on her lips. "And He does seem to scatter us in a thousand directions, doesn't He? Salt of the earth, and all that. Add a little seasoning here and a little there." She looped arms with both of them, pulling them along beside her. "Speaking of seasoning, come on, my darlings. We'd better grab ourselves some hamburgers before they're all gone!"

Joshua went up into the hills and sat where he could look out over Haven. The campground had a dozen tents pitched with families starting barbecues. The Riverfront parking lot was full, teenagers lazing on beach blankets while families picnicked under the redwoods and children splashed in the roped-off swimming area.

Since graduating last month, he'd devoted all his time to his carpentry apprenticeship with Jack Wooding. He loved the sounds of saws and hammers, the smell of sawdust. He liked seeing houses go up, knowing he was playing a part in making it happen. But by the time he got home, showered, and made himself dinner, he barely had enough energy to talk with Dad.

It wasn't often he had a day off, but when he did, he came up here to breathe fresh air and pray. The future seemed so uncertain. North Korea had invaded South Korea, and the United Nations had taken police action, which meant America was being pulled into war. Several men Dad knew who were in the Army Reserves had already been called up for service. And the draft had been reactivated. Joshua felt a restlessness in his soul, a yearning he couldn't define.

Priscilla had taken him aside at church on Sunday and said she and Peter were concerned about Abra. "She spends all her time in her room reading or over at Mitzi's practicing piano. She says she's fine, but I don't think she is. Peter tried to talk with her, but she only lets us get so close and then she puts up this invisible wall." She didn't ask, but Joshua knew she was hoping he'd come by and talk with her, find out what was going on inside her.

It shook him how much he wanted to. She was only thirteen, for heaven's sake. And he was eighteen. She was still a kid, though he had noticed at her graduation party she was growing up fast. Her hair was darker red, and she showed the first hint of womanhood. Dad had noticed him noticing her and given him an odd look. He'd laughed at himself. He'd almost told Priscilla to find someone else, but he didn't want her to think he didn't care. He just wasn't sure how to encourage a thirteen-year-old girl without giving her the wrong impression.

He'd loved her as far back as he could remember. When Dad gave her to Peter and Priscilla, he'd grieved. Now he was worrying. He couldn't get Abra out of his mind. He couldn't squelch the concerns Priscilla had unwittingly, or perhaps wittingly, put in his head. *Abra is suffering, Lord. Is it because of the past? Or is it because of something that's happening now? And what might that be all about?* Was it just teen angst? Conflicts with Penny? How would he know unless he spent time with her?

Abra needs a friend. No more than that. And no less, either.

Joshua was driving back into town when he spotted Abra walking across the bridge. She didn't even notice his truck coming up behind her until he tooted his horn and called her name through the open window. "Do you want a ride?"

"Oh. Hi. Sure." She yanked open the door and hopped in.

"I was just thinking about you, and there you were." Joshua put the truck in gear. "I haven't seen you in weeks."

"You've been busy."

Her hair was damp and her cheeks sunburned. "You've been swimming at Riverfront Park."

"Today was the first time I went. I'm not going back."

"Did you get into a squabble with Penny?"

"No." She lifted a shoulder and stared out the window. "I just don't like going there."

Oh. He knew why, but thought it better not to say any more. "So . . . what are your plans for the rest of the day?"

"Me?" She gave him a sardonic look. "Plans?"

"Good. I'm starved. How about a hamburger, fries, and a milk shake? You can call home from Bessie's and let your folks know you're with me. I don't think they'll mind."

All the angst left her face and she gave him a smile that melted his toes.

The new waitress, Susan, took their order. Joshua understood now why Dad was having more meals at Bessie's. He asked Abra how her summer was going, and she said, "Slowly." He told her she was getting better at the piano every Sunday, and she said she still felt sick to her stomach every time she played in church. "Mitzi insists I'll get over it, but I haven't yet."

"How did she talk you into it?"

"She said if I played for church, she'd teach me ragtime. I'm holding her to her promise."

He chuckled. "It could be interesting if you got the two styles mixed up."

She gave him a mischievous smile that reminded him of Mitzi, then changed the subject. "What have you been doing all summer? Are you and Lacey Glover still going together?"

"We broke up two weeks ago."

"Is your heart broken?"

He put his forearms on the booth table. "We're still good friends."

Abra's sympathetic smile turned sour. "I'll tell Penny. Her heart will be all aflutter knowing you're available again. And she'll forget all about Kent Fullerton."

He didn't like the catty tone. "Don't be a brat."

She looked ready to defend herself and then sank back against the seat. "I get tired of pretending sometimes."

"Pretending what?"

She looked at him and then shook her head. "It doesn't matter."

"You matter. To me." He leaned forward. "What's bothering you?"

"Everything. Nothing. I don't even know. I just want . . ." He could see the inner struggle and frustration on her face. She gave up trying to explain and shrugged. "My hamburger, fries, and shake." She smiled politely as the waitress delivered their orders.

"You're new, aren't you?" Joshua said before the waitress headed off. When she said yes, he extended his hand. "I'm Joshua Freeman, Pastor Zeke's son, and this is my friend, Abra Matthews. I'll bet Bessie is glad to have you on board."

"So she says." Susan gave a mirthless smile. She looked from him to Abra. "Nice to meet you both." Did she sense something amiss?

Joshua said grace and picked up his hamburger. "Do you have a crush on the lifeguard, too?"

"Penny would murder me in my sleep." She pounded the end of the bottle of ketchup until it came in a flood.

Joshua chuckled. "Nothing like a little hamburger with your ketchup."

She giggled.

"So, how did you guys meet Kent Fullerton?"

She picked up her hamburger. "Well, we haven't exactly met him yet. He's a lifeguard at the park. He'll be a senior next year, and he's on the football team. All the girls are crazy about him."

"Including you?"

She swallowed and gave him a droll look. "He's a sun-bleached blond Adonis who would look perfect with Penny." She shrugged and took another bite.

He changed the subject.

Abra told him about the list of classics Peter had given her. She'd read six so far. She relaxed and did witty imitations of conversations in Jane Austen novels. Joshua laughed.

After eating, they went over to the square and listened to the band. Families gathered. A few older couples danced on the patio in front of the gazebo. Joshua took Abra's hand. "Come on. Let's join them."

"Are you kidding?" She dug her heels in. "I don't know how to dance!"

Joshua half dragged her. "Don't be such a chicken. I'll teach you." He showed her a simple box step, then put her hand on his shoulder and pulled her into dance position. She apologized every time she stepped on his toes. "Lift your head, Abra. Stop staring at your feet." He grinned at her. "Trust me. Close your eyes and feel the music." She caught on quickly after that.

Other couples crowded in. The clock in the bell tower chimed. The song ended. Joshua let her go. "I'd better get you home."

Abra walked alongside him. The dismal expression he'd seen at the bridge was gone. She looked happy and relaxed, more like the kid she ought to be.

"Are you up to a hike on my next day off?"

"Sure." She beamed a smile at him. "When will that be?"

"Sunday. And I'm talking about three miles uphill, not a walk around the block." The truck sputtered and died twice before he got it started. "Are you up to it?"

"I don't know." She grinned. "Are you sure you don't have to work on this piece of junk?"

He grinned back. "Never on a Sunday."

Joshua knew Dad wouldn't be home yet. He had said he was driving out to the MacPhersons' to talk with Gil, who'd been struggling ever since he'd come home from the war. Sadie called every few weeks and asked Dad to come. He never said what it was about, other than Gil had been a medic and saw more than any man should.

Joshua took the mail from the box and headed up the steps, flipping through envelopes. The one at the bottom of the pile, addressed to him, felt like a kick in his stomach.

He set Dad's mail on the kitchen table, his heart drumming a hard beat, and opened his letter. Refolding it, he slipped it back into the envelope. He looked around and then decided to tuck it into his Bible for safekeeping.

The roar of the Packard sounded. Joshua didn't want to tell Dad, not yet. He wanted to pray about it and let it soak in first. He needed a little time before he broke the news. He felt like an elephant was sitting on his chest.

Summer suddenly looked a whole lot different from the way he'd envisioned it a couple hours ago while dancing with Abra.

Maybe God wanted to close that door.

CHAPTER 3

Forgive your enemies,
but never forget their names.
JOHN F. KENNEDY

ABRA WAS PLEASED when Joshua kept his promise and took her for a hike on Sunday afternoon. During the next few weeks, whenever he got off work early, he would pick her up and drive her to Bessie's for fries and a shake. He told her to stop complaining about Penny and Priscilla and talk to him about books, or what classes she was going to take, or what she wanted to do when she grew up.

Most Sundays they hiked together. He pushed her to keep up, not stopping until she felt like she had a spear in her side and could barely breathe.

"Okay. We'll stop here."

She sat, feeling sticky with sweat. Joshua smiled and shrugged off his pack. "Next week, we're going all the way to the top of the mountain."

"Assuming I'll ever take another hike with you." She flopped onto her back, arms spread.

"A half mile and we're there. The view will be worth it. I promise."

"Tell me about it on your way back." She sat up, opened her canteen, and would have emptied it if he hadn't taken it away.

"A couple of swallows or you might get sick." He opened his pack and handed her a sandwich. The peanut butter and jelly had melted into the bread. It tasted like heaven.

She took another couple of swallows of water and looked at him. "You haven't said much today."

"I've got a lot on my mind."

"Such as?"

"Hike to the top of the mountain and we'll talk about it." His smile teased, but his eyes looked serious. He ate without speaking. He sat right next to her, but seemed to be a thousand miles away.

Abra finished her sandwich and stood. "Let's go." He looked up at her as though having second thoughts. "Come on. You said you wanted to make it to the top and show me the view. So let's go."

He stuffed the pieces of wax paper into his pack, shouldered it, and took the lead. Abra felt dread nibbling at her as she followed. A quarter of a mile and she was huffing again. Her legs ached. Her feet felt hot inside her red canvas sneakers. Gritting her teeth, she didn't complain. She felt triumphant when she saw the top. Joshua shrugged off his backpack and dropped it on the ground. Abra looked out over Haven. "You can see everything from up here."

"Almost." He seemed to be drinking in the sight.

She'd been thinking of all kinds of possibilities. "So. You and Lacey Glover are back together and you're getting married."

"Married? Where did you get that idea? I'm not dating anyone. I've been—"

He stopped so abruptly, she knew she wasn't going to like whatever he had to say. "You've been what?"

He looked grim. "Drafted."

Abra closed her eyes, her lips trembling. She remembered standing in the graveyard and watching Marianne's coffin being lowered into the ground.

She sat heavily on the ground, put her elbows on her knees and her hands over her head. She sucked in a sobbing breath. "Why do you have to go?"

"Because I've been called." He sat beside her. "It doesn't mean I won't be back."

It hurt to breathe. "So you brought me all the way up here to tell me that."

"I've been putting it off for weeks. I didn't want to spoil what time I had left with you."

She was afraid to ask, but she had to know. "Are you going to Korea?"

He shook his head. "I don't know. Boot camp first; then I'll get orders to wherever I'm to serve." He frowned. "We have bases in Europe and Japan. I'll let you know as soon as I do."

She leaned against him and he put his arm around her shoulders. She scooted even closer, until her hip was against his. "I love you."

She felt him kiss the top of her head. "I love you, too. I always have. I always will."

"How many people know you're going?"

"Dad. Jack Wooding. Now you."

"What about Penny? Peter and Priscilla?"

"You can tell them. I think Priscilla has already guessed." He rubbed the top of her head with his chin. "When are you going to start calling them Mom and Dad?"

Abra snuggled herself against him and cried. "Promise you'll come home."

"I promise to try."

———

Abra ran home from school, eager to see if another letter had arrived from Joshua. He had arrived at Fort Ord. He described the base near Monterey Bay and said he'd been assigned to a holding barracks, then a training barracks, where he received his uniform. An NCO platoon leader would oversee the training for the next eight weeks. More letters followed.

> *Our NCO is tough, but every man here respects him. He made it through D-day, so everything he says carries weight. We march everywhere and exercise several times a day. The obstacle courses are a challenge I enjoy, but I'm getting tired of running miles in formation every day, rain or shine. . . .*

He said he missed having time alone in the hills. Every hour of his day was scheduled, and all of it in the company of the other men.

> *My bunkmate is from Georgia and a Christian, too. He's got a better voice than I do and sings so loud at chapel some men laugh at him. He says, "Amen" every time the chaplain makes a point, which startled me at first. I'm getting used to it. He worked for a peanut farmer, but joined up when he heard President Truman desegregated the armed forces.*

Joshua took his first leave and spent it down at Cannery Row with buddies from the barracks. Abra went to the library and checked out John Steinbeck's *Cannery Row*. In her next letter, she asked if he was looking for the Bear Flag Restaurant. Joshua wrote a swift response.

> *If you're asking what I think you're asking, the answer is no! I was not looking for a girl. I was looking for something better to eat than mess food. Tell Bessie I miss Oliver's cooking.*

Mitzi wanted Abra to practice on the church baby grand. So every Saturday, they met there. Mitzi would give her instructions and then leave her to practice while she checked the hymnals in the pews or found something to do in the fellowship hall. Pastor Zeke often came into the sanctuary to sit and listen. "You get better all the time, Abra."

She found herself watching for him. He always waited until she finished practicing before he asked if she'd heard anything from Joshua.

"I got a letter yesterday. He said he's discovering muscles he didn't know he had. And he went down to Monterey again."

"He makes Monterey sound like a beautiful place, doesn't he?"

"Is he coming home after boot camp?"

"We can hope so."

She hadn't talked to Pastor Zeke this much since she was living in his house.

Joshua loved mail call. Dad wrote frequently, but Abra was writing less and less, and her letters were brief and stilted.

Dear Joshua,
How are you? Fine, I hope. I am well and working hard.

She wrote about homework assignments and teachers, never about Penny or her other friends.

Tearing open Dad's envelope, Joshua unfolded the single sheet filled with his father's neat cursive writing.

My dearest Joshua,
May this letter find you well in body and in spirit. I miss our long talks over morning coffee. I'm glad you've found buddies willing to spend time in Bible study. When two or three are gathered in His name, Christ is among you, and He will comfort and strengthen you when you need it most.

Priscilla and Peter came by the house. They are very concerned about Abra, as am I. She goes to Mitzi's every day after school now. She hardly speaks to Penny. Priscilla thinks Abra is jealous over some boy who likes Penny. I pray that both girls will come to care for each other as sisters should. They were so close before Peter and Priscilla adopted Abra. We all hoped their friendship would grow into a true sisterly bond.

Abra has a good friend in Mitzi. She is a good woman who loves the Lord. I know she'll do all she can to keep Abra in the boat while going down the rapids.

On a happier note, Abra is becoming a wonderful pianist. She told Mitzi she no longer feels like throwing up every time she plays in front of the congregation. Sometimes I think she wants to talk to me, and I leave my door open. Mitzi gives us space, but Abra stays silent. I broke Abra's trust, and I can only pray and wait and hope someday she will accept my love again.

―――――――

Dear Joshua,

You'll be happy to know that Penny and I are on speaking terms again. We both liked Kent Fullerton. Remember the Adonis I told you about? He's our star quarterback with half the girls in school pining for his attention. He showed some interest in me, until Penny decided to steal him. But easy come, easy go. Now her heart is broken because he's going out with Charlotte. Penny said it had to do with Peter's no-dating-until-16 rule, but I think it has to do with wanting a girl who will sit in the back row of the Swan Theater. You know what they do in the back row, don't you? Penny is doing a passable job of acting like she doesn't care.

I miss you, Joshua. I haven't had a hamburger and shake since you left! But I'm mad at you, too. You invited your dad to your boot camp graduation ceremony. Why didn't you invite me? I would have come. I wouldn't care if I missed church for the rest of my life! And don't tell me I should be ashamed of myself for having such a bad attitude. I hear that enough from Mitzi.

I am mad at her right now, too. She already made me learn to play every hymn in the book, but that's not good enough for her. Now she's making me memorize a different one every week. I was so mad I wanted to punch her. She just smiled.

I took her copy of "Maple Leaf Rag" and said I wasn't giving it back. She came right out on her front porch and yelled loud enough for everyone in the neighborhood to hear that I'd never get the rhythm right without her. Priscilla and Peter said I can practice at the house, but I know that won't last. There's always the piano at church, but I don't think your dad or the board would approve. Do you? Ha-ha.

Write soon. I love you.

Abra

Zeke entered Bessie's café and found the booths all full of early morning customers. He spotted Dutch on a stool at the counter and took one next to him. "Good morning."

Susan Wells stood a few yards away, jotting down an order. She glanced at Zeke. "Be right with you, Pastor Freeman."

Dutch looked at him solemnly. "Any word from that boy of yours?"

"He's in Texas, training to be a medic."

Dutch rubbed his head and rested his arms on the counter. "Not much I can say to that, is there?" He sipped his coffee.

"How's Marjorie?"

"She won't set a date yet."

Zeke knew what the problem was. "Have you put away Sharon's picture?"

Dutch frowned as though thinking about it. "Is that what's bothering her?"

Bessie came out of the kitchen with plates stacked up her arm and delivered the breakfast platters to a booth near the front. "Mornin', Zeke. Susan, see he gets what he wants."

Susan set a mug in front of Zeke and filled it with steaming hot coffee. She refilled Dutch's. A bell sounded, and Susan headed for the kitchen.

She came back and asked Zeke if he was ready to order. He said he'd like the lumberjack breakfast with orange juice. She didn't linger.

Dutch watched her go. "I don't think she likes you."

"I make her nervous."

He laughed. "You used to make me nervous, too. I knew you were after my soul." Dutch raised his hand for the check. "Gotta get back to work." Susan put his bill on the counter in front of him. As she headed for the register, Dutch stood and slapped Zeke on the back. "Good luck, my friend. I think you're going to need it."

Zeke took Joshua's latest letter out of his jacket pocket. He'd read it a dozen times already and would read it a dozen more before he received another.

He wondered what war would do to Joshua. Some men survived physically, but came home soul-wounded. Gil MacPherson still had episodes of deep depression. The onset of the Korean War had stirred up his nightmares again. The poor man still dreamed of the carnage of Normandy and friends who'd died there, one in his arms. Several others manifested battle fatigue in lesser degrees. Michael

Weir worked constantly, leaving his wife alone and lonely. Patrick McKenna drank heavily.

Oh, Lord, my son, my son . . .

His son was a man of peace being called into war. He'd be in the middle of the fighting, traveling with his unit, carrying medical supplies. He had to be ready to give emergency aid to the wounded. Zeke had to remind himself frequently that no matter what happened, Joshua would never be lost. His future was safe and secure, even if his body wasn't. Despite knowing that, fear could be a relentless enemy, attacking him when he was tired and most vulnerable.

"A letter from your son?"

Startled, Zeke glanced up. Susan held his breakfast platter and a pot of coffee. "Yes." He folded the letter and tucked it into his jacket pocket.

She set his plate down. "I'm sorry. I shouldn't have asked."

"I see it as a kindness that you did." He smiled. "He's doing well, but asking for prayer that he will be up to the job they're giving him."

"What job will he have?"

"Medic."

"Oh." She closed her eyes.

Her reaction allowed one of Satan's darts to get through a chink in his armor. Fear clawed at him. *Lord!* Zeke prayed. *Lord, I know You love him even more than I do.* "God is sovereign, even in times of war." He took up the napkin and unrolled the silverware.

"You're not afraid for him?"

"Oh, I know fear, but every time it hits me, I pray."

"Prayer never did me any good." Her expression grew troubled. "But I guess God listens to ministers more than someone like me." She moved away before he could comment, and she kept her distance. She filled his cup one more time and left his check on the counter. Zeke left enough to cover breakfast and a generous tip. He turned over the check and wrote, *God listens to everyone, Susan.*

1951

Dear Joshua,

Peter said training to be a medic means you will be going to Korea. Is that true? I hope he's wrong about that. If he isn't, I hope the war ends before you finish training! Peter listens to the news every night, and Edward R. Murrow never says anything good about Korea.

Christmas was nice. Mitzi helped with the pageant. Mr. Brubaker played piano this year. Did you know he used to be a concert pianist? Mitzi says he played at Carnegie Hall. She told Priscilla and Peter I should take lessons from him once a week. I asked her if she wants to get rid of me. She says we can concentrate on ragtime now. Penny and I went to Cinderella.

Other than that, I study and do my chores and practice piano like a good little girl. That is the sum total of my boring, pathetic life. Haven is the dullest town on earth.

When I grow up, I am moving far away to a big city. You will have to come and visit me in New York or New Orleans and see the Mardi Gras! Maybe I'll go to Hollywood and become a movie star. I want to live somewhere exciting where people have fun! You owe me two letters now.

Love, Abra

Abra came home from Mitzi's after a long lesson with Mr. Brubaker. Priscilla greeted her and went on peeling potatoes. "There's a letter from Joshua on your bed."

Abra ran upstairs. She hadn't seen or heard from Joshua since he came home on leave before Thanksgiving. He had taken her to Bessie's Corner Café once, and she felt oddly shy with him. He looked different. He stood straighter and seemed older, more reserved. He wasn't a boy anymore, and she was very aware of their five-year age difference. She had never before been tongue-tied with Joshua, nor felt the strange swirling tingles in her stomach when he looked at her.

Dumping her books on the desk, she grabbed for the thin blue- and red-striped military mailer. She tore it open carefully. Only a few lines this time.

> *Dear Abra,*
>
> *By the time you read this, I'll be in the air and on my way to Korea. I told Dad I didn't want anyone knowing I had my orders. It would have spoiled my time at home. I'm sorry I didn't say good-bye. I thought it best at the time. Now I'm sorry I didn't.*
>
> *I'm praying you will fix your mind steadfastly on Jesus and trust Him no matter what happens. God has a plan for each of us, and this is His plan for me. I will do my best to fulfill my duty and come home in one piece.*
>
> *Please thank your mom for the picture.*
>
> *I'll love you forever.*
>
> *Joshua*

Abra wept.

—————

Zeke took his place in the pastor's chair to the right of the pulpit as Abra finished a medley of hymns and the congregation settled into their seats. Abra's playing had improved markedly since Ian Brubaker had begun working with her. She played with more skill than Marianne ever had, but mechanical skill could not replace the outpouring of one's spirit into the music. Zeke prayed as he watched and listened. *Lord, what will it take to open this child's heart to the depth, breadth, and height of Your love for her?*

Zeke spotted a new face among the familiar. Susan Wells sat in the back pew, moving slightly to the right to hide behind the Beamers and the Callaghans. Zeke almost smiled, but thought better of it. Let her think he hadn't noticed her. He didn't want her to slip out the door and run away. She had been running for a long time, and she looked weary of it.

Opening his Bible, Zeke turned to the Sermon on the Mount. Pages rustled as Zeke began to read aloud. "'Blessed are the poor in spirit: for theirs is the kingdom of heaven. Blessed are they that mourn: for they shall be comforted. Blessed are the meek: for they shall inherit the earth. Blessed are they which do hunger and thirst after righteousness: for they shall be filled.'"

Everyone sat waiting as Zeke sent up a silent plea for the Lord to give him the words that needed to be said, and then he began to speak. Ross Beamer settled back in the pew, and Zeke caught a glimpse of Susan behind him. Nothing showed in her face, but he sensed her brokenness and yearning.

His heart ached at what he saw in her expression. Would she be gone before he had an opportunity to welcome her? Perhaps others would offer friendship if she wouldn't accept it from him.

The service was at an end. People stood and moved toward the center aisle as Abra played the postlude. Zeke thought Susan would be gone before he passed the last pew, but she was hedged in by little old Fern Daniels, who always kept watch for newcomers. Mitzi would be along soon, too. Zeke hoped their focused, loving attention wouldn't frighten Susan away. He stood outside, shaking hands and speaking with parishioners as they filed out of the church. Most thanked him, made kind observations, or chatted briefly before heading for the fellowship hall, where refreshments awaited.

Marjorie Baxter slipped her arm through Dutch's as they reached him. "We have good news, Zeke." She looked happy. So did Dutch.

"I saw the Haven *Chronicle* announcement of your engagement. Congratulations."

Fern Daniels had Susan by the arm as she introduced her to Mrs. Vanderhooten and Gil and Sadie MacPherson. They all moved toward the front door. Susan avoided looking at him. Fern smiled brightly. "Zeke, I want you to meet Susan Wells. Susan . . ."

"We've met," Susan said, and Fern looked surprised and then so interested, Susan was quick to explain. "I work at Bessie's Corner Café. Pastor Freeman comes in for breakfast a couple times a week."

"Oh, no one calls him Pastor Freeman, dear. He's Pastor Zeke to everyone in town." She gave him a motherly pat. "We're all family around here, and we'd love to have you join us."

"I'm just visiting, ma'am."

"Well, of course you are. You visit as many times as you want. Oh, and here's our little Abra. Honey, come on over here." She beckoned. "Susan, this is Abra Matthews. Isn't she a marvelous piano player?"

"Yes. She is."

"Not as good as Ian Brubaker, Mrs. Daniels." Abra shook hands with Susan.

"Oh, stuff and nonsense." Fern waved the comment away like a pesky fly. "He went to Juilliard. You shine, too." She leaned toward Susan. "Abra's been playing since she was knee-high to a grasshopper. She used to be scared half to death sitting up there in front, but she just keeps getting better every week." Fern looked around for others to introduce. Susan seemed ready to duck for cover.

"Mitzi! Come here. There's someone I want you to meet."

Zeke chuckled. "You'll be fine, Susan. They don't bite."

Mitzi and Fern both guided Susan toward the fellowship hall.

Abra lingered. "Have you heard anything from Joshua, Pastor Zeke?"

Joshua was the only common ground they trod. "I had a short

letter that said he made it to Japan and would be transported by ship across the Korean Strait to Pusan. How about you?"

"Nothing." She looked worried. "Peter said Hoengseong was destroyed. Joshua wouldn't be there, would he? Peter said the Communists were overrunning our units like a human wave."

Zeke had been reading the paper and listening to news broadcasts, too. "Hoengseong is in the middle of South Korea. He wouldn't have been there when the battle happened, though he may have gone in after. He didn't say whether he'd be with a unit or in an aid station. We'll just have to wait until he writes, and pray God keeps him safe."

She looked angry now, close to tears. "Well, I hope God hears you. He's never listened to me." Turning away, she rushed down the steps.

═══════

Joshua had only been in country a week and already felt dead on his feet. And it got worse every day. He'd never been so tired in his life. The advance on Chipyong-ni and mountains to the southeast had been grueling. His back and legs screamed for relief. The terrain was rough, the temperature barely warming to fifty degrees by midday. Joshua carried a metal kit, pouches, and an M1911 .45 ACP he would only use to save himself or a patient.

He'd already been warned Communists didn't respect the Geneva Convention and would use the red cross on his white helmet as a bull's-eye. As a precaution, he covered it with mud, but rain just washed it away. He'd been pinned down more than once, enemy fire plucking the ground around him. His comrades said they were lucky the Commies were lousy shots, but Joshua credited God and whatever band of angels He'd sent for keeping him alive.

Gunfire came from the hill above. Joshua dove for cover. "Keep your heads down!" Grenades were flung up the hill. A man cried out and went down. An explosion hit nearby. Surging to his feet, Joshua bent low and ran uphill to get to the fallen man.

"Boomer!" They'd prayed together and talked about their families back home. Boomer's folks raised corn and eight kids, five of whom were sons, back in Iowa. Boomer shared Joshua's faith, but he'd had a feeling things wouldn't go well for him today. He'd given Joshua a letter to send home if anything happened to him. Joshua had it in his jacket pocket.

Boomer lay sprawled on his back, a red blossom in the center of his chest, his eyes wide-open, staring up at the steel-gray sky. Joshua gently closed them as a machine gun rat-a-tatted. Explosions shook the ground on which he knelt. He heard other men cry out.

"Medic!" someone shouted from higher up the hill. Joshua snapped the chain around Boomer's neck. He wedged one dog tag between Boomer's two front teeth and pocketed the other. Shifting his pack, he made the run. Two men had been shot. Joshua called for help, signaling another medic to take the closest wounded while he headed for the one farther up. Bullets pelted the ground around him. He saw a blast from above, heard shouts and screams. Heart pounding, legs burning with exertion, he kept running, fixing his mind on reaching the men who needed him.

Abra hadn't received a letter from Joshua in a month, and all Peter could talk about was the number of men dying in Korea. He turned on the radio the minute he came in the door, eager to hear the latest news reports. President Truman had relieved General MacArthur of duty. The Communist Chinese forces drove through the 2nd, 3rd, 7th, and 24th divisions and on toward Seoul while MacArthur faced congressional hearings for his outspoken views on how the war should be fought.

Joshua's last letter had been short, almost perfunctory, as though he wrote out of duty. He asked about her. Had she worked things out with Penny? Life was too short to carry a grudge. He hadn't answered any of her questions about his life as a soldier or his friends or what was happening around him. And Pastor Zeke wasn't sharing his letters anymore. She had been rude to him. Maybe this was his way of punishing her.

When she apologized, he still wouldn't let her read Joshua's letters. "I'm not withholding them out of spite, Abra. Joshua writes different things to me than he does to you. That's all."

She grew even more determined with that. "That's why we've been sharing, isn't it?"

"Some things you don't need to know."

"Like what?"

"What it's like to be in the middle of a battle."

"You could tell me *something*, couldn't you?"

"I can tell you Joshua needs your prayers. I can tell you he's been transferred to an aid station near the front."

Peter thought being in an aid station sounded safer than being on a battlefield. "At least he's not running with a unit and taking fire." She worried less until she overheard him talking to the next-door neighbor about the Communists targeting MASH units. She didn't have to ask if that meant Joshua might be in danger. She had nightmares of him lying in a casket and being lowered into a hole in the ground next to Marianne Freeman's marble headstone.

Priscilla awakened her in the middle of the night. "I heard you crying."

Abra went into her arms, sobbing.

Penny, bleary-eyed, stood in the doorway. "Is she okay, Mom?"

"Just a nightmare, honey. Go on back to bed." Priscilla's arms tightened around Abra, and she spoke softly. "I know you're worried about Joshua, Abra. We all are. All we can do is pray." Priscilla did just that as Abra clung to her. She could only hope the God who hadn't been there for her wouldn't let Joshua down.

Staring into the darkness outside her bedroom window, she prayed, too.

If You let him die, God, I'll hate You forever. I swear I will.

———————

Dear Dad,

It's been rough. Had no sleep for 92 hours. Woke up a little while ago in the tent barracks and didn't know how I got here. Joe said I collapsed. I don't remember anything. Gil often comes to mind. I understand him better now. I pray for him every time I think of it.

I'm under orders to rest for eight more hours, but I wanted to get a letter off to you. It may be a while before I can write again.

I thought the freezing rain and snows were bad, but now we have the heat. Insects are a problem, fleas the worst. Every patient we get in from the front is infested. We have to dust and spray them with DDT. Every Korean in the country is infested with worms and parasites. The minute a doc opens up a Korean patient, worms start crawling out, some more than two feet long. The docs just drop them into a bucket.

We're short on water, and what's available is polluted with night soil. Lots of men down with dysentery and enteric fever. Even had a couple of cases of encephalitis. Lots of refugees in poverty, hungry, looking for shelter anywhere they find it and living in filth. Women turn to prostitution to survive. Every soldier who goes looking for "comfort" comes back with VD. Doc is doing short-arm inspections on every man coming back from leave.

I have my pocket Gideon Bible on me at all times and read it every chance I get. It calms me, gives me hope. Men call me "Preacher," and not in the mocking way they did in boot camp. When death hunts men, they look for God. They want to hear the gospel.

Pray for me, Dad. I've seen so many die, I no longer feel anything when it happens. It's probably just as well, though. I need a cool head. I need to work fast. One dies, but another waits on a gurney.

Tell Abra I love her. I dream about her sometimes. Tell her I'm sorry I'm not writing much. The truth is, I don't know what to say to her anymore. I live in a world so different from hers, and I don't want to invite her into it. All she needs to know is I love her. I'm still doing my best to serve God and my country. I'm alive.

I love you, Dad. Your words are my lifeline. They keep me sane in an insane world.

Joshua

———

Joshua wrote to Abra once from Japan, where he was on R & R. It was the longest letter she had received in months. He said he spent most of the time sleeping while others went out on the town. He'd put in for an extension of his tour of duty because he felt needed.

Abra wrote back, furious that he was willing to cause everyone so much worry. She listened to the news almost as much as Peter. Talks of truce started in July, but by late August the Communists broke off negotiations and the Battle of Bloody Ridge hit the headlines. Peter thought the Communists were posturing for peace, but really just wanted time to recoup their losses. His concern proved true when fighting intensified, the peace negotiations having allowed time for the enemy to hide supplies in sandbag bunkers in their plan to take all of Korea.

School started, giving her more to think about than piano lessons and obsessing about Joshua. Penny made the varsity cheerleading squad and spent most afternoons practicing new cheers. When the girls went to see *The Day the Earth Stood Still*, Abra kept saying, "Klaatu barada nikto!" over and over again because Patricia Neal couldn't remember what she was supposed to say to save the world from the space robot.

Meanwhile, the Battle of Heartbreak Ridge raged in Korea. Within weeks, three US divisions attacked Communist forces along sagging boundary lines and successfully drove the enemy back. Communist losses were so heavy, peace talks resumed at Kaesong. Abra didn't hear a word from Joshua, but she knew things weren't going well because Pastor Zeke looked gray and gaunt.

1952

Peter and Priscilla gave Penny a record player for her sixteenth birthday. Abra got sick of listening to Hank Williams singing "Your Cheatin' Heart" and Rosemary Clooney's "Come on-a My House." In self-defense, she swam alone in the backyard pool. They saw *High Noon*, and Penny started wearing her hair up like Grace Kelly.

Abra didn't expect a birthday celebration, but Peter and Priscilla surprised her by inviting Pastor Zeke, Mitzi, and Mr. Brubaker to join the family for dinner. Mr. Brubaker gave Abra sheet music to the Broadway hit *South Pacific*. Mitzi had wrapped up her beautiful Spanish shawl. Penny gave her a Kit-Cat Clock. When she opened Pastor Zeke's present, she found Marianne's worn Bible wrapped in tissue paper. She opened it and saw Marianne's neat handwriting in the margins; passages underlined, circled, and starred. When she looked up, she saw hope and moisture in his eyes. She thanked him, but she couldn't lie and promise she'd read it.

"And now, our gift." Priscilla handed Abra a beautifully wrapped present. Removing the ribbons and papers, she found a blue velvet case with satin lining.

Penny gasped. "Pearls! Oh! Let me see." She reached for them, but Peter reminded Penny she'd gotten a nice record player. He took the pearls from the case and put them around Abra's neck, securing the clasp.

The evening wasn't even over before Penny asked to borrow them when she went to *The Quiet Man* with Jack Constantinow, one of the varsity linebackers.

"Not until I've had a chance to wear them." Abra tried to make the words light, but she resented Penny's assumption that everything in Abra's drawers and closet belonged to her, too. When Priscilla brought in the birthday cake and told her to make a wish, Abra wished Joshua home from the war and blew out all the candles.

Peace talks continued; small battles continued along the Main Line of Resistance. Losses mounted up as the negotiations dragged on.

Joshua's letters slowed to a trickle and then stopped.

CHAPTER 4

War is hell!

WILLIAM TECUMSEH SHERMAN

1953

Sweat ran cold between Joshua's shoulder blades as he rose and ran with his unit. Breech-loaded field guns boomed behind him, shells exploding. Muzzle-loaded mortars fired shells into enemy battlements, sandbags bursting, fire flashing, men screaming.

A man went down in front of him. Another was flung backward, arms spread wide like wings. A sobbing soldier tried to haul a buddy to safety. Joshua helped him get over and behind the rocks. "Jacko!" the soldier wailed. "Jacko! Come on, man. Wake up! I told you to keep your head down."

Joshua didn't need to check for a pulse. He snapped off the dog tags, tucked one in his pocket, and set the other between the man's teeth.

Joshua pulled the grieving soldier against his chest like a father comforting a child. The man leaned heavily against him, racked with sobs. An explosion hit so close, they were both thrown back. Joshua's ears rang. He heard shouts and machine-gun fire. Rolling over, he saw the other man unconscious from the blast. He dragged him to safe cover and radioed for assistance. Within minutes two medics came up the hill with a litter.

The smell of dirt, blood, and sulfur surrounded Joshua. The ground moved every time field guns fired. Something hit the side of his helmet. He felt a hard punch in his side.

"Preacher!" someone shouted.

Joshua skidded into the cover of rocks. One man leaned back, pale and panting, while two others fired their guns. Someone was screaming profanity as a machine gun spent dozens of rounds in the space of seconds. Shrugging off his own pack, Joshua peeled off the wounded man's gear. He wiped moisture from his eyes and opened the man's jacket and shirt to get to the wound and stop the bleeding.

"Preacher." Face covered with dirt and grime, the man's eyes held relief and confusion.

Joshua knew him. "Don't try to talk, Wade. Let's see what's what." He assessed the damage. "Shoulder wound. Missed your lungs. Thank God. You're going home to your cornfields, my friend."

Joshua wiped his face again, and his hand came away covered in blood. He pulled a gauze pad from his supplies and jammed it up inside his helmet. One of the men threw a grenade. The explosion brought a rain of rocks and dirt. "Got 'em! Let's go!"

Joshua and Wade were left behind. Joshua tried to radio for help, but he couldn't get through. The wounded man had passed out. Joshua shifted and drew in a sharp breath. His side burned like fire, moisture seeping into his waistband. Grabbing another gauze pad, he pressed it hard against his side to stanch the flow of blood, using a length of bandage to keep it in place.

His radio crackled, then fell silent. No one was coming.

The firing had moved farther away. He might make it down the hill if he went now.

Joshua pulled Wade up and across his shoulders and staggered to his feet. He headed across the barren, rocky ground, avoiding pits, rocks, and detritus. Dog tags jingled in his pocket. How many had he carried in his pockets since stepping foot on Korean soil?

He stumbled once and fell to his knees, pain shooting up his legs and back. Wade's weight bore down on him like a sack of stones. Searing pain spread across his side. *God, give me strength!* The aid station had to be close. His vision blurred, but he thought he spotted the blacked-out school building and tents.

Wade's weight was lifted from him. Joshua hit the ground face-first. Strong arms lifted. He tried to walk, but his toes dragged as two men half carried him. Everything went black.

"Abra." Priscilla stood in the bedroom doorway. "Pastor Zeke is downstairs. He wants to talk to you."

Abra's chemistry text and notebook bounced onto the floor as she flew off the bed and raced downstairs. Neither she nor Pastor Zeke had heard anything from Joshua in weeks.

Pastor Zeke looked pale and drawn. Fear flooded her, anger in its wake. "He's dead, isn't he? Joshua's dead." Her voice broke. "I knew he'd get killed. I knew it!"

Pastor Zeke gripped her by the shoulders and gave her a gentle shake. "He's been wounded. But he's alive."

Abra felt weak with relief. "When can I see him?"

"He'll be at Tripler hospital in Hawaii for a while; I don't know how long. Then he'll be flown to Travis Air Force Base. He'll let us know when he arrives." Half a day's drive from Haven. She started to cry. She couldn't stop herself. Pastor Zeke drew her into his arms. "He's coming home, Abra."

She kept her arms at her sides. Pastor Zeke's hand cupped the back of her head. She had forgotten how the sound of his heartbeat comforted. "Pray the war ends soon, Abra." Pastor Zeke rested his chin briefly on top of her head before letting her step back. "For Joshua's sake as well as all the other men in Korea."

The relief dissipated. "He's wounded. They won't send him back."

"We can hope the Army won't listen to his request." Pain flickered in Pastor Zeke's eyes. He'd aged since Joshua left. His dark hair had streaks of gray. He'd lost weight. "It's in God's hands."

"All you ever talk about is God. You could tell Joshua to stay home and he'd listen to you."

"I can't do that."

"You can, but you won't!"

"That's enough, Abra." Peter spoke firmly. "Go to your room."

She ran out the front door instead, racing down the steps. She ran three blocks before the pain in her side made her slow down. Anger pulsed through her and she wanted to aim it at someone. Volunteer to go back? Was Joshua crazy? Did he *want* to die?

Gasping for breath, she continued at a fast walk until she reached the town square. She sat on a bench, looking at the patio where Joshua had danced with her. No bands today. Summer was long over. Rain drizzled; dark clouds promised heavier ones coming. Her body cooled and she shivered. Bessie's would offer shelter.

Few customers came between breakfast and lunch. The bell jangled over the door as she went in. The dark-haired woman at the counter glanced up in surprise. What was her name? Susan Wells.

"Can I have a drink, Mrs. Wells?"

"Call me Susan." She put crushed ice in a tall glass, filled it with water, and set it in front of Abra. "If you don't mind me asking, are you all right?"

"I'm all right. Joshua's been wounded." She gulped the water.

"Pastor Zeke's son. Nice young man. You've been in here with him, haven't you?"

"He's my best friend. Or he was. I don't know anymore. He hardly writes. He tells Pastor Zeke all the important stuff and just asks me a bunch of stupid questions." She spoke in mockery. "'How's school, Abra? How are you getting on with Penny? Are you doing your homework? Are you going to church?'" She bit her lip to stop the rush of words, afraid tears would follow. Why was she rattling on to a stranger?

"Maybe he doesn't tell you some things because he knows you'd worry."

"I'm not going to worry about him anymore." She drank the rest of the water and plunked the glass down on the counter. "I don't care what he does. He can go to perdition for all I care."

"That's usually what we say when we care a whole lot." Susan gave a mirthless smile as she refilled the glass. "He's a medic, isn't he?"

Abra slumped onto a stool. "He's an idiot!"

"How badly wounded?"

"Enough that the Army is sending him home, but not enough to keep him from going back again!"

"Oh." Susan sighed, staring off into space. "He did look like that sort of young man."

"What sort?"

"The sort that cares more about other people than himself." She smiled sadly. "Not many men like that around anymore. That's for sure."

Abra covered her face and gulped down a sob.

Susan took hold of her wrists and squeezed. "I'm so sorry, Abra. I'm so, so sorry." She spoke so close Abra could feel the warmth of her breath. "If there's one thing I've learned over the years, it's that you've got no say in what other people do with their lives. Everyone makes their own choices, good or bad."

"I don't want him to die."

Susan's hands loosened and lifted away. "All you can do is wait and see what happens." She put several napkins on the counter in front of Abra.

Abra took one and blew her nose. "I'm sorry I'm making a fuss."

"Don't worry about it."

Abra looked out the window. No drizzle now, just a cold, hard, pelting rain. "Can I stay awhile?"

"Stay as long as you want." She put a menu in front of Abra. "You might feel better if you had something to eat."

"I don't have any money."

"My treat." Susan smiled. "Unless you want a steak."

———

Joshua felt fear bubble up inside him like soda in a shaken can. It made no sense. He was stateside and on a Greyhound bus heading home. Soon after he'd arrived at Travis, he'd tried to volunteer to go back to Korea, but he'd been told he'd have to reenlist. He prayed about it, but instead of feeling peace about returning to the front, he'd felt the strong pull to go home.

Everything was so quiet, so normal, while inside, he felt anything but. He couldn't stop thinking about the men still in Korea, still fighting, still dying. He felt like he'd gone through a meat grinder and been spewed out the other side.

Most of the bus passengers slept. One snored loudly in the back row. Joshua dozed and dreamed he was running up a hill, his lungs burning for air, explosions going off to the right and left of him. He could hear screaming and knew he had to get to the wounded. He made it to the top and looked down into a valley of shadows and death—Americans, Koreans, and Chinese all tangled together. The air was filled with the stench of rotting flesh; the sky was black with circling carrion birds ready to feast. He fell to his knees, weeping, and heard dark laughter.

A figure came out of the darkness, malevolent and mocking. He spread his wings, triumphant. *I'm not done yet. This is just the beginning of what I will accomplish before the last day comes.*

Joshua stood. "You've already lost."

Ah, but then, so have you. You couldn't save them all, could you? Only a measly few. This is my domain. I hold the power over life and death.

"You're a liar and a murderer. Get away from me!"

The sneering voice came closer. *I see you, Joshua. I see her, too.*

Joshua reached for his throat, but the creature laughed and disappeared.

Joshua awoke, his heart pounding a war beat. No one stood beside his seat. No one was speaking to him. No incoming mortar shells blowing men to pieces. Just the screech of the bus brakes.

He leaned back and stared out the window. He didn't want to close his eyes again. He'd been on American soil for a month, but sleep still brought nightmares of Korea.

Joshua breathed in deeply and exhaled slowly. He cast his mind back, remembering. His muscles relaxed; his mind focused. *You called and I answered, Lord.*

He felt warmth and stillness. *And I call you again to lay down your burdens. I give peace, Joshua, not as the world gives, but a peace beyond all human comprehension. Abide in Me.*

The Greyhound bus pulled off the main road. Joshua saw Riverfront Park off to the left. His heart drummed with excitement as the bus crossed the bridge to Haven. *Rat-a-tat, rat-a-tat,* the wheels whispered against the steel and macadam.

Joshua leaned forward as the Greyhound pulled to a stop on Main Street, across from the town square. Joy burst inside him when he saw Dad standing on the sidewalk, and then a sharp stab of disappointment. He didn't see Abra.

"Haven!" the driver called out as he opened the door and went quickly down the steps.

Joshua rose, straightening his uniform jacket as he made his way off the bus. Dad embraced him firmly. "You'll see Abra in a few minutes. Peter and Priscilla insisted we come for dinner." Dad took the duffel bag from his hand and led the way to Mitzi's roadster parked around the corner.

Joshua grinned as he slid in and closed the door. "Either you haven't been driving this baby or you just had it washed and polished."

Dad laughed as he turned the key. The engine roared to life. "I thought it was a good time to give her a spin."

A *Welcome Home, Joshua* banner was stretched along the white picket fence. He saw cars parked up and down the street. Dread filled him. "What is all this?"

"I'm sorry. You know what's waiting for you and you'll survive it. I tried to tell them to give you a couple of days, but people love you, Son. They want to welcome you home." The parking space in front of the house had been reserved for them.

Friends poured out the front door onto the porch to cheer and clap. Joshua barely made it around the car before they swarmed through the gate, surrounding him, hugging him, slapping his back. Priscilla cried and waved others ahead of her. Joshua took in the familiar faces: Mitzi, the Martins, Bessie and Oliver Knox, the Lydicksons. Jack and the crew he'd worked with.

"Give the man room, folks!" Peter shouted. "Let him get inside the house!"

And then Joshua saw Abra. His heart leaped when she came through the front door and stood on the porch. She'd grown taller and filled out while he was away. Even with a girlish ponytail, she looked like a young woman and not a girl anymore. Seeing her coming down the steps, he pressed his way between friends and caught her when she threw herself into his arms. "Joshua!" Arms wrapped around his neck, she pressed herself full against him. He drew in a sharp breath, caught off guard by the shock of sensations coursing through his body. She kissed his cheek. "I missed you so much!" Could she hear how hard his heart pounded against hers or feel the heat radiating through him?

He set her down firmly and stepped back, forcing a laugh. "I missed you, too." His voice came out tight and hoarse. He wished they were alone so he could talk to her. Her recent letters had been so cautious and cold. He hadn't known what to expect when he came home—certainly not a welcome like this, not this heat in his belly, nor the racing blood.

Abra grabbed his hand, tugging him up the steps, acting more like the girl-child he had left behind. "Come on! Everything's ready inside!"

He laughed uneasily. "What everything?"

"The decorations, the buffet in the backyard, the cake!" When they entered the house, she slipped her arm around his waist and squeezed hard. "I was afraid you'd never come home."

He slid his hand under her ponytail and gently gripped the back of her neck. "So was I." She turned exuberantly and kissed him on the corner of his mouth. When she drew back, he saw something indefinable and intoxicating in her eyes. Did she sense her budding power? He looked away, deliberately breaking the moment. Dad stood off to one side, watching them.

Joshua didn't fully relax until people lined up for the buffet. He'd been to a hundred banquets at the church, and he'd lined up for grub in Army mess halls. Everyone insisted he go first. They had all brought something to add to the feast. Joshua hesitated until Mitzi grabbed his plate and his arm. "Come on, boyo. You need more meat on your bones."

———

Penny pulled Abra off to one side. "Cover for me, would you?"

"Where are you going this time?"

"Michelle and I are going to Eddie's."

Abra had half expected the sight of Joshua in his Army uniform to resurrect Penny's old crush. Other than saying he looked handsome, she hadn't been bowled over. Abra looked at him standing at the buffet table, Mitzi snatching his plate and serving him. He had changed. It wasn't just in the leanness or muscle of his body, the cropped hair, or the tension in his jaw. It wasn't the uniform. It was something else, something pressed down deep inside him. She'd seen it when he got out of the car. Did everyone? He had suffered, greatly. He carried deeper wounds than the one in his side. He was still Joshua, just not the same Joshua who had left Haven nearly three years ago.

"Abra!" Penny pressed, impatient. "Will you cover for me or not?"

"All this drama for a hamburger and milk shake with Michelle?"

"There's this guy I want to see."

Abra gave her a droll look. "Of course. Who is he?"

"No one you know. He's from LA and absolutely gorgeous. I want to meet him. If Mom asks—"

Abra laughed. "If anyone asks, I'll say you're on the telephone. That'll give you the whole afternoon all to yourself. How's that?"

"Perfect!" She kissed Abra's cheek. "Thanks. I'll do you a favor someday. And I'll tell you all about him when I get home." She took two steps and turned back with a teasing grin. "Then again, maybe I won't."

"As if I care." Abra rolled her eyes. "Go on. Get out of here." She shook her head as Penny headed through the gathering and went into the house. Abra picked up a plate and took a piece of fried chicken. She looked over at Joshua. People kept stopping by his table. Joshua seemed uncomfortable, tense. If she'd had her way, she'd have met Joshua alone at the bus station and they'd be at Bessie's right now, having hamburgers, fries, and shakes—chocolate for her, strawberry for him.

She glanced at Joshua again. He was looking right at her. She felt an odd twinge in her stomach. He smiled. She smiled back, hoping the war hadn't changed him too much.

A shiny red Corvette convertible with white leather bucket seats was parked in front of the house when Abra came home from Mitzi's a few days later. As she opened the gate, she heard voices and spotted a young man leaning against the porch railing. This must be the "guy from LA" Penny was all atwitter about. When the gate snapped shut behind Abra, he glanced at her.

Abra had never seen a young man more stunningly handsome. He could have stepped out of a movie poster. When his mouth tipped, she realized she'd been staring. He looked Abra up and down with dark, hooded eyes. Her whole body went hot, and breath caught in her throat.

He straightened and walked toward her. "Since Penny has forgotten her manners, let me introduce myself. Dylan Stark." He held out his hand. "And you are . . . ?"

"Abra." His fingers closed around her hand, and she felt the warm pressure all the way down to her toes.

"My sister," Penny said brightly, eyes hot.

"Really?" he drawled. His brown leather jacket was open, revealing a fitted white T-shirt tucked into snug belted Levi's. He'd look better in a bathing suit than Kent Fullerton ever did. She averted her gaze, but not before he noticed. His expression gave Abra the feeling he knew exactly what she was thinking—and feeling. He grinned, showing perfectly straight white teeth. "It's a pleasure to meet you, Abra." The tingling awareness unsettled her.

"Abra." Penny glared at her. "Don't you have something to do?"

Abra gave Dylan another glance before opening the front door. "It's always a pleasure to meet one of Penny's new boyfriends." She escaped inside and almost ran into Priscilla in the entry hall.

Priscilla looked toward the front door. "What do you think of him?"

Abra tried to come up with an answer, but her emotions were boiling over inside her. Priscilla studied her expression and frowned. She opened the screen door and went out onto the porch. "Penny, why don't you ask your friend to stay for dinner?"

"I don't want to put you to any trouble, Mrs. Matthews."

"We'd love to have you join us." Priscilla sounded almost insistent. "Peter and I always like to get to know Penny's friends."

Dylan laughed softly. "Well, how can I say no? But I'll need to call my father, in case he's already made plans."

"Of course. The phone is in the kitchen."

Embarrassed at the thought of being caught eavesdropping, Abra raced up the stairs. Closing her bedroom door, she leaned back against it, heart pounding. Was this what the romance novels meant about meeting someone and knowing immediately you were made for each other? She had never felt it before. Did Penny feel this way every time she was "in love"?

Abra brushed her hair fiercely. Why should Penny get every boy she wanted when Abra hadn't even had a date yet? Let Penny chase down and tackle someone else. Abra had been infatuated with Kent Fullerton, and that hadn't stopped Penny from charming him until he succumbed.

Stripping off her white blouse, blue jeans, bobby socks, and tennis shoes, Abra rummaged through her closet and decided on the green dress she wore to church. Mitzi said it was just the right color for her. Abra didn't wait to be called down for dinner. She volunteered to set the table. Priscilla seemed startled when she saw Abra's change of clothes and her hair down around her shoulders. Penny was clearly furious, but one look from Priscilla kept her from saying a word about it. Peter talked briefly with Dylan in the living room before they all took seats around the dinner table.

Every nerve in Abra's body told her Dylan's attention was fixed on her, though he didn't even look at her. Her heart drummed; her body hummed. Peter started asking questions. Penny protested, but Dylan said he didn't mind. He answered with a smile while passing mashed potatoes and pork chops. He had taken some classes at USC, mostly business and marketing. He was twenty years old and taking a break before finishing school and jumping into a career. He liked the idea of having his own business someday, but what business, he didn't know. He was spending the summer with his father, who owned vineyards in the area.

"I don't know any Starks around here." Peter sounded perplexed.

"My father is Cole Thurman. He owns Shadow Hills Winery."

"Oh." Peter's tone was flat. Only those who knew him well would recognize he had any sense of misgiving.

Abra hadn't seen that expression on Peter's face before. She glanced at Priscilla and saw she was troubled, too. Who was Cole Thurman?

Dylan continued. His parents had been divorced since he was a boy—not an amicable parting of ways, unfortunately. He gave a soft, sad laugh and said that was why he went by his mother's name rather than his father's. He thought it was time to come north and get to know him, make his own judgments.

Peter sawed at his pork chop. "How long do you plan to stay?"

"I don't know yet." Dylan shrugged. "Could be a week. Could be a lifetime." His mother wasn't happy about his coming at all, but he needed time to make up his own mind. Everyone had the right to know the truth about their parents, didn't they? His dark eyes found Abra. She felt the jolt. Had Penny been telling him stories about where her sister came from?

Peter asked what Dylan thought about the war in Korea. Penny groaned. "Dad!"

Priscilla interrupted. "Why don't we all go into the living room and be more comfortable."

Penny shoved her chair back. "Daddy, Dylan wants to take me to the movies tonight. *The Beast from 20,000 Fathoms* is playing."

"I thought you didn't like horror movies."

"Oh, this one is supposed to be really good. Please . . . ?"

"I promise to have her home by ten, Mr. Matthews."

Penny would probably drag Dylan into the last row. She'd pretend to be terrified and in desperate need of a protective arm around her. Abra watched Penny walk down the steps with Dylan. He opened the car door for her. She smiled at him as she tucked her white skirt around her thighs before he closed her in. Abra lowered her head, afraid he'd see her staring out the window at him, and didn't raise it until she heard the roar of the Corvette pulling away from the curb.

She headed for the stairs. In her room, Abra stripped off the green dress and hung it back in the closet. She'd made a complete fool of herself by being even more obvious than Penny. She put on her pajamas and threw herself across her bed.

The doorbell rang. She sat bolt upright, suddenly remembering Joshua was supposed to stop by tonight. She ran to the head of the stairs before Priscilla opened the door. "Tell him I'll be down in five minutes!" She ran back to her room and pulled on her new black Audrey Hepburn capri pants and black flats. She buttoned on a short-sleeved green blouse, raked her fingers through her hair, and put on a bit of lipstick.

She'd ask Joshua to take her to the Swan.

———

Joshua caught his breath when Abra raced down the stairs, her cheeks flushed, her eyes so eager. What a difference three years could make in a girl. He felt off-balance, shaken. Why couldn't she have stayed a little girl instead of becoming this disturbing young woman who threw her arms around his neck and hugged him like a friend when he was feeling so much more. *Too soon,* he told himself, hoping the heat would cool and his heart slow to its normal rhythm.

"Can we go to the movies, Joshua? Please. Please!"

"What's playing?"

"*The Beast from 20,000 Fathoms*," Peter called from the living room. He appeared in the doorway and gave Abra an odd look before extending his hand in greeting. "Good to see you, Joshua." He raised a brow at Abra. "Planning on keeping an eye on your sister?" He gave a bleak laugh. "Not that it's such a bad idea. I'm having second thoughts about letting her go."

Joshua looked at Abra in question and saw her cheeks bloom hot pink. Peter walked them to the door, told them to have a good time, and closed the door after them. Joshua opened the front gate for her. "I thought you didn't like horror movies."

She shrugged. "I don't. Usually. This one is supposed to be really good."

Something else was going on, and he wanted to know what it was before he walked into the middle of it. "Who said?"

"Everybody!" She opened the truck door and hopped in. "We need to hurry or we'll miss the first few minutes."

Joshua glanced at her as he drove downtown. "What's the deal with Penny?"

"No deal. She's on a date. Some guy who just came to town."

Some guy. She said it in a breezy tone, like it didn't matter to her. He felt an uncomfortable pain in his chest. "Sure you don't want to go to Bessie's and just talk?"

"I'm sure." Her hands clasped and unclasped in her lap.

"What's this new guy like?"

"Younger than you. From LA."

She said it as though Joshua were forty and Los Angeles the most exciting town in the universe. Joshua clenched his teeth and didn't ask any more questions.

The pimple-faced boy inside the ticket booth said they'd already missed ten minutes of the movie. Joshua suggested they go bowling instead. Abra insisted she wanted to see the movie. They couldn't have missed all that much, she said, and if they had, they could always stay and see the first part when it ran the second time. Couldn't they? "*Please*, Joshua!"

He'd always indulged her, but now he wanted to shove her in his truck and get her a hundred miles from the Swan. *Be rational,* he told himself, trying to calm down. He bought the tickets. He wanted to see his competition.

The usher turned on his flashlight and led them into the darkened theater. Abra looked toward the back rows. Joshua took her firmly by the arm and gave a nod. "If you're looking for Penny, she's four rows down on your right." Her platinum hair almost glowed in the dark. She was leaning into a boy who had an arm draped around her shoulders.

Eyes fixed on them, Abra stepped into a row and sat. When the dinosaur awakened by an atomic test in the Arctic started its devastation of the North Atlantic seaboard states, she didn't even notice it. Penny jumped and let out a shriek, and then pressed closer to the boy she was with. Joshua glanced at Abra and saw her mouth tight, eyes blazing. Annoyed, he leaned close. "Are you enjoying the movie?"

"Sure." She crossed her arms and slouched in her seat. "It's great."

Joshua had never felt jealousy like this before, and it unnerved him. He closed his eyes tightly. *Lord, this doesn't feel right. Who is this guy?* He opened his eyes and concentrated on Penny's companion. The fellow leaned toward Penny, whispering something in her ear. Abra's hands clenched in her lap. Joshua knew exactly how she felt.

The dinosaur was successfully vanquished from New York City, and the anti–atomic weapon message was pounded home. Evil America was at fault for dropping the A-bomb twice on Japan, and who knew what monsters still lurked in the future? Joshua rolled his eyes. He was struggling to control his rising anger. He kept seeing men who'd died on the battlefield in Korea. A well-placed A-bomb dropped farther north might end the carnage. *Lord, help me. My flesh is getting the upper hand.* He shifted in his seat and glanced at Abra. "Can we go now?"

"Not yet."

The lights came up and Joshua got a good look at the boy both Matthews girls wanted. Not a boy—a young man. Affluent, confident, charismatic. Penny looked at him with worshipful eyes. Only half-interested in his conquest, he was already checking out the other women in the theater. When he spotted Abra, his mouth curved in an all-knowing smile that made Joshua want to punch him. He took Abra by the arm this time. "Let's get out of here."

She had already planted her feet. "Just a minute."

Joshua made eye contact. The other man's brows rose slightly as he acknowledged the warning. Then, looking past Joshua, he stared at Abra as though claiming her even while holding Penny by the hand.

Joshua extended his hand and introduced himself. The younger man accepted the gesture and politely reciprocated, though his hooded obsidian eyes held nothing but disdain. Joshua wanted to tighten his hand until he crushed every bone in Dylan Stark's. He let go before the impulse became too much. He reminded himself it wasn't his right to judge anyone. Maybe his initial dislike of Dylan would disappear if he knew him a little better. "Why don't you and Penny join us at Bessie's? We can talk over hamburgers and shakes."

Stark's smile grew wry. "Unfortunately, I must decline." He put an arm around Penny. "She'll turn into a pumpkin if I don't have her home by ten." He glanced at his gold watch. "Which gives me fifteen minutes before Daddy calls the cops." He grinned at Abra. "I take it you're under a different set of house rules."

"Only when she's with me." Joshua put his hands on Abra's shoulders and drew her back from Dylan. She was trembling, her body radiating heat. One look at Stark's face told Joshua the reprobate knew exactly what effect he had on her.

As soon as they went through the theater doors, Abra looked right and then left. Joshua heard the roar of a powerful engine and knew before he looked who'd be at the wheel. A red Corvette convertible pulled up to the stop sign. Stark grinned at him and revved the engine. Everyone on the sidewalk turned to look. The boys noticed the car, the girls the guy driving it. Joshua tried to recapture Abra's attention. "Would you like to go to Bessie's for something to eat?"

"Not really. It's late. I think I should go home."

He gave a soft, cynical laugh. "I never knew you could be so easily distracted by a handsome face." He was sorry as soon as the words left his lips and not just because of the look on her face. *Shut up, Joshua!* If she hadn't guessed how he felt before, she'd know now. "He's too old for you, Abra."

"He's only twenty. You're twenty-two!" She yanked her arm free. "Peter let Penny go out with Dylan, and you know what a stickler he is about who's good enough for his daughter."

"If I take you home now, he and Penny will both think you're chasing after him." It was a crime she had often leveled at her sister. Hadn't she written that Penny had stolen Kent Fullerton? Joshua pulled her inside Bessie's. Maybe a glass of ice water would cool her off. If she didn't drink it, he might pour it over her head.

The café was packed with high school couples who'd just been at the movies. Susan smiled at them and pointed out two chrome-and-red-vinyl stools at the counter. She handed each of them a menu and told Joshua it was good to see him home in one piece. Abra perched on her stool as though ready to fly.

He frowned and put the menu down. "Do you want to stay or go home?"

"As if I have a choice."

He strove for patience. "I'm giving you a choice."

"I don't want to stay, but I don't want to go back to Peter and Priscilla's either."

Peter and Priscilla's. "Stop talking about them like they're strangers."

"They might as well be."

"They're your parents. They love you."

She glared at him. "They've never been, and never will be, my parents. I don't have any parents. Remember? I don't belong anywhere or to anyone." She slid off the stool and headed for the door. Susan gave him a worried look. He shook his head in frustration and followed Abra. She was already at the corner getting ready to cross the street.

"Wait a minute!" Joshua caught up with her in the crosswalk. "What's going on inside your head?"

She faced him under the streetlight, eyes glittering. "I'm sick of being told how I should feel and what I should think about everything! I'm sick of seeing Penny have *everything* she wants, whenever she wants it! And I'm sick to death of you and everyone else defending her all the time and telling me I have to make the best of things."

"Hold on a minute." He had to take a breath and fight to stay calm. "You're not being fair."

"Just leave me alone!"

He caught her firmly by the arm and yanked her around to face him. "You want to go home? Fine! I'll take you!"

"It's only six blocks. I'd rather walk." She tried to pull free.

"Oh, no you won't."

"I'm a big enough girl now, in case you hadn't noticed! I can take care of myself!" she screamed at him.

"From where I'm standing, you're acting like a bratty two-year-old throwing a fit because you're not getting your way." He marched her back to his truck. "Get in!" She did, slamming the door so hard he thought it would pop off its rusty hinges. Joshua slid into the driver's seat. "We're going for a ride."

"I don't want to go for a ride!"

"Tough! You're going to cool off before I take you home."

She crossed her arms over her chest and glared out the window.

Joshua drove around town for half an hour. They didn't say a single word to each other. His temper cooled. Abra finally wilted, and tears poured down her cheeks. "You just don't get it, Joshua." She sounded broken. "You don't understand!"

"About seeing someone and feeling light-headed and turned upside down and inside out?" He shook his head. "Oh, yeah. I do." He felt her looking at him as though she understood him. He knew she assumed he was talking about Lacey Glover. He didn't want to correct her. She was breaking his heart and didn't even know it.

He pulled up in front of her house and shut off the engine. "I don't want you to get hurt, Abra."

"I've been hurting my whole life. I can't remember a time when I haven't felt like I wasn't enough."

When he started to put a hand out to touch her cheek, she turned away and opened the truck door. He got out quickly and came around to walk her to the house. She was already through the gate. He caught up and swung her around. "Listen to me, Abra. Please." When she tried to wrench free, he held both her arms and leaned down to look her in the face. "Guard your heart. It affects everything you do in this life."

"Maybe you should've practiced what you preach." She gave him a sad smile. "Lacey Glover doesn't deserve you." She ran up the steps and went inside.

Zeke heard Joshua come in. The back door closed with a hard thud. Keys jangled onto the table. Water ran in the kitchen sink. Zeke rose from his easy chair and went into the kitchen. Joshua was bent over the sink, splashing water in his face. Zeke took the towel from the oven handle and put it in Joshua's questing hand. "Thanks," Joshua muttered, drying his face. Zeke had never seen his son so angry.

"Something wrong?"

"You could say that." He gave a mirthless laugh. "Abra fancies herself in love."

"It had to happen sometime."

"I don't like him."

"You met him?"

"For about two minutes. Long enough to know he's bad news."

Zeke chuckled. "It took that long to make up your mind?"

Joshua threw the towel onto the counter. "Okay. Maybe I wouldn't like any guy she fell in love with, but this one . . ." His eyes were dark with pain. "There's something about him, Dad. I don't usually have a visceral response to people, but he set my teeth on edge." He rubbed the back of his neck. "She just met him today." Joshua let out his breath. "I'd like to know more about him. His name is Dylan Stark. Ever hear of him?"

Zeke frowned. "Does he have family here?" The name didn't ring a bell.

"Peter might know something. I doubt he'd let Penny out the door without asking twenty questions first." Joshua smiled slightly, hopefully, then shook his head. "I don't want Abra having anything to do with this guy."

Zeke went by the elementary school the next day to talk with Peter. "He was forthright with information," Peter said. "He's Cole Thurman's son. It was before your time, Zeke, but he almost ripped Haven Community Church apart when he had an affair with the choir director. He wrecked that marriage and then started up with another woman before he got the message and left the church. I see him around town once in a while. I'm not saying Dylan is a chip off the old block. But I will say he has managed to pit my daughters against one another. I don't like him."

"Is Penny going out with him again?"

"If I say no, he'll be forbidden fruit. I'm making him welcome." He looked grim. "I'd rather have my enemy close, where I can keep an eye on him. I know Penny is a flirt and flighty at times, but underneath all that, she has a good head on her shoulders."

"And Abra?"

Peter was grim. "She's never understood how much we love her." He didn't have to say what he meant. She might look for love somewhere else.

Zeke thought of Joshua, but knew it wasn't the time for his son to make any declarations. She was too young, Joshua still too broken from the war. His heart ached already, seeing what the war had done to his tenderhearted son. What would it do to both of them if Abra followed the deceiver rather than the lover of her soul?

Zeke knew he had only one way to do battle for this child he and his son both loved. He prayed.

CHAPTER 5

The devil tempts us not—'tis we tempt him,
Beckoning his skill with opportunity.

GEORGE ELIOT

THE DAY BEFORE SCHOOL STARTED, Abra withdrew money from her college savings and went to Dorothea's Dress Shop just around the corner from the square. Mitzi called Dorothea Endicott the town's best dresser. She'd been a model in New York back in the day, every inch of her slender six-foot frame declaring her an expert in fashion. She took one look at Abra and smiled. "I've been hoping you'd walk into my shop someday. You have all the right stuff in all the right places, my dear, and I can't wait to teach you how to dress."

The next morning, Abra ignored Penny pounding on the bathroom door and telling her to hurry up. She'd put on the flared skirt and button-up blouse and red leather belt Dorothea had chosen for her. She pulled up the collar just so and left her hair down. It hung loose over her shoulders and down her back.

They weren't even out the gate when Penny told Abra she was meeting Dylan. A quick glance over Abra's new outfit added a silent statement that all her primping wouldn't matter one bit. They walked three blocks and Abra heard the growl of a powerful engine come up alongside them.

"Two gorgeous girls and I only have room for one. What a sad state of affairs."

Penny opened the car door and slid in. Dylan ignored her and grinned at Abra in a way that made her toes curl inside her new shoes.

Penny put a pink bandanna over her hair. "Don't tell Daddy, Abra."

Dylan winked at her before he peeled out, leaving Abra to smell burning rubber and smoke.

During lunch break, Abra saw Penny sitting with Michelle and Pamela and several football players. Michelle waved Abra over to join them. Penny smiled as though Dylan wasn't between them. The bell rang and they all got up to return to class. Penny fell into step with Abra. "The gang is going to Eddie's after school. Do you want to come with us?"

By "gang," Abra knew she meant Michelle, Charlotte, and Pamela and probably Robbie Austin and Alex Morgan as well. "Aren't you meeting Dylan?"

She grimaced. "No."

"No?" Was she really supposed to believe that?

"Daddy doesn't really want either of us going out with him."

"That didn't stop you from getting into his car this morning."

"I learned my lesson."

"What are you talking about?"

Penny looked unsettled. "Dylan isn't Joshua, Abra. He . . ." Charlotte caught up with them and Penny frowned. "Dylan sort of scares me," she whispered. "I'll tell you about it later." She walked backward down the hall toward her next class. "Come with us to Eddie's." She grinned. "Alex said you're a knockout. He'll probably ask you to homecoming." Penny turned and hurried through the other students.

Abra rolled her eyes. Who cared what Alex thought? And she didn't believe for a minute Penny had lost interest in Dylan Stark. She was just pretending, the way Abra had pretended she didn't care about Kent Fullerton.

When school let out, Abra walked downtown instead of home or to Mitzi's. She felt restless and edgy as though waiting for something to happen. When she heard a familiar engine purring, she knew why. She didn't turn and look. She walked to the next shop, pretending interest in the books in the window. The silence told her Dylan had parked his car. The sound of the car door slamming filled her with excitement. She opened the door of Bessie's Corner Café.

Susan glanced up from washing the counter and smiled. "You're looking very pretty today, Abra." The place was almost empty. "Sit anywhere you like." She tossed the washrag under the counter and waved her hand over the clean counter.

"Thanks, but do you mind if I sit in a booth? I have homework."

"Sure." She looked surprised, but pleased. High school students only came into Bessie's on Friday and Saturday nights after the movies. "What can I get you? Fries? A soda?"

"Just a soda, thanks." She slid into one of the back booths as the bell jangled over the front door. Her nerve endings tingled. She didn't have to look to know it was Dylan.

She kept her head down, pretending to sort through her text-books. The closer the footsteps, the faster her heart beat.

"Mind if I join you?" Dylan slid into the seat facing her without waiting for an answer. He folded his hands on the table and gave her a slow, taunting smile. "And don't pretend you didn't know I'd follow you."

Pride jabbed, she lifted her chin. "If you're looking for Penny, she's at Eddie's Diner across from the high school. Do you need directions?"

"Are you telling me to leave you alone? Just say the word and I'll go." He waited. When she didn't answer, he studied her face and everything else he could see above the table. "I'll bet you turned a lot of heads today, Abra. Always happens when a girl lets down her hair for the first time."

It wasn't what he said. It was the way he said it that brought heat into her cheeks. She looked away out of self-defense and saw Susan watching them. The waitress frowned and shook her head at Abra. Dylan looked over his shoulder and gave a soft laugh. "I'll bet she's a friend of that PK you're dating. Right?"

"PK?"

"Preacher's kid. Penny told me all about him on the way home last night. A war hero. I'm so impressed." He tilted his head slightly. "Would you like to go for a ride with me? See what I'm like?" His expression teased. "I promise not to take you any further than you want to go." His smile dared her. "And you'll be safely home in plenty of time to get all your homework done and have supper with your mommy and daddy. They won't even know you've been missing."

Abra's heart raced. She glanced at Susan and then looked back at Dylan. "Where do you want to go?"

"Take a risk." He slid out of the booth and held out his hand.

"What about your soda?" Susan spoke up from the counter.

Abra didn't even remember ordering one. Dylan pulled a quarter from his pocket and slapped it on the counter. "That should cover everything." Holding Abra's books under one arm, he spread his hand against the small of her back and guided her to the door. He opened it for her and stayed right on her heels. "Seems like everyone in this town wants to protect you."

It was a broad statement, and far from true. "No one in this town cares what happens to me."

"Is that so?" He gave her an odd smile. "You really are an innocent, aren't you?"

Was he mocking her? "Where are we going?"

"You'll see." Dylan dumped her books onto the floor in front of the passenger seat and opened the door for her. "Are you ready to live dangerously, little girl?"

"I have to be home by five." She felt infantile as soon as the words came out.

Dylan laughed. "We'll make it quick." He leaned over the stick. "Hang on, baby. I'm going to give you the ride of your life." He peeled out of the parking place, shoved the stick into gear, and shot toward the stop sign, braking for barely a second before the car squealed onto Main Street. He stayed at the speed limit until he turned onto the bridge. Shifting gears, he hit the gas.

Wind whipped at Abra's hair as he raced out of town. Laughing, she tried to hold it. When the air current caught beneath her skirt and lifted it, she grabbed it and tucked it under her thighs. Dylan watched. "Spoilsport!" He grinned. He took turns so fast the wheels screamed. A green blur of trees and bushes flew by. Abra's stomach tickled when they raced up and over a hill and down into a dip, then up again and around a sharp curve. She felt a jolt of fear when he accelerated, tearing up the road like a race driver. His grin looked more like the baring of teeth as he shifted again.

Vineyards spread out on both sides of the road. Abra's pulse shot up when Dylan downshifted quickly and took a hard right. The Corvette slid as he compensated. Dylan shifted again and cranked the wheel so hard the Corvette swung around in a full circle and skidded to a stop in a cloud of rubber-scented dust. He leaned over and raked his fingers into her hair. "Now I'm going to do what I've wanted to do since I laid eyes on you." He kissed her long and hard. She gasped when he let her go. Grinning broadly, he ran his hands over her hair.

Some intense, basic instinct rose up inside her when he stared at her. His hand curled over her hip. "I love the way you look at me." He kissed her again. It wasn't the same as the first time. He parted her lips and devoured her. When he drew back, he looked amused. "Never been kissed like that before, have you?"

"No." Had he kissed Penny that way?

"You're delicious. Let's try it again."

━━━━━━━

Nothing stayed hidden in a small town for long. Zeke knew Abra had gone for a ride with Dylan Stark before they crossed the bridge. Susan Wells called him. "He followed her right in here and sat at her booth. Five minutes later, he had her in his car. She's just a baby, Pastor Zeke, and he's . . . I know his kind only too well."

Mitzi called the next day. Her son had told her he'd seen Abra in a red Corvette. "Hodge said that boy was driving like a maniac. He said he must have been going sixty by the time he passed Riverfront Park. Is Peter out of his mind letting Abra go off with a boy like that?"

He'd no sooner hung up than Priscilla called. "Peter told Dylan both girls are too young for him. I've never seen Peter so angry."

"What did Dylan say?"

"Nothing. He just got in his car and drove away. Peter talked with the girls. I thought Penny would go through the roof, but she was fine. It's Abra who was furious."

Peter had told Abra she was never to speak to Dylan again, and she said she'd do whatever she wanted, and he said, "Not under my roof, you won't!" and she said she'd leave. She could go live under the bridge! That's where they all thought she belonged anyway, wasn't it?

"I don't know what to do, Zeke. Peter is out of his mind with worry and hurt. I don't know what Abra is. Crazy in love. Isn't that what they call it?" Priscilla wept. "I've never seen her like this. Will you please talk with her?"

He tried. She sat in stony silence, hands fisted, staring straight ahead. When he fell silent, she got up and walked out of the room.

Peter and Priscilla came out of the kitchen and looked at him. He shook his head.

Joshua was the last to hear what was going on and the most deeply disturbed.

———————

Joshua rang Peter and Priscilla's doorbell. His hands were shaking. Dad had asked if he'd go by and speak to her. Joshua reminded Dad that he'd already tried to warn Abra about Dylan Stark, and he hadn't even seen her since that night at the movies. But he figured it was worth a try.

Priscilla answered the door. "Thank God." She stepped back so he could come inside. "I hope she'll listen to you, Joshua." She kept her voice low. "She's grounded, but I'm worried the minute she goes out that door to school, she'll be in Dylan's car. She won't listen."

"How's Penny?"

"Upset. Of course. She had a crush on Dylan, but I think it's already over. I'm not quite sure how that happened." She looked at him. "I thought all the melodrama over Kent Fullerton was trying, but this is frightening. We don't know what to do, Joshua. Abra wouldn't even speak to your father yesterday. I don't think she heard one word he said."

"She can be stubborn."

"Can't we all?" She gestured weakly. "She's upstairs in her room. She must be hungry. She wouldn't come down for dinner." She gave a bleak laugh. "She said she didn't want to eat with hypocrites." Her eyes filled with angry tears. "Some people are very difficult to love."

Which meant they needed love even more.

Joshua went upstairs. Penny's door was open. She lounged on the window seat, flipping through a movie magazine. She got up when she saw him and came to the door. "Good luck. You'll need it. She's an idiot!" Her voice rose. "Abra wouldn't listen to God if He appeared in a burning bush." She threw the magazine on the floor, raising her voice another notch. "She thinks I'm jealous. I'm not!" she yelled. "You're going to be sorry you ever met Dylan, Abra!"

"Penny!" Priscilla called from downstairs. "That's enough!"

In tears, Penny slammed her bedroom door.

At least one Matthews girl had seen through the disguise.

Joshua tapped on Abra's door. "Abra? It's Joshua."

The lock turned and the door drifted open. Abra walked back to her unmade bed. She didn't look at him as she sat cross-legged on the bed and picked up her hairbrush. "Are you here as a friend or foe?" She sounded hostile.

"When have I ever been your foe?"

She kept her face turned away as she yanked the brush through her hair. "Then close the door. I don't want that little witch across the hall to hear anything we say to each other."

No matter how long he'd known her, it felt wrong to be closeted alone with her in a bedroom, even if Peter and Priscilla approved under the current circumstances. "Maybe we should go out for a walk."

"I'm grounded."

Joshua shrugged and closed the door. He took the chair from her small desk and turned it around, straddling it. Abra continued brushing her hair. He looked around the room. It felt like a hotel room, not her personal living space. Everything matched perfectly except for the bulletin board with pinups of old-time movie stars more suited to Mitzi's generation than Abra's. His heart lifted when he spotted two pictures of himself, one in his high school graduation cap and gown and the other in uniform. At least he still mattered somewhere in the scheme of things. Maybe there was still hope.

"So . . . what's going on?"

She lifted her chin, pale-green eyes spitting fire. "Nothing." She clenched the brush as though she intended to throw it at his head. "Yet."

"Yet?"

"Dylan and I have a lot in common."

"Like what?" He kept his tone cool, though everything inside him tightened up for battle.

"His father left him when he was a baby."

"What else do you know about him?"

Her eyes flickered. "He plans to get his degree in business and marketing."

"Sounds like a family thing." He tried to sound neutral, but her eyes flashed again.

"What's that supposed to mean?"

"Cole Thurman is reputed to be a consummate businessman. That's all I meant."

She went back to brushing her hair. "He's trying to make up for the years he lost with Dylan."

Joshua fought against the anger rising in him. It had been boiling beneath the surface since he came back from Korea. "How well do you really know Dylan Stark?"

"He doesn't like pretense. He wants me to be myself."

"Oh, really." Sarcasm dripped this time and he knew he was already defeated.

"He understands me!"

"He understands you're attracted to him. I saw that much at the Swan. This isn't about love, Abra. It's about sex, the basest kind."

Her mouth fell open and her face flamed red. "You're disgusting!"

He stood so quickly the chair toppled. "I'm telling you the truth!"

"Dylan says I'm beautiful. Dylan says I'm smart. Dylan loves me!"

"Dylan will say anything to get what he wants!"

"He wants *me*."

"I don't doubt that! But for how long? His affection for Penny didn't last a week."

She smiled and lifted her chin. "He said Penny is water, and I'm wine."

Dylan seemed to know exactly what Abra wanted to hear. It infuriated Joshua that she didn't know what the guy was up to. He righted the chair and sat again, hands clasped between his knees this time, fighting his emotions. "Listen to me, Abra. Hear me out. We're friends. Give me that much." When she didn't say anything, he prayed as he spoke. "A man who loves you will strive to bring out the best in you."

"I *am* my best when I'm with Dylan."

He gripped his knees. "Vain and rebellious? Completely self-centered, without a thought of what you're doing to your family? This is your best?"

Abra's eyes filled with tears of accusation. "You're supposed to be my best friend, and you can say that to me?"

"I say it because *I love you*." She had no idea how much.

"You know what, Joshua? I used to think you were the only real, true friend I had." Her eyes went cold. "Now I know you're just like all the rest."

The wound in his side throbbed. "I'm still your friend, the best friend you'll ever have." And more, so much more. "And I always will be."

She tossed the brush on the unmade bed, got up, and went to the door. She opened it and stood aside. "Thanks ever so much for coming by." She spoke in a sugary tone, then added ice. "Don't bother ever coming back."

Joshua stepped over the threshold. She uttered a choked cry, slammed the door, and locked it.

Joshua stood in the hallway, stunned. It was over before it had ever begun. *I've lost her, Lord. Oh, God, I've lost her.*

Joshua's nightmares returned, worse than ever. He dreamed he was back in Korea, suffering through a cold white winter, running—

always running—to save someone he couldn't quite reach. Dad awakened him almost every night and sat and prayed over him while Joshua lay panting, fighting the panic that lurked just under the surface.

Gil MacPherson called and invited Joshua out to the ranch. Dad had suggested it. "He was a medic at Normandy. I think he might understand better what you're going through than I can."

Gil did.

Dad still went out every morning for his long walk around town. Joshua knew he still stopped at Peter and Priscilla's gate. He still prayed for Abra.

And Dylan Stark still showed up in town. A high school teacher friend of Peter's said he'd seen a red Corvette parked at the cyclone fence on the far side of the high school football field. Dylan Stark had also been seen near Eddie's Diner, where students liked to hang out.

Joshua knew Dylan wouldn't give up. Dylan was biding his time, waiting for an opportunity to take what he wanted. Peter couldn't keep Abra grounded forever.

Abra felt like she was going crazy. All she could think about was Dylan and when she could see him again.

Classes let out for lunch break; the halls and corridors swarmed as students made their way outside, sitting in clusters on the lawn, sitting at picnic tables set up under the trees near the shop building, or gathering in groups on the football field. When Abra spotted Dylan standing by the cyclone fence, she darted a look around and went to him. She gripped the wire. "It's good to see you."

His fingers curled over hers. "That's all you've got to say?" He looked angry, frustrated. "When are you going to break out of that prison they've locked you in?"

"Peter grounded me for a month, Dylan. I still have two weeks to go."

"I'm not waiting around for another two weeks, baby. I'm sick of this town."

Her heart knocked hard and fast. "Please don't go."

"Come with me." His fingers tightened, hurting her.

"Where would we go?"

"Does it matter? You love me, don't you?" At her breathless nod, he stepped closer. "I want to get my hands on you. We were barely getting started that day I took you home. We're going to be good together, baby. We could go to San Francisco, Santa Cruz, wherever we want to go."

She didn't doubt he loved her. "You know I want to get away, Dylan."

He let her go and stepped back from the fence. "Then meet me at the bridge at midnight."

Tonight? "I can't!" She couldn't think that fast.

"Can't or won't? Maybe I was wrong about you." He walked away.

"Dylan! Wait! I'll be there."

He looked back then and smiled. "If you're not, you'll spend the rest of your life wondering what you missed." He kept walking this time and didn't look back.

———

Abra ate even though she wasn't hungry. It was Penny's turn to do the dishes, and Abra asked to be excused. She had homework to do and was a little tired. Maybe she'd go to bed early.

Peter looked at her, a faint question in his eyes. "Sure you don't want to join us in the living room? Watch a little television?"

"I wish. I have a report due on Friday." Two lies in a row and it didn't even bother her.

With everyone downstairs, it was easy for her to slip into Penny's room and steal a suitcase from the set Priscilla had given her for Christmas. Penny wanted to go to Mills College. Ian Brubaker said Abra should go to Juilliard. But she only wanted one thing now. To be with Dylan.

The suitcase wasn't big enough for everything, but Abra packed what she could and hid it under her bed. It was after nine o'clock before Peter came upstairs. An hour after that, Priscilla came up. She tapped lightly on Penny's door. "Lights out, Penny. School comes early."

The house fell quiet. Abra lay in the darkness. Joshua's words came back to her, and doubts followed. Did Dylan really love her? He'd never said so in so many words. But could he kiss her like that and not love her?

The clock ticked. Time crept by. She got up and paced, then stopped because someone might hear and come and knock on her door and ask if anything was wrong. She sat on the end of her bed, heart thumping wildly. She should leave a note, at least. She went to her desk and found paper. She turned on the lamp and wrote quickly. The wind came up, the maple tree outside the window rustling and startling her. The wind chimes danced under the patio arbor. The downstairs clock chimed eleven. She took out envelopes. She tucked in a note addressed to *Mr. and Mrs. Matthews*, another to *Reverend Ezekiel Freeman*, and a far kinder farewell to Mitzi. She wanted to write to Joshua, too, but didn't know what to say. Best to leave well enough alone. As an afterthought, she took Marianne's Bible from the bottom drawer and scribbled a quick note to tuck inside: *Marianne would want Joshua's wife to have this.*

Pulling the suitcase out from under the bed, she slowly opened the door and tiptoed down the hallway, heart skipping a beat when the stairs creaked. She hurried to the front door and closed it quietly behind her.

Her side ached by the time she reached the bridge. Dylan was there, leaning against his car. He straightened when he saw her. He tossed her suitcase into the small trunk and slammed it. "I knew you'd come." He pulled her close and kissed her until she was breathless. "Wouldn't you love to see their faces in the morning?" His hands spread over her breasts and she felt a moment of panic.

"Still wearing this?" He broke the chain holding Marianne's cross and tossed it aside. "You don't need any reminders of the past, do you?" He didn't give her time to think before he kissed her again. His hands took liberties that shocked her, but she was afraid now to protest. "I'm going to have so much fun with you." He shifted her so he could open the car door. "Get in."

She slid down, swinging her legs in before he closed the door.

He came around and got into the driver's seat. "Tonight, we start living." He gunned the engine and honked the horn as they crossed the bridge out of Haven. "Just so they all know!" He looked so delighted, she laughed, exultant.

———

Joshua sat in the kitchen, still shaken by his nightmare. Head in hands, he tried to concentrate on Psalm 23. *"Yea, though I walk through the valley of the shadow of death, I will fear no evil: for thou art with me; thy rod and thy staff they comfort me."*

The telephone rang. Adrenaline shot through his body; he felt a premonition and tried to push it away. Just because the telephone rang at four in the morning didn't mean something had happened to Abra. Dad often got calls in the middle of the night. Joshua scraped the chair back and went into the living room to answer.

"Joshua, it's Peter. She's gone."

He didn't have to ask who had taken her. "When did they leave?"

"Sometime after we went to bed. Priscilla woke up and thought she heard something. I've been out driving around town for the last two hours, but I haven't seen her."

Joshua hung up, flipped through the telephone book, and dialed Cole Thurman's number. The telephone rang ten times before a groggy voice answered with a foul curse.

"Mr. Thurman? Joshua Freeman. Where's Dylan?" Joshua barely restrained himself from shouting.

"How would I know? I'm his father, not his keeper."

"Abra Matthews is with him. She's sixteen."

"That girl was trash the day your father found her. He should've left her under the bridge."

Joshua slammed the receiver down.

"There's nothing you can do, Joshua." Dad stood in the doorway, dressed for his morning walk. His face looked even more pale and worn than it had when Mom died.

"I can't just do nothing, Dad! I have to go after her!" He grabbed his jacket and keys and headed for the door.

———

Abra felt warm and velvety enclosed in Dylan's sports car. He drove fast, radio blaring rock and roll. Her nerves tingled every time he looked at her. When he downshifted, then shifted again, her stomach clenched with excitement. Penny and all her friends had tried to win his attention, but he'd picked her. They'd be together forever. He only had to look at her to make the heat flood her veins.

His hand glided up her thigh. "You look excited."

Abra felt consumed with need. "I'm still taking it all in." She looked at him, hoping he would say he loved her.

"Taking what in?"

Dylan had the most beautiful, gleaming smile. She laughed, a little breathless. "Running away with you, of course." He was so handsome. Picture-perfect.

"I can't wait to get you into bed."

Would the earth move, like Penny's hidden romance novels said?

She felt a shiver of fear. She didn't know anything about sex, other than it was a great mystery.

She studied his profile. "Where will we go to get married?"

"Married!" He gave a short, derisive laugh. "What gave you the idea I was going to marry you?"

His words felt like a slap. "You asked me to come away with you, Dylan. You said you wanted me."

"Oh, baby. I do. I want you in the worst way." He caressed her burning cheek with the back of his hand. "More than I've wanted anyone in a long time." He focused his attention on the road ahead. "Who knows? Maybe I will get married someday. Wouldn't that be something?" He laughed as though the whole idea were impossible. "Hey." He gave her a sneering smile. "Do you think Reverend Freeman would perform the ceremony?"

"I doubt it."

He laughed. "I was kidding."

Maybe it was the way Dylan was driving—taking the curves so fast the tires screeched, jamming the gearshift, accelerating—that made her feel sick to her stomach.

"Well, we'd invite him anyway, wouldn't we?" Dylan spoke dryly, mockingly. "And that sanctimonious son of his, too. What was his name?"

"Joshua."

"Yeah. Joshua. Nice Bible name. Maybe I'll marry you just to see two grown men weep." He laughed.

For a split second Abra wanted to tell him to turn the car around and take her home. She didn't want to talk about Pastor Zeke or Joshua. She didn't want to think about how disappointed they'd be in her. She thought of the notes she'd left. No turning back now.

Dylan looked at her. "You know what I love about you, baby? You went after what you wanted. You didn't chicken out."

She studied the hard, handsome angles of his face, illumined by the dashboard lights. Would she ever find anyone like him again? Someone who made her feel such a wild sense of want and need? "I love you, Dylan."

Dylan grinned. "I know you do, baby. I knew the minute I saw you, we were made for each other."

She'd hoped her declaration would encourage Dylan to make a declaration as well. Her stomach trembled, no longer with desire. "Do you love me, Dylan?" She held her breath, waiting for his response. She had turned her back on everyone in Haven to come with him, and now, sacrificed her pride as well.

Dylan gave a careless shrug. "I'm not sure I know what love is, baby." He gave a curt laugh. "I'm not sure I want to know. From what I've seen, love makes a man weak." He downshifted and took a hard curve, accelerating again. "One thing you'd better learn about me right now—" he gave her a warning glance—"I don't like being pushed."

She got the message. If she wanted Dylan to love her, she'd better do whatever it took to keep him happy. She looked out the window, fighting the struggling emotions inside her. She should count herself lucky. Every girl in Haven had wanted him. He had chosen her. And he had chosen her over Penny. That was important, wasn't it?

Resting her head against the seat, she pushed down the swelling weight of disappointment. This wasn't what she wanted. This wasn't what she thought it would be like. Instinct told her not to cry in front of Dylan. He had as much as told her he didn't like cowards.

Dylan turned up the radio, and Nat King Cole's "Pretend" filled the car. He sang "That's Amore" along with Dean Martin. He had a good voice, but not nearly the quality of Pastor Zeke's or Joshua's.

Why was she thinking about Pastor Zeke and Joshua again? She told herself to put them out of her mind. She'd seen them for the last time.

"You're awfully quiet all of a sudden. I can't stand it when a girl sulks."

She forced a smile. "I'm just enjoying the ride."

"Are you, now?" He pressed down harder on the gas pedal, grinning at her and not letting up until the car began to vibrate with the speed. "Feels like it's going to come apart, doesn't it?"

Her heart thundered in her ears, but she made herself laugh. "Can't it go any faster?"

Dylan looked surprised and pleased. "You're a wild girl!" He slowed the car. "We'll try her out on a straightaway sometime."

"Where are we going?"

"San Francisco. I made reservations." He gave her a bright-white grin. "It'll be nicer than any place you've ever been."

As the hours passed, the fog of infatuation seemed to burn away. How much did she really know about Dylan? All she'd thought about over the past weeks was the way she felt when he looked at her. Even now, when he turned his dark eyes on her, she felt a little breathless. Dylan didn't ask how she was feeling or why she was silent. He was too busy beating a rhythm on the steering wheel.

"Dylan sort of scares me." Penny's whispered words rose up to mock her.

Niggling doubts chipped away at her confidence. But what did Penny know? She and Dylan had only gone out twice before he lost interest and dropped her. Thinking about Dylan with Penny made her stomach clench. Why was she letting herself even think about these things now? Dylan was all that mattered. He had chosen her, not Penny. He'd take care of her.

Had he said so?

What if he hadn't?

The road climbed. Dylan raced up the hill, then down, entering a tunnel. The Golden Gate Bridge came into view on the other side. Heavy morning fog poured over the mountain and across the road like white foam. The City by the Bay was all lit up, beckoning. Dylan slowed to pay the toll when he reached the bridge, the *ta-tick-ta-tick* quickening Abra's pulse. After going so fast, forty-five felt like a slow crawl across the mile-plus expanse. Dylan drove along Doyle Drive toward the marina, then turned down Van Ness. He ran two stoplights and made a hard left onto California, shooting up the hill. "We're almost there, baby."

A cathedral loomed above them. She'd dreamed she'd have a white wedding someday. She made a promise to herself to make Dylan so happy tonight, he'd want to marry her tomorrow morning. Her fingernails dug into her palms. She'd make it so he never wanted to let her go. The car flew up Nob Hill. A block past the cathedral, Dylan made a sharp left, and parked in front of the Fairmont Hotel. Abra gaped. She'd never seen anything so grand.

"Here. Put this on." He pulled a ring from his little finger and handed it to her. "Turn it around, so only the band shows. If anyone asks, we're on our honeymoon." He shoved his door open and got out. Cold humid air hit her.

Abra quickly slipped on the ring with the crest of a winged beast before the man in uniform opened her door. "Welcome to the Fairmont." His smile altered when he got a good look at her. She blushed. Clearly the man knew she and Dylan weren't married. He knew why they were here. She lowered her eyes as she got out of the car.

"Hey! You!" Dylan tossed the keys to the man. "Park it." He came around and took Abra by the arm, leaning down to whisper, "Try not to look like such a schoolgirl." Dylan swept her inside the hotel.

Abra wanted to hide when they entered the lobby, though only hotel staff was around at this hour.

"Sit over there and wait for me. Don't talk to anyone. I'll be right back." She did what he told her, sinking into a plush velvet chair behind a palm. Dylan walked away.

He had such confidence, as though he belonged in places like this. Heart hammering, palms sweating, Abra looked around at marble pillars, gilt staircase, red carpets, the sculptures tucked into corners, the paintings on the walls. It was like a palace! She remembered what Mitzi had taught her when she got the jitters before playing piano at church. *"Take a deep breath and release it slowly through your nose. It'll calm you down."* Abra put away the thought that anyone was looking askance and imagined herself a princess, Dylan the prince who had brought her to this castle.

She heard him laugh. Peering around the palm, she watched him flirt with the attractive receptionist. The woman smiled back at him and went to work while Dylan leaned forward on the counter. Whatever he said flustered the woman and made her face turn pink. Jealousy and hurt surged through Abra's body. Had he already forgotten he'd left her hidden in an out-of-the-way corner?

What would Dylan do if she got up and walked out the door right now?

Where could she go if she did? It was cold outside, and she hadn't thought to bring a coat. She'd have to call Peter and Priscilla and beg them to come and get her.

Would they?

Dylan appeared, grinning. "Piece of cake. Flirt a little and she didn't even bother to look your way." He studied her face. "You didn't think I was attracted to her, did you? She's got ten years on me at least. Then again, it could be interesting." He put his arm around her and tucked her close against his side. "Relax. I'm all yours. They're sending champagne up to the room so we can celebrate the nuptials." He kissed her temple. "You look scared."

"I am. A little."

He knew exactly where the elevators were located. Had he been here before?

"I don't know anything, Dylan."

"Oh, you will, baby. You will." As soon as the doors closed, Dylan pulled her into his arms. "I love the way you look at me. Like the sun rises and sets on my command." His mouth devoured hers as he pushed her back against the wall. Up, up, up they went. His body felt like a furnace.

The elevator stopped. Dylan took her by the hand. She had to take two steps to his one as he strode down the carpeted hallway. He unlocked a door and pushed it open. "Home, sweet home."

Her heart stuck in her throat, and she didn't move until he put his hands on her hips and pressed her forward. The door wasn't even closed before he started pulling at her clothing. She gasped, backing up. Buttons popped. Unzipping her skirt, he shoved it down over her hips, and it dropped to the floor around her ankles. She said his name in frightened protest when he yanked the straps of her bra down from her shoulders.

Someone knocked on the door. She scrambled to cover herself.

Dylan said a foul word, his breath coming hot and heavy. "Go in the bathroom and stay there until I tell you to come out."

Abra fled and closed the door behind her, shaking. When she looked in the mirror, she didn't recognize the flushed, dark-eyed, disheveled girl staring back at her. She could hear Dylan through the door, talking to someone. He sounded in complete control again, amused. The other man spoke in a low, respectful voice. Footsteps headed for the door. It closed with a snap.

Dylan walked into the bathroom. "We have our luggage. Coast is clear, baby." When he lifted the lid of the toilet and unzipped his pants, she hurried to the bedroom. Hands against her hot cheeks, she stood at the windows, staring out at the city lights, the narrow streets, the Bay Bridge. She felt a thousand miles away from Haven. She heard the toilet flush.

In a panic, she opened Penny's suitcase and rummaged for her baby-doll pajamas. When Dylan came back out into the bedroom, she ducked by him and went into the bathroom again, locking the door this time.

Dylan laughed and drummed his fingers on the door. "You're not going to be one of those girls who locks herself in the bathroom all night, are you?"

Another knock on the door to the suite saved her from having to answer. Dylan opened it and talked to another man. She heard the rattle of a cart, glassware, the men talking in low voices, the pop of a cork, the door closing. Dylan tapped again. "Champagne's arrived."

She opened the door cautiously. "Is anyone else going to come?"

"Not until we order breakfast in bed." He held out a crystal glass of champagne and lifted his. "Here's to enjoying life to the fullest." He clinked her glass with his. "Drink up, baby. You look like you need a little liquid courage." He watched through veiled eyes as she sipped experimentally. The bubbles tickled her nose and she didn't like the taste. "Try it with this." He fed her a strawberry. He replenished her glass. After two, she felt light-headed.

Dylan ran a fingertip down her bare arm, raising goose bumps. "You look more relaxed." He took the glass of champagne away and put it on the room service cart. "Enough bubbly." He gave her a teasing wink. "I want you conscious."

Abra had never seen a man undress before and turned her back. Dylan chuckled. "Don't be shy. You can look." He turned her around to face him and grasped her hand. "And touch." When she pulled back, he took hold of her baby-doll pajamas and ripped them down the front. She raised her hands to try to cover herself, but he grabbed her wrists and pulled her arms apart so he could look at her. "I knew you'd be beautiful."

"You're hurting me, Dylan."

"It's your own fault. Stop fighting me."

"Please. Wait."

"Why?" His eyes were like black coal, his smile mocking. "Baby." He wedged his knee between hers.

How could someone so beautiful become so ugly and frightening?

The curling warmth in the pit of Abra's stomach became a cold lump of fear. Everything felt wrong.

Dylan was strong and relentless. He was neither kind nor gentle.

Unable to escape, Abra retreated inward, shutting down, going numb. She felt as though she floated above, witnessing the devastation. *This is making love? This vile, profane act of violence? This is what novelists describe as making the earth move?*

Finally, it was over. Dylan pulled back abruptly, leaving her to feel the cold. Had his fingers left bruises? She felt battered inside. She wanted to cover her face in shame.

Dylan sprawled on his back and went straight to sleep. He snored like an old man.

Abra lay still, afraid to move, afraid to awaken him. She stared at the ceiling, tears flooding her eyes, seeping down her temples into her hair. In the darkness she remembered. *"I don't want you to get hurt, Abra."* Joshua had tried to warn her. She'd always been an outcast, a castaway. Now she was defiled, as well.

Oh, God, what happens now?

A dark voice in her head whispered, *What do you think? You make your bed. You sleep in it. Remember? This is what you wanted. You'd better make the best of it.*

CHAPTER 6

Be careful what you wish for.
You might just get it.
KING MIDAS

JOSHUA DROVE through the night to San Francisco. He found a gas station and filled his tank, trying to think what to do next. Should he start looking in the maze of streets that laced the hillsides? He didn't know where to begin, how to find her. Would Dylan have taken her to a fancy hotel or a cheap motel? Would he have kept driving? Doubtful. He'd have wanted to take what he was after as soon as possible. But then what? Leave Abra somewhere on her own? Take her with him to wherever he intended to go next?

Dawn came and Joshua parked along the beach. He stared at the endless ocean, the waves lapping the shore. People came out and strolled, a few with dogs. Joshua put his head against the steering wheel. "Lord, please, make her call home." Defeated, he started the engine and headed back to the Golden Gate Bridge.

———

Abra filled her lungs and breathed out all her expectations and dreams. Her tears dried. She cautiously eased out of bed, went into the bathroom, and locked the door. Hands shaking, she turned on the shower. She stepped under the stream and turned up the heat gradually until her skin reddened like a boiled lobster. The room filled so thick with steam, she breathed in liquid air. She washed thoroughly and still felt dirty.

Dylan awakened when she got back into bed. "Hmmmm, you smell so good." He wanted her again. She didn't dare say no. Even if she had, would he have listened? When he finished, she pulled the blanket over herself and curled into the fetal position.

Abra, an inner voice whispered. *Get up. Go downstairs and call home.*

I can't.

Call Pastor Zeke.

She pressed the heels of her hands against her ears.

You're just a child.

Not anymore. Peter and Priscilla would be too ashamed of her to look at her, let alone speak to her. Penny would spread it all over school that she'd run away with Dylan, spent one night in a hotel, and come home with her tail between her legs like a whipped puppy. Pastor Zeke would tell her she was bound for hell. And Joshua . . . Oh, what would Joshua say to her? She shuddered at the thought of facing him.

Call—

She closed her ears to the voice. *I can't go home. I don't have a home anymore. Wherever Dylan goes, I go.*

Exhaustion finally took over. She dreamed she was a baby again, so weak, she couldn't raise herself, with barely enough strength to cry. A man stood on the bridge above her. Hope came and she raised her hand, fingers spread, beseeching. She wanted to call out, but she had no voice. He leaned forward, looking over the rail, but a beast with dark wings approached her. All Abra could see now was the great, dark shape looming over her. It had burning red eyes and a bright-white mocking smile.

Dad opened the back door when Joshua came up the steps. He didn't have to ask if Joshua had had any luck. Joshua went into the living room and sank onto the couch. "I didn't even know where to start looking."

"She's in God's hands, Son."

"She's in Dylan Stark's hands, Dad!" Anger surged. "He'll break her to pieces." He felt like he was choking on rage. "If he hasn't already."

"Maybe that's what it's going to take to reach her."

Joshua stared at him. "You don't mean that."

"I don't like the idea any better than you do, Son, but love and kindness and reason haven't moved her. She's closed her heart to everyone, except this boy."

"He's not a boy. He's a son of a—!"

"If you oppose her, she'll feel like a martyr."

Joshua came to his feet. "Then tell me what to do!"

"You've done all you can do. That's what I'm telling you. It's time to let her go."

"Give up on her?" Joshua's voice came out ragged, broken.

"Letting go isn't giving up. It's trusting God to do whatever He has to do. Remember what you know to be true. God loves her more than you do. He loves her more than I do or Peter and Priscilla, more than all of us put together." He sighed. "Sometimes God has to destroy in order to save. He has to wound in order to heal."

"Destroy? Wound? I can't let that happen."

"It's already happening, Joshua. It's not your choice. It's hers. All you can do is trust in God's unfailing love."

"I have to *do something*, or go crazy." Joshua sank onto the couch again, covered his head, and wept.

He felt his father's hand firm on his shoulder. "We will do something." His hand tightened. "We'll pray for her."

———

Abra awakened when Dylan pulled the covers from her. "Come on, baby. Get up." They ate breakfast in the room, and Dylan had her wait outside while he checked out. He said they'd stay another night or two in San Francisco in a hotel near North Beach. It wouldn't be as grand, but all they really needed was a bed, right?

He drove her to Fisherman's Wharf. He talked about the last time he'd been in the city with fraternity friends. When he said they'd had fun, she knew he meant with girls. She liked the smell of the sea. Dylan bought fresh crab in a small cup. "Open up, little bird." He forked it into her mouth. He said he wanted to buy her something as a souvenir and decided on an inexpensive pink zip-up sweatshirt with *Fisherman's Wharf* printed on it. Pink was Penny's favorite color.

"Rumor has it Joe and Marilyn will get hitched soon. They live someplace around here. If we're lucky, we might run into them."

"Are you telling me you know them?"

"I've met Marilyn." He grinned at her openmouthed surprise. "She's been to my house. My mother knows everyone in Hollywood."

"Is your mother an actress, too?" She'd never heard of Lilith Stark.

"She's a columnist. She makes and breaks actresses. She throws the best parties in the industry. Anybody who wants to be somebody comes. She knows all the dirt people try to hide. Everybody wants to be on her good side. When she says come, they ask when." He smiled sardonically. "Marilyn may come off like a witless blonde, but she's smarter than she looks."

Dylan took her to dinner in Chinatown, and then to a nightclub in North Beach. "I've got a whole new world to show you." The man at the door took one look at her and shook his head. Dylan leaned forward and spoke in the man's ear as he slipped some money into his hand. He stepped aside and let them enter.

It was dark and smoky inside. Abra's mouth fell open when she spotted two naked girls gyrating on a small stage. The place was packed with people, mostly men. Dylan pulled Abra along behind him until he found a place for them to sit. Men looked at her. She felt her skin crawl. A topless waitress came to take their order, and Abra quickly looked down at the table. Dylan ordered and leaned back in his seat to watch the show.

"Can we go?" Abra pleaded, mortified.

"Quit acting like a Sunday school girl. Watch the act." He caught her by the chin and turned her head toward the stage. "You might learn something." When Dylan got up, she panicked. He leaned close. "Don't worry. I'll be right back." She watched him weave his way between the tables and speak to a man on the other side of the room. The man took something from his pocket and handed it to Dylan. Dylan handed something back. Abra didn't breathe easily until Dylan returned to the chair beside her. He winked at her. "Did you think I was leaving you already?"

The topless waitress returned with a tray of drinks. Dylan took one and handed it to Abra. "Drink up." She obeyed and felt the kick as soon as she swallowed. Her stomach grew warm. He took a small envelope from his pocket and removed a pill. "Take this. You've been uptight all day. This will help you relax." She did as he said to please him. When he nodded at her drink, she took another swallow.

Abra did relax. The rhythmic beat of drums pounded through her blood. Dylan pulled her up and danced with her. When he took his hands away, she didn't stop. She felt exhilarated, just moving to the music. Men shouted encouragement. Colored lights were in her face. She closed her eyes and turned around, arms in the air, body moving to the beat. The noise grew louder. She heard angry shouts, a commotion, but didn't care. She didn't want to think about anything but the music, the movement.

Someone grabbed her wrist and pulled her. She stumbled down steps. Had she been on a stage? "Come on." A woman half dragged her into a dimly lit hallway. Abra stumbled and bumped into a wall. The woman slapped her face lightly, once, twice. "Snap out of it, honey. What'd that devil give you?"

Abra heard Dylan. The woman cried out. He grabbed Abra. The woman protested, and he called her a foul name and told her to mind her own business. Wobbling, Abra kept walking, running her hand along the wall to find her way. Everything was blurry. Dylan caught up with her and put a firm arm around her waist. "Let's go." He opened a door at the end of the hall. The air was cold, the sky dark, so dark. She swayed, everything going black.

Awakening with a pounding headache, Abra heard a shower running. She hurt all over, inside and out. Where was she? She didn't remember this room. It had one old dresser, a mirror, a worn chintz chair by a curtained window, and a picture of the Golden Gate Bridge on the wall.

Dylan came out of the bathroom with a towel wrapped around his waist and using another to dry his hair. "What a night!" He grinned at her like a feral cat ready to pounce on a mouse. "You made a splash last night."

"What happened?"

"What didn't?" He laughed at her. "You went wild!"

She didn't remember much after that pill Dylan had given her. She sat up and pressed her hands against her temples. "My head hurts."

"I'll give you something to take care of it." Dylan smirked. "You surprised me, baby. I didn't know a good little Christian girl could dance like that."

Like what? She remembered enough not to want to ask. "What did you give me?"

"Just a little something to take the edge off." He sat on the bed and pushed the hair back from her shoulders. He kissed the curve of her neck. "You wore me out, baby." He nipped her earlobe. "I asked for late checkout, so we have until two. That gives you thirty minutes to get ready."

Abra felt dread. "For what?"

"To keep going."

They headed south on Highway 101 toward Santa Cruz and stopped at the seaside boardwalk at the mouth of the San Lorenzo River. Dylan was in high spirits. He asked her what she wanted to do. She rode the carousel and grabbed the brass ring. Dylan took her on the red-and-white Giant Dipper roller coaster. She went from abject terror one minute to hysterical laughter the next. After that, they made the rounds of boardwalk games. Dylan bought two colorful towels, swimming trunks for himself, and a bikini for her. "You've got it, baby. Flaunt it."

They swam toward the platform. Dylan told her she was taking too long and lengthened his strokes, leaving her behind. The water was cold. She felt a shiver of fear, imagining what might be swimming in the depths. She swam faster and was tired by the time she reached the pontoon. Dylan was already basking in the sun. He became bored quickly and dove back into the water. She followed, dismayed when he reached the shore and walked away without looking back. He wiped the water from his shoulders and shook his head like a shaggy dog. She wondered if he knew a dozen girls were staring at him. A slender blonde in a one-piece pink suit walked over to talk with him. He turned to her and drank up the attention.

When Abra reached shallow water, she walked out without looking in his direction. Striking a pose, she raked her fingers through her wet hair and wrung it out, then shook it loose. Even Dylan turned to watch. When a young man headed her way, Dylan reached her first.

"Back off. She's mine." He slung an arm around her shoulders as they walked up the beach. "We've been invited to a party."

Cars were parked up and down a narrow street, music blaring from inside a beach house, the place mobbed with kids. The blonde from the beach called out to Dylan, and Abra resisted the urge to cling to his arm. He let go of her hand as soon as he was inside the door and wove his way through the throng ahead of her, holding up a quart of Kentucky bourbon and earning cheers. The girls all seemed to be wearing flimsy tops over swimming suits, some bikinis skimpier than hers. Dylan was soon surrounded. When he kissed the blonde, Abra felt a kick in her stomach.

She went out the sliding-glass doors to where others gathered around a campfire, their faces bronze in the firelight. Waves crashed and raced up the white slope, lost power, and retreated to the sea.

Abra had watched Penny flirt often enough to know how it was done. But it seemed more natural to her to let the boys who approached her talk. She smiled, pretending to listen, hoping the door would slide open and Dylan would appear. What was he doing inside the house with that blonde? When he finally did appear, she laughed at nothing and said something low so the boys standing with her had to lean in a little closer.

"Here you are, baby. I've been looking all over for you."

Liar. Abra didn't take the drink he offered, lifting another someone else had given her. When he took it and set it aside, handing her the one he'd brought outside, she wondered if he'd put another pill in it. She heard shrieking laughter as a naked boy and girl came out of the house and made a run for the ocean. While Dylan watched and laughed, Abra poured the drink into the sand. He looked at her. "Come on back inside when you're finished pouting."

When she did, Dylan was standing among a cluster of boys and girls, most her age. He looked grown up and sophisticated in comparison. They gazed at him worshipfully.

"I didn't expect to see *you* here." Kent Fullerton stood next to her, a beer in his hand. "I saw you at the beach. I thought you might have come with Penny Matthews."

"I don't live with them anymore."

"Since when?" Kent sounded troubled.

"A couple of days ago. I'm with Dylan now."

He lifted his beer as he studied Dylan. "Another older guy."

She looked at him. "What do you mean?"

Kent's smile was rueful. "Penny told me you were in love with Joshua Freeman. That's why you wouldn't give me the time of day."

"Joshua was a friend of the family. And I would have given you the time of day if you hadn't lost interest so fast."

"I didn't lose interest. Every time I looked at you, you turned the other way. Penny said you were shy. I waited for you outside class once. You took one look at me and ducked into the girls' bathroom. I felt like an idiot chasing a girl who didn't even want to talk to me."

"No one even knew I was alive until then. I didn't know what to say."

Kent studied her face. "Well, we're talking now."

"It's too late."

Kent looked from her to Dylan. "Are you sure you aren't making a mistake?" When she didn't answer, he peered down at her again. "Do you want me to get you out of here?"

After hours of watching Dylan with his growing throng of admirers, she'd like nothing better.

They hadn't gone more than a few feet when Kent was yanked away. The look on Dylan's face before he hit Kent terrified Abra. When Kent tried to get up, Dylan dove at him like a wild animal. People moved back and shouted. Rolling, Kent managed a few blows before Dylan straddled him and used both fists. Others moved in then, grabbing Dylan by the arms, dragging him back.

The music blared on as Dylan fought them, teeth bared, veins bulging on his forehead, face livid. "Okay," he said. "Okay! Let go of me!" He shook off restraining hands.

Kent groaned and tried to sit up. Abra took a step forward, and Dylan grabbed her by the arm. "You and I are leaving!" He propelled her toward the door. People made a path for them. Even the girls who had been so enamored drew back, frightened now. The blonde met Abra's eyes, and there was a look of worry, not envy.

Dylan's fingers dug into her as he strode toward the car. Abra had to take two steps to one of his. He yanked open the passenger door and almost flung her inside. She barely had time to pull her legs in before he slammed the door. Planting the flat of his hand on the hood, he swung over, yanked open the driver's door, and slid in. The engine roared to life. Swearing, Dylan revved it, then peeled away from the curb. He sped down the street, barely missing parked cars. The tires squealed as he turned corners.

"You were leaving with that guy."

Abra closed her eyes, terrified. Dylan shifted gears again. Two days ago, that move had quickened her pulse. Now it stopped her heart. "He was one of Penny's old boyfriends."

"What'd you plan to do with him?"

"No more than what you were doing with all those girls standing around you."

He laughed, but it wasn't a mirthful sound. He didn't say anything else, and Abra stayed silent, wanting him to concentrate on his driving so he wouldn't get them both killed.

Abra had no idea how many miles they traveled before Dylan relaxed. "I broke his nose. I wanted to knock his teeth out." He gave her a cruel smile. "Maybe I did." He mocked the girls he'd met on the beach. The blonde had wanted to show him the house, but when push came to shove, she lost her nerve. Abra looked away, knowing what he meant by that.

Dylan looked at her and grinned. "Just like Penny." He swerved sharply, and she sucked in her breath. Gravel pelted the underbelly of the car as it skidded to a stop at the edge of a cliff. He grabbed her by the hair, yanking her toward him. "I could throw you down on those rocks and no one would even miss you." The look in his eyes made Abra's heart jump like a fleeing rabbit. "What do you say to that?"

She'd make sure she left marks on him if he tried.

His expression changed. "Most girls would be crying right now, begging." He gave her a punishing kiss. "You're something, you know that?" Smiling, he shook his head and pulled back onto the road. "I don't think I'm going to get tired of you anytime soon." He drove on into the night.

Resting her head against the seat, Abra studied Dylan. He was so beautiful. He'd been jealous of Kent. Maybe that was a sign he did love her, but just didn't know it yet. He gave her the smile that had made her fall in love with him—or made her imagine that she had, anyway.

"What're you thinking about, baby?"

"Just enjoying the ride. Where are we going, Dylan?"

"Does it matter?"

She looked out into the endless darkness. "No."

"I want to have a few more days with you before I head home and face the music."

Abra shook her head. "You don't have to worry, Dylan. No one will bother looking for me."

"I wasn't talking about you." He gave a dismissive laugh as though the people in Haven were the least of his worries. "Let's just say I left a little situation for my mother to clear up. That's why I came to Haven, to give things time to cool off."

"What things?"

"Some girls just don't know when to let go. My mother said the wounded dove flew off and is spending a few months on the Italian Riviera." He put his hand on her thigh. "So the coast is clear." He took his hand away. "Problem is, my mother is going to take one look at you and want my head on a platter."

———

Zeke walked to the bridge and rested his forearms on the rail. Clasping his hands loosely, he prayed, eyes open, soothed by the sound of water coming down from the mountains and flowing to the sea. Memories of Abra washed over him—hearing her newborn cry, seeing her helplessness, feeling her heartbeat beneath his fingertips; the breath of life he blew over her; her cold flesh pressed against his chest. He'd known fear before, but never as he had that night when he held Abra, slick from birth, close to death, in his hands.

I remember the way she looked at me with complete trust and love. And I remember the day that all changed.

He gripped the railing.

Lord, I won't pretend to understand what You're doing through all of this, but I trust You. Joshua is struggling. A battle is going on inside him. He's just come home from one war and now faces another. He listens to me, Lord, but his heart is broken. Put a hedge of protection around him, Father. Shore him up. Encircle him.

Zeke straightened and looked east. Abra had been gone a week and no word. The horizon softened with faint light, announcing sunrise. Pushing his hands into his pockets, he started back. A glimmer on the walkway caught his eye. Curious, he stooped and picked up the item. Marianne's cross, the chain broken. With a sigh, he slipped it into his shirt pocket.

When he let himself into the house, Joshua was sitting at the kitchen table, dark circles under his eyes, his hands wrapped around a mug of steaming coffee. He gave Zeke a bleak smile. Zeke squeezed his shoulder and went over to the counter to pour himself a cup of coffee before he sat across from his son.

Joshua shut his eyes. "I wonder where they are now."

It would do no good to tell Joshua he had to stop thinking about Abra and Dylan. He might as well tell him to stop breathing. "Are you working today?"

Joshua shook his head. "Not at the subdivision. We're waiting on more lumber. I thought I'd go out to Gil's and help repair the barn."

"Good idea." Hard work would keep Joshua's mind occupied. He'd have to learn for himself that only time would ease the pain.

———

Dylan ran low on money and checked them into ever-cheaper motels. They ate at greasy spoons. Once, he gave her some money and told her to buy bread and cheese while he looked through the magazines. When they got back into the car, he pulled a stolen bottle of bourbon from under his jacket and tossed it in her lap. He found a place to park for the night and made a bed from two blankets he'd stolen from the last motel. He drank the bourbon while staring at the surf. Abra was afraid to go to sleep, afraid if she did, she'd wake up and find him gone. Exhaustion drained her resolve.

The sun came up and she felt Dylan's hands combing through her hair. He searched her face, his expression bemused. "I'm usually tired of a girl by this time. But I still want you."

She heard what he didn't say. *It's only a matter of time until I'm done with you.* Dylan would do exactly what he wanted to do. Ironically, that had been one of the things that had most attracted her to him.

Eyes hooded, he ran a fingertip down her forehead, over her nose and lips, down her throat. "I've got enough money for gas to get me home. I guess it's time to face the dragon."

Dylan hardly spoke after that. Abra grew more nervous with each passing mile he drove along the Pacific Coast Highway, though she did her best not to show it. He took San Vicente to Wilshire, turning off at South Beverly Glen to Sunset Boulevard. Pristine neighborhoods with green lawns like carpets and clipped hedges flashed by.

Bakeries and dress shops, shoe and tailor shops, jewelry stores and steak houses, and more houses, then another turn onto Benedict Canyon Drive. He sped up and the Corvette hugged the road. Houses were set farther back, grander, more hidden.

He made a hard right turn onto Tower Road, sped up, then down-shifted and made another hard right, screeching to a stop by a raised box in front of two huge stone pillars and a massive, ornate iron gate. He punched a button. A man's voice crackled. Dylan called the man by name and told him to open the gate, then waited, his hand on the gearshift. A muscle twitched in his cheek as the minutes ticked by. Abra knew she wasn't the only one on edge.

Dylan revved the engine and bumped the gate. "Come on, Mother. Enough stalling." Tires screeched as he backed up and slammed on his brakes. He revved the engine again. The gate opened slowly. "About time!" As soon as it opened enough for the Corvette to fit through, he gunned it.

A man rode a car-size lawn mower in the woodland. The estate reminded her of Golden Gate Park—carefully manicured grass, trees, shrubs, flowers. The road curved and an enormous Mediterranean mansion with a red tile roof came into view.

Dylan sped up, swinging the car in a sharp circle and skidding to a stop in front of the house. Leaving the keys in the ignition, he shoved his door open and got out. He came around and acted like a perfect gentleman. He took her hand and kissed it as he helped her out. "Mother always stressed good manners." He winked. "She's probably watching us from her tower." Slipping his arm around her waist, he kissed her cheek. "Be brave. If she starts breathing fire, just get behind me. I can take the heat."

A servant opened the front door and greeted Dylan deferentially. She gave Abra a polite nod. Dylan led her across the threshold into a red marble, white-pillared entryway with potted palms in color-ful terra-cotta pots. An enormous, elegantly furnished living room spread out before them with plate-glass windows overlooking a courtyard with a huge swimming pool. On the other side lay formal gardens that sloped toward the valley view.

"Where is she?" Dylan asked the doorman.

"Upstairs office, Mr. Stark. She rang when the gatehouse let her know you'd come home. She wants you to come up."

Dylan grasped Abra by the elbow. Tiny beads of sweat stood out on his brow. Was it the Southern California heat, or was he really that afraid of his mother? His hand tightened as they walked down a corridor lined with oil paintings and marble statuary tucked into alcoves. It felt like a museum. He stopped in front of a large carved door, his fingers biting painfully into her flesh. "Don't say anything. Let me do the talking."

Muffled voices came from behind the door.

Dylan let go of Abra and, without knocking, opened the door wide and strode in. "Hello, Mother." A man in a suit and tie and a young woman in glasses, a black skirt, a button-down blouse, and black pumps retreated through a door off to the right.

A reed-thin woman in an elegant pink suit stood at windows overlooking the front drive, her blonde hair immaculately arranged in a chignon. She turned and tilted her head to one side. "Dylan, darling. The prodigal, home at last." She presented her cheek for him to kiss. "So good to see you." She sounded anything but pleased. She stepped away from him, her cold blue eyes fixed on Abra, standing in the doorway, where Dylan had left her. "And you brought a friend with you. Isn't that wonderful?" Her tone dripped sarcasm.

Dylan made a formal introduction. Abra offered the suitable salutations, embarrassed that she sounded like a frightened child.

Lilith turned on Dylan. "Are you completely out of your mind? How old is this one? Fifteen?"

This one?

Dylan laughed it off with a shrug. "I forgot to ask." He looked at Abra and raised a quizzical brow.

"Seventeen." It wasn't too much of a lie, since her birthday was in two weeks.

Dylan's mother glared at her like a laboratory technician examining a plague-causing germ under a microscope. She gave a sound of disgust. "Another tangled web to unweave. I like to write about scandals, not be in the maelstrom of one."

"No one cares about her."

"Your father called and said the police came to see him. And then I got a call from a man wanting to know where you were."

"When was that?"

"A week ago."

"Anyone call since?"

"No."

Dylan gave her a smug smile. "Like I said. Nobody cares."

Abra felt Lilith Stark's cold blue eyes on her again. "Why wouldn't anyone worry about you?"

Dylan answered for her. "She doesn't have any parents."

Lilith Stark ignored her son. "What do you say I give you some money? Dylan can put you on a Greyhound bus and send you back to wherever you came from."

Abra felt a moment of panic and looked at Dylan. Would he do it? How could she face the people of Haven after what she'd done? Everyone would say, "I told you so."

"I'm keeping her, Mother." Dylan sounded furious.

"What is she? A pet?" Lilith studied him. "You usually go for willowy blondes, Dylan. What do you see in this girl?"

"It's not something I can put into words. She's just got . . . something."

"And how long will *something* last this time?"

"As long as I want."

"Always your answer, Dylan." Lilith picked up diamond-studded reading glasses. "I give this affair a month." She flipped through a book. "Fine. Keep her. She can stay in the blue bedroom."

"I want the guesthouse."

Lilith pulled her glasses down her nose. "All right. The guesthouse. She's your cousin, daughter of my sister."

"You don't have a sister."

"Who would know?" She glared at him. "I don't want anyone thinking I approve of seedy affairs under my own roof."

Dylan laughed, really laughed. "I won't mention the banker from New York or the artist from Mexico or—"

"Careful, Dylan." Her eyes narrowed. "This is *my* house."

"And you know how much I adore and admire you, Mother." Undaunted, Dylan chuckled. "Seedy affairs are the way you make your living. Oh. I need some money. I'm all out."

"I'll give you money. After you work for it." Lilith leaned back and gave him an indulgent smile. "I have a big party scheduled for Saturday. I expect you to attend."

"Who's coming this time?"

"Everyone, of course."

Dylan grinned at Abra. "You're in for a treat, baby. All those country bumpkins back in Haven would die to be in your shoes right now."

"Speaking of shoes . . ." Lilith looked with distaste at Abra's and wrote something on a tablet. She tore off the page and handed it to Dylan. "Call Marisa and have her do something with your little friend." Lilith grimaced. "She looks like something the cat dragged in."

"We've been riding with the top down."

"Is that what you call it?"

"How much can I spend on her?"

"The sky's the limit." Her bright-white smile was the same as her son's. "The bill will be sent to your daddy." Her attention drifted briefly and then fixed on him again. "Oh, and another thing, darling. Take her to our doctor and make sure she has protection." Her expression filled with heavy meaning. "If you create another little problem, Dylan, you'll be the one making and paying for all the arrangements this time around."

The telephone rang. Lilith clamped a bejeweled hand on the receiver. Her voice changed when she answered. "Darling, what juicy bits of news do you have for me?"

<hr />

Zeke sat forward on Mitzi's couch as she handed him a delicate porcelain teacup and saucer. "You look like you could use something stronger than tea, Pastor Zeke. I've got some good brandy in my cabinet—only for medicinal purposes, of course."

Her wry tone made him chuckle. "Tea is fine, Mitzi." He watched the old woman cross the room. She'd lost weight she couldn't afford to lose. She eased her thin body carefully into the faded-red velvet chair near the front windows. Her ankles were swollen, her fingers twisted with arthritis. Ian Brubaker was filling in for Abra at church, and while he had retained all the skills of a concert pianist, Zeke missed the lighter touch Abra had learned from Mitzi. Mitzi had a wonderful way of sneaking in humor now and then—to the consternation of Hodge and a few others. "How are you, Mitzi?"

She gave him a droll look. "I'm just fine and dandy, Pastor Zeke. Have Peter and Priscilla had any word on Abra?" When he shook his head, she sighed and rested hers against the back of her easy chair. "I was afraid of that. Teenage girls can be so stupid." She gave him a pinched look. "I ought to know. I was one once."

"Abra might call you before she calls anyone else."

"If she does, I'll let you know, but I can't promise I'll tell you what she says or where she is, if she asks me not to."

"She trusts you, Mitzi. So do I." He'd always liked Mitzi. Hodge seemed to be torn between mortification and pride. He adored his mother, but said she drove him insane at times. He admitted once he never knew how his hardworking, somewhat-shy, prim and proper father had even met her, let alone married her. Not that he wasn't glad it had happened, being the only product of the union.

Zeke knew Mitzi as a woman of wit and wisdom, one who might seem flighty if not so solidly grounded in faith. Life experience didn't always bring wisdom. In Mitzi's case, it brought a great deal more. She said she'd been passionate in sin, but she was even more so in repentance. She had the gift of compassion for outcasts to prove it. "I will never ask you to break Abra's trust, Mitzi."

"I know. I have a list of names I could call that Dylan Stark, but I won't. Who is he, anyway? He appeared out of nowhere, and I got a whiff of sulfur smoke from the pit. Where did he come from? Do you know anything about him?"

Mitzi had made the tea strong and hot and laced it heavily with honey. "He's Cole Thurman's son."

"Oh. The wolf's cub." She looked at Zeke with those wise old eyes. "Poor Abra." She shook her head and stared into her cup of tea. "She's in for a rude awakening." She sipped her tea. "How's Joshua?"

"Grieving. Working hard. Taking long walks in the hills. He doesn't sleep much."

"Sounds like a chip off the old block. Even when you know the train is coming, you don't always know how to get out of the way, Zeke." She looked ready to cry. "I worry about that boy of yours."

"He has strong faith."

"He'll need it. It could be a long time, you know."

"I still have hope."

"You hold on to that. God isn't finished with Abra, even if she wants to be finished with Him." Her smile held the old hint of mischief. "I'm going to pray she remembers every single line of every hymn I made her learn." She chuckled. "I'm sure she'll want to forget, but I believe God will bring it all to mind when she most needs it." She tapped her temple. "It's all right there inside her head, Zeke. God can use it."

Zeke leaned back, relaxing into the cushions of the old settee. "Sounds like you knew this day was coming."

She sipped her tea again. "Abra and I may be decades apart, but we have a lot in common. Besides, aren't you the one who told me nobody is born a Christian? The war over a soul begins before a baby even draws breath." Mitzi put her teacup and saucer on the coffee table. "I can't walk all over town like you do, or wander the hills like Joshua, but I sure can sit right here in my easy chair and pray all day long. The devil can take that and shove it. I may be the oldest dame in town, Zeke, but I haven't taken my armor off since the day I put it on." Her aging face crinkled with a gentle smile. "And I'll tell you something else. I'm not the only one in this town willing to come alongside you and Joshua to go to battle for Abra. I'm not just talking about those other two grieving souls, Peter and Priscilla. Abra has friends in this town she doesn't even know about."

Zeke hoped so.

He stayed for another hour.

He had come to comfort. He went away comforted.

CHAPTER 7

Stone walls do not a prison make,
Nor iron bars a cage . . .
RICHARD LOVELACE

1955

Jack Wooding's son drove into the construction site, windows down, radio blaring the Doris Day hit "If I Give My Heart to You." Abra flashed into Joshua's mind, bringing a stab of pain with her.

She'd been gone over a year and no word from her. Peter had contacted the police after the first week. Chief of Police Jim Helgerson went out to Shadow Hills and talked with Cole Thurman, who said he didn't know where his son was or who he'd taken with him when he left. Why not call his mother, Lilith Stark? He handed over the telephone number. Lilith Stark said she hadn't seen her son in several months. He was an adult, responsible for his own life, but she doubted he would take any girl who wasn't willing to go with him. Who knows? Maybe they got married.

Chief Helgerson told Peter there wasn't anything more he could do. Runaways had a way of disappearing for as long as they wanted.

They could have been married in another state by now. He didn't have the time or resources to keep looking. "If she wants to come home, she'll come home." The chief's words were hardly cheering to anyone who loved Abra. Even Penny worried about her.

The last anyone heard about Abra came from Kent Fullerton. The high school football star came home from college at Christmas and called Penny. He'd seen her sister at a beach party in Santa Cruz. It had to have been just a few days after she'd left Haven. When Joshua heard, he went by the Fullertons' to talk with Kent. "I asked her if she wanted to leave. Before I knew what hit me, I was on the floor with a broken nose. I think that guy would have killed me if a couple of my friends hadn't pulled him off. I have this to remember him by." He touched a scar on his cheekbone.

Joshua's nightmares returned with a vengeance.

"Will you give me all your love? Will you swear that you'll be true to me?" Doris Day's voice sang out, the truck idling as Jack's son delivered some paperwork. Joshua clenched his teeth at the lyrics and wiped sweat off his brow. What kind of promises had Dylan made to Abra? Had he kept any of them? Did Abra still feel the same way about Dylan, or had the infatuation worn off by now? Were they still together, or had he dumped her someplace? He thought of war-torn Korea, starving girls left on their own, and how many GIs he had treated for venereal disease. He sent up another shotgun prayer for God to watch over and protect Abra.

Joshua fitted a freshly sawed board into place and pulled his hammer from his tool belt. He found pleasure in the scent of sawdust, the grain of the wood, the way each piece fit together like a jigsaw puzzle. The Doris Day song had ended, and now Rudy Eckhart, working a few yards from Joshua, was singing along with the Chordettes: "'Sandman, I'm so alone; don't have nobody to call my own. . . .'" Thankfully, street bulldozers started up, drowning him out with the racket of grading new sites for the next phase of Pleasant Hills.

Trucks rumbled in, loaded with concrete and ready to pour slab foundations. Joshua and his crew would be busy framing those houses in the weeks ahead, then putting in doors and windows and installing siding while subcontractors went to work on roofs, wiring, and plumbing. The insulation and trim came next, followed by the plaster guys and painters. The electricians and plumbers finished off their work before bathroom and kitchen counters were installed. More subcontractors arrived to lay carpet and flooring. Once the hookups to water and sewer were done, the bosses would get the punch list and check for any deficiencies or issues that needed to be addressed. Before that day came, Joshua would do his own walk-around inspection.

A piercing whistle stopped the hammering. "That's it for the day, gents!" Jack waved the handful of checks his son had delivered from the home office.

Rudy gave a cheer. "Hey, guys! What do you say we go on over to the Wagon Wheel and soak up a couple of ice-cold beers? You coming with us this time, Freeman?"

"I've got a prior engagement." Joshua slipped his hammer into his work belt as smoothly as a gunslinger holstering his Colt .45.

"News flash, everybody!" Rudy shouted to the others stowing tools and heading for Jack. "Joshua has got himself a date tonight!"

Joshua laughed. "A date with a roof early tomorrow morning." The church had needed a new one for several years, but money was scarce. He had connections and enough money put aside to get the job done. Dad, Gil MacPherson, and Peter Matthews would be part of the work crew.

"Don't you ever stop working, Freeman?" Rudy yelled.

"I'm off all day every Sunday."

"And spend it in church. All that singing gives me a headache."

One of the men called out, "Hearing you sing 'Earth Angel' gives me a headache!" Others laughed.

Rudy broke into "That's All Right" and imitated Elvis's infamous hip moves. Men booed and shouted protest. "What's the problem, Eckhart? Got ants in your pants?"

Laughing, Joshua collected his check and walked with his buddies toward their parked vehicles. Everyone had plans for the weekend. Two were going out to the coast to fish. One had a hot date with a girl he'd met in a bar. Another said his wife had a long honey-do list, and if he didn't get it done before his in-laws arrived, he'd be living in the doghouse. Two others liked Rudy's idea of meeting up at the Wagon Wheel after showers and having a couple of cold beers and steaks to celebrate payday.

Joshua stopped off at the church on his way home. He wanted to make sure the roofing materials had been delivered. Irene Farley's old Plymouth was parked in front. She'd been the church secretary for as long as Joshua could remember. Dad called her "the FLM"—first line of ministry—because her warm telephone voice brought more than one weary soul into church on Sunday, if only to meet the lady with the sweet voice. Mitzi's roadster was parked in front, too, which meant Dad must have been doing visitation outside the town limits.

Bundled stacks of asphalt shingles, a box of nails, and rolls of black tar paper and copper flashing had been left on the lawn between the church and the fellowship hall. Two extension ladders leaned against the church. The hardest part of the job would be stripping the old shingles. The debris would be dropped and loaded into his pickup. Hodge Martin would make the runs to the dump.

The door to the church office stood open. Irene glanced up when Joshua walked in. "Well, howdy-do, Joshua!" She smiled when he leaned down to give her a peck on the cheek. Dad's office door was slightly ajar. He heard the low mumble of a woman's voice. Dad never met with a woman unless Irene was in the front office, and even then, he never closed his door all the way.

Slouching into a chair, Joshua chatted with Irene while he waited for Dad to finish with his counseling appointment. He was surprised when Susan Wells came out, her eyes red and puffy. Susan blushed when she saw Joshua. She said a quick, pained hello, thanked Irene, and headed for the outer office door. Dad followed. He put his hand on Susan's shoulder before she could escape and spoke in a low voice. Susan stood still under his touch, but didn't raise her head. She nodded once and left.

Irene looked at Dad. "Is she going to be all right?"

"She's learning what it means to trust God." Dad thanked Irene for staying late. Gathering her purse and some files, she said she'd see them both Sunday morning.

Joshua followed Dad back into his private office. "You look exhausted, Dad."

"So do you." Dad smiled. "Ian Brubaker sent the supplies over. Do we have everything we need?"

"Yes, but promise me you won't go up on the roof again." He'd almost slid off last time, barely managing to catch his heel in the gutter.

"I planned on handling the pulley." He picked up his jacket. "What do you say to dinner at Bessie's?"

Joshua cocked his head and studied his father's face. Irene said he'd been in his office for over an hour. "You like Susan, don't you?"

"Yes. I do."

It was a decisive statement. Joshua started to ask if he meant that in a personal way, but his father interrupted his speculations. "Just leave it at that."

Joshua stifled his curiosity. "I need a shower before we go out to dinner." He wondered how Mom would feel about Dad's interest in another woman.

Dad took his Cardinals baseball cap from the hook by the door. "I'll walk down now and get us a booth."

"I'll be quick. Order whatever the special is."

"No hurry, Son. I'll wait until you get there."

Joshua went home and stood under the stream of cool water, washing away the dirt and sweat of a hard day's work. He kept thinking about Dad and Susan Wells. Dad was still a man in his prime. Had he finally met someone he might consider marrying? Joshua dressed in fresh Levi's, a button-down short-sleeved shirt, and loafers and decided to pay closer attention to their relationship.

He pulled into a space around the corner from the café. The bell jangled, and Bessie called out a greeting as he walked in. "Two Freemans! My lucky day! You both eat like horses!"

Dad had his usual spot, closest to the swinging doors into the kitchen. Susan stood by the booth, talking with him, hands pushed into her apron pockets. She turned as Joshua approached. She no longer had puffy eyes, but she still seemed unsettled. "Hello, Joshua. What can I get you to drink?" It wasn't the first time someone had been embarrassed to be found in the pastor's office.

"Lemonade, lots of ice please." He slid into the booth. "And I'll order whatever special Oliver is cooking up for tonight."

"Roast beef, mashed potatoes, and mixed vegetables. Dinner comes with tomato bisque soup or a green salad."

"Salad with vinegar and oil."

Chuckling, Dad handed Susan his menu. "Make that two, Susan, if you will."

"Coming right up, Pastor Zeke." There was new warmth in Susan's voice and an expression that hadn't been there before. Joshua studied his father surreptitiously and saw nothing out of the ordinary. He looked relaxed, content. Every time the door opened and the bell jangled, Dad smiled a greeting. He knew everyone in town. Some called out a hello; others came over to talk for a few minutes. Joshua had grown up in the midst of interruptions.

Dad set his baseball cap aside. "I hear Gil is coming tomorrow morning to help out."

Joshua counted Gil as one of his closest friends, despite the disparity between their ages. They'd both been through hell and struggled to make sense of the carnage they'd witnessed. They both knew what it meant to be haunted with regret simply because they'd survived when others hadn't. Abra's departure had added to Joshua's postwar stress. Gil suffered, too, and had for years. Somehow, talking things through had helped them both lay down the burden of what they couldn't do, and let go of the ghosts of those they couldn't save.

Dad had been trying to fan a dying spark of faith in Gil. When he'd sent Joshua out to meet with him, something changed in the man. He was needed, desperately, by another who had suffered as he had. They gained strength from one another. Joshua saw faith flame in the older man. They both had someone closer than a brother standing with them, someone who died to save everyone, someone who knew what it was to grieve over those lost in the battle for men's souls.

Being with Gil made Joshua remember things he'd been taught. "I forgot the rules," he'd admitted to Gil during one of their early conversations.

"What rules?" Gil had asked.

"Rule number one: young men die. Rule number two: you can't change rule number one. I heard it in training, but forgot it in battle."

Joshua and Gil could talk freely about what they'd seen and experienced on the battlefield. They could share things they couldn't speak of with anyone else. As time passed, they talked less about what they had lost, and more about what needed tearing down and rebuilding. Gil's neighbor had a new barn. In a few days, the church would have a new roof.

Susan came through the swinging doors with their salads. Dad blessed the food. "And we pray for our beloved Abra, Lord. Let her remember who she is."

Head bowed, Joshua added, "And to whom she belongs."

"And to call home," Susan said, still standing close enough to hear every word. Joshua glanced up and she grimaced in apology. "Sorry. I didn't mean to intrude."

"You didn't." Dad smiled.

She went away and came right back to refill their glasses of lemonade.

Dad watched her walk away. He caught Joshua watching him. "God is working, Son."

Joshua grinned. "Looks like it."

"He is always working." Dad tucked into his salad.

Joshua believed that. He just wished God would work a little faster on Abra.

Abra lay on her back, staring at the cottage ceiling. Dylan had already left, dressed in his immaculate white tennis clothes, for a day at the country club. He never took her. He never said who he would be with or when he would be back.

A week after he'd moved her into the guesthouse, Abra had given in to tears and complaints when he went out again without her. Dylan accused her of nagging. When she raged at him, he caught hold of her arms and shook her. She saw the barely controlled fury in his eyes, felt it in his hands, and remembered what he'd done to Kent Fullerton when he lost control. When she showed up at the house for a party that night, Lilith noticed the bruises and sent her back to the cottage. She could hear Lilith tearing into Dylan before she reached the door. He returned that night, but he didn't apologize. And long before the sun came up, Abra knew never to question him again. He would do whatever he wanted, whenever he wanted, and that included whatever he wanted to do to her. He could do even more damage with words than with his hands.

Lilith expected Abra to look pretty and polished, act friendly—but not too friendly—and eavesdrop. "Just move around the room and listen in on conversations."

And Abra did. She overheard all kinds of things.

"They ought to turn that studio into a bomb shelter. It hasn't had a hit in years."

"From what I hear, they aren't doing any productions, just renting old movie rights to television."

"Television won't last."

"You're a fool if you believe that. Television is here for good. Nobody's going to turn it off. You wait. You'll see I'm right."

"Yeah, yeah."

Lilith treated Abra like a favorite niece at parties and ignored her the rest of the time. She enjoyed Lilith's parties—dressing in expensive gowns and being in the same room as the rich and famous, even if they barely noticed her. Lilith preferred it that way. She told Abra to move around the room, be quiet, unobtrusive. Men liked young women who hung on their every word. "Encourage them to boast. Be all ears and eyes." Penny would have given anything to be among these people. Penny would be bragging to everyone if she were in the same room as Natalie Wood and Robert Wagner and Debbie Reynolds and Gene Kelly.

Sometimes Abra thought of writing a letter to Penny just to talk about the people she'd met. She'd say she was still with Dylan, living in a lovely little cottage on a huge estate owned by his mother, a famous Hollywood columnist. She wanted Penny to know her life was bigger and better than Penny's would ever be. So what if it wasn't the truth? Penny didn't have to know Dylan could be cruel, his mother merely tolerated her, and none of the famous people in the room knew or cared enough to carry on a conversation with her because she was a nobody. They were polite because she was Lilith's "niece." She'd been nobody in Haven and she was nobody here, too. So what was new? Dylan's friends, those she had met, didn't even know she was his girlfriend. The closest he'd ever come to telling anyone was at a pool party when he got drunk, put his arm around her, and kissed her and then laughingly called her his kissing cousin.

Lilith always invited Abra to come for coffee and a chat the morning after a party. Dylan typically remained in bed, hungover. Lilith would ask what Abra had heard and jot down notes as Abra talked. Dylan smirked when he read the columns. When he was gone, Abra read them and understood what part she played in spreading innuendos and outright scandals, how a tidbit of seemingly harmless information could be twisted and used to reward or punish people.

It hadn't taken more than a few parties to realize "stars" weren't so different from other people. They were insecure, jealous, sometimes nice, sometimes shy. They were more beautiful and had more money, but their lives weren't as perfect as Abra and Penny and Charlotte and the others had always imagined.

Eventually Abra stopped sharing with Lilith all the things she heard. How could she be party to spreading such rumors, when her own life had begun as a scandal? Her birth had made headlines and the story still haunted her. She didn't want to help Lilith dig for dirt, but she knew better than to admit her attack of scruples.

Lilith sensed the change and became a little less tolerant, even less inclined to give Dylan money to spend on her upkeep, as she put it. "If you want her at the party, you buy her dress this time."

"You always brag about being so generous, Mother," Dylan argued. "What will people think if your 'favorite niece' has to stay in the cottage for lack of a decent gown? You'll be like the wicked stepmother in *Cinderella*." He laughed.

Lilith didn't look amused. "I doubt anyone would miss her."

Abra had the feeling Dylan only insisted she come to irritate his mother. Most of the time he left her on her own while he went off to charm and flirt with young movie actresses and drink with their handlers. During the first months, she had burned with jealousy and ached with hurt. She had to remind herself he was playing a role, working a room the way his mother wanted. As long as he did it well, the money would keep rolling in.

The longer Abra was with Dylan, the less handsome he seemed. The beauty and charisma that had so attracted her began to fade. Dylan commented on the change in her and played games to keep her enthralled. He wasn't as rough. He acted the gentleman. She wasn't fooled anymore. She only pretended to be.

"I never know what you're thinking behind those green eyes of yours. I never know whether I really have you or not."

Maybe that was the only thing that kept him interested. Not knowing. Once he boasted of having slept with someone else. He gave her all the details. She listened, detached, and asked if he would mind if she did a little experimentation of her own. She'd seen this man at one of his mother's parties—

That was as far as she got. She never said anything like that again.

Her heartbeat still sped up when he came into the cottage. Was it love or fear that made her tremble when he took her in his arms? It was better to convince herself it was love.

Restless, Abra got up and opened a dresser drawer. Dylan had told her to be ready by ten to go shopping. He'd be taking her to Marisa's. Lilith was having another party and expected her to do her part. Marisa Cohen was far less elegant than Dorothea Endicott back in Haven, but the middle-aged woman knew how to dress movie stars.

Dylan usually stayed to enjoy the fashion show. Today, he pulled up to the curb and, without even the pretense of manners, reached across and shoved the door open. "Have Marisa call a cab when you're done. I've got someplace to go."

Alarm bells went off inside her head, but she did as he said. It took all her willpower not to turn around and watch him drive away.

"Dylan wants something special for tomorrow evening," Marisa announced. "He was very specific. Nice that he has good taste." She looked like a schoolteacher with her black-rimmed glasses and her dark hair pulled back in a prim bun. Only the simple slacks, cream silk blouse, and double strand of pearls shouted money.

She had a rack of gowns waiting for Abra to try on. The white was too virginal; the red nice, but a little too revealing. One dress drifted like cloud layers over Abra's curves. Marisa told her to walk around in it. "Head up; roll those shoulders back. Imagine you're a queen. That sea-green chiffon is gorgeous on you! Perfect for those amazing eyes of yours and all that red hair."

Distracted, Abra confessed, "I've always hated my hair. I'd rather be a blonde."

"Why?" Marisa looked askance at Abra. "Blondes are a dime a dozen in Hollywood, especially since Marilyn Monroe came to town."

"Dylan likes blondes." She couldn't remember one of Lilith's parties where he hadn't gravitated to one. Sometimes she wondered why he'd ever lost interest in Penny and turned to her.

"Dylan likes women. Don't change yourself to suit a man. Dylan probably chose you because you are different. And he hasn't tired of you like he has the others. Most of his girlfriends last a month or two. You've lasted more than a year. That's saying a lot. He must love you."

Did he? Or did he keep her around for another reason? He'd never said the words, and she'd never seen that tender look she'd seen between Peter and Priscilla.

Marisa touched her shoulder lightly. "Don't look so sad. You're a beautiful girl, Abra. Even if he does lose interest, there are plenty of other fish in the sea." She turned her to face the mirror. "Look at what you have to offer."

Abra stared at her reflection. The dress was beautiful.

"You can change now. Wear your hair up for the party."

Abra hadn't been back in the cottage ten minutes when Dylan stormed out of the house, his mother on his heels. Dylan stopped and faced her, livid. Their voices carried across the pool to the open windows of the cottage.

"Veronica bores me to death!"

"You had a thing for her last year."

"It was a game, Mother. I won. It's over!"

"It's not over! And I don't care how you feel about her! You're lucky her father doesn't know what had to be done. And luckier still the girl doesn't have the courage to tell him. You are going to apologize and beg her forgiveness. You are going to be your most charming self. You're going to be a gentleman."

"Aren't I always?" he sneered.

"You cannot treat the daughter of the president of one of the biggest studios in Hollywood like a common strumpet!"

"She *is* a common—"

"Shut up, Dylan! She has a far better pedigree than that mongrel you have in the cottage. Don't think I don't know everything about where she came from. When are you going to get rid of her?"

"When I'm ready!" He stepped forward, thrusting his face toward hers. "Stay out of my business, Mother. I was finished with Veronica before I went north."

"Yes, but you left me holding the bag. If you're nasty to her, she may just go crying to Daddy. And he'll want to know why."

Dylan told her to go to blazes.

Lilith Stark swore back at him. "Lucky for you Veronica still has a thing for you, buddy boy. Find a way to let her down gently, or set her up with one of your frat friends, *or her daddy will send goons to rearrange your handsome face.* He might just cut off the only thing that seems to matter to you. Do you understand me *now?*"

"All right!" Dylan turned away, rubbing the back of his neck. He faced his mother again. "I'll play nice. Happy now?" His sarcasm dripped. When he turned toward the cottage, Abra ran into the bedroom and flung herself on the bed, curling on her side and

pretending to be asleep. The door slammed. Dylan swore again and shattered something against the living room wall. She couldn't pretend not to hear that.

When she came into the living room, Dylan was sitting on the edge of the sofa, pouring himself a glass of whiskey. She could feel the heat of his wrath and see it in the tension in his shoulders. He glanced back at her and then downed the liquor. He'd taught her how to give massages, but she knew better than to touch him in his present mood.

"How'd it go today with Marisa?"

"Fine." She kept her tone neutral, but adrenaline poured into her bloodstream. She looked at the shattered Grecian urn and wondered if he'd take his temper out on her next. She judged the distance to the door.

Dylan emptied a second glass and set it down with a hard thump. "Come here." His dark eyes narrowed and burned. When she sat down beside him, he shifted, making himself comfortable. He extended his arms along the back of the couch and gave her a look she had come to dread. "Make me happy."

When Dylan left an hour later, Abra stayed in the cottage. She didn't go to the house for dinner. No one called to ask why.

———

Dylan didn't come back that night, and a breakfast tray was sent the next morning with a note from Lilith that the chauffeur would take her to Alfredo's Salon. Alfredo was Lilith's hairdresser, a handsome, somewhat pale young man who assured Abra he would make her a goddess. He talked and asked questions, most rhetorical. He offered her lunch. Apparently it was a small matter to order it brought in from one of the exclusive restaurants in the area. He named Lilith's favorite. Abra said she wasn't hungry.

When Alfredo finished with her, she thought it overdone, but didn't say so. Marisa had said to wear her hair up with the sea-green chiffon dress. Lilith's chauffeur gave her an admiring glance before opening the car door. The Mexican maid showed up at five with one plate on the dinner tray. It wasn't the first time Abra had dined alone. Dylan showed up as she was dressing. He leaned against the doorway, watching. He looked like a movie star in his tuxedo. Even given all she knew about him, sometimes she was still struck by his physical beauty.

"I'm only here for a few minutes." He'd forgotten his wallet and keys. "I have to pick up someone." Veronica. The girl who still burned for him, despite having suffered at his hands.

How many of us are there in the world? Abra wondered.

"I'll see you at the party, but I won't be able to spend any time with you."

She almost reminded him he seldom did.

"You look beautiful, by the way." He came over and tipped her chin, kissing her. He stared into her eyes. "I'll be watching you."

Lilith looked stunning in a black dress. Her brows lifted a fraction as her gaze flickered over Abra. "You do have something." It sounded like a small concession. "Do *not* distract Dylan. He has important business to do this evening. I'd better warn you so it won't be a hurtful surprise. He's bringing another girl. It's very important you stay out of the way."

As people were ushered in, Lilith became effervescent, warm, full of laughter. She gave air kisses to everyone. They all smiled and chatted gaily. Despite the pleasantries and shows of affection, Abra had the feeling there were few in the room who liked Lilith Stark. Everyone knew the power of her pen, and no one wanted it dipped in poison at his expense. Dylan came in with a willowy blonde clinging to his arm. Many knew and greeted her. Trays of hors d'oeuvres were served, glasses of champagne replenished. Abra stayed as far away from Dylan and Veronica as she could get in the living room.

She sensed he was searching for her. He spotted her and whispered something to the girl on his arm, then led her across the room. Lilith saw what he was doing and tried to intercept them. He stepped around her, and Lilith gave Abra a withering look of warning. Abra headed for the door open to the outer courtyard. When Dylan said her name, she had no choice. Turning, she smiled.

"Veronica, I want you to meet my cousin. Abra, this is Veronica." He leaned down and kissed her cheek. She blushed with pleasure and looked at him with adoring eyes. Abra's heart pounded. The devil still had the power to hurt her. A server in a black tuxedo approached, offering champagne. Dylan took two glasses from a tray, handing one to Veronica and one to Abra. He took another for himself. "You don't look like you're having much fun, Abra."

She smiled stiffly. "Enough."

"She's a budding actress." His mouth tipped on one side.

"You're fortunate to have Lilith as your aunt." Veronica sipped champagne. "She knows everyone in the business." She looked Abra over and glanced at Dylan.

Lilith called Abra, beckoning her over to meet someone.

Dylan laughed. "Tell her all her efforts are for naught."

Abra had already turned away, but she heard Veronica. "That's not very nice, Dylan. Your cousin is very pretty."

Lilith made the introductions and kept the conversation going. Abra stood with half a dozen people and felt utterly alone. "You look a little wan, dear." Lilith pretended concern. "Why don't you go back to the cottage?"

Abra wasn't willing to do that. Dylan was the only hope she had. She took another glass of champagne and stood near the windows where she could watch and not be noticed. Dylan was playing his games with Veronica, and the girl was obviously under his spell. Abra felt desolate.

"And who might you be?"

Startled, she noticed the man sitting in a chair near the wall. He was attractive and older. She guessed him in his early forties. He rose. He was taller than Dylan, with the broad, muscular shoulders of a mature man. His brown hair had a light sprinkling of gray at the temples. He raised one brow. "Cat got your tongue?"

"My name is Abra." She didn't ask for his.

"Abra." He said the name as though testing it. "An interesting name. Well, Abra, how do you fit in here?" He gave a nod that included the entire room.

"I don't." She almost forgot who she was supposed to be. "I'm Dylan's cousin. From up north."

"Are you really?" He looked amused. "Dylan's cousin. From up north. It's all in the details, isn't it? Which side of the family?"

"Franklin Moss!" Lilith moved between guests, zeroing in on them. "Darling! There you are! I've been looking for you all evening."

He faced her, his mouth curving. "Who dares hide from Lilith Stark?"

"I was so sorry to hear about Pamela."

"Ah, Pamela. I'll bet you were." He sounded droll. "Pretty girls come and go."

Lilith grazed Abra with a brief look before she shook her head and gave Franklin Moss a reproving half smile. "You're not trolling the waters, are you, darling? Everyone here already has an agent."

Mr. Moss cocked his head and looked at Abra again. "Even Dylan's cousin?"

Lilith covered her irritation with a lifted hand. A servant appeared like a genie from a bottle, offering champagne. Mr. Moss shook his head and said he was drinking bourbon on the rocks. Lilith told the waiter to get him another. She plucked the champagne glass from Abra's hand and said, "Naughty, naughty. She's too young to drink, Franklin, and too young for you."

"I didn't know you were so protective."

"She's my favorite niece. And yes, she is lovely, and I daresay she has some kind of talent, but she's going home soon." She sipped champagne, her eyes fixed on Abra. "Her family misses her."

"And which family would that be?"

Lilith's eyes narrowed. "We've known one another a long time, Franklin. I'm sure you understand." She tipped her chin. "Now, tell me about Pamela. I won't be satisfied until I hear every detail from the horse's mouth. You know I would rather hear the truth from you than depend on gossip."

"That hardly seems your style, Lilith."

Her pink lips tightened. "Rumor has it she fired you and went with another agency. I can't believe that's true. After all you've done for her."

Abra felt the unpleasant undercurrents and withdrew. Dylan was immersed in conversation with Veronica and several others. Abra felt like a ghost, moving invisibly among the glittering crowd. A few looked at her, frowning slightly, as though trying to place her. She took a cracker with a slice of boiled egg and caviar.

Elizabeth Taylor was stunningly beautiful beside her husband, Michael Wilding, as they talked with Debbie Reynolds and Eddie Fisher. Robert Wagner was even more handsome in real life than on celluloid or a poster.

Abra edged around the various groups, listening to bits and pieces of conversation: actors' chitchat about auditions gone bad or good, a part they were playing, or talking up their credits to some man in a dark suit, some asking about auditions. She could always spot the studio executives.

Dylan was laughing at something someone had said. He still had his arm around Veronica.

Depressed, Abra quietly slipped out of the house and returned to the cottage. She hung the Grecian gown in the closet, pulled on a T-shirt, and went to bed. She couldn't sleep.

Dylan came in after midnight. "I need the bed. One last hurrah with Veronica before I dump her."

A tide of jealousy and hurt swept over her. "It's bad enough I had to watch you with her all evening."

"Get up."

"No!"

"Don't ever say no to me." Dylan ripped the covers off the bed. Emotions she'd held in check for months brought her up and at him, hands like claws. She'd never felt such wrath or hate.

Dylan caught her wrists and pinned them against the mattress. "It's been a long time since you sounded like a jealous girlfriend." Grinning, he straddled her. "I knew fire still burned inside you."

She managed to get one hand free and slapped him across the face. His eyes changed. Grabbing a pillow, he covered her face. Terrified, she bucked and fought. Just before she blacked out, Dylan tossed the pillow aside and grabbed her by the hair. "You ever slap me again and I'll kill you. I could, you know. No one would even miss you."

Gasping air, she sobbed, terrified. He sat back on her hips. Her muscles stiffened when his hands ran over her body, but she didn't fight him. "You pretend indifference, baby, but your heart still pounds for me. You still love me. I can still have you whenever I want."

His weight lifted from her. He sat on the edge of the bed and released his breath. He stroked her hair in a gentle caress, the cruel glint disappearing from his eyes. "You were already burning inside. I just stoked the fire." He stood, a look of wariness in his face. "Sometimes I'm not sure how I feel about you. I feel something, more than anyone else has ever made me feel. Maybe that's why I'm not ready to let you go." He sighed as though the admission angered him. He jerked his head. "Take a swim."

Still shaking, Abra got up. "Veronica knows I'm not your cousin."

"That's probably why she's so intent upon pleasing me tonight."

She removed her clothing while he watched and put on the bikini he'd bought for her in Santa Cruz. "Have your fun, Dylan."

"I always do."

Abra sat on the edge of the pool, shivering, as Veronica came out of the shadows. How much had she overheard? What did it matter other than that she might change her mind about Dylan? Maybe he'd said and done it all for that very purpose.

Fighting tears, Abra slipped into the warm water. Letting out her breath, she sank to the bottom and sat cross-legged on the white gunite. It felt rough against her tender flesh. Her long red hair floated around her like seaweed. Would Dylan care if she drowned herself? Giving vent to her anguish, she screamed under the water, hands fisted.

Her body, traitorous, rose. She treaded water. She felt someone watching her and looked toward the side of the pool. A man stood in the shadows, smoking a cigarette. He tossed it on the cement and ground it out with his foot before going back to the house. He turned slightly before he went inside, his face illuminated. It was Franklin Moss.

Joshua's face swam in Abra's memory, his words whispering in the palm fronds stirring in the night breeze. *"Guard your heart."*

Too late. She had been so certain when she ran away that she loved Dylan and he loved her. She learned the truth the hard way that first night in San Francisco. What he felt wasn't love. She'd hoped his lust might turn to something better, something more tender and lasting. She'd given him everything in the hope of that happening.

He said he still felt something. But what? He said he wasn't ready to let her go. She could hold on for a while longer, hope a little more.

She floated on her back, legs and arms spread like a dead woman, eyes wide open, staring up at the night sky. The air was chilly; the moon was full. Water covered her ears and she couldn't hear anything except her own mind.

She couldn't go back to Haven anyway. She'd been such a fool.

What was it Mitzi said once? *"No man buys a cow when he can get the milk for free."* Even the waitress at Bessie's Corner Café tried to warn her about Dylan.

I was blind, but now I see. The words of "Amazing Grace" ran through her mind. She'd played that hymn dozens of times. Other lines came, unbidden. She didn't want to remember them. She didn't want to think about God.

Thinking about God only made her feel worse.

―――――

Zeke awakened in the darkness. His heart hurt. He sat up slowly, rubbing his chest. Turning the Baby Ben, he read two fifteen. He listened intently and heard the twittering hoots of a screech owl in the backyard, but knew that wasn't what had awakened him. He rubbed his face, slipped his feet into his slippers, and padded into the kitchen. Joshua's Bible was open on the table, notes jotted in his neat hand. Zeke pressed his fingers against his sternum again, as if he could rub away an old wound.

Is it time yet, Lord? It's been eighteen months.

Silence.

Is there anything I can do, Lord?

Joshua came into the kitchen, barefoot and dressed in his pajama bottoms. "I heard you get up. Bad dream?"

"No. You?"

Joshua slumped into a chair and raked his fingers through his short hair. "It's easier during the day. I can focus on work."

"You work at night, too, in a different way. Our work is to believe God." He took the coffee from the cabinet. "The battle is always over the mind, Son."

"Do you think she thinks about us at all?"

"She probably tries not to."

"I just don't get it, Dad. She's known the Lord all her life."

"She knew what we told her about the Lord, Joshua. That's different from knowing Him." He turned on the tap water. "None of us hear His voice until we listen."

Dylan came and went as he pleased. Sometimes he still stayed all night. "Have you missed me, baby?" At least she could pretend for a few hours someone loved her. Lilith kept him busy with constant demands. He was always on the go, "doing research," as he mockingly called it. There wasn't a hot spot or hideaway he didn't know about. No one could bury a secret deep enough that he couldn't dig it up. He had spies in private hospitals who called to whisper what star had checked in and why. Lilith made lots of money. Abra wondered if most of it was for keeping certain stories under wrap. She was generous, however, sharing a percentage of her income with Dylan.

"Mother is giving another party."

Was there ever a weekend when she wasn't? Dylan had something on his mind, and Abra knew she wouldn't like it. "Marisa will see to everything. I want you to outshine everyone."

"Why?"

"I have my reasons." He got up and took a shower, dressing in his white tennis shorts and shirt. "I'll always take good care of you." He tipped her chin and leaned down to kiss her. "I promise." He brushed cold fingers against her cheek and left.

Dylan had given Marisa Cohen specific instructions, and Abra found herself wearing a halter-neck Chantilly white dress. "It shows off your tan beautifully." Abra had been spending a lot of time alone by the pool. "It's casual for an evening party, which will make you stand out even more. Leave your hair down."

The telephone rang as she was walking in the door. "Maria is bringing your dinner. Be ready by seven, but don't come to the house until I call you." It was almost eight before she heard from him.

She entered through the French doors off the courtyard and found the living room packed with people in formal attire. Women wore floor-length gowns and glittering jewelry; the men wore tuxedos. Her informal white dress immediately drew attention. She spotted Dylan and was wondering what game he was playing now, when a familiar voice spoke from behind her.

"A dove among the peacocks." Franklin Moss put a cigarette between his lips, inhaled deeply, and crushed it out in a marble ashtray. He exhaled slowly as he studied her face. "You look virginal." When she pressed her lips together, he shook his head. "No insult intended. Lilith made it sound like you were on your way out the door last time we met. I didn't expect to see you again."

She lifted one shoulder. "I'm still in the cottage."

"Lucky you." He took out a silver cigarette case and offered her one. She shook her head and said she didn't smoke. "Smart girl. Nasty habit." He withdrew one for himself, tapped it on the case. He put the case in his pocket and took out a lighter, glancing toward Dylan. "How did a nice girl like you ever get tangled up with Dylan Stark?"

Nice girl? She almost laughed. "He's my cousin."

"And I'm your uncle." He looked around the room and then back at her. "Lots of uncles in the world. This isn't the place for you."

"Probably because I'm not an actress."

"Oh, I think you are, and better than most in this room, even the ones who get the starring roles. Mind if I tell you something?"

"What?"

"For a smart girl, you are really stupid."

She turned her head away.

"Why do you stay? Is it his looks? He's got them in spades, that's for sure."

"Love?"

He grinned at her sarcasm. "Yeah. *Love.*" He chuckled. "Or is he that good in bed?" When she didn't answer, he gave a weary sigh.

"Even when you get the monkey off your back, the circus always comes back to town."

She didn't know what he was talking about.

Dylan wove his way through the crowd toward them. "Franklin, good to see you, as always." He put his arm around Abra's waist and looked between them as though something shady had been going on. "I didn't know you two knew each other."

"We don't." Mr. Moss crushed another cigarette, ready to leave.

Dylan squeezed Abra's waist. "Franklin worked for one of the most elite agencies in town until one particular actress defected and he got fired."

"Like mother, like son. You know everyone's business."

"Nothing secret about a high-profile starlet diving into an affair with the director of her latest movie. Pretty hard to do damage control after that, wouldn't you say?"

"Pamela will go far."

"Do you think so?" Dylan's expression turned to one of deep sympathy. Abra knew it was all show. "I heard your wife filed for divorce. Which makes me wonder if the rumors about you and your client commingling . . . ?"

The older man's eyes flickered with anger as well as pain, but he covered his feelings quickly. He shrugged. "As I told your mother, women come and women go."

"This man is a legend, Abra. They used to say he could take a girl off a street corner and make her into a movie star."

"I still can, though I'm more selective these days."

"Found anyone?"

"Still looking." His gaze drifted to Abra.

"How selective? What are you looking for? Another blonde bombshell?"

"Loyalty. That's what I'm looking for. Unfortunately, it's nonexistent these days."

"You're wrong." Dylan grinned at her. "Abra is as loyal as a Labrador. Aren't you, baby?" Abra knew what was coming and saw no way to avert the inevitable.

Franklin Moss looked at her again, and not just her face this time. "Does she have any talent other than dogged faithfulness?"

"Her sister told me she plays piano."

"How well?"

"I have no idea, but she must have been good." Dylan laughed. "She played for a church." He let go of her when someone called his name from across the room. He raised a hand in response and called back for them to give him a minute. "Take her back to your place and see what she can do." He winked. "Who knows? She might surprise you."

"You think so? I don't surprise easily."

"Nothing ventured, nothing gained, as they say."

"Dylan." Abra hated how small and desperate she sounded. She reached out and clutched at his arm.

He leaned down. "Go. It's better than being put on a Greyhound bus." He brushed his lips against her ear. "I promised I'd take care of you, didn't I?" She watched him walk away, too shocked and hurt to speak. Dylan plucked a glass of champagne from a tray and joined a foursome of beautiful girls.

Abra's body shook. It was over. Just like that. She'd lost him. She'd known she would. Eventually. Someday.

Not tonight. Not here. Not now.

She'd told herself over and over the day would come, but now that the moment had arrived, the shock set in, the devastation.

"Are you game?"

"What?" Abra gave Franklin Moss a blank look.

One brow lifted. "To show me what you can do."

What choice did she have? She lifted one shoulder. "I guess."

"Come on, then. Nothing ventured, nothing gained."

CHAPTER 8

For everything there is a season,
a time for every activity under heaven.

ECCLESIASTES 3:1

FRANKLIN MOSS KEPT a hand beneath Abra's elbow as they went out Lilith Stark's front door. Abra had the feeling he thought she'd bolt. It entered her mind, but where would she go? Run off into the dark? Sleep on a bench somewhere? Then what? Return and beg Dylan to take her back? He would love that. Her stomach was quivering with tension. Was she making another wrong decision? Should she tell this man she'd changed her mind?

"I know you're scared. I can feel you shaking." Mr. Moss gave her a sad smile. "But let me give you fair warning. If you go back inside that house, Lilith will have Dylan drive you to the closest bus station. They both want to get rid of you."

"How do you know?" Was Dylan merely carrying out his mother's instructions?

"You know it, too." He let out his breath in disgust. "That was the coldest kiss-off I've ever seen, and I've seen a lot."

Tears began to gather and burn. Her breath came faster. Dylan had dumped her into the hands of an older man without so much as a warning, and out of bravado, she'd agreed. Mr. Moss put his arm around her waist and leaned down. "Don't give them the satisfaction of looking over your shoulder or shedding any tears where they can see you. Hold your head up." It was a command.

She obeyed. "I don't know if I'm doing the right thing going with you." Her voice quavered.

"At the moment, there is no right thing. There's just escape." He spoke in a matter-of-fact tone. "Hold it together until we're out the gate. Then you can cry buckets and rant and rave. Just not now. Not here. Look up at me. Smile. Do it like you mean it. That's my girl."

A shiny new black Cadillac pulled up in front, and the young attendant in black uniform and cap got out. "Your coach awaits, Cinderella."

Abra slipped in quickly. The trembling got worse. She felt cold all over. She clenched and unclenched her hands, half-reaching for the door handle. *See it through, you coward. Nothing ventured, nothing gained.*

She watched Mr. Moss walk around the front of the car. He talked briefly to the young man, handed him a folded bill, and then slid into the driver's seat. "You're off to see the wizard, the wonderful wizard of Oz." He sang softly, on key, and winked at her as he put the car in gear and punched the gas. As soon as he passed beneath the gate and turned left onto Tower Road, he spoke softly. "Now you can cry."

Abra turned her face away so he wouldn't see the tears pouring down her cheeks. She gritted her teeth. Her rescuer dropped a pristine white monogrammed handkerchief on her lap. She snatched it gratefully. "I hate him."

"Not yet, but someday you'll recognize Dylan for what he is. You can take some consolation. You lasted longer than any other girl I've heard about, and as far as I know, he's never made any kind of arrangements for the others."

"Lucky me."

Mr. Moss glanced at her. "You've got spunk. I like that."

She closed her eyes tightly. *I am such a fool.*

"Give yourself credit where credit is due. You survived the scorpion and her son. They both grab hold and sting. Lilith feeds on ruined lives. It's her business to know the latest and greatest scandal."

How much had Dylan told her? Abra wondered. But then, who would care anyway? "I thought Dylan loved me." She'd wanted so desperately to believe someone could.

"Dylan Stark is incapable of love. Forget him."

"You make it sound easy."

"Not easy. Necessary."

"And if I have no talent? What then?" Would this man toss her out on the street?

His gaze moved pointedly over her body. "We'll start with what you do have, which is very nice—very nice indeed." He gave her a rueful smile. "Don't look so scared. I'm not after what you think."

Emotions still roiled inside her. Would he be as rough as Dylan? He was taller and broader. She didn't feel like asking questions. Thankfully, Franklin Moss didn't ask any of his own. He didn't turn on the radio either. She'd never gone anywhere with Dylan that he didn't have it blaring.

She looked away. Had Dylan ever loved her, even for a second? She'd only seen lust, sarcasm, and fury. She'd stayed because she was too ashamed to call for help. She'd stayed so she wouldn't have to hear how she'd made her own bed and would have to sleep in it. She'd stayed out of fear. She'd stayed because she didn't know where else to go. She'd stayed for a hundred reasons that made no sense, not even to her. Now, she felt lost. And the feeling had nothing to do with location.

This man handled a car differently than Dylan. He didn't drive at breakneck speed, careening around corners, passing cars with inches to spare. He drove fast, but with complete control. He didn't beat a rhythm on the wheel, but held it firmly.

Was he really offering her a chance to salvage herself—or merely a change of beds? A cold wind of realization blew through her. Would it matter?

They went through a yellow light. "Do you want to go back?"

"To Dylan?"

"To whatever life, or family, you had before you met him."

"No." Even if anyone had bothered to try to find her, she wouldn't have gone back. She'd never go back to Haven. "I didn't have a life."

"None at all?" He looked dubious.

"None worth talking about."

"What about your family?"

"I don't have one. I've never really belonged anywhere."

He considered her words and her, then looked straight ahead at the road. "It's one of the things I noticed about you first, that air of mystery. You stood out. You stood back, too, observing and observed."

"Observed?"

He chuckled at her look. "You don't believe me? The only reason no one came on to you is because Lilith said you were her niece. No one wanted to risk her wrath."

"She would have been dancing in the street if someone had taken me from Dylan."

"Then you don't understand anything." He gave her a cool look. "Even she won't cross Dylan."

They didn't talk anymore. Remote, pensive, Mr. Moss sped through the streets of Los Angeles. She didn't know where he was taking her and didn't care. What did it matter now anyway? The buildings were bigger and taller, the lights brighter. Cars jammed a boulevard. An art deco theater shone with neon lights, the marquee boasting *Lady and the Tramp*. It had let out. People strolled along sidewalks. Her life had just fallen apart, but the world around her went on as usual. If she dropped off the face of the earth, she wouldn't even be missed. She might as well do whatever she could to survive.

They pulled up in front of an eight-story gray building with Egyptian men and women carved in stone relief. A uniformed doorman emerged as Mr. Moss came around to open Abra's door. "Good evening, Mr. Moss."

"Yes, it is, Howard." Mr. Moss handed him the keys and said he wouldn't be needing the car again tonight. Abra felt the heat rushing into her face. She supposed she should be grateful he would let her spend the night even if her audition didn't turn out to be what he hoped. She felt his large hand spread against the small of her back, pressing her forward through the door Howard held open for them. "Fill up the tank and check the oil, would you, please?"

"Yes, sir."

Abra felt more embarrassment than the night Dylan had checked her into the Fairmont Hotel. Mr. Moss was as old as Peter Matthews, or close to it.

The Otis elevator took them to the top floor. Mr. Moss stepped across the hall and unlocked a door. There was only one other door, farther down and on the other side of the hallway. "Home, sweet home." He inclined his head and she stepped forward into a black-and-white world. The living room looked Spartan; furnishings utilitarian, expensive, and modern. A bank of windows opened to the dark night and a sleeping apartment building across the street. The only color in the room came from three large framed pictures hanging on a white wall: three different views of a man in a short robe embracing a marble figure that had apparently just come to life.

Mr. Moss shrugged out of his black suit coat, folded it shoulder to shoulder, and laid it over the back of a white leather chair. He loosened the black tie and unfastened the top button of his white shirt. "Jean-Léon Gérôme's work. What do you think?"

A tiny warning bell went off inside her. She silenced it. It seemed a perfectly appropriate set of paintings for a talent agent. "Pygmalion and Galatea."

"Smart girl."

Pulling her gaze away from the prints, she went to a baby grand in one corner. "Do you play?"

"Some, but you didn't come to hear me." He'd stepped behind a counter. "A drink first. Take a seat. You're wound up tighter than a two-dollar clock. I'm not going to compromise your virtue."

As if she had any virtue left to compromise. She sat on the edge of a white sofa. How could she relax when the next hour would determine what happened to the rest of her life? She heard the clink of glass and ice, the grate of a cap being unscrewed. Mr. Moss walked toward her, studying her as he handed her a glass of dark sparkling liquid. She frowned at it, remembering the nightclub. "What's in it?"

"So suspicious. I suppose it comes from experience."

She held the cold drink in cold hands. "Dylan gave me a drink once that had me dancing on a stage."

"Where was this?"

"North Beach. San Francisco."

He made a derisive sound. "Dylan has always been a class act." His expression changed to one of curiosity. "Were you any good?"

"Good enough to start a fistfight and get the place busted by police." Or so Dylan had told her. She didn't remember much from that night.

He nodded toward the glass in her hand. "It's rum and Coke. You didn't look like a Scotch-on-the-rocks girl. And I'll never give you drugs unless you know about it and they're prescribed by a doctor."

He talked like everything was already settled. She took a tentative sip. She usually didn't like alcohol, but this tasted good.

Mr. Moss sat at the other end of the sofa, his expression pleasant. He looked full of confidence, perfectly at ease. Despite the distance between them, she felt a tension in him, an undercurrent of excitement, expectation. He said this audition wasn't about sex, but she still wondered. He rested his arm on the back of the couch. "A few things you might want to know about me before we get to your audition." His smile was wry, as though he could read her mind.

He gave a monologue, summarizing his life. He'd graduated from Harvard Business School, apprenticed in a New York agency geared for Broadway performers, before coming west and joining the most prestigious and powerful Hollywood talent agency in the business. He'd done well, bringing in several clients who became big stars. He had never been fired in his life—despite the rumors to the contrary. He had made a lot of money, still had most of it. Since leaving the agency, he had signed contracts with several actors, every one of whom now had steady work, which meant a steady income stream as well. He liked to gamble. He had been looking for another project. And yes, he'd had an affair with Pamela Hudson of the bright lights, and yes, it had caused a lot of grief, not the least of which was his wife walking out on him and taking his two children with her. Not that he minded all that much. They'd married young and grown in different directions.

"Divorce is never simple and sometimes expensive. My biggest regret is what the affair did to my children. They haven't forgiven me for cheating on their mother."

"And your wife?"

"She has the house in Malibu, which makes her and my children very happy. They like the beaches. I have this apartment, which makes me happy. I like being close to the action."

Everything he had said had come too fast for her to absorb. "How many children do you have?"

"A boy and a girl, ages fifteen and thirteen." He finished his Scotch and got up to pour another. "My daughter would like to lop off my head and give it to her mother on a platter. My son doesn't speak to me. The fallout from Pamela."

"Are you still in love with her?"

"I have more regret over my wife than her. Oh, well." He gave a harsh laugh. "Right now, my only interest in any woman is professional. It took the golden goose flying to another man's nest to bring me to my senses. Good thing I invested the commission I made from Pamela before she spread her wings to fly." He smiled without humor. "Not that she went far. She's pregnant. By the time she has the baby and gets her body back in shape, she'll be forgotten. And I give her marriage two to three years max. She'll come out of the divorce with a couple of million, but not the career she envisioned when she snagged her director. Not what she could have had if she'd stayed the course." He shrugged. "At least she'll have enough to keep her from ever having to work as a carhop at a drive-in again."

"Is that story true?" She and Penny had read about Pamela Hudson in a movie magazine. "You really met her at a drive-in?"

His smile was full of cynicism. "She leaned over to take my order. Let's say I got a good look at her assets and lost my head." He got up and took Abra's half-empty glass. "You look like you're feeling better."

Perhaps it was his openness, his businesslike manner. "Would you like me to play for you now, Mr. Moss?"

"Go ahead." He poured himself another drink. "I'm all ears."

She ran an experimental hand over the keys and found the piano perfectly tuned. Making herself comfortable on the bench, she played scales and chords to warm up. It was a lifetime ago that she had played. She felt more at home now than she had since leaving Haven.

She relaxed. Music poured into her mind and she played what she knew best, a medley of hymns. Every note reminded her of Mitzi, Pastor Zeke, Joshua, the church filled with people she'd known all her life. She lifted her hands abruptly, clenching them.

"Something wrong with the piano?"

"No." She paused. "I don't think I'm playing what most people want to hear. That's all." He was sitting on a barstool, watching her closely. "What would you like me to play?"

He looked surprised. "You're giving me a choice? Play whatever you want."

She started with Bach's Toccata and Fugue in D minor. Then Debussy's "Clair de Lune" spilled through her hands. She thought of Dylan and played Hank Williams's "Your Cheatin' Heart" and the Orioles' "Crying in the Chapel." Pulling her mind away from him, she sought for some other inspiration and Mitzi popped into her head. Holding back tears, Abra launched into an impassioned rendition of "Maple Leaf Rag." When Mr. Moss started to laugh, Abra stopped. She lifted her hands away, fingers splayed, heart breaking. What was so funny?

"Well, you are a surprise! And believe me when I say I'm not surprised very often." He finished his drink and left the glass on the bar. He came over to the piano. "Dylan had no idea you could play like that, did he?"

"He knew I played for the church."

"Definitely not his kind of music. You already said you can dance. Can you sing?"

She corrected him. "I danced when I was drunk on something and didn't even know what I was doing. And I guess I can sing, as well as anyone else. I could probably yodel, too, if someone taught me how."

He lifted a hand as though to stop her from saying more. "It doesn't matter. You move like a dancer. You have nice tone to your voice. You know what? You're the real deal." He looked excited, eyes glowing. "We can do it."

"Do what?"

"Make you a star."

She stared at him. Was he serious? Her heart pounded.

"It's going to take hard work on both our parts. I'm willing. Are you?"

She caught his excitement. "I can work hard, Mr. Moss." She was eager, but nervous. "But where would I live?"

"Here. With me. And don't look at me like that. I have two extra bedrooms and they have locks on the doors. Come on." He nodded the way. "Take a look."

Still nervous, Abra followed him down a hall. He passed an open door to a room with masculine blues and browns, a double bed, and signed, framed posters of Yogi Berra, Bob Grim, and Joe DiMaggio on the wall. He swung another door open, revealing a more feminine bedroom beautifully decorated in pastel pink, green, and yellow. It had white French provincial furniture—a queen-size bed, dresser, side tables, and lamps. It even had a private bathroom with a claw-foot tub and separate shower, everything in pink-and-white tile with gilded-framed mirrors and pale-green towels and rugs. Penny would love it.

"This is my office." Mr. Moss opened another door across the hall, revealing a bigger room with a large brown leather swivel chair, mahogany desk with stacks of files, telephone. Next to it was an iron safe. Four filing cabinets stood against one wall. Movie posters and glossy portraits were on display, Pamela Hudson noticeably absent. A typewriter sat on one side of his desk with stacked trays of writing supplies. He gave her a few seconds to take it all in and then led the way to the door at the end of the hall.

"This is my room." He opened the door into a suite much bigger than Peter and Priscilla's living room. It was filled with dark wood, rich fabrics, and masculine identity. When he went in, Abra didn't follow him. He looked from her to his king-size bed and back, with a sardonic smile. "No?"

She wondered if everything hinged on her saying yes. She swallowed hard. Mr. Moss didn't press the issue or look disappointed.

He came out of the room and closed the door behind him. "Another first." He smiled at her. "Good girl." She followed him back to the living room.

"Decision time, Abra." He sat at the end of the couch again, relaxed, watchful. "You can go back to Tower Road and beg Dylan to take you back, knowing he won't. Or you can move in tonight, work with me, and become a star. Which is it?"

Was it really such a sure thing? She stood on the edge of a precipice, trembling.

"Take the leap." He gave a soft laugh. "Any other girl would be diving at the opportunity I'm offering. But you're not like other girls, are you? I knew that the first time I saw you. I've been watching you for a while."

She remembered him standing by the pool. "Did Dylan know?"

"Most likely." His smile held no humor. "What do you want, Abra?"

"I want to be . . ." A little catch in her throat kept her from saying the rest.

"Rich and famous?"

"Somebody."

She wouldn't be invisible anymore. She wouldn't be the disposable child. She wouldn't be Dylan's cast-off girlfriend. Dylan would regret throwing her away. Penny and her gang of friends would envy her. She'd be *somebody*.

"I'll make you that and more." He rose with an air of satisfaction, everything decided. "Come on back to my office." He walked with purpose. He opened a file cabinet, fingered through files, and pulled out two documents. Dropping them on the black leather desk blotter, he plucked a silver-and-black fountain pen from the top drawer and put it on top of the papers. He pulled the chair back. "Sit. Read. Take all the time you need. Ask anything you want."

"I don't even know what to ask."

He looked inexplicably sad. "Where on earth did you come from, little girl?"

"I was born under a bridge and left to die." She hadn't meant to say that.

He tilted his head, studying her. "Nice story."

"True."

"Obviously, someone found you."

"Then gave me away." And now, Dylan had given her away as well. What would this man do with her? "No one has ever wanted me around for long."

He frowned slightly, searching her face, then dismissing the notion. "If you sign that contract, you're putting yourself in my hands for a long time. And I'll make you into someone the whole world wants."

Could he really do that? She studied him for a moment and saw he believed it. She wanted to believe it, too. Abra picked up the pen, flipped through the pages, and signed the blank line.

"Impetuous youth." Mr. Moss's tone was enigmatic. He took the pen from her fingers. When he leaned over her, she felt the heat radiating from his body, the warmth of his breath in her hair. He signed the line below hers with a flourish. He flipped through the second copy and pointed. She signed again. He signed and put the pen back into the drawer, opened the iron safe, and tucked one copy inside. He nodded toward her copy, still on the desk. "You should keep that safe."

"Where do you suggest? In my underwear?"

He laughed and held out his hand. "Give it to me." He tossed it into the safe with his copy, closed the door, and spun the dial. He opened a box of file cards, pulled one up, jotted a telephone number on a tablet, picked up the telephone, and dialed. Smiling confidently, he winked at her. "Dylan! My young friend. I called to thank you. Who? Franklin Moss here. Who else? . . . Two in the morning? I had no idea you'd be in bed so early. . . . No, I'm not drunk. Quite the contrary. I'm feeling better than I've felt in a long, long time." He listened again, then laughed. "In answer to that question, yes, she surprised me. I just signed her." He leaned his hip against the desk, grinning at her. "You still there, Dylan? . . . Yes. That's exactly what I said." He tore the telephone number off the notepad, wadded it, and pitched it into the trash can. "I always know what I'm doing. . . . No. Don't bother sending anything over. She's starting fresh." He dropped the telephone receiver into the cradle. "Finis. That, my girl, was the end of a dark era. A new dawn has come."

If she'd had any thoughts of turning back, it was too late now. "What did Dylan say?"

"He wanted to know how well you played."

"He didn't mean the piano."

"True." Mr. Moss's eyes took on a hard gleam. "But he doesn't know that's all you did."

He gave Abra another drink, then said it was time for her to go to bed. He tapped on her door a few minutes later, and her heart jumped in alarm. "My wife left a few things behind." He handed her a pile of clothing. "They'll do for now. We'll go shopping tomorrow." He looked faintly amused. "Lock the door if it makes you feel safer."

Abra barely slept. She kept looking at the clock on the side table. She waffled between despair over Dylan and hope that the dreams Franklin Moss had planted in her head could actually come true. If she worked hard enough, could she find retribution?

"I'm done!" Gil called, coming up from the other side of the American bungalow roof. "How about you?"

"Two more to go." Joshua nailed down the last shingles and stood, slipping the hammer into his tool belt. He took off his knee pads and tossed them down.

"Looks great from down here!" Harold Carmichael called from

the sidewalk, where he sat watching from his wheelchair. "You two boys have done a grand job! Donna and I are mighty grateful."

His elderly wife stood behind him, holding the chair by the handles. "There's lemonade and cookies in the kitchen when you two gentlemen are ready."

Gil started down the ladder. "You've got one taker, Mrs. Carmichael." Joshua followed. As soon as his feet touched the ground, he unsnapped the locks on the extension ladder, folded the sections, and carried it over to his truck. Harold and Donna's American bungalow was weatherproof now. No chance of another leak when winter rains came.

Mr. Carmichael looked troubled. "We should pay you something, Joshua."

Joshua grasped his hand gently, careful not to hurt the man's crippled, arthritic fingers. "It's our way of thanking you both for all your years of faithfulness to the church family."

"Did I ever thank you for the ramp?"

Joshua laughed. "Yes, sir, you did." About a hundred times.

"I love my home, but it was beginning to feel like a jail cell."

Mrs. Carmichael started to push the wheelchair. "What do you say we go on inside so Joshua and Gil can have some refreshments?"

Joshua brushed her hands away. "Allow me." She gave him a grateful look and went ahead as he wheeled Mr. Carmichael up the ramp. She held the screen door open. Gil followed behind.

Mr. Carmichael had other things on his mind. "I'm going to have to order some firewood."

"Tell me how much you want," Gil volunteered quickly. "I can bring it next week. I wouldn't mind getting rid of a cord. It's going to rot otherwise. There's always a tree falling somewhere in the woods, and I like to keep as much cleared as I can to cut the fire hazard. You'd be doing me a favor taking it."

"I still want to pay you something."

"Okay. I want two dozen snickerdoodles and a couple of jars of those pomegranate and quince jellies your wife makes."

Donna Carmichael beamed. "I can give you the jars of jelly today, but I'm afraid you'll have to wait for your snickerdoodles. I made two dozen, but Harold got to them first." She patted her husband's shoulders. "He has a sweet tooth."

Gil laughed. "So do I." He finished a cookie and downed the glass of lemonade. "Sorry, folks, but I've got to run. I'll bring a pickup full of wood on Wednesday. How's that?"

"Anytime, Gil, and thanks again." Mr. Carmichael turned his wheelchair around and escorted him to the front door.

Donna took Joshua's glass and refilled it without asking. She had something to say. He expected it to be about her husband's health. "I've had Abra on my mind for days. Have you heard anything from her?"

It had been almost two years, but the mention of her name still roused emotion in him. "Not a word." No one had received so much as a note from Abra in all that time. Had she forgotten everyone who ever loved her? Had she forgotten him?

Joshua drained the glass of lemonade, rinsed it, and set it on the counter. "Abra will come home when she's ready. Just keep praying." He squeezed her shoulder. "Thanks for the lemonade and cookies."

Mr. Carmichael was headed for the kitchen doorway. "Are you going, too?" He didn't try to cover his disappointment.

"Harold." His wife spoke gently. "The poor boy has been working on the roof all morning. It's Saturday. He probably has a date."

Joshua had only been out a couple of times since he and Lacey Glover had decided to stop seeing each other. Maybe he should start looking around. He wasn't getting any younger. "I'll see you two in church tomorrow."

On his way back through town, he spotted an old friend walking along the sidewalk and pulled over. Leaning across the front seat, he rolled down the passenger window. "Sally Pruitt! When did you get home?" She had slimmed down and cut her brown hair in a short bob that looked good on her.

Sally smiled in happy surprise. "Funny coincidence. I was just hoping to run into you, Joshua." She came over to rest her forearms on the truck door. "You're a sight for sore eyes."

"You're looking pretty good yourself. Do you want a ride?"

"I'd love one." She opened the door and slid in. "You know what I'd like even more? A strawberry shake at Bessie's. I've spent the last two hours walking around town, and I think I need something to cool me off."

"From the heat or trouble?"

"Children can't come home without parents wanting to become parents again, and I'm a big girl now. I left home the week after high school graduation, in case you don't remember."

He didn't, but he knew better than to admit it. He put the truck in gear. "Are you up for the weekend or longer?"

Her open expression of pleasure closed. "I'm here to . . ." She shrugged. "Think."

"Should I ask what you're thinking about?"

"What I want out of life."

"Do you have any ideas?"

Sally looked at him. "I've always had one idea, but it just never worked out the way I dreamed."

Joshua parked around the corner from Bessie's. Sally got out before he had a chance to open her door. They walked side by side. When Sally reached for the door, Joshua beat her to it. "Allow me to be a gentleman."

She laughed as she walked in ahead of him, talking to him over her shoulder. "I've been living in a city where most men let the door slam in your face or hit you from behind."

"It wasn't always that way."

"Times change, Joshua. I've changed with them."

"Not too much, I hope."

Susan and Bessie called out greetings. Bessie hugged Sally and said how good it was to see her. Had she brought her homework along? They both laughed. Susan told Joshua to say hello to his father for her. Bessie seated them in the back corner by the windows looking out onto the side street where he'd parked. She handed Sally a menu and smirked at Joshua before handing him one. He shook his head. What was it about women? Bessie always wanted to pair him up with someone.

Sally set her menu aside, folded her arms on the table, and studied him. "You look different, Joshua."

He put his menu on top of hers. "I'm older."

"Older, wiser, a little battered and bruised."

"I was a medic in Korea."

"It's more than the war, Joshua."

Joshua knew where she was headed. She had heard about Abra, and like so many others, she was fishing for information.

Bessie came over. "What can I get you two?"

Sally ordered a strawberry shake; Joshua asked for his usual, black coffee. Sally watched Bessie walk away and then faced Joshua again. "Bessie says your dad comes here a lot. Any particular reason?" Clearly, her head had already been filled with an idea.

"Dad prefers Oliver's cooking to his own."

Sally raised her brows. "You're saying it has nothing to do with Susan Wells?"

"I'm saying you can't stop people from speculating." Joshua knew Susan never did anything that might raise any question about her behavior or Dad's. Maybe that was why Dad liked her enough to seek her out so often. Sometimes Joshua wondered where their deepening friendship might lead. Mom's picture still sat on his bedside table, and their wedding portrait hung above the mantel.

"How about you, Joshua? Are you seeing anyone?"

"Yes." He laughed. "I'm seeing you."

"You know what I mean. I heard you and Lacey Glover dated for a while."

"I'm not going out with anyone at the moment." Serious, he met her gaze. "Lacey and I are still friends."

"All right." She sighed and gave a slight shrug. "We'll play it your way."

Some things needed to be clear from the start. "I don't play, Sally, especially when it has to do with someone's feelings. I never did. I never will."

She blushed. "I always liked you, Joshua." Her smile was tinged with sadness. "I never had to wonder where I stood with you."

Bessie delivered their order. She nodded to Sally. "Let me know if that shake is okay." She filled Joshua's mug with steaming fresh black coffee. Sally dutifully dipped a long-handled teaspoon into the frosty steel beaker. She rolled her eyes dramatically and said it was heavenly, absolutely heavenly. Bessie arched a brow. "How are you and your mom doing?"

Sally shrugged. "We're adjusting to one another. We still butt heads, and hers is still harder than mine. I might be coming in here on a regular basis again."

"You come on in here anytime, honey. You're always welcome." She went to check on other patrons.

Sally asked if Joshua ever saw Paul Davenport, Dave Upton, or Henry Grimm. Paul Davenport worked on his father's apple ranch and didn't come into town much. Dave Upton had gone to USC on a football scholarship. Shortly after graduation, he married one of the Trojan cheerleaders. Joshua had heard her father was a studio executive. Paul told him Dave and his wife settled in Santa Monica. Henry and Bee Bee Grimm had a rough start, but were very happily married now and expecting their third child. He didn't mention that their first child had arrived only six months after the wedding. Brady Studebaker had taken over his father's sign business on Main Street. Sally had kept in touch with Janet Fulsom. She was married now and settled down in the Central Valley and had two children. Her husband ran a gas station on Highway 99 in Bakersfield.

Sally stirred her shake with the straw. "I came close to getting married once. Did you know I was engaged two years ago?"

"Lacey mentioned it. Wasn't his name Darren?"

"Darren Michael Engersol. We broke up two months before the wedding." She lifted one shoulder in a half shrug and sipped her shake. "He decided he wasn't ready to commit to a lifetime with anyone, then married someone else four months later."

"Ouch." Joshua winced. "That must have hurt."

"Not as much as one might think." She looked serious. "Better to know sooner rather than later. And to tell the truth, Joshua, I was having second thoughts myself. Darren was a nice guy—a really nice guy—but . . ."

"But what?"

"I kept thinking about Mom and Dad and all that yelling. I didn't think they loved each other at all. Bicker, bicker, bicker—that's all they ever did. Then Dad died and I came home and saw how things were. Mom has come completely undone without him. I've never seen anyone grieve like her." Her eyes grew moist. "Surprise, surprise. She did love him after all." She let out a quick breath and shook her head, as though shaking off the emotions rising up inside her. "It's been a revelation, I can tell you."

She poked the straw up and down in the shake. "Darren and I never fought. I can't remember either of us ever raising our voices to one another." She gave a short laugh. "No fire. Not even a spark. All in all, we had a pretty boring relationship."

"So you're looking for a sparring partner?"

"No! Well, maybe. Oh, I don't know." She gave him a self-deprecating grin. "That's the sad part of it all. I have no idea what kind of guy I'm looking for."

"Maybe you should stop looking and let God bring him to you."

She met his gaze steadily. "You do know I had a gigantic crush on you from kindergarten through senior year of high school."

Heat flooded Joshua's face. "Is that so?"

Her face lit up. "I didn't know a man could blush."

"Thanks. That's real helpful."

She laughed. "You knew. Your buddies teased me unmercifully until you told them to stop."

"I was flattered, Sally."

"You were flattered." She gave him a droll look. "So flattered you never even asked me out. Not even once, Joshua. I was so hurt." She made it sound like she was teasing, but he wondered. She tilted her head and smiled slightly. "You didn't want to lead me on. Right?"

"I wasn't interested in girls back then."

She laughed. "Oh, yes, you were, but only Abra."

Just when he thought things couldn't get any worse. "She was just a kid."

"Yes. Well, I heard you had a huge fight with her when you came out of the Swan Theater one night, and it wasn't long after that she disappeared with some bad boy from Southern California." Sally was watching his face, searching for answers. She looked impatient. "Were you in love with her?"

"Yes."

"Are you still?"

"I don't know. She's been gone a long time."

"That's not an answer, Joshua."

He knew this wasn't a casual conversation. They weren't schoolkids anymore. Most of their friends were married and had started families.

She wanted to put things on the table. So be it. "I'm not waiting anymore, if that's what you're asking."

She finished her milk shake and set the beaker on the edge of the table.

Bessie came over. "How was it?"

Sally grinned. "The best ever, Bessie!"

"You say that every time." Bessie looked between the two of them. "It's good to see you two sitting here nice and cozy together, having a good chat."

"Forget it, Bessie." Sally put on a mournful face. "I threw myself at Joshua and he dodged."

Joshua took his wallet out. "And just when I was about to ask you to the movies."

Sally laughed in surprise. "Are you kidding?"

"Unless you'd rather go bowling. There's a new alley at the other end of town." Joshua slid out of the booth and held his hand out to help Sally. As soon as she straightened, she let go of his hand, falling into step beside him as they walked to the door. She didn't reach for it this time, and smiled at him as she went out. He'd always liked her dimples.

"Do you even know what's playing?"

"Sure." He grinned. "*Lady and the Tramp*."

"Ohhhh." She widened her eyes effectively. "Sounds racy!"

They stood in line talking for almost half an hour before reaching the ticket booth. Joshua stood in line again to buy hot dogs, popcorn, sodas, and Junior Mints before they went into the theater. Sally tucked her arm through his. The theater was filling up fast and they found seats on the right side, halfway down. Joshua remembered the night he brought Abra to the movies and she'd stared hungry-eyed at Dylan, who looked straight at him, smug and triumphant, daring him to try to hold on to her if he could.

Wherever Abra was now, whatever she was going through, he

couldn't let his imagination come up with answers. It would drive him mad if he thought about all the grim possibilities.

Sally looked at him. "Are you okay?"

Joshua let the past and Abra slip away. There was a time for all things. He couldn't come to her rescue. Only God could save her. "It's been a while since I've been inside this theater." Not since Abra. Not since a last friendly date with Lacey before she moved away. He pulled himself into the present.

"Me, too."

The lights dimmed and the music started. Joshua relaxed, enjoying Sally's company.

———

Abra awakened when Mr. Moss tapped on the door the next morning. "Open the door." She pulled on a robe and turned the lock. He handed her a small paper bag. "Toothbrush, toothpaste, cotton undies. Hope they're the right size. There's a hairbrush in the bathroom drawer. Take a shower. Don't bother washing your hair. Just get dressed and come on out to the kitchen."

She washed and dried herself quickly. The white panties fit perfectly. His wife's bra and white blouse were both too small; the black capris hung on her hips; the flats flip-flopped. She brushed her hair and swept it up in a ponytail, using one of the rubber bands she found in a bathroom drawer.

Mr. Moss set a newspaper aside and stood. He was dressed in tan slacks and a white shirt. He pulled a chair out for her. "Sit. We don't have much time. You have an appointment at Murray's Mane Event this morning. The wizard himself will be working on you, not one of his minions." He set a box of shredded wheat cereal in front of her. "Eat."

She poured cereal into a blue-and-white porcelain bowl. "May I have milk and sugar?"

He set a carton in front of her. "Yogurt is better for you."

She frowned. "What is it?"

"Just put it on your cereal and eat it. We don't have time for a science lesson." He'd already finished and put his bowl in the sink. "We have a big day ahead of us." He laid out a schedule and talked so fast, she wondered if she should be taking notes. Her hair appointment was just the first stop. "I've already told Murray the look I want."

A blonde, no doubt. Men seemed to be crazy about blondes.

"He'll have someone do your makeup and your nails." He was looking at her like a bug under glass. "Then we'll do a little shopping, get you an appropriate outfit before going to lunch in Toluca Lake so we can test the waters." He didn't give her time to ask what that meant. The telephone rang. He got up, crossed the room, and answered. "We're on our way down." He hung up. "Let's go."

A yellow cab waited at the curb. Mr. Moss gave instructions to the driver and paid him in advance. He put his hand on her shoulder. "Take the elevator to the sixth floor and tell the receptionist I sent you. Murray will ask lots of questions. Do not tell him your life story. I haven't made it up yet. In fact, the less talking you do, the better. Remember that. It's important." He smiled slightly as he assessed her. He patted her cheek in a fatherly way. "Be brave, little girl. You're about to go on a journey others only dream about."

Murray's salon had a waiting area with plush chairs and stacks of magazines and a stunning receptionist behind the counter. Abra told her Franklin Moss had sent her. "I'll let Murray know you're here." The young woman smiled. "Please make yourself comfortable." Abra sat and looked over copies of *Photoplay*, *Silver Screen*, and *Movie Spotlight*.

"And you would be Franklin's new protégé." A man spoke from the doorway. He came into the waiting room and extended his hand. "Murray Youngman." He wasn't what she'd expected. Alfredo had been effeminate and effusively friendly, his bleached-blond hair slicked back like a greasy DA's. Murray stood six foot, wore Levi's, a button-up white shirt, and cowboy boots, and had a crew cut much like Joshua's. His fingers closed around hers firmly, and he looked at her intently. "Franklin told me what he wants, but I can't say I agree. How do you feel about it?"

She didn't know what ideas Mr. Moss had, and she wasn't in a position to rebel anyway. "Franklin's the boss."

"You'll hardly know yourself."

"That's not such a bad thing in some cases."

An odd expression came into Murray's brown eyes. "Are you sure you know what you're doing?"

"I don't, but Franklin does." She looked to the right and left as he led her into the salon. It wasn't one big room with stations down each side. It was a series of small private cubicles, with only a few of the doors open.

Murray answered her silent question. "Our clients like privacy until they're camera ready." He ushered her into a small room. The first thing he did after seating her was to rake his fingers into her hair. "Nice and thick, natural wave, feels silky already." His smile was genuine and warm. "Wash first." He turned the chair and lowered the back, pumping a lever at the bottom as he combed his fingers into her hair at the nape of her neck, lifting the mass and draping it into the sink. Leaning over her, he turned on the water, testing the temperature in his hand as he studied her face. "You and I are going to become good friends."

She wasn't so sure.

He asked a lot of questions as he worked. She gave evasive answers.

She glanced at the clock on the wall. He noticed. "It's an ordeal, isn't it? Keeping secrets." He stood behind her, raking his fingers back through her hair and binding it loosely. He put his hands on her shoulders. "We'll finish as soon as the makeup artist is done with you. Sit tight." He ran a finger over her brow, tucking in one errant lock. "No peeking."

He'd told her before he started mixing his magic that he wanted to see her honest reaction when she saw the finished look. To that end, he had turned the chair away from the mirror. Murray stepped out into the hallway. "Tell Betty she's ready."

A gorgeous blonde came in with a box that opened into tiers of makeup. "You have perfect skin." She studied Abra with a professional air and began to take tubes and brushes from her supplies. "Don't worry. I won't take nearly as long as Murray."

He came back the moment the woman began to tuck her things away. She didn't ask what he thought. It wasn't necessary. He worked briefly on Abra's hair. "Franklin knows what he wants." He turned the chair around. "Now, let's see if you agree."

Abra stared at the beautiful ebony-haired girl in the mirror. "Is that me?"

Murray smiled. "That's the first unguarded thing you've said since you sat in that chair."

She had never looked more beautiful in her life. "I thought he'd make me a blonde."

"I would have kept you a redhead." Murray put his large, strong hands on her shoulders, kneading them as he met her gaze in the mirror. "Franklin didn't want you to be one more blonde among a sea of blondes. In my opinion, a lighter red would've been beautiful, but black makes you exotic, especially with those pale sea-green eyes of yours. You're like a mermaid from the mists." He dug his fingers into the thick mass of wavy curls, lifting it. "Men will see your eyes first, then the rest of you." He let her hair spill from his hands over her shoulders and breasts, leaving her in no doubt of what he meant.

The receptionist appeared in the doorway. "Franklin Moss is here."

"Your Svengali awaits." Murray turned the chair so she faced him. He took her by both hands, and drew her up from the chair. He stood so she couldn't get past him. His expression turned grave. "Be careful." He let go of her. "I will see you in two weeks."

"Two weeks?"

The grin didn't reach his eyes. "We don't want your red roots to show, now, do we?"

Mr. Moss's eyes glowed when he saw her. "Exactly what I want." He gave something to Murray that made the hairdresser's brows rise.

Abra was eager for praise when they got into the car. "You like it?"

"I see you do."

"I've never felt so beautiful in my life."

"We're just getting started."

Mr. Moss took her to a boutique, where he introduced her to Phyllis Klein. The woman looked her over the same way Dorothea Endicott had back in Haven. "I see that gleam in your eyes, Phyllis, but I didn't bring her here as a model. Something understated that will make people look at her, not the clothes she's wearing."

"As if anyone wouldn't."

Mr. Moss looked at his wristwatch. "And we don't have much time."

"I won't need more than a few minutes. I know exactly what you have in mind." Phyllis whisked Abra into a dressing room, took quick measurements, and went out again. She came back with a simple gray dress and high heels.

Abra began to undress. Phyllis took one look at the bra and told her to wait. She came back with another. She tossed the black capris, flats, and white blouse into a corner like rags for the trash bin and helped Abra dress. "Perfect."

The dress fit every curve, the belt accentuating her small waist. The high heels added three inches to her height and defined her calf muscles. Phyllis opened the door. "Let's see what Franklin thinks, shall we? Not that I have any doubts."

His brows rose slightly, and he told her to turn around so he could take a look. Like a marionette on strings, Abra put her arms out and turned slowly. Phyllis's laugh held a touch of smugness. "I don't have to ask if you like it."

"The other items we talked about this morning?" Mr. Moss sounded all business.

"I have her measurements. I'll make a few alterations. We can have a fitting on Friday. I'll send over a few outfits this afternoon. Did you want the black capris and—?"

"Throw them away." His eyes hadn't left Abra. "The gown. We haven't talked about colors."

"Trust me, Franklin." Phyllis assessed Abra again. "Lavender, I think." Mr. Moss was already guiding Abra to the door.

The Southern California sunshine blinded Abra. She felt his hand at her elbow. "We'll have to get you sunglasses." He gently guided her.

"Where are we going now?"

"For a little walk."

"I'm not used to high heels."

"Take my arm. I'm parked two blocks down." He put his hand over hers. "Set your own pace. We're in no hurry."

"Aren't we going to be late?"

"We don't have a set meeting time." She felt the air of excitement about him. "Don't look at your feet. Chin up. Look straight ahead."

"I might trip."

"No, you won't. We're just taking a little stroll. I have hold of you. Take a deep breath. Let it out."

She gave a nervous laugh. "My piano teacher used to say the same thing."

A man in a business suit walked toward them. He slowed as he came closer. Abra ignored him. Mr. Moss glanced back briefly and chuckled under his breath. Two more men passed. Abra felt relief when they reached the black Cadillac. Mr. Moss unlocked the passenger door. He didn't say anything until they were both seated inside the car. "You'll get used to the attention."

"Will I?" She felt a breathless mixture of pride and discomfort.

Mr. Moss pulled easily into traffic. "When we get to the restaurant, walk the way you just did—chin up, shoulders back. Don't look around. Don't look at anyone unless it's me. Got that? If anyone approaches us and asks you a question, let me do the talking."

The restaurant was small with an open-air feel to the dining room, which flowed together with potted ferns tucked here and there. The manager recognized Franklin. "This way, Mr. Moss." Abra felt his hand at her back again, warm and gently guiding. He greeted several people casually in passing. He made no introductions. When they were seated, he ordered for both of them. She didn't like fish, but didn't argue. Her neck and shoulders ached with tension.

Mr. Moss kept telling her what to do. "Turn your body a little to the right. . . . Cross your legs. Slowly. We're in no hurry. . . . Tilt your head a little to the left. That's it. . . . Smile as though I've said something witty. . . . Lean forward. Look at me. . . . Breathe, little girl. Breathe." Abra wished he would stop calling her that.

"We're about to have some company." A conspiratorial smile touched his lips. "Albert Coen is one of the biggest producers in Hollywood. He's had his eyes on you since we walked in the door. Don't speak. Stay seated. When I introduce you, nod graciously and smile. And don't look surprised when I say Lena Scott. That's your new name."

She drew in a soft gasp of protest. "Why did you change my name?"

"It suits the new you." His eyes held a glint of warning, though he looked calm and self-possessed, all business. "Get used to it." He lifted his fluted glass of champagne. "To the Franklin Moss and Lena Scott partnership." When she lifted her champagne glass of orange juice, he touched it lightly.

A man's deep voice spoke and Franklin glanced up, feigning surprise. "Albert. It's good to see you." Standing, he shook hands with a balding man with a dark mustache and a nice suit. The man looked at the other chair, but Mr. Moss didn't invite him to join them. Abra smoothed her skirt over her knees and folded her hands loosely in her lap. She acknowledged the introduction with a slight nod and a remote smile. She crossed her legs. Mr. Moss was pleasant, but offered little information. When Coen asked a question about her, he expertly changed the subject.

In the last twenty-four hours, the girl who had run away from Haven with Dylan Stark had completely disappeared. She looked different. She felt different. She had a new name. *Who am I? Who am I going to be?* Whatever story Franklin Moss made up for her, she doubted it would be anything close to the truth. He would get around to telling her soon. He'd have to if she was going to play the role that would make her into the person they both wanted her to be. A movie star. Someone desirable. Someone people would remember. Someone no one would ever forget. Or want to throw away.

Norma Jeane Mortenson had become Marilyn Monroe, hadn't she?

She drew in a slow, deep breath as the men talked above her, and let it out slowly. *Abra Matthews is dead. Long live Lena Scott.*

CHAPTER 9

A pedestal is as much a prison as any small, confined space.
GLORIA STEINEM

ABRA JOINED MR. MOSS for breakfast, trying not to grimace when she saw the box of Post Grape-Nuts and a container of yogurt waiting for her. He'd told her the camera added five to ten pounds. Better to be under rather than normal weight, as long as it didn't lessen her other attributes.

Mr. Moss closed *Daily Variety* and tossed it on the table. "We have a busy day ahead of us: pictures with Al Russell, lunch at the Brown Derby, dinner at Ciro's. Eat quickly." He glanced at his Vacheron Constantin. "We're leaving in fifteen minutes."

"I don't know what to wear, and I've only brushed my hair."

"Your hair is fine. A makeup artist will be at the studio, and Phyllis is sending over a wardrobe. Now, let's move."

She finished her bowl of cereal. He put the box in the cabinet and the yogurt in the refrigerator. She guessed she wouldn't be having any more than a cup of food before tackling a full day.

Al Russell didn't look much older than Mr. Moss, and he was equally lean and fit in casual slacks and a button-down blue shirt unbuttoned at the collar, a tie pulled carelessly loose. Mr. Moss made the introductions. Abra held out her hand, and Al took it, an amused smile touching his lips. He held on to her hand as he scrutinized her from head to foot. "She's got that special something, hasn't she?"

Mr. Moss looked noncommittal. "We'll see. Everything arrive?"

"Racked and ready in the dressing room. Shelly's laying out her war paint and brushes as we speak, but I don't think this girl is going to need much to make her camera ready."

Mr. Moss led her past the receptionist watching them, through the gallery of framed photographs of famous actors and actresses, and into a large studio with partitioned sets, cameras on tripods, mounted lights, reflective umbrellas, fans, and props. He knew his way around. "Over here." He opened a door into a small room where a brunette with a flawless, polished-perfect face stood dressed in a white-belted red polka-dot dress and high heels. A carrying case lay open, displaying a vast array of beauty supplies.

The woman smiled brightly. "Franklin! It's so good to see you again."

"And you, Shelly." He drew Abra forward between then. "This is Lena Scott. We're working on a full portfolio today. Go for the siren look."

The woman studied Abra's features with a professional air. "Nice cheekbones, patrician nose, flawless skin, mouth a little full, and eyes to die for."

"Make her sizzle." He closed the door as he left.

Shelly shook her head. "I would have suggested ingenue. You have that wide-eyed look right now. When did you sign with Franklin?"

"A few days ago." Since then, he'd changed the color of her hair and her name.

"Well, Franklin seems to have made up his mind what he wants to do with you." She waved Abra into a raised chair and draped her with a shiny black cape. "Where did he find you? Waiting tables at a restaurant? Carhopping on skates?"

"We met at one of Lilith Stark's parties in Beverly Hills."

Shelly looked surprised. "So you were already in the business and had connections in high places. Not his usual modus operandi." Shelly stared intently at her in the mirror, waiting for more information.

What story did Mr. Moss want Abra to tell about Lena Scott? She didn't think he'd want her to admit she'd been Dylan's live-in girlfriend and he had tricked Franklin with a bet he couldn't refuse. She could say she was part of the hired help. It was partially true. She'd had room and board as long as she kept Dylan happy and snooped for Lilith, until her conscience got in the way. Abra felt Shelly's silence and knew she had to say something. "I was just visiting."

Shelly began wiping away the makeup Abra had applied. "Well, wherever Franklin discovered you, he'll know exactly how to market your talent."

"I'm not sure I have any talent."

"Oh, honey, you have plenty." Shelly laughed before turning to look over the various shades of foundation. "Look what Franklin did with Pamela Hudson, not that she ever appreciated his efforts."

"Did you know her?"

"I still know her. She's beautiful and ambitious, and I thought she was smart until she dumped Franklin and married Terrence Irving, one of the top directors in Hollywood. I'd bet a million dollars she'll never star in another one of his movies."

"Why not?"

"Because he only casts the best, and she's barely mediocre."

Hadn't Shelly just said Mr. Moss could spot talent a mile away?

Shelly applied foundation, her expression serious as she got down to work. "I must say, you have lovely skin. You wouldn't believe the spots and blemishes some stars have." She mentioned a few and then turned to her brushes, tubes, compacts, and pencils.

The time passed quickly as Shelly regaled Abra with stories of the private lives of well-known young actresses she knew. Abra decided never to tell Shelly anything she didn't want spread around.

"You're lucky to have an agent like Franklin Moss," Shelly said. "You won't end up being a five o'clock girl."

"A five o'clock girl?"

"Under contract to a studio and under an executive or producer at five in the afternoon, if you know what I mean. Pretty girls are a dime a dozen in Hollywood, honey. Hundreds arrive starry-eyed and hopeful for any part in any movie. They come hoping to be discovered. Some smarten up and go home. Some end up with a contract and get no further than a casting couch. Precious few end up with an agent who knows what he's doing. Sad fact of life in Tinseltown." Shelly stepped back to survey her work. "You are absolutely gorgeous. I can definitely see your face on the silver screen and your name on a marquee."

"If Mr. Moss knows what he's doing."

"Take a little advice from someone who's been around and seen a lot. Give Franklin free rein, and he'll get you where you want to go." She winked. "He's the best sugar daddy anyone could have." She laughed. "You're not going to ask me what that means, too, are you?" She removed the cape from around Abra and gestured toward the mirror. "So? What do you think?"

Abra stared at the stunning girl in the mirror. "Is that me?"

Shelly laughed. "That's all you with just a bit of my magic."

Mr. Moss was deep in conversation with Al Russell when Abra came out of the makeup room. Both men glanced her way and then stared, Mr. Moss with paternal pride, Al grinning boldly. "I can't wait to get to work on that face!"

Shelly touched Abra's arm and showed her into a dressing room furnished with a full-length mirror and a rack of evening gowns, swimming suits, and airy lingerie, along with several shoe boxes. On top sat a gold foil box tied with a red ribbon. Mr. Moss had followed her into the dressing room. He stepped around her, flipped through the hangers, and pulled out a black satin gown. "This one first." He hooked the hanger on the mirror. He picked up the gift box and offered it to her. "First photo shoots can be unnerving. This is a little something from Paris to help get you in the proper mood."

Untying the box and opening it, Abra lifted a red teddy out with one finger and stared, heat filling her face. "You want me to wear this? In front of Al Russell?"

His smile was almost tender. "He won't see it, but what a woman wears underneath her clothing shows in her eyes." He tipped her chin. "It'll be our little secret."

"But . . ."

He put two fingers over her lips. "You promised to trust me. So trust me. Get dressed." He closed the door behind him when he left.

The murmur of men's voices outside the door fell silent when she came out. The black satin gown fit every curve of her body. Feverish with nerves, Abra felt Al's and his assistant Matt's eyes fixed on her. She remembered Mitzi's training and breathed in through her nose, exhaling slowly through parted lips. She tried not to hunch her shoulders.

Mr. Moss poured her a glass of champagne. "It's early, but this will help you relax." He leaned close. "Roll your shoulders back. Chin up. A little more. That's it. Try to remember that from now on." The champagne tickled her nose and warmed her stomach. "Drink it all." He jerked his chin. "Al's ready."

Abra downed the champagne like soda pop and handed him the glass.

"Wait." Mr. Moss turned her around. "You look like you just came from a beauty salon." He raked his fingers into her hair. "I want it tousled, a bit wild." He lifted her hair and shook it gently. "That's my girl."

Al stood deep in conversation with Matt, who lost concentration as Abra approached. Al noticed and turned to face her. "You look loaded for bear."

Abra lifted an eyebrow. "Where do you want me?"

Matt blushed crimson. Al gave a throaty laugh. "That's a dangerous question from a girl who looks like you." His gaze swept over her. "And dressed like that." He pointed her toward a mattress covered in waves of white satin. "I want you on your back in the middle of that."

She tried not to show panic when she looked around. "Where's Mr. Moss?"

"I'm right here, Lena. It's all right. Do what Al says."

Al chuckled. "Better give her another glass of champagne, Franklin."

"Better give me the whole bottle," Abra muttered, earning a laugh from both men.

"Good girl!" Al winked. "She's going to do just fine, Franklin. You can go now."

Mr. Moss spoke from the darkness. "I'm staying so I can keep an eye on things."

Abra breathed in relief as Al climbed a ladder to the scaffolding above. Gathering her courage, she hitched up the ankle-length satin gown and crawled to the middle of the mattress. She lay on her back, legs crossed, arms outstretched. She looked at Al. "Like this?"

"You look like you're about to be crucified." Al gave quick, businesslike instructions. "Curve one arm; turn your head to the right, body to the left; stretch out your left leg, right leg bent over the left. Relax. Point those pretty toes. Look at me. Now smile as though you're hoping I'll come down and join you on that mattress."

"I feel like a pretzel."

"Take my word, you don't look like one. Your hands are in fists.

Loosen your fingers. That's it." He offered over-the-top compliments as he snapped shots.

The champagne began to do its work and she started to have fun. She vamped several actresses she'd always admired, hardly daring to believe she might soon be one of them. Al came down off the ladder and moved in close. "Close your eyes partway. I want a sleepy look, like Venus awakening. There you go! Beautiful!"

Mr. Moss moved in closer and gave instructions. "Arch up into a sitting position, Lena. Did you get that shot, Al? Stretch out on your side, Lena. Prop your body up a little, hands flat on the mattress. Tilt your head. There's what I want."

Al came in for another close-up.

Mr. Moss again, from the shadows. "Shake your hair, Lena. Lean back on your elbows. Let that hair be like a waterfall. That's it."

Al interrupted. "Bend one leg."

Abra felt the satin slide and heard Al's sharp intake of breath. "Betty Grable has some competition." He spoke in a low, husky voice.

The fear had left Abra, the shyness. She was desirable, in control, powerful. The room felt steamy. She moved seductively and looked into the lens. "Is it getting hot in here?"

Al chuckled low. "Hotter by the minute. Hey, Matt! Wake up. Turn on the fans."

They came on abruptly, blasting cool air. Abra's flesh tingled. Al clicked away. She forgot her inhibitions and relished the male attention, the rain of compliments, the sense that her body held Al and Matt captive. She moved languidly into whatever pose they wanted, imagining herself as Marilyn Monroe, Elizabeth Taylor, Rita Hayworth. She smiled, pouted, looked breathless with anticipation.

"Enough." Mr. Moss spoke roughly from behind the lights. He came forward, took her by the hand, and helped her off the mattress. "Put on the strapless ballet dress." Leaning down, he whispered, "No red teddy. No nothing."

Her heart plummeted.

Shelly refreshed Abra's makeup. "Matt's in love with you."

"We haven't even been introduced!"

"As if that mattered. You're going to have hordes of men in love with you when you hit the silver screen."

Abra's excitement grew. Was she really going to become a star loved by thousands? Would people want her autograph? She laughed at herself. She had to be in a movie first.

Brushing her hair, she pulled it into a ponytail and wound it around into a prim bun on the crown of her head.

Mr. Moss grimaced. "What in hades did you do to your hair?"

"I'm in a ballet dress. My hair should be in a bun, shouldn't it?"

He removed the pins and rubber band. "Shake it out." He guided her to a low bench. "Sit knees a few inches apart, toes in and touching." He plucked at the net skirt so it fluffed around her like a cloud of white. "Lean forward. A little more." He stepped behind the lights. He said something low to Al, then gave Abra more instructions. "Elbows pressed against your sides. Hunch your shoulders a bit."

She gasped, afraid she'd spill out of the front of the dress. *Click. Click.* Al said something to Franklin. "Tilt your head, Lena." Franklin moved to one side where she could see him. "Chin down. Look into the camera, not at me. Wet your lips."

Shelly laughed from somewhere in the studio. "Matt needs a cold shower."

Abra felt an increasing sense of her own power as the morning wore on. She played whatever role Mr. Moss wanted, knowing she was safe as long as he stood guard.

When they decided it was time for a break, Mr. Moss had her change into a new dress Phyllis had tucked in among the gowns. He took her to the Brown Derby. Abra wasn't quite sure whether he was serious when he said there was another Brown Derby restaurant that actually looked like the hat it was named for.

The proprietor recognized Mr. Moss, gave Abra an admiring smile, and showed them to a table, where a waitress offered Abra a menu. Mr. Moss took it and said he'd order for both of them: a French red wine for himself and water with lemon for her.

He glanced at her over the menu. "You're having a bit of fun, aren't you?" The possibility seemed to please him.

"Yes. I am." She felt bold enough to admit it. "I was a little self-conscious. I think the champagne helped."

His eyes grew amused. "And the French lingerie?"

"Until you told me to take it off."

"You gave me the exact look I wanted: virginal fear and steamy heat." He set the menu aside.

It had been five hours since she had eaten the small bowl of cereal and yogurt. Her stomach growled and she pressed her hand against it, embarrassed. "I'm starving."

"I'll feed you." He leaned back. "I've known Al Russell for ten years, and I've never seen him sweat the way he has in the last two hours. If you can do that to a seasoned Hollywood photographer, we're going to do very well with a few directors I know."

"Really?"

He smiled. "Really."

"I don't know how I'm ever going to thank you for all you're doing for me, Mr. Moss."

"You can start by calling me Franklin."

She felt an odd flicker of misgiving, but pushed it away. "Franklin. I wouldn't have had the courage to pose like I did if you hadn't been standing right there every minute, making sure no one made a pass at me."

The tension eased inside her. Their wine and water were delivered. Abra squeezed the lemon. "Shelly said I'm lucky to have you as an agent."

His eyes narrowed slightly as he sipped the wine. "I'll have to remember to thank her."

Abra's gaze drifted and she drew in a startled gasp. "Is that Cary Grant over there?"

"Yes, and don't stare."

She tried to be surreptitious about it. On further exploration, she spotted Mickey Rooney laughing and talking with friends. John Agar, Shirley Temple's ex-husband, sat a few tables away with his second wife, model Loretta Barnett Combs. Abra felt bubbles of excitement. She was sitting among stars!

The waitress returned for their order. Mr. Moss—Franklin— ordered two salads, a medium rare steak for himself, and grouper for her.

Abra grimaced and spoke quietly. "I'm not fond of fish."

Franklin didn't change the order, and the waitress left. He faced her. "Fish is good for you. It has fewer calories. Learn to like it."

Like cereal and yogurt. She stifled the disappointment, admonishing herself. She should be thankful. He was paying; he had the right to decide. Besides, he knew better how she should look and act in order to be a star. If she had to lose five or ten pounds, so be it. It wouldn't cost her anything. Or would it? "How much will the photographs cost?"

"Nothing for you to worry about. All bills are on my tab until you're suitably employed. Then we'll figure out how you can pay me back."

How could she not worry? "And if I fail?"

"You won't." He leaned forward, his manner confident and paternal. "Your job is to be teachable. I can help you with a lot of things, and for those I can't, I'll make sure you have the right people to train you. We're in this together. Our relationship will be mutually beneficial."

"You're spending the whole day with me. What about your other clients?"

"Let me worry about them." He changed the subject. He had managed to get an invitation to the premiere of a major movie. Phyllis would send over an appropriate gown, shoes, jewelry. The more he talked, the more excited and hopeful Abra became. Maybe everything would happen simply because Franklin Moss willed it.

Their meals were served, and Abra tried not to stare at Franklin's succulent steak with open envy. The grouper wasn't bad, but then a sautéed slice of cardboard would have satisfied her after so many hours with so little food. "How much weight do I have to lose?"

"No more than a few pounds."

People stopped by their booth to greet Franklin and to be introduced to her. One mentioned Franklin's long vacation. Another said he hadn't seen anything of Pamela Hudson in a while. Franklin shrugged and said it would be up to Irving what she did in the future. "Not much," came the response. Each visitor looked at her with open curiosity. One director grinned at Franklin and said he still had a good eye for what studios wanted.

Franklin smiled. "You know my number. Give me a call." The man gave her an over-the-shoulder look before going out the door.

Franklin put his napkin on the table and paid the bill. "Time to get back to work with Al." He helped her out of the booth and kept a protective closeness as they made their way out of the restaurant.

The one-piece black bathing suit Franklin chose was sexier than the bikini Dylan had purchased in Santa Cruz. Al positioned her in front of a wooden helm wheel while Matt pulled down a sky-blue screen painted with clouds. Al put his hands on Abra's hips and moved her back against the wheel. She had nowhere to go and felt the warmth of his mint-scented breath on her face. "I want you right here."

"Knock it off, Al."

A malicious gleam came into Al's eyes. "Pretty protective of you, isn't he? Better watch out." He let go and stepped back. She frowned slightly, remembering Murray's similar remark. What were they trying to say to her? Franklin Moss behaved like a perfect gentleman.

Strictly business, he'd said. She hadn't seen anything to indicate he wanted to change the arrangement.

"Grasp the spoke handles behind you, Lena." Franklin gave directions.

Al winced. "Not so hard. Loosen those elegant fingers of yours." He moved her hands to the spokes he wanted before backing off. "Put one foot against the wheel. Now stretch up on those pretty little toes."

Franklin spoke again. "Left shoulder up, chin down. A little more. Get that shot, Al."

"The man knows exactly what he wants from you."

They worked through the afternoon. On the drive back to the apartment, Franklin told her they'd have time for showers and a quick change before they headed out for dinner at Ciro's. She hoped he'd allow her to eat more than salad and fish. "You'll see a lot of familiar faces there. Try not to look like an eager fan. When we get to the apartment, take a five-minute shower. Don't get your face or hair wet."

"Should I put my hair up?"

He cast an assessing look. "Brush it and leave it down."

She did exactly as he said. The knee-length black dress he'd picked out fit perfectly. She brushed her hair quickly and went out to the living room. Franklin stood by the windows. He looked distinguished in black slacks and a crisp white shirt. His hair was still damp and slicked back.

"Do I pass inspection?" Abra turned around.

Franklin crossed the room slowly, his expression enigmatic. She noticed the lion's head gold cuff links when he reached out to brush a wayward strand of hair over her shoulders. A matching tie tack held his black tie. He stepped back and smiled. "Classic and classy." He gave a single nod of approval.

Abra touched her hair. "Is it all right now?" The glistening black waves hung to the middle of her back.

"Perfect."

Franklin talked about the movie business, directors they might see, the one they had met at the Brown Derby, and how he wanted her to act when they went into Ciro's. Abra drank in every word, eager to be a part of the exciting world he knew so well. Dylan had hidden her away. Franklin Moss wanted to show her off.

The plain exterior of Ciro's gave no hint to the baroque interior or the glamorous patrons. Abra's heart raced with elation as she spotted Humphrey Bogart and Lauren Bacall. Wasn't that Frank Sinatra with Ava Gardner? Everywhere she glanced, she recognized faces of the rich and famous.

Franklin guided her as though he belonged here. As long as she was with him, she did, too. When men and women greeted him, he paused and introduced her as Lena Scott. As they moved on, Abra sucked in her breath and looked back over her shoulder at Lucille Ball and Desi Arnaz. Franklin's hand tightened, and she almost tripped over her own feet. He steadied her as she faced a platinum blonde in a body-hugging white dress and fur stole. It took only a second to recognize Lana Turner. "Oh! Hello." She was even more beautiful in person than on a movie screen.

"Hello to you, too." The actress laughed softly and smiled at Franklin. "Another sweet young thing." They exchanged quick air kisses on each cheek. "It's good to see you again, Franklin."

"You're as ravishing as ever, Lana."

"Pamela was a fool to leave you, darling. But I see now how easily she's been replaced with something even more lovely." Smiling, she admired Abra. "More curves than Pamela, raven hair rather than blonde, and those sea-green eyes so full of mystery." She laughed and gave Franklin a smile that hinted at conspiracy. "Are we ready? I chose this spot because Hedda is less than twenty feet away. Her photographer is inching over."

"I owe you one."

Abra looked at Franklin. "Who's Hedda?"

Lana Turner's laughter sounded real this time. "Where did you find this innocent? At the Greyhound bus station?"

"I got her out from under the roof of Lilith Stark."

Lana grimaced. "Lilith is a nasty piece of work."

"Lana!" A man spoke from behind Abra. "How about a picture?"

"Of course." Lana slipped an arm around Abra's waist. "Smile pretty." She turned Abra and leaned close as though they were the best of friends. A flash of bright light half blinded Abra. Lana withdrew her arm immediately and raised her hand in friendly adieu. "Have fun, you two."

Franklin reclaimed Abra, guiding her to their table, where a waiter stood ready to take their drink orders—Scotch neat for him, iced tea for her. Abra gave a breathless laugh, her heart pounding. "I can't believe I had my picture taken with one of Hollywood's biggest stars!"

Laughing, he patted her hand. "We're just getting started." He ordered for her, salmon this time. She didn't care. She was too happy and excited to be in Ciro's among the stars to think about eating. They watched a floor show while finishing dinner. Their waiter cleared their table as the dance band started. Franklin took her by the hand. "Let's dance."

She cast a nervous look at the couples doing the rumba.

He helped her up from her seat. "Just relax and follow my lead." He escorted her onto the dance floor and took her into his arms. He kept his eyes on her face, but she had the feeling he knew exactly what was going on everywhere in the room. He drew her closer. "Are you happier now? Even though you're living in a fifteen-hundred-square-foot apartment with a man old enough to be your father, rather than a pretty little Beverly Hills bungalow with Dylan?"

"Are you kidding?" She shook her head. "I've never been so happy in my whole life! I'm still trying to figure out how I got so lucky."

His expression warmed. "I'm glad you feel that way."

She imagined the days and months ahead with Franklin as her mentor and friend. From now on, she would awaken with the expectation of something good happening, rather than being constantly on edge, wondering what mood Dylan would be in when he walked through the door. She had a chance to make something of herself. "I don't think I'll ever be able to thank you enough for what you're doing for me."

Franklin gave her a cool smile. "They all say that in the beginning."

"I mean it."

"I've been waiting for a girl like you for a long time. I thought Pamela was the one, but she was weak and too easily distracted. I need someone smart, ambitious, willing to be trained. I need a girl who won't complain when she has to work hard. There's no limit to what I can do with a girl like that."

"I'm that girl."

Franklin gazed at her, eyes glowing. "Yes, I believe you are."

―――――――

Joshua sat beside Sally in the middle row of the Swan Theater. Sally's tears unnerved him. News had hit the papers last month that James Dean had been killed while speeding in his Porsche 550 Spyder. Now everyone was lining up for *Rebel Without a Cause.* Judging from the sniffles throughout the theater, Sally wasn't the only one who couldn't stop crying. Joshua couldn't wait for the movie to end. Noting Sally's soggy hankie, he pulled out his own and offered it to her. "Are you going to be all right?"

She blew her nose. "I'm fine."

When the movie let out, they went to the café for a light supper. Bessie took one look at Sally's red-rimmed eyes and grinned. "I saw the movie, too."

Sally grimaced. "I'm a mess! This is ridiculous. I never cry at movies."

"I cried buckets when I went two days ago." Bessie put her hands on her ample hips and raised her voice, making sure it carried through the open kitchen door. "I had to go *alone* because Oliver doesn't go to a movie unless it's a Western with guns blazing!"

Brady Studebaker came in. By the look on his face, Joshua guessed he wished he was the one sitting in the booth with Sally. When Bessie welcomed him by name, Sally swung around just enough to catch a glimpse before she turned back again. Her expression was hard to read, but Joshua felt an undercurrent of something. "Brady." Joshua waved their friend over. "Why don't you join us?"

Brady slid into the booth so he was facing Sally. "Have you been crying?" He speared Joshua with a threatening gaze.

Joshua lifted his eyebrows. "We've just been through two hours of James Dean."

Sally blushed. She said men didn't understand about romance.

Brady muttered two foul words under his breath and turned away.

Sally glared at him. "What do you know about it?" She seemed about to say something more, but she pressed her lips together.

Brady returned her glare and slid out of the booth. "You two look good together. Be happy." It sounded like an indictment, not a blessing. "See you around." He didn't sit at the counter. He walked out the front door.

"He makes me so mad!" Sally said through her teeth.

Bessie looked from the door to Joshua. "Did you say something to chase a customer away?"

"Not me." Joshua shook his head. "I guess he had somewhere else to go." Sally looked ready to cry again, and he had a feeling her emotions had nothing to do with James Dean's tragic death. He crossed his arms on the table and leaned forward. "What's going on, Sally?"

"Nothing." She wilted under his scrutiny. "We can talk about it later." She seemed determined to forget Brady had ever walked into the café.

Sally was quiet on the ride home. Joshua glanced at her. "Ready to talk now?"

"It's nothing." She sighed. "Brady and I ran into each other at Eddie's last Friday."

"Eddie's?" He laughed.

"I know it's a high school hangout, but I was feeling nostalgic. Brady saw me and came in. We talked. He took me for a drive." She gave him a guilty glance. "I haven't been out with him since high school, Joshua. He took me to the senior prom. Remember?" She gave a bleak laugh. "No. Why would you? You were all hot and bothered over Lacey."

"Was I?"

She looked at him. "Weren't you?"

He laughed. "We're getting off subject. We were talking about you and Brady."

"He kissed me. He said he loved me."

"In high school or last Friday?" He could almost feel the heat of her blush.

"Both," she said quietly and then got mad again. "Of all the nerve!" She sat up straighter. "I told him I was dating you. He wanted to know why I let him kiss me. As if it was my fault! I said I didn't. He said . . . Oh, never mind what he said. He's an idiot!" She spent the next five minutes ranting about Brady and what a big head he had and how he didn't know the first thing about love. And what sort of guy kisses a girl when she's not even expecting it and he knows she's going out with someone else?

Joshua tried not to smile. Poor Brady. Joshua had been dating Sally for almost six months and hadn't had a clue about Brady's feelings until tonight, when he walked into Bessie's. He sighed. He and Sally had done some necking in his truck a few times. They might have gone further once if Abra hadn't come into his mind. What sort of man kisses and fondles one woman while thinking of another? He'd been ashamed. When he let go of her, she asked what was wrong. He didn't tell her he was afraid he was using her to forget someone else.

He remembered the day he came home from Korea and saw Abra on her front steps. One look at her, and his pulse had rocketed. Sally had never elicited that kind of a response in him. Tonight he realized he wasn't making Sally's heart race, either. But Brady was.

It was time to change this relationship. They needed to get back to being friends again, and give up pretending it could lead to anything more. "You blushed when you saw him."

"I did not!"

"Your head snapped around when Bessie said his name. I saw your face, Sally."

"You don't have to be jealous about Brady."

That was just the problem: Joshua wasn't jealous. He felt relieved. "Maybe it's time we talked about what is and isn't happening between us."

"I don't know what you mean."

She seemed distracted, not crushed. Joshua smiled slightly. "Yes, you do. We've gone as far as we're ever going to go."

She flared. "Are you saying this just because Brady Studebaker came into Bessie's tonight and made a scene?"

A scene? "I'm saying it because you're all worked up right now, and it's not because of me."

"I've had a crush on you since grammar school, Joshua Freeman. I used to sleep with your picture under my pillow and dream about marrying you someday." She sounded more angry than hurt.

He could be blunt, too. "And now you know, just like I know, we're not in love with each other. We wanted to be. We gave it a good try. The problem is we're both tied up in knots over other people."

She leaned her head back in exasperation. "Brady makes me feel all riled up inside. I feel comfortable with you."

"Is comfortable what you want?" He pulled up in front of her house and stopped. "Or are you just worried you'll have a relationship like your mother and father's?" Joshua got out and came around to walk her to the door. "A friend offers comfort, Sally. And encouragement." He leaned down and kissed her cheek. "Call him."

She shook her head. "I can't."

Joshua went by the Studebaker Sign Company the next day. Brady was dialing Sally's number before he left. The day after that, on his way home from work, he saw Brady and Sally sitting together in the town square. He laughed, glad they hadn't taken too long.

1956

Abra tried to ignore the pounding in her temples as Murray parted and painted dye into her hair. She closed her eyes against the pain, knowing it came from the endless tension and stress of playing Lena Scott for Franklin. He had taken her to another party last night. They'd been at parties every night this week. It was all about being seen, never about relaxing with friends—not that she had any. Franklin used parties the same way Lilith Stark had, except he wasn't looking for dirt. He was on the hunt for new opportunities.

Directors and producers treated Franklin with respect. He might have made a fool of himself with Pamela Hudson, but he knew talent when he saw it. Word got around he had a new protégé. People wanted to meet her. Franklin introduced Lena, and received a few offers. He told her she wasn't ready to work yet. She still had a lot to learn, and he threw her into twelve-hour days of acting lessons and a tutor to work with her on elocution. He paired her with a personal trainer who worked her until she begged for mercy. She had fittings for a new wardrobe, photo sessions, a doctor who prescribed vitamins, as well as uppers and downers, which Franklin doled out judiciously.

Over the last year, the luster of meeting movie stars and studio bigwigs had begun to wear off. It hadn't taken Abra long to realize everyone was looking for a way to climb higher, get more publicity, a better part, a new contract, sometimes a new agent. One woman had offered Franklin *"anything"* if he'd take her on as a client. He recommended someone else, but not before Abra felt a little less secure, a little more easily replaceable.

She still did whatever Franklin told her to do, but would that ever be enough? She hadn't counted the cost of putting her life in someone else's hands. Sometimes, Dylan's cruelty seemed less frightening than Franklin's growing demands for perfection.

Murray set the bowl of black dye aside. "You're wound tight today." He stripped off his gloves. "Things not going well?"

"On the contrary. I've already had one walk-on part, and Franklin is getting calls. I have an audition tomorrow for the lead in a new movie." She didn't say she'd end up a zombie if she got the part.

"That's good news." Murray's tone implied otherwise.

Her shoulders sagged. She was too tired to sit up straight, too tired to care if her posture wasn't exactly the way Franklin wanted. When Murray put his hands on her shoulders, she started in surprise.

"Lena, you need to relax." He clipped her hair up to let the dye set. "And a massage wouldn't hurt."

"I don't have time."

"Tell Franklin to add one to your schedule." He looked concerned.

Everything was going so well. Franklin said so. His instincts and knowledge had worked with Pamela Hudson. Abra could trust him. She loved wearing beautiful gowns and having her hair and makeup done. She enjoyed being in the same room with famous movie stars like Susan Hayward and Victor Mature and meeting directors like Billy Wilder and Stanley Donen. She even enjoyed attending acting classes. Franklin coached her. Whatever he told her to do, she did.

She cooperated, remembering the bargain she'd made and the promise she'd given him to work hard.

What she hadn't understood was how very hard it would be . . . and how much of her life Franklin wanted to take over.

He controlled her daily schedule. He was either with her, waiting for her, or had someone ready to take her where he wanted her to go. He told her how to act when they arrived at whatever he had set up. Parties served as a place to make contacts with people who could help move her career forward. They didn't waste time with people who didn't matter. Before each introduction, Franklin told her what to say, what subjects to avoid. He maneuvered her in close when pictures were being taken. "It's all about being in the right place at the right time with the right people." And he made sure she was. She had movie magazines to show for it. Maybe Penny would see one. But would Penny even recognize her?

It was a heady feeling to be among so many rich and famous people, a rarefied atmosphere, an environment of competition and caution, hope and disappointment. Everyone looked like they were having a marvelous time, but there was always the undercurrent of more than small talk and light laughter, handshakes and drinks.

If there wasn't a party going on somewhere worthwhile, Franklin took her to a club where stars hung out, big stars who might like her and mention her name in the right ear. He got her in the door the same way Dylan had. Men approached, but Franklin was always close, watchful, protective. She drank Coke; he drank Scotch neat. If anyone asked for her telephone number, he gave them his card. "You're not here for romance. You're here to work."

Sometimes Franklin reminded her of Lilith and Dylan Stark. He knew how to work a room.

Murray kneaded her shoulders. He hadn't said much, but then how would she know if he had? She hadn't been paying attention as he had first rinsed, then conditioned her hair. Now she felt his concentrated stare, but she avoided looking at him in the mirror.

"You look depressed." Murray studied her face. "What's bothering you?"

She gave a shrug and a practiced smile. "I wish I knew."

He checked the roots of her hair. "Thinking about your past life?"

Franklin had come up with her story and had kept it uncomfortably close to the truth, because "reporters will always dig into your past when you're famous." He made her into Cinderella: A child with no parents, passed from one family to another, she grew up, talent and potential beauty unnoticed, in a small northern California farming community. A friend offered her a ride to Southern California. Franklin spotted her in a crowd. Shades of truth. He laughed and said a story like hers would bring a thousand girls to Hollywood, hoping to be the one in a million noticed by an agent or director who knew how to make a star. They'd believe it didn't matter if they'd never been off a farm or out of North Dakota. They could be discovered in a diner or a bus station or walking along a sidewalk.

Murray dropped his hands to her shoulders again. "Lena, you can talk to me. Despite what Franklin may have told you, I can keep secrets."

"'To whom thy secret thou dost tell, to him thy freedom thou dost sell.'"

"Ben Franklin, right? Did Moss make you memorize that?"

"I have an appointment to get my nails done."

"Okay." He lifted his hands. "Have it your way." He whipped off the silky covering that protected her clothing. "Only you'd better find a way to unwind or you're gonna break."

Abra stood, smoothing the designer dress that fit her like a second skin. "Maybe I should run an extra five miles."

"I think you've run too far already." He wadded the cloth and tossed it into a basket in the corner. "I'll see you in two weeks."

CHAPTER 10

God whispers to us in our pleasures,
speaks in our consciences, but shouts in our pains:
it is His megaphone to rouse a deaf world.

C. S. LEWIS

1957

Zeke sat in the church office, Bible open as he went over notes for the Sunday sermon. Typewriter keys clacked in the outer office, telling him Irene Farley was preparing the weekly bulletin. She'd need a title for his sermon. It was a game they played every week. She wanted more than the Scripture references, and sometimes he had to draw the line. "Born to Raze Hell" hadn't been his idea of an appropriate title for a Christmas sermon, though he had to agree there was truth in it.

The typewriter fell silent. Irene peered in through the doorway. "Ready yet?"

"John, chapter 11."

"Ah. Lazarus, isn't it? How about 'Rude Awakening'?"

"Rude?" Zeke raised his brows.

"Well, just think about it. Would you want to be called back from paradise to serve more time on earth? I wouldn't. I would've been arguing. 'Oh, Lord, please let me stay here.' Jesus calls, and out of the tomb Lazarus comes." She frowned. Zeke could almost see the wheels in her brain going round and round. "He was wrapped up like a mummy. He would have had to hop out." Her lips twitched. "Can you see it? It'd be hard not to laugh if you weren't screaming in holy terror. I mean, really. Who says God doesn't have a sense of humor?"

"You never cease to amaze me. No to 'Rude Awakening.'"

"How about 'Mummy Love'?" She snickered.

He laughed. "I should've fired you years ago."

"'Jesus Called, Lazarus Answered'?"

"Getting warmer."

"I'll think of something and run it by you before it goes to print."

"You'd better."

He'd spent weeks on the Gospel of John and barely scratched the surface of what God had to teach his growing flock. Susan Wells had asked more questions than he could answer when he stopped in to buy dinner at Bessie's. She'd clearly been studying the Bible he had given her and was eager to learn. She attended services every week now and had joined the ladies helping out with refreshments afterward. She wasn't sitting in the back row anymore, either. All it took was a little fake light-headedness on Mitzi's part to get Susan out of that back pew. Mitzi said she didn't want to leave, but would appreciate a supportive arm. Susan complied and ended up smack-dab in the middle of the sanctuary with the Martins. Once Mitzi had her there, she didn't let go. Hodge and Carla welcomed Susan like a long-lost sister, probably figuring one more adult might be needed to help keep an eye on Mitzi. Susan had been sitting there ever since.

Zeke could see everyone from his vantage point at the raised pulpit—the daydreamers impatient for the service to end so they could go fishing, the whisperers with a new story to tell, the artists doodling on prayer request notepads, the seemingly intent who stared at him with glazed eyes while their minds wandered hither and yon, and plenty of hungry and thirsty ones feasting on the Word of God. God forgive him, he had his favorites: Mitzi; Peter and Priscilla; Dutch, frowning in concentration while Marjorie helped him find places in the Bible; Fern Daniels, the oldest saint in the congregation. She always sat in front, alert and smiling up at him the same way she had the first day he'd preached in Haven Community Church. On the way out the door, she always said something to let him know she appreciated the time and effort he'd put into his sermon.

"Hey, Dad." Joshua tapped and entered the office. "You look serious."

"Just thinking."

"I'm taking a couple of the teenagers to the roller-skating rink tonight. Sally and Brady are coming along. We'll probably go out afterward. Don't expect me home until late."

"Thanks for letting me know." He leaned back after Joshua had left. Had Joshua's love for Abra begun to fade with time and distance? It might be God's mercy if it did. He still felt the pain of loss, but it wasn't the sharp blade cut it had been when he left her with Peter and Priscilla. Now, it was a dull ache in his chest. He'd learned to trust God in every circumstance. God had a plan and it encompassed everything. He clung to that promise like ivy to a stone wall.

Irene stepped in and told him the bulletin was done. She was heading home. He thanked her and said he'd see her in the morning. He glanced at his wristwatch. He was hungry. Maybe he'd go by Bessie's again, order another special. It was easier to talk with Susan there. What would she ask him this time? She made him think and search. He enjoyed the challenge. He just wished she'd make a decision.

Susan was teetering. He'd give a shove if it would make a difference, but too often hard pushing made people run and hide rather than receive the gift offered. In his mind, the choice was simple: do you want to be held in the talons of Satan or the scarred hands of Jesus?

What would Marianne think of Susan? Would she be able to bless his growing affection?

Someone tapped on his door, startling him from his reverie. "Priscilla." He stood and came around his desk to give her a fatherly hug, then gestured for her to take one of the comfortable chairs. "How is Penny doing at Mills?"

"She's doing well. I can't believe she's already a junior. She changed her major." She gave a soft laugh. "Education."

He smiled, pleased. "So she'll be a teacher like Peter."

"Despite all her protestations to the contrary. She wants a job here in Haven."

"Last I heard, she wanted to stay in the Bay Area."

"She and Robbie Austin are engaged." Priscilla winced a smile. "Penny reminds me he is Robert now, all grown up."

"They do have a way of doing that, haven't they?" He had seen the young couple in church whenever Penny was home from college. He'd seen them dancing to the band music in the square on hot summer nights. They'd looked very much in love.

"He didn't finish college, but he has a good job with an insurance company. He saved enough to buy one of those nice American bungalows Joshua helped build out on Vineyard Avenue."

"Robert is a young man with plans." All of the Austins were hard workers.

"Needless to say, Peter and I couldn't be happier Penny will be settling in Haven." Her eyes clouded, revealing a pain he understood. They were both thinking of Abra. Priscilla rushed on. "So many young people are moving away these days. Aren't they? I'm beginning to understand how my parents felt when Peter and I moved to California. I only see them once a year now. We keep trying to convince them to sell and move out here close to us, but they love

Colorado. If Robert and Penny do get married, we'll be able to see them anytime we want. And when grandchildren come along . . ." She shook her head. "I'm getting ahead of myself."

Priscilla didn't usually talk this much unless something was on her mind. Zeke suspected it had to do with Abra.

Priscilla let out a deep sigh and opened her purse. "I wanted to show you something." She pulled out a movie magazine. "I don't usually read these things." She blushed as she thumbed through the pages. "I was standing in line at the grocery store and picked it up to pass the time." She held the magazine out to him and pointed to a picture. "Is that Abra?" Her voice caught.

Zeke took the magazine. He recognized her immediately, even with her hair pitch-black and loose over her shoulders. A strapless, ankle-length navy-blue dress with white embroidered and beaded blossoms accentuated every curve. She was standing beside a tall, handsome young man in a tuxedo, his arm around her waist. His smile looked genuine; hers, sultry and enigmatic.

"Yes. It's Abra." He could hardly believe the difference in her. The slender redheaded teenager had turned into a shockingly exotic and provocative young woman. Was this what Dylan had done to her?

"She changed her name." Priscilla blinked back tears. "She's not Abra Matthews anymore. She's Lena Scott now and going out with movie stars." She dug through her purse. "I'm sorry, Zeke. I didn't mean to start crying again."

Zeke set the box of tissues close enough for her to reach.

Priscilla blew her nose. "Does she look happy to you?"

He studied Abra's eyes. They both knew that smile. "She's trying hard."

Priscilla pulled out another tissue. "I still picture her as a little girl with a thick red ponytail. She and Penny were such kindred spirits. Those two little girls. I thought they'd be like peas in a pod forever." Her voice choked with tears. "We loved her, Zeke. We wanted so much for her to love us back." She blew her nose again. "Penny will be envious when she finds out Abra knows Elvis Presley."

"Elvis Presley?" He hadn't bothered to read the caption. The "Hound Dog" man? The one with gyrating hips who had thousands of girls screaming for him?

"He's all the rage these days. That's something, isn't it? Our little Abra is among the stars." Clutching the damp tissue, she pointed at the offensive movie magazine. "And she's been in a movie apparently. 'A notable walk-on,' they call it—whatever that means." She fisted the tissue in her lap. "I have to show it to Peter and Penny. Someone is bound to see that picture and know it's her. I don't want them caught off guard."

Zeke thought of Joshua.

Tears ran down Priscilla's cheeks. "I just wish I could tell her I'm sorry for whatever we did wrong."

"It wasn't you."

"Peter and I would've jumped in the car and raced anywhere to bring her home."

"She knew that."

"I don't think she did, Zeke. She took so little with her, and that horrible note she left you. It's as though she wanted to stab us all in the heart." She pulled half a dozen tissues from the box. "My heart still aches every time I think about her. It's the same for Peter. And Penny . . . she just gets mad." She raised watery, hopeful eyes. "Has Joshua ever heard anything?"

"He would've told us if he had, Priscilla."

"I thought she would at least write to him. They were so close. She used to wait for his letters when he was in Korea. Peter and I always thought they'd end up married someday." Priscilla clenched the damp tissues in her fist. "That boy Dylan! I knew he was trouble the minute I laid eyes on him. Why did she have to fall in love with someone like that? He sat right there at our dinner table, accepting our hospitality, and setting our girls against one another. All that charm and he was so handsome, like a—" she waved her hand at the magazine—"movie star. He knew exactly what he was doing. We should have done something more to protect her."

"She was just shy of seventeen, Priscilla. She had a mind of her own." Zeke's mother had been married by that age.

Priscilla's anger cooled. Her shoulders drooped. "He's not anywhere in the picture. I don't know if that's good or bad." She held out her hand and Zeke returned the magazine. Priscilla stuffed it back in her purse like a dirty diaper needing to be dumped in an outdoor trash can. "At least we know she's alive and well. Peter might not have those awful nightmares again."

Peter had dreamed Dylan raped and murdered Abra. After hearing Kent Fullerton's story, he'd had recurring nightmares of Dylan shoving Abra off a cliff into the ocean.

Priscilla rose. "You have to tell Joshua, I guess."

Zeke rose, too. "I know." He walked her through the outer office. Should he go downtown and buy a copy of the magazine? He felt bleak. The clerk would wonder why and comment. What could he say?

"Is there anything we can do, Zeke?" Priscilla's tone was filled with hope and despair.

"We can pray."

She looked impatient at that. "I have prayed. I've prayed until my knees ache."

"Prayer brings us into the throne room of God, Priscilla. And it puts Abra there with us, whether she knows it or not. Don't forget what you know to be true. Abra is never out of His reach. Never."

She hugged him. "I think that's what I needed to hear." He held her firmly, like a father. She rested her head against his chest for a moment before she withdrew. "Thanks, Zeke." She offered him a tremulous smile and left.

Zeke saw a note on top of the Sunday bulletins. *I saw Priscilla coming in. I hope you don't mind me picking a title. It's the message we always need.* He picked up a bulletin and opened it. *Resurrection Faith.*

———————

Abra tried to relax while Murray lathered and washed her hair, but her neck ached with tension. She closed her eyes, hoping that would help. It didn't. She only had one more appointment today, with a new manicurist, and then she'd be on her way home to Franklin. Maybe he'd give her something for the headache before they went out. Where were they going tonight? She couldn't remember.

Tomorrow night they'd attend the premiere of *Dawn of the Zombies.* Would reviewers like it? Or hate it? Would they say awful things about her acting? Franklin had worked with her through the entire shoot, drilling her on her lines, telling her how to look, what to do. She always felt sick to her stomach before going on set. All those cameras, like eyes staring at her, and the director and crew. Franklin said to put them out of her mind. When she couldn't, he said she'd get used to it. She didn't. He asked how she managed to play piano in front of a church, and she told him she never had to worry about Mitzi standing up and yelling, "Cut!" and telling her to do it again, from the beginning.

Murray put a firm hand beneath her neck as he lifted her from the sink. "You look like you have a splitting headache." He rested his hands on her shoulders as he looked at her in the mirror. "It's a hard job, jump-starting a career. This is supposed to be a place where you can relax and let your hair down, so to speak. No one is watching you here, Lena."

"You are."

His smile was gentle. "Not with an eye to criticize. I don't have any motives other than to make you look and feel better." He began to work the tight muscles in her neck and shoulders. "Take a deep breath and let it go."

Quick tears burned her eyes. Mitzi used to say the same thing. Abra lowered her head and closed her eyes. Anyone looking at her might think she was praying, but she hadn't done that since the night she saw Pastor Zeke walk away from Peter and Priscilla's front gate.

Eighteen months of hard work had produced one walk-on part, a portfolio of glamorous glossy pictures, and one starring role in a movie not yet released. Franklin claimed it would send her name into orbit. She didn't see how. Everything hinged on the critics' response to what would be shown tomorrow night, despite the talk in town— talk that Franklin had generated. Abra felt Franklin's growing excitement like a train racing along the tracks. Where exactly was he taking her? Sometimes she'd see something in his face that made her nervous. She tried not to think about it, but worry had been niggling at her for the last few weeks.

Sometimes she just wanted to be alone. She wanted to find a place where she could hide from Franklin's driving ambition, his determination, his push, push, pushing because she wouldn't be young forever and they only had a small window of time to get her name up in lights. She wanted to be still. She wanted to be someplace quiet. Like up in the hills when she'd hiked with Joshua.

Joshua.

She pulled her mind away from the past.

Sometimes she just wanted to be left alone in the apartment. She'd open the piano and play all day.

Murray's hands were strong. She groaned, though he wasn't hurting her. He spoke quietly as he continued the massage. "The world thinks it's all glamour, but it's hard work."

"Harder for some than others." She didn't fit in. Even as an insider she felt outside.

"Feeling any better?"

Her head was still throbbing. "I think I'm just hungry."

"We can fix that. What would you like to eat?"

She gave a bleak laugh. "A big, juicy hamburger!"

He grinned. "That's easy enough. I can send someone across the street and—"

"Don't. I can't." Franklin would have a fit. "I need to take off another two pounds."

He frowned. "Every woman I've ever met has been on a diet, especially the ones who don't need to be."

"Tell that to Franklin. I look five pounds heavier when the cameras roll."

"So what?" His hands stopped working her muscles and rested lightly on her shoulders. "Most men like women with a little meat on their bones."

"The problem is, the camera doesn't."

"You looked just right to me the day you walked in here."

She caught an unveiled look in his eyes before he let go and moved away. He sat on a stool near the wall. Abra turned the chair and faced him. She'd been around enough men over the last year and a half to know when a man felt stirred. Instead of flirting with her, Murray had backed off. He looked her over on occasion, but always averted his eyes quickly. He'd always treated her with respect, never making an effort to deepen their relationship in any way. She knew that was her fault. Franklin had told her how to act with Murray that first day, and she'd done exactly what he told her. Murray respected the line she had drawn and had kept the conversation light, general. Sometimes he didn't speak at all, and she wondered if he was waiting for her to break character.

"I haven't been very nice to you, have I?" Franklin had warned her not to trust anyone, but she found herself wanting to trust Murray. "I'm sorry for the way I've acted. It wasn't my idea."

He didn't pretend not to understand. "Franklin doesn't want you to get personal." He looked sad as he studied her. He seemed to be debating whether to break the rules. "I remember the first day I met you." He shook his head. "All that beautiful red hair. I thought Franklin was crazy, wanting to change it."

She didn't smile or play the usual flirtatious games Franklin told her to play with other men. "What do you think now?"

"Hard to say. Red seemed to suit you, but then, how would I know? I don't really know you at all, do I?"

She felt the prick of hot tears again and swallowed. No one really knew her, Abra Matthews. She'd always kept the walls up, just the way Franklin told her. She was so tired of being Lena Scott all the time. Why couldn't she be Abra for an hour or two now and then?

Murray sat silent. She knew the course of their relationship was being left to her. She took a shaky breath and stepped over the line. "There's not much to know. I met a bad boy and fell in love. He brought me south and moved me into a little bungalow in Beverly Hills. He did whatever he wanted with—or without—me. I guess you could call me his beck-and-call girl. When he got tired of me, he made a bet Franklin couldn't refuse."

"What was that?"

"Franklin said he could make a star out of anyone. My boyfriend said, 'Try her.' My life in a nutshell."

Murray didn't look shocked or disgusted. Maybe a hairdresser was like a priest. They'd heard it all before.

"He will make you a star, if that's what you want to be."

"It never even occurred to me, until Franklin put the idea in my head." She lifted her shoulders. "It would be nice to be somebody."

"You are somebody, Lena."

She shook her head and looked away.

"Well, then, you're on your way, aren't you?"

"Lena Scott is on her way." She was sorry the moment she said it. She was sharing too much of herself. She put her fingers to her temples and closed her eyes. Franklin wouldn't be happy if he knew she was talking to Murray like this. She waited for him to pry. When he didn't, she felt oddly bereft. Maybe he wasn't interested. She opened her eyes and saw that he was. Blinded by tears, she told him what she'd wanted to say for a long time. "My real name is Abra."

"Abra." Murray tested the name. "I like it." His mouth curved. "Thank you."

"For what?"

"For trusting me enough to tell me."

"I'm sorry I didn't tell you before."

"You're telling me now."

Her heart began to pound. "Don't tell Franklin—"

"You don't have to say it, Abra. What you say to me stays with me."

The habitual caution still had a firm grip on her. She hoped she hadn't made a mistake trusting him. She changed the subject. "How did you end up in Hollywood?"

"I was born in Burbank. My mother was a hairdresser. My father left when I was two. I spent most of my life in the salon where she worked." He smiled. "At first, women were lifting me out of the play-pen or sitting me on their laps while Mom worked on their hair. As I got older, they played board games with me or read me stories while they sat under a dryer. I had two dozen aunts, big sisters, and grannies."

"Sounds nice."

"It was. My mother had big dreams for me. She wanted me to go to college, become a doctor or a lawyer. Just like most mothers, I guess. I did well in school, but what I really enjoyed was watching my mother work and seeing the difference a couple of hours in a salon could make for a woman." He shrugged. "My life was school, the salon, and church on Sunday morning. Until I hit high school. Then it was baseball and girls. I kept my grades up. Mom was tough and made sure of that. I hung out with friends, went to parties, necked with girls, but never went too far."

When Murray fell silent, emotion tightening his jaw, Abra waited, not pressing him. "I was a sophomore when my mother went through a radical double mastectomy and radiation for cancer. She didn't even have enough energy to fix her hair." He looked grim and angry. "She'd cry and say she didn't feel like a woman anymore, as though breasts and perfect hair were all that mattered."

Aren't they? Abra almost asked. She felt his pain and anger, was touched by his words. Would Franklin or anyone else in the world care about her if she didn't have big breasts and raven hair?

"I bought Mom a wig and fixed it up for her. She looked and felt better. One of her clients came to visit and commented on how nice she looked. Mom sent me out to buy more wigs. Training me gave her something to think about other than cancer. She would be a blonde one day, a redhead the next, a brunette with hair down her back, or a platinum blonde with a bob." He chuckled at the memories. "We had some great times together before she died."

"How old were you when she passed away?"

"Seventeen. Still in high school. One of Mom's older patrons took me in so I could finish. I quit baseball and got an after-school job at a hamburger joint. I saved money for beauty college. Not that I told anyone about my plans." He laughed. "Most of my friends thought male hairdressers liked men better than women, if you get my drift. They were applying to colleges or trade schools, or enlisting in the Army or Navy."

Grinning, he shook his head, his expression wry. "I was one of four guys in beauty college, and the only one who loved women, which made me pretty popular. I might have given in to temptation. Fortunately, my future wife was one of my fellow students."

She stared in surprise. "You're married?" He didn't wear a wedding ring, and she'd always sensed he was available.

"Widowed. I lost my wife the same way I lost my mother."

Abra caught her breath. "That's not fair."

"Life never is."

"I'm so sorry, Murray."

"Yeah, so am I. Janey was . . ." He didn't speak for a moment. "No word is good enough for what she was. I blamed God for a while, thought it was a bad joke He'd played on me." He stood and turned Abra's chair around, meeting her eyes in the mirror. "And then I remembered we had five wonderful years together. I'm thankful for the time I had with her."

"Do you have children?"

"No. The salon had only been open two years. We wanted to make sure the business was solid before starting a family. Logical choice when we thought we had years ahead of us, but one we both regretted later when we ran out of time." He worked conditioner into her hair. "You reminded me of Janey the first time I saw you."

"How so?"

"Red hair." Murray smiled wistfully. His hands in her hair were strong, yet gentle. "Walls up like I was Casanova at her door. Little did she know, one look at her and I was a one-woman man. Still am." He ran his fingers through Abra's hair and looked into her eyes. "Don't let Franklin remake you completely, Abra. And try to remember you're more than a face and body. You are a soul."

"Hollywood says otherwise."

"Hollywood and Franklin Moss aren't the whole world. They aren't right about everything." He turned on the water again, testing the temperature. "You are who you are, my young friend. And you were already beautiful."

"More so now, don't you think?"

"You're Lena-Scott beautiful. Is Lena Scott who you want to be?"

"Lena Scott is the one who'll become a star."

Murray looked like he wanted to say more, but didn't. He rinsed her hair, raised the back of her chair, and wrapped her head in a warm towel. He rubbed gently before removing it and letting her long, thick, damp hair lay against the cape covering her back. He dug his fingers in, lifting tresses, shaking them loose. He reached for the blow-dryer.

Abra looked at him in the mirror. "How long have you known Franklin?"

"Ten years." He held the blow-dryer at his side, but didn't turn it on. "He knows the business. He's dedicated. I'll give him that."

"You don't like him, do you?"

"I don't dislike him. We just don't agree on some things."

"Like what?"

"My vision has always been to enhance who a woman is. Franklin . . ." He pressed his lips together and shrugged.

She finished what he didn't seem willing to say. "Franklin makes them someone else."

Murray turned on the blow-dryer and went to work on her hair. She couldn't talk to him with the appliance going. She sat still, eyes downcast, wondering if he wanted to end the conversation. Maybe they shouldn't have started it in the first place. She looked up at him. He didn't meet her gaze this time. He looked grim with concentration, troubled. It always took a long time to dry her hair. When he finally turned off the blow-dryer, he tossed it carelessly on the counter.

"Murray?" She waited until he looked at her in the mirror. "You told me once to be careful. What did you mean by that?"

"Don't lose yourself."

"And you think I have?"

"It doesn't matter what I think. You have to decide who you are, who you want to be."

"What if I don't know?"

He put his hands on her shoulders and squeezed gently. "Try praying about it."

She gave him a bleak smile. "God wants nothing to do with me. He never did."

"What makes you say that?"

"I prayed once. I put my whole heart and soul into it." She shrugged. "He did the opposite of what I asked."

Murray took his hands away, unsnapped the cape, and removed it. "Maybe He has a better plan."

She got up without looking at the finished result in the mirror. Franklin said Murray was the best in the business, and she didn't want to look at Lena Scott.

"I'll see you in two weeks . . . Abra."

She paused in the doorway and looked back at Murray. "Did you know Pamela Hudson?"

"I still know her."

Franklin said Pamela Hudson had been a shooting star, gone and almost forgotten. "Is she sorry she left Franklin?"

Murray looked at her, but didn't answer. It took a moment to understand, and then she smiled. "Anything anyone says to you stays with you, right?"

"Call me if you ever need a friend to talk to."

———

Abra went into the room where manicurists had stations. Her usual girl wasn't there, and the receptionist apologized and led her to an attractive brunette in the salon uniform. "Miss Scott, this is Mary Ellen. Mary Ellen, Miss Scott." Abra wondered if she could relax with yet another new person in her life. She'd gotten used to the innocuous Ellie, who was too enamored with her own life to ask prying questions about Abra's.

Mary Ellen looked straight into her eyes and shook hands with her. Most of the manicurists looked like fashion models, but Mary Ellen looked normal, her brown hair cut in a simple pageboy. Abra noticed her nails were cut short and squared off rather than rounded, the way she used to wear her nails when she played piano. Franklin said long nails were sexier, especially when painted red.

Mary Ellen smiled and held out her hands. Ellie usually had a bowl of soapy water ready and talked while Abra soaked her fingertips. Mary Ellen studied Abra's hands, turning them palms up and then over again. She massaged one hand and then the other. "You can tell a lot about a person from their hands. Your hands are cold."

Abra felt increasingly uncomfortable. "So I have a warm heart."

"Or poor circulation. Or you're nervous." She gave Abra a quick smile. "Or my hands are the cold ones because it's my first day. Are they?"

Abra didn't answer. Mary Ellen set out a bowl of warm, sudsy water. Abra put one hand in while Mary Ellen removed nail polish from the other. She wore a simple gold wedding band. "You have beautiful hands, Miss Scott. If you played piano, you could stretch a full octave without a problem."

"I did."

Mary Ellen glanced up. "So did I." She gave a self-deprecating smile. "Not very well, I'm afraid." When she finished Abra's right hand, she began on the left. "Music is good for the soul." She glanced up again. "Did you play classics or popular songs?"

"A little of everything. Mostly hymns." She hadn't meant to say that.

"Did you play for church?"

"A long time ago."

Mary Ellen's brown eyes warmed with humor. "You're not that old, Miss Scott. In fact, I think I'm probably a few years older than you."

Abra wanted to change the subject. "So this is your first day . . ."

"It's really by accident I'm here. As a matter of fact, it was going to church that got me this job. Or coming home from church. We saw a car parked alongside Arroyo Seco Parkway and a man trying to change a tire. Charles pulled over." She gave a soft, embarrassed laugh. "I'm sorry to admit I tried to talk him out of stopping. He was wearing a suit, and all I thought about was how much it'd cost to get it cleaned." She gave Abra an amused look. "You'd have to know Charles to understand. If he sees someone in trouble, he wants to help. Anyway, it was Murray. The two men got to talking and Charles told him we were new to the area. We came because Charles was offered a better job, but we didn't know anyone here. I had a list of clients in San Diego. Now, I'm starting over again. Murray said I should come in. He was one manicurist short. So here I am." She finished cleaning and preparing Abra's fingernails. "Clear or a color?"

"Red." Abra pointed out the one Franklin liked.

Mary Ellen took it out and shook it. "It's a beautiful shade."

"Like blood." Abra spread her fingers on the rolled towel.

"Or rubies."

Mary Ellen hummed while she worked. Abra recognized the tune and remembered all the verses. "Fairest Lord Jesus" had been one of Mitzi's favorites. Thinking of Mitzi brought Pastor Zeke to mind, and then Joshua. A wave of homesickness swept over her. Mary Ellen glanced up and apologized. "I'm sorry. It's a habit, humming all the time. That hymn has been stuck in my head since Sunday. I used to whistle, but Charles teased me about it all the time. 'Whistling women and cackling hens always come to very bad ends.'"

"It's all right. It wasn't you."

Mary Ellen bowed her head over the work again. "Where do you go to church?"

"I don't. Not anymore."

"Did you lose your faith?" Mary Ellen looked troubled.

Abra gave a wistful smile. "I'm not sure I ever had any." Afraid Mary Ellen might launch into a gospel message, she added, "And please don't start quoting Bible verses." She tried to keep her tone light. "I grew up on them."

Mary Ellen had clear brown eyes, like melting milk chocolate. "I'll try not to hum."

"Hum all you want. It doesn't bother me."

But it did. Hearing that one hymn brought a rush of others to her mind—and memories with them, pulling her into an undertow. Joshua taking her for a ride in his rusty truck, Pastor Zeke in the pulpit, Priscilla in the living room doorway inviting her to join them while they watched *Life with Elizabeth*, Joshua buying her a chocolate shake and fries, Peter watching *Victory at Sea*, Joshua taking her for a hike in the hills, Mitzi making cocoa in her kitchen, Penny sprawled on her bed poring over the latest movie magazines, and Joshua . . .

Joshua.

She closed her eyes. The last two times she'd seen him, they'd ended up fighting over Dylan. Sometimes she wanted to write to him and tell him she was sorry for the things she'd said in anger. She'd slammed the door in his face the last time she saw him. He was probably married to Lacey Glover by now, or some other girl. Why did that bring a sharp pain to her heart? Maybe she would write to him. She could swallow her pride and tell him he'd been right about Dylan. He had every right to say, "I told you so." She could also tell him she'd met someone a lot nicer who believed in her, someone who was going to make her into someone important, someone people would recognize and envy, someone people could love.

But she knew she wouldn't.

What if he wrote back?

The receptionist came to Mary Ellen's station. "Mr. Moss called. He's been delayed. A driver is waiting for you downstairs." Abra thanked her.

Mary Ellen had finished the final coat. "Shall I set up another appointment?" She looked so hopeful, Abra couldn't say no. She'd need another, same time next week. Mary Ellen wrote it into her appointment book. She stood as Abra did and smiled warmly. "I look forward to seeing you again, Miss Scott."

"Call me Ab—" She blushed at the near mistake. "Lena."

Somewhere on the walk to the elevators, Abra gave in to impulse. Instead of meeting the driver out front, she stopped on the second floor, found the stairs, and left through the emergency exit. The alarm went off, and she ran to the end of the alley and looked out before walking quickly to the end of the block and around the corner. She knew she'd regret it, but she had to be alone for a little while. If she went back to the apartment, Franklin would be there.

She slowed and wandered. All she had with her was a clutch bag with a handkerchief, lipstick, and a key to Franklin's apartment. She didn't even have a dime to make a telephone call, let alone enough money to hire a cab. Franklin said it wasn't necessary for her to carry money around with her.

The sun was bright and she put on her sunglasses. She didn't have to worry about anyone recognizing her on the street. She doubted she'd be recognizable even after the premiere tomorrow. It was such a ridiculous movie. Another melodrama in black-and-white.

After six blocks, her high heels made her feet ache. She could feel sweat trickling down her back and wondered if it was soaking through the white linen jacket. Desperate to get off her feet for a few minutes, she went into a department store and found the ladies' room. After resting on the love seat for a while, she washed her hands and patted her cheeks with the cool water. Mary Ellen had done a beautiful job. Her fingertips looked dipped in blood. *Franklin is going to kill me when I get home.*

It was late in the afternoon when Abra reached the apartment house. Howard looked worried. "Are you all right, Miss Scott?"

She had a throbbing headache and wanted to take off her shoes. "Is Franklin still home?" Howard didn't know. He'd just gotten back from his break. He held the elevator door for her.

As soon as the doors closed, Abra took off her high heels and sighed in relief. She unlocked the apartment door, feeling as though she'd been walking for days. Maybe a warm shower would make the headache go away.

"Lena!" Franklin's footsteps came down the hall. "Where have you been? You've been missing for hours!" His expression changed from worry to suspicion.

She tried to remember what she'd learned in the elocution class he'd had her take and kept her voice smooth and cool with dignity. "I'm sorry. I should've told the driver I wanted to take a walk."

"A walk?"

"Yes." The courage she'd mustered shrank with each step he took toward her. "I went for a walk." He'd been drinking. Not a lot, but enough to fuel emotions she had glimpsed over the past few weeks. His blue eyes looked like steel.

"Who went with you?"

She blinked, surprised. "No one." Then she knew what he was thinking. "I was alone, Franklin. I didn't have any money, or I would have called for a cab to bring me home." It sounded like an accusation. She softened her tone. "I'm sorry you were worried."

She stepped around him. Cold sweat trickled between her shoulder blades.

"Where are you going?"

"To the kitchen. For a drink of water. I'm thirsty." She had been walking in the sun for two hours with frequent, but brief, sojourns into stores. Now her head felt as though it would explode.

Franklin followed. She could feel his eyes boring into her back. "Do you really expect me to believe you've been alone all this time?"

Hand shaking, she turned on the tap. "I've never lied to you, Franklin." She gulped water, then felt light-headed. She set the glass in the sink and turned to face him. "I'm never with anyone unless you've arranged it." Her head swam. She leaned back against the counter, afraid she'd faint.

"You were with Dylan, weren't you?"

"I never want to see Dylan again. You, of all people, should know that."

How wonderful that Dylan had shown up at a Hollywood party they attended. Franklin had seen him first and warned her. When she'd turned, there he was, grinning at them, saying it was so nice to see them both looking so well. In a way, she'd been relieved. She realized that she despised Dylan more than she had ever loved him.

"Don't ever lie to me, Lena."

She'd signed Franklin's contract. He should trust her. She knew why he didn't. Over the past two months, he'd stopped looking at her like a client. What was it Mitzi used to say? The train was coming and she didn't know if she could get off the tracks.

Lena. Abra pressed damp palms against her throbbing temples. That's how he saw her now. As Lena. She wasn't Abra anymore. Abra had disappeared from the face of the earth as far as Franklin was concerned, and that's the way he wanted it. The star maker thought he'd hammered away chunks of Abra. He'd gone to work with chisel and mallet. Why couldn't she be Abra in the privacy of this apartment? Why did he insist she play the role of Lena everywhere?

She'd asked him once, and he'd laughed. Did Roy Scherer sound sexy? Did Archibald Leach? Rock Hudson and Cary Grant sounded better. Lena Scott was a name for a star. That was her name now. She'd better get used to it.

Something inside her balked. She wanted to be known for herself. Abra was flesh and blood. Lena Scott was a figment of Franklin's imagination. Or had started out that way. She knew better than to argue with him. He'd made up his mind. Lena Scott, not Abra Matthews, was the woman he could make into a star.

But his vision of what she would be had grown in the last few weeks. She had felt the subtle change in him. Lena was becoming more real to him than Abra. And he wanted Lena.

He was watching her. "Tell me where you went."

She could feel the heat radiating from him. Was it anger or something else? "I don't even know, Franklin. I just wanted to take a walk and be alone for a little while."

"You're alone every night, in your bed."

There was something about the way he said it that stretched her nerves taut. "Maybe I wanted to defy you, just once." She'd wanted to break his strict dietary restrictions and buy a hamburger, fries, and a milk shake, but she didn't have any money. So she walked. She went to a park and sat on a swing. She wandered away and then came home. "Sometimes this apartment feels like a prison." She didn't say he acted like a warden. "I'm grateful. Really I am. But sometimes . . ." She shook her head. "It's so hard."

Tears of exhaustion blurred Abra's vision. She hadn't had a day off in a year and a half. But then, neither had he. "Don't you ever get tired, Franklin?"

"We'll have time to rest someday."

Someday. "I do everything you ask. Everything. I'm so tired, I can't sleep." She'd been on edge for weeks, awakening at every sound in the apartment.

"So tired you supposedly walked miles when you should have been coming home."

A fissure cracked open and she erupted. "Tired of being told what to do every second of every day! Tired of having every minute of my existence under your control!"

"Calm down." He moved closer.

"I've done everything you want, and you still keep hammering at me!" Her voice rose and she realized how shrill she sounded. Lena wouldn't talk like this. She fell silent. She was shaking again, little shivers of nerves. *Why am I never enough?*

Franklin took her gently by the arms. "I know what's wrong with you. It's what's wrong with both of us. We can't go on like this, Lena. We'll both go mad if we do."

Abra looked at him and drew in her breath softly.

She had met Pamela Hudson at the last party a month ago. Franklin had been cordial to her and her husband, a sure sign he didn't love her anymore. When someone drew Franklin's attention, Pamela spoke to her in quiet haste. "You need to be careful with Franklin." Abra asked what she meant. Pamela frowned. "Don't you notice the way he looks at you? Everyone thought he was in love with me. The truth is he loved what he made me. Take some advice from someone who knows Franklin better than he knows himself. He's on the edge. He has been for a long time." Pamela touched her arm lightly. "Be careful he doesn't pull you over with him."

Less than five minutes later, Abra's ex-lover showed up. Franklin hadn't been bothered by Pamela's appearance on the arm of her husband, but the sight of Dylan roused him. She'd seen it in his eyes, felt it in the firm hand he kept beneath her elbow. It was as though he was telling Dylan, *She's mine. Stay away from her if you know what's good for you.*

Dylan enjoyed himself, pouring on the charm and flattery. He'd already seen the new movie. How? He had studio connections, didn't you know? "Bravo, *Lena.*" His dark eyes mocked her new name. "You're going to be one hot property now, baby. Good for you, Franklin. You're still the wonderful wizard of Oz."

Abra had kept silent. Her role in *Dawn of the Zombies* required no acting skills. At the audition, the director had merely asked her to put on a period costume and then a negligee. He wanted to hear her scream.

After Dylan's appearance, Franklin was ready to leave the party.

The tension had been building in the apartment ever since that night. They both knew why. Franklin's blue eyes lost their steely intensity. "I want you." He said it simply, almost in apology. "I have for a long time."

Today, in the bright Southern California sunshine, she'd known what she'd face if she came back. Franklin had been preparing her for the role he wanted her to play in the movie running inside his own head.

Torn by gratitude and frustration, familiarity and fear, she shook her head. She owed him everything. Where would she be now if not for him? She would be on the streets, selling her body like a dozen girls she'd seen on the long walk home. She was thankful; she was. But why did he have to keep pushing so hard all the time?

She pressed fingers to her throbbing temples. "I have a headache, Franklin." She moved away from him, wanting distance and time.

"And you don't think I have a headache from worrying about you all afternoon? You don't think I worry about who you're with and what you've been doing?" He moved closer again. She felt trapped. "Look at me." When she did, his eyes caressed her face. "You are Lena Scott. You can't just go out for a walk. It isn't safe."

"No one knows me from Adam." She saw the pulse throbbing in his throat and her own quickened, but not with desire.

"The premiere is tomorrow night. I give it one week and you'll have crazy fans trying to find you. You'll be getting love letters in the mail." He kept hold of her arm with one hand and with the other stroked the hair back from her damp brow. The touch wasn't platonic. "I want to protect you." He brushed the back of his knuckles against her cheek. "I promised you a fresh new life, didn't I? I'm keeping my promise. Have you seen how people already look at you? You walk into a room and every man notices. Even Dylan looked bewitched. And it gave you pleasure, didn't it?"

It had. Revenge had been sweet—for about two seconds, until that mocking look came into his eyes. He'd never loved her. He never would. He was incapable of love. It had been in that moment she felt relief, realizing she didn't love him either. He still made her heart beat faster, but not out of love. She felt instinctively that Dylan was dangerous, that he had enjoyed hurting her, and would love to hurt her again. She'd never give him that chance, not ever again.

Franklin's first signs of jealousy had shown the night she met Elvis Presley. Of course, she'd been in awe, but it took only ten minutes in his company to know he was just a nice guy who liked girls and was enjoying the attention. He wasn't any happier than she about having others telling him what to do all the time. She'd liked his sultry Southern drawl, but she noticed how his gaze drifted quickly from one pretty girl to another. He was like a little boy in a candy shop. A photographer appeared and he put his arm around her waist. She saw Franklin scowling and thought he wanted her to smile. So she did. It wasn't two seconds later that another aspiring starlet with a pushy manager moved her aside. Franklin had made some crack about her swooning, and she had to remind him he'd been the one to move her in close so she could have a personal conversation with Elvis.

And now Franklin was touching her. He cupped her face. "I've fallen in love with you."

She grasped his wrists tightly. "You're in love with Lena, Franklin."

"You are Lena." His hands shook slightly when he ran them softly over her hair. "Do you know I haven't been with a woman since you moved in with me?"

Would he trust her more if she gave in? Would he relax his iron grip and loosen the chains? She played for time. "I'm afraid of you sometimes."

"Why? I'd never hurt you."

She lowered her head. "I know, but . . ."

He tipped her chin. "Everyone in this building thinks we're already sleeping together."

"Is that any reason why we should?"

"I'm a man, Lena, not a eunuch."

Abra felt the rising flood in him, the need. A soft whisper inside her heart said, *Run*. A louder voice told her to measure the cost if she walked out that door. Did she want to be destitute and walking Hollywood Boulevard like so many other girls who'd come to this humanity-devouring town to fulfill a dream? Franklin had offered her everything, if she'd play her part.

She felt impelled to be honest. "I'm not in love with you, Franklin."

"Not yet." He spoke with such confidence.

Maybe she would fall in love with him. She respected him. She liked him, most of the time. She groaned at the throbbing in her head. He said he'd give her something for her headache. He guided her down the hall and into her room. "Just rest. I'll be right back." He gave her a pill and a glass of water and sat on the edge of the bed. "We won't go out tonight." He ran his fingers across her forehead. "Don't get sick. We're going to the premiere tomorrow night." He lingered for a moment and she was afraid he'd lean down and kiss her. "I'll let you sleep." He stood and quietly left the room.

CHAPTER 11

Though none go with me, still I will follow;
No turning back, no turning back.

S. SUNDAR SINGH

DESPITE ABRA'S FEARS, a crowd waited to see the premiere at the Fox Village Theater. She and Franklin arrived in a black limousine and stepped out to flashbulbs and microphones. She posed in her forest-green satin gown while Franklin held her mink stole, then posed again with Tom Morgan, the leading man. Franklin moved in and told her it was time to go inside.

The movie wasn't a work of art, but most guests seemed to enjoy it. One critic turned around and spoke to Franklin. "The movie is a piece of rubbish."

"But . . . ?" Franklin grinned, undaunted.

The man laughed. "You've done it again, Franklin. She's star material." He winked at her and turned back to watch the rest of the movie.

Franklin was high on her success. They went to the producers' party to celebrate. He toasted her with a glass of champagne. "Well done, Lena."

Abra had been too nervous to eat anything all day, so Franklin went to the buffet and prepared a small plate of food. She ate and had another glass of champagne. A band was playing and she wanted to dance. She would have stayed hours longer, but he said it was late and they had appointments in the morning. They were both still in high spirits when they returned to the apartment house.

When Franklin unlocked and opened the door, Abra raised her arms and waltzed in, singing, "'April in Paris . . .'"

Laughing, Franklin closed the door. "We'll have to work on your singing."

She turned to him, grasping his lapels so she wouldn't tumble. "I was a success, wasn't I?"

"Yes." He leaned down and kissed her. She gave a soft gasp of surprise and swayed to one side. He caught hold of her. "Lena." He drew her fully into his arms this time and slanted his mouth over hers. He stopped after a moment and caught hold of her hand, leading her down the hall. She stopped at her bedroom door, but felt pulled along.

"Franklin."

"Shhh." He kissed her again, pulling the mink stole away and tossing it on the floor. He let go of her long enough to shed his jacket. "Lena." He must have seen something in her eyes because he stopped undressing to caress her face, her shoulders. "I won't hurt you. I swear."

He kept his word. He didn't hurt her. He didn't move her, either.

When it was over, he held her close. "I wanted to wait. I wanted to take more time." He sighed, relaxed. "Next time will be better."

Next time. Abra knew there would be no going back.

Dylan had always moved away after he'd finished. Franklin held her close. When he went to sleep, she tried to get up. He awakened and pulled her down again. "Where are you going?"

"To my room."

"This is your room from now on." He slipped his arm under her neck and put his leg over hers. "I love you." He nuzzled her neck. "Hmmm. You smell so good." He sighed. "Go to sleep, Lena." She fought the urge to free herself from his embrace and forced herself to relax. He loosened his arms so she could turn onto her side and use his arm as a pillow; then his other arm came around her possessively.

She lay wide-awake in the darkness, listening to his breathing, feeling the heat of his body against her back.

Life would be perfect if she could fall in love with him.

She would try.

First, she'd have to forget Abra Matthews ever existed.

———

Life settled into the old routine for Joshua—work, enjoy time with his friends, read his Bible, hike up into the hills on his days off—but he felt a restlessness growing in him, a feeling that there was more to life and more to God's plan for him than this.

Dad left a note that he had a board meeting and would be home late. Joshua warmed up leftovers for supper. Edgy, he decided to go to a movie. He didn't know what was playing, but he drove downtown anyway. Cars had filled the spaces around the square and he had to park around the corner. The Swan's marquee announced *Dawn of the Zombies* in big red letters. He grimaced and headed for Bessie's, giving a cursory glance at the glass-encased advertisement in passing. He went hot, then cold. He stepped back and looked again.

Joshua never expected to see Abra advertised as the star of a horror movie. She had long black hair now, not a mass of red wavy hair. The advertisement depicted her screaming and fleeing in terror from a zombie with outstretched arms.

He read the credits. *Lena Scott.* Dad had said she'd changed her name. He had told him about the movie magazine Priscilla had shown him. Joshua went to the ticket office and recognized one of the teens from church. "What time does *Dawn of the Zombies* start?"

The kid looked shocked. "Started ten minutes ago."

"One ticket, please."

"You sure? It's not your kind of movie."

"Have you seen it?"

"Yeah . . . well . . ." He blushed. "Three times, actually."

It was a Friday night and the Swan was packed. He found one seat in the back row between two couples who didn't look happy he was sitting with them. He ignored them and fixed his eyes on the big screen. It was Abra, all right, dressed in a crinoline with a cinched waist and a scoop neck that revealed far too much.

The story, set in New Orleans before the Civil War, moved slowly. Her fiancé had a plantation and slaves who practiced voodoo. A wedding took place, Abra dancing happily with her dashing groom, who died tragically when he fell from his horse a few days later. While she grieved, her mother-in-law went to the slaves, who performed a ritual that guaranteed her son would be raised from the grave. And arise he did, as a zombie who strangled a prospective suitor of his buxom young widow before he disappeared into the bayou. Later, he came back on a rampage, lurching out of the darkness to grab one victim after another. Thankfully, the producers left the feasting to the imagination, though whenever someone screamed on-screen, a dozen girls in the audience screamed right along with her.

The music changed, warning the audience that the dead scion's beautiful bride—attired in a flimsy, frothy chiffon and lace gown and asleep in the canopy bed—was in danger. Twice before, the zombie had stood on the lawn gazing up tragically at her window. This time, he opened the creaking gate door of the mausoleum and began his slow, clumsy, plodding walk toward the mansion. The girl tossed in bed and then sat upright, her nightgown barely covering her ample breasts.

Joshua felt a jolt seeing her in such dishabille. The heat spread and centralized when she swung the sheets aside, revealing slender, shapely legs. How many other guys in this theater were feeling what he was?

The girl called out for the servant, who was at that moment being attacked downstairs. Pulling on a flimsy robe, she ran to the window, looking out into the moonlit night. A wolf howled.

Joshua rolled his eyes, wondering if a werewolf was about to come bounding out of the woods to save the day.

The zombie climbed the stairs. It opened the door and moved sluggishly into the lamplight. The girl would have to be deaf as a post not to hear the thud and drag of those feet coming across the wooden floor of her bedroom, but there she stood, leaning out the open window, yearning for something, or someone, her black hair in waves down her back. She turned. Of course, it was too late.

Abra's scream went right through Joshua. It sounded so genuine it raised goose bumps all over his body.

The funeral scene was held in an old cemetery. The casket was open, Abra playing dead in a white wedding gown and veil, bougainvillea blossoms scattered across her breasts like dark drops of blood. Her brothers wept as they slid her casket into the shelf of the family mausoleum and then locked the door behind them. Fade out to night. Moss hung from the trees. Mists rose as the moon rose. The zombie stood at the mausoleum gate. He broke the lock with his bare hands and entered. In the next scene, he had somehow managed to extricate his bride from her casket. She had turned into a zombie, too, of course, but unlike her ghoulish on-screen husband, she was exquisite, though her facial expression and eyes were devoid of life, her face death-white in the moonlight. When the zombie took her in his decaying arms, she moaned in ecstasy. In the last scene, the couple walked hand in hand through the mists of the bayou. Together. Forever.

Joshua thanked God the movie was over.

A boy sitting two rows in front of Joshua snorted loudly. "Man, was that ever dumb!"

"There'll probably be a sequel."

"The movie stinks, but did you get a load of that girl? Va-va-voom!"

"Oh, yeah. She's worth the price of another ticket."

"When she leaned out that window, I thought she was going to fall right out of her dress."

The boy laughed. "Let's watch it again."

Feeling sick, Joshua went outside to get some air. The sun had set while he was inside the theater. He got in his truck and drove out of town. He parked where he always did and hiked into the hills. Sitting with his back against a boulder, he looked up at the stars. He wanted to drive down to Hollywood and find her. He wanted to make her come home. Then what? Hog-tie her?

His heartbeat slowed, but his thoughts still tumbled. Abra looked so different. Only someone who loved her and knew her well would recognize her. Others might think Lena Scott looked remarkably like Abra Matthews, but they would dismiss the very idea that a Haven girl could ever become a movie actress, let alone one who oozed sex like a practiced courtesan.

Maybe Lena Scott was Abra's doppelganger.

Joshua raked his hands into his hair and held his head. He was a man and he wasn't blind. She'd grown up and filled out over the last three years. She was no longer a red-haired, dewy-faced teenager, but a raven-haired, sultry woman who played innocence with worldly eyes. It wouldn't just be teenage boys lusting over her. And those two boys weren't the only ones who wanted to watch her again.

Abra was a B movie star.

But that scream. The look in her eyes. Was that acting?

Joshua grabbed a rock and heaved it into the dark shadows on the hill below. Letting out his breath, he stopped and looked up at the night sky, the stars cast across the heavens like sparkling dust particles. He'd wait. He'd keep on waiting until he felt the nudge to do something more than wait. Even if that never happened.

Joshua parked on the side street. Dad was still up. The kitchen light was on. Joshua came in the back door and found him sitting at the table. "Sorry I'm so late."

"I wasn't worried."

"Have you eaten?" Joshua pulled sandwich fixings from the refrigerator. "I could fix you something."

"I had dinner at Bessie's."

His dull tone made Joshua glance at him. "You saw the movie poster."

"Yes."

"I went to the movie." He took out a butter knife, opened a jar of mustard, and smeared some on a slice of bread.

"And?"

"She's a good actress."

"She always was."

Franklin poured himself a glass of Scotch and sat on the couch with a script. "Play something." Abra moved to the piano bench. "Not scales." Franklin looked irritated. He'd been reading scripts for days, looking for the right vehicle for Lena Scott's next sojourn into the celluloid world of make-believe. "Something soft."

She played quietly, humming like Mary Ellen. *"I'm pressing on the upward way, new heights I'm gaining ev'ry day; still praying as I'm onward bound, 'Lord, plant my feet on higher ground.'"*

She hadn't realized she'd begun singing until Franklin spoke. "The voice lessons are helping. I like that piece you're singing." He'd set the script aside. "Sums up our quest, doesn't it? Trying to reach higher ground."

Abra lifted her hands from the piano, realizing she'd been playing a hymn medley Mitzi had put together as a prelude. She got up and stood at the windows looking down over the busy street. Franklin hated ragtime and she hated the blues. She hadn't intended to play hymns, but they seemed to come out of nowhere. Was God playing some kind of cruel joke? "Can we go to a music store so I can pick out some sheet music?"

"You haven't got time for that. We're trying to make you into an actress, not a concert pianist." Franklin picked up the discarded script, tossed it on the coffee table, and patted the space beside him. "Come here." His tone raised her hackles, but she went like a dog called to its master. Franklin draped an arm around her. "You're far away today. What're you thinking about?"

Franklin controlled too much of her life already. She didn't want him inside her head, too. "Is the script good or bad?"

"Forget the script." He tipped her chin and kissed her. She fought the desire to draw back, get up, and move away. He'd be hurt or angry; one always led to the other. He'd say things that would make her feel even guiltier. "Hmmm, you smell so good."

"Murray's trying some new products on me."

"Tell him I approve."

She wasn't in the mood for what he had in mind, and she tried to distract him with business. "Tell me about the script."

"Pretty good Western."

"Can you see me riding a horse and shooting a gun?" He'd probably arrange more lessons to make sure she could do both, if he thought the script good enough.

"You'd play a prostitute with a heart of gold like Miss Kitty Russell on *Gunsmoke*."

Nice. Right up her alley. "Miss Kitty is a saloon proprietress, not a prostitute."

"Two years with Dylan and Lilith and you're still naive." He got up and went to the bar. She followed, watching him replenish his glass with Chivas Regal. He mixed rum and Coke and slid it across the counter to her. He always gave her a drink before broaching unpleasant subjects. Like acting. He was beginning to realize she might never be comfortable in front of cameras. It took two months to shoot *Dawn of the Zombies* and she had been sick every day of it. She'd never get used to people watching her through a lens. She felt like a germ under a microscope. Everything was studied, criticized.

"Did you ever see *Stagecoach*?" Franklin clinked his glass with hers. "This is down that same dusty road."

She sipped. He'd made the drink strong. "I hate acting, Franklin."

"Everyone is an actor, Lena, and you're a natural."

Didn't he ever listen? "I get sick every time we go on set."

"Stage fright comes with the territory. A lot of actors get it. Sometimes it gives your performance a certain edge."

There was no point in arguing. He wasn't going to let her say no. She stopped sipping. Just thinking about making another movie made her tense up. All those people standing behind the lights watching every move she made. It was especially disconcerting when she had to wear a gauzy nightgown.

Franklin straddled the stool beside her and talked about the script. She finished her drink and got up. He made another while she paced. He kept talking.

"Can we go out for a walk, Franklin? I feel cooped up in here."

He set another rum and Coke on the counter, told her to sit down and drink it. He said it would help relax her, make her think straight.

She picked it up, drained it, and set it down. "Are you happy now?" She stretched out on the sofa. Her muscles did relax. She felt warm and fuzzy. He talked about business, movie reviews, competitors, auditions coming up. She hated auditions.

He sat on the edge of the sofa and brushed the hair back from her forehead. "You're not even listening, are you?"

"I hate acting, Franklin."

"I know." His hand moved down over her body. "But you're very good at it."

She didn't like the way he said it. "I'm good at screaming." The reviewers praised that part of her performance, though not as much as how she looked in a flimsy nightgown. "I'm never going to be Susan Hayward or Katharine Hepburn." Why not say it aloud? "Or Pamela Hudson."

He took his hands away. "Didn't you read the papers? Her last movie was a bust. Her career is over."

"I don't think she cares, Franklin."

"Oh, she cares. Take my word for it. I know her. You forget I slept with her for a year before she took off like a witch on a broom. She married to further her career."

Abra felt languid. "She's expecting another baby."

"Yeah. She didn't realize her middle-aged Romeo wanted a family."

Pamela's husband wasn't much older than Franklin, but Abra thought better than to mention that fact.

"Babies are the kiss of death for a career in this business." His laugh had malice in it. "I can imagine what she was thinking when her husband suggested you as the star of his next movie."

She stared at him. "Is that true?" She couldn't help but feel flattered.

"Ah." He grinned. "I see a little spark for acting in your eyes." He shifted away and stood. "I said no, of course. You're on your way up, not down."

"I thought he was one of the best directors in the business."

"A director is only as good as his last movie. His mistake was putting Pam in the lead role. She always thought her looks would carry her."

"You had faith in her once."

"As long as she listened and learned, she had potential. Now she has nothing."

"She has a husband. She has children. She has a life."

"A life? You call dirty diapers and chasing kids a life? Your life is exciting. You're going to be bigger than she ever dreamed she could be." He'd made her another drink.

Abra sat up and took it. Liquid courage. "All this hard work you're doing isn't really about Lena Scott, is it, Franklin? It's about getting back at Pamela Hudson."

His eyes turned glacial as he considered her, but he warmed quickly. "Maybe it is, a little. Wouldn't you like to get back at Dylan, make him regret throwing you away?" He laughed and swallowed his Scotch. "We're a pair, aren't we?"

"Vanity of vanities; all is vanity." Good old King Solomon knew what he was talking about.

He changed the subject. The new acting coach had told him she was a quick study. Franklin knew she was good, but he intended to make her better. She knew he had lofty goals. He would wheel and deal until Lena Scott was number one in the box office, and then he'd shoot even higher. Why not an Academy Award? What about a play on Broadway, and a Tony? He'd never be satisfied.

"I'm twenty years old, and I don't even know how to drive a car."

He gave her a surprised look. "Where would you go?"

"Anywhere. Nowhere. Somewhere away from this apartment!" *And you,* she wanted to add. She wanted to get away from his constant demands, his insatiable ambitions, and his physical hunger.

He came over to her. "You're all tensed up again." He touched her body like the sculptor in the painting, admiring his work.

She got up and sat at the bar.

Franklin stood, too, and looked annoyed. "I told you it wouldn't be easy. You said you could do the work. I spelled it all out for you. You signed the contract. I'm just keeping my part of the deal." He came over and stood in front of her, hedging her in again.

"I know, Franklin." She felt so tired sometimes. She was running a race she couldn't win.

"So there it is. We're in agreement. It takes time and dedication on both our parts. We made a pact. I've dedicated my life to you."

"You have other clients, don't you?"

"No one like you. They're all bit players, character actors, and they're all doing fine, I might add." He cupped her face. "You're special, Lena. I love you. I'm doing all this for you." He looked so earnest, so sincere; she knew he believed everything he said.

She flinched when the telephone rang. He gave her a light kiss. "It's the offer I've been waiting for." He stood by the telephone and winked at her. He let it ring three more times before answering. "Tom! Good to hear from you."

Abra went back to the piano. It was the one place in this black-and-white world where she felt at home. She played a few notes. Franklin snapped his fingers at her and shook his head. She wanted to pound out "Maple Leaf Rag," but she closed the piano like a good little girl and headed for her bedroom. Franklin cupped the receiver. "Sit on the couch."

She flopped onto the couch, stretching out full length. She closed her eyes, wishing she could close her ears, too. Then she wouldn't have to listen to him selling her like a used car. *Lena can do this; Lena can do that; Lena can do anything you want.* If she couldn't, Franklin would make sure she learned how.

"Can she swim?" He didn't even look at her. "Like a fish." He listened for a minute and then laughed. "A mermaid? Sounds intriguing. Send the script over. Can't this week, Tom. No way. Her schedule is packed. You'd better send the script by messenger if you want her to read it anytime soon. Offers are flooding in."

A slight exaggeration. There were only seven scripts on the table. A mermaid? How long would the director want her to stay underwater? She was already drowning.

"Are you kidding me?" Franklin's laugh was genuine this time. He listened and gave a cynical chuckle. "Well, I didn't see that coming. It sounds right up his alley. I suppose Mommy can make it happen." He hung up, his mouth twisting. "Dylan turned in a treatment for a TV game show. He's trying to line up sponsors."

Franklin launched into the story line of a mermaid who rescues a fisherman who fell overboard in a storm.

Abra sighed. "So now I'm going to be a mermaid instead of a prostitute with a heart of gold?"

Franklin rummaged through the scripts and tossed one onto her stomach. "Sit up and read through it. That one will show another side of your talent."

Abra recognized the title and dropped it on the floor. "I don't know how to sing or tap-dance."

"You're learning."

"Franklin!" She felt a bubble of panic. "You just told Tom Somebody-or-Other to send over his script by messenger!"

He picked up the script she'd dropped like a hot potato and waved it at her. "This is better for your career, and Tom's production won't be ready to roll for four months. You'll have time to do both movies, providing Tom's script is as good as he says it is."

Abra's heart fluttered like a trapped bird in his hands. The more she struggled, the tighter his fingers closed around her. "I'm not Debbie Reynolds."

"She didn't know how to dance either when they signed her for *Singin' in the Rain*. She learned on set when Fred Astaire found her sobbing under a piano after a dance scene with Gene Kelly."

"I'm not Esther Williams, either!"

"Stop worrying all the time! You can do it."

"I can't!"

He lost patience. "You can and you will. I get you the parts and you learn what you have to learn to do them. That's your part in our plan. Remember?" He tossed the script on the couch. "Read it! It's a good movie, good money, and we're not turning it down!"

Good money? She shook inside, fear and anger driving her. "I haven't seen a dollar from all my work on that zombie movie yet."

He turned, eyes narrowing. "Are you suggesting I'm cheating you?"

"I didn't say that!"

"You better not. Just so we're clear. I've already invested a lot of my own money in you. What little you've made is in safekeeping. You'll have a nice nest egg someday."

"I wouldn't mind enjoying a little deviled egg right now."

He smiled slightly. "And what would you spend it on? Shoes?"

"Driving lessons!"

He laughed like she was joking. "I've got a few more calls to make." He headed for his office. "Read the script! Who knows? You might find you love tap-dancing."

It sounded like he'd already closed the deal. She felt the weight of heavy chains. She couldn't throw the script away even if she wanted to. She'd signed her life away. Franklin owned her.

At least he loved her. Or she thought he did. At least he didn't leave her on her own and go off with other women the way Dylan had. He wasn't out to break her heart and ruin her life. Quite the contrary. Frustrated, she told herself to stop whining and complaining. She raked her fingers through her hair, pulling it all up and making a ponytail. She got up and rummaged through a kitchen drawer for one of the rubber bands from the morning newspaper. She sat cross-legged on the couch and opened the script.

Franklin came back into the room. "What the . . . ?" He crossed the room and reached for her. Frightened, she drew back. He hooked a finger in the rubber band and yanked it off, taking a dozen strands of hair with it. She gasped in pain as her hair tumbled around her shoulders. "What are you playing at?" He glared down at her.

She stared at him, shocked by the intensity of his anger. "I wasn't playing at anything." It was the first time in a long time she'd been just plain Abra.

———

Students from the Thomas Jefferson High School class of 1950 packed the Haven Hotel. Seventy-eight had made it for the reunion, organized by Brady and Sally Studebaker, Henry and Bee Bee Grimm, and Joshua, all of whom had spent weeks playing detective, tracking down fellow classmates. It had only been seven years since graduation, but they thought it time to get friends together. Sally and Bee Bee wanted a formal dinner dance. Brady, Henry, and Joshua wanted a casual picnic at Riverfront Park. They compromised on a buffet and dance at the hotel, with a local DJ keeping the music rolling.

Most out-of-towners had arrived a few days ahead, some staying at the hotel, others with parents who still lived in Haven. Janet Fulsom and her husband, Dean, drove up from the Central Valley. Steve Mitchell brought his family down from Seattle. He and his wife said they hadn't had a night out since they had the twins, and were thankful Steve's parents had the little ones corralled for the evening. Lacey Glover had married a real estate agent from Santa Rosa and was seven months pregnant.

Joshua saw Dave Upton arrive with his wife. He hadn't sent an RSVP, and the party was in full swing when they came through the door. Dave looked every inch the successful businessman in his dark suit, white shirt, and tie. All he lacked was a black leather briefcase. He had his arm around his wife, a slender blonde in a simple black dress. Dave looked around, as if searching for someone. When their eyes met, Joshua smiled and raised his hand in greeting. Dave leaned down to speak to his wife and guided her in the opposite direction.

Old grudges died hard, Joshua guessed. He hoped they'd have an opportunity to talk. Joshua talked with Lacey and her husband while Sally and Brady bebopped like a couple of teenagers.

Sally's laughter made Joshua smile. Sally had gotten along better with her mother since she and Brady got together. Brady and Sally brought Laverne to church and then went back to her house for Sunday dinner. Sally said she was beginning to see how two people could fight and still love each other. Mitzi had invited Laverne to a ladies' luncheon where Laverne found herself drafted into the quilting club. She had plenty to keep her busy, which made Sally's life less complicated.

Joshua had taken a seat at a vacant table when he heard a deep voice close by. "I heard you and Sally were an item for a while." Joshua glanced up and saw Dave standing with his wife. Joshua stood out of respect. Dave raised the beer in his hand. "Sorry things didn't work out for you." He sounded anything but sorry. His wife looked at him in surprise and then at Joshua to judge his reaction.

"Actually, I'd say things worked out very well." Joshua nodded toward Sally and Brady, now embracing for a waltz and looking blissful. Joshua pulled a second chair back. "Would you like to join me?" He smiled at Dave's wife. "I'm Joshua Freeman, by the way."

"Kathy." The willowy blonde introduced herself and held out her hand. Her smile reached her blue eyes. "David seems to have forgotten his manners." She had a firm handshake.

Joshua liked her already. "It's a pleasure to meet you, Kathy."

"David's talked a lot about you over the years." Dave gave her a look, but she didn't notice. When he put his hand to her elbow, Joshua knew he wanted to be anywhere but here. Kathy tugged free and sat in the chair Joshua had offered.

Dave didn't hide his anger. "I thought you wanted to dance."

She looked up at him. "You said you'd rather not."

"I've changed my mind."

"Then go. You have lots of friends here. Dance with one of them. I want to get to know Joshua." She faced Joshua again. "David said you were in Boy Scouts together."

Livid, Dave gave a short, cold laugh, scraped a chair back, and sat. "Joshua was a fanatic about it. He had to earn every badge. Didn't you? He made it to Eagle Scout before he graduated from high school. Built a ramp for the library so crippled veterans could check out books." His eyes narrowed. "You didn't go to college, did you?"

"Couldn't afford it."

"Too bad. You can't go far without a degree these days." Dave paid no attention to Kathy's obvious embarrassment. She stared at him, but Dave kept on. "You've never even been out of Haven, have you?"

"I spent three years in the Army."

"Oh, I forgot. You joined up, didn't you?"

"I was drafted."

"I thought maybe you'd join up to make up for your father." Joshua felt the heat rise, but pushed it down.

"David!" Kathy put her hand on his knee. "What's wrong with you?"

Dave clamped his hand over hers, but glared at Joshua. "A carpenter. Isn't that what you are?"

"Yes. I am."

Dave gave a derisive laugh. "Joshua was voted most likely to succeed. And now he builds those ticky-tacky bungalows that are spreading like blight everywhere. Do you still live with your father? I'll bet you can't even afford to buy a place of your own."

Kathy pulled her hand from beneath his and stared at him as though she didn't know him, let alone like him. A fleeting apology crossed Dave's face. "Come on." He put his empty beer glass on the table and grabbed Kathy's hand. "Let's dance."

She yanked free. "I'd rather talk to Joshua."

"Suit yourself." He got up and walked off.

Kathy watched him go. "I don't know what's bothering him." She faced Joshua again. "I'm sorry David was so rude. He's not usually like that."

"No need for you to apologize." Joshua noticed Dave had joined a couple of football buddies at the bar. He hoped things wouldn't go from bad to worse.

Kathy noticed, too. "We've only come up to Haven a couple of times to visit his parents." She smiled at Joshua. "I've met Paul Davenport and Henry Grimm. They talk about you. Paul said the four of you were best friends when you were in grade school. He said there was a fight, but he wouldn't tell me what it was all about. Will you?"

"Better if you ask Dave."

"I did. He says he doesn't remember." She frowned. "Obviously, he does. What did he mean about making up for your father?"

"My father spoke out against putting Japanese Americans into internment camps. Dave's uncle was on the USS *Arizona*." Joshua could see Kathy jumping to conclusions.

Kathy still seemed troubled, but she didn't press. She asked questions about Haven, instead, and Riverfront Park. She wanted to hear about bike-riding escapades. It was half an hour before Dave joined them. Kathy smiled and took his hand. Dave sat beside her. He looked a little mellower. "Joshua was just telling me about the good old days when you and he and Paul and Henry used to ride up in the hills together. He said you had a bull after you one time."

Dave looked like he wanted to say something. Kathy gave him openings, but he stayed silent.

Joshua tried to make it easy for him. "Your father gave Dad your address. That's how I knew where to send the invitation."

"They know each other?"

"They're friends, have been for some time. They both like to fish."

Dad had come across Dave's father on the banks of the Russian River shortly after Dave left for college. Michael Upton knew about Dave beating up Joshua. It hadn't been his idea. He talked about his brother who'd died on the USS *Arizona*. Dad told him about the hardworking Nishimura and Tanaka families and how Bin Tanaka had served honorably in Europe. While they were in an internment camp, their property had been repossessed and sold off to Cole Thurman. The two men ended up talking a long time that day, and then got together to fish a few weeks later. Dad and Michael Upton had become good friends.

Joshua gave Dave a few seconds to absorb that before adding his own feelings. "I hoped you'd come tonight, Dave. It's been a long time, buddy." When Dave said nothing to that, Joshua stood. "It was good to see you." He gave Kathy a nod. "It's been a pleasure, Kathy."

CHAPTER 12

Why should I not, had I the heart to do it,
Like to the Egyptian thief at point of death,
Kill what I love? a savage jealousy
That sometimes savours nobly.
WILLIAM SHAKESPEARE

JOSHUA FELL ASLEEP as soon as his head touched the pillow. He awakened in darkness. The telephone was ringing, but that wasn't unusual. Midnight calls were part of Dad's job as a pastor. Rolling over, Joshua put a pillow over his head. He had just fallen back to sleep when Dad put a hand on his shoulder. "It's for you, Son."

"Who is it?"

"He didn't say."

Groggy, Joshua sat up and rubbed his face. He pulled on a T-shirt and went into the living room. "Hello?"

"It's me."

Dave. "Are you okay?"

"I'm drunk, but I wanna talk to you." His tone wasn't belligerent.

Joshua had tried to talk to him over the years. Dave had never been willing. Now he wanted to talk, drunk and in the middle of the night? "Where are you?"

"In a phone booth down by the railway station. How about tomorrow?" He said a four-letter word. "It's already tomorrow, isn't it? How about today? Kathy and I are leaving this morning. I have to be back in LA Monday morning." He slurred. "What time is it, anyway? I can't see my watch." Joshua told him. He spit out another foul word. "Any place open this early?"

"Bessie's café." She would have the coffee on. "Does Kathy know where you are?"

"Yep. Told me she doesn't want to talk to me until I talk to you."

Great. Joshua would have liked it better if this chat had been Dave's idea. "I'll meet you at Bessie's in half an hour." That would give Dave time enough to walk from the station. The cool night air might clear his head.

The bell jangled when Joshua walked into the café. He spotted Dave sitting in a booth, shoulders hunched, hands wrapped around a mug of steaming coffee as if it held the elixir of life. He was still in his Brooks Brothers suit, but his Italian tie was missing and his top two shirt buttons were undone. Joshua slid into the booth. Susan set a mug on the table and filled it with steaming, fresh hot coffee. She refilled Dave's without asking. Dave muttered a bleak thank-you but didn't raise his head until Susan was behind the counter, not close enough to hear. "What happened to us, Josh?"

"You tell me, Dave."

Dave shook his head, eyes red and bleary. "You were my best friend in the world."

"I'm still your friend."

"No, you're not." He didn't look happy about it.

"What makes you think that?" He watched Dave's eyes fix on the scar he'd put on his left cheekbone. It had faded with the years.

"I called your father a traitor. I beat you up. In front of everybody. You wouldn't fight. I wanted to grind you into the dust, but after the first couple blows, you just ducked and parried. I called you a coward. You wouldn't hit back. *Why?*"

Dave looked angry and frustrated, but Joshua knew it was shame that bothered him most. It hadn't been a fair fight. Everyone watching had known it, and he'd paid a price. "I knew Dad wasn't a traitor. And I didn't want to fight my best friend, especially when I knew you were still dealing with your uncle's death."

Dave didn't like that answer. "You were always faster than me. You could've ended the whole thing with one well-timed punch."

"Would a punch have changed your mind?"

Dave rubbed the back of his neck. "No. Maybe." He swore under his breath. "I don't know." He looked away.

"It was a long time ago."

Dave shoved his fingers through his hair. "I don't know what to say."

"You know." Joshua sipped his coffee. "You just don't have the guts to say it." When Dave's head came up, Joshua grinned. "Just spit it out and get it over with." Pride had always gotten in Dave's way. "It won't kill you."

Dave called him a name, but it lacked sting. "Okay. I'm sorry." He looked and sounded sincere.

"Apology accepted." Joshua set his mug aside, put his elbow on the table, hand up and open. They'd arm-wrestled as boys. "You used to win. Remember? I think I can take you now."

"You think so?" Dave took the challenge.

The match ended quickly and Dave laughed. "I guess carpentry builds muscle."

"You've been sitting at a desk, getting soft."

They reminisced, laughing about good-natured pranks they'd pulled on one another, the places they'd ridden with Paul and Henry. They drank coffee until Dave was sober and hungry, then ordered the lumberjack breakfast.

Dave worked on his steak. "You ever think of leaving Haven, Joshua?"

"A time or two." In the months after Abra ran off with Dylan. He wanted to go hunting.

Dave cut off a chunk of meat. "My father-in-law is in the movie business. Bigwig. Knows everybody. The studios hire carpenters to build sets. If you're ever interested in living in Hollywood, just let me know." He dipped the piece of steak in A.1. sauce. "I could get you a job."

Joshua felt something shift inside him. Was God opening a door? "I'll think about it."

"Sorry about what I said about those bungalows you build. Anything you ever built was first-rate. Even that ramp." He dipped another piece of meat. "I can't drive a nail in straight. Just ask Kathy."

"You knew how to throw a football." It had earned Dave a full scholarship.

He frowned slightly. "You could've gone to college after serving in Korea. Why didn't you?"

"I guess this is where God wants me."

"Are you sure about that? I mean, you're not exactly making a fortune."

Joshua laughed. "I'm richer than Midas, Dave." He could see his friend didn't understand.

That evening, Joshua told Dad about the morning spent with Dave before he went home to collect his family. Kathy would be driving most of the way until Dave slept enough to take over.

Dad took off his reading glasses. "Did you two work things out?"

"Took long enough."

"Something else on your mind?"

Joshua didn't tell Dad about Dave's offer to find him a job in Hollywood. He needed to pray about it. It might not be a good idea to start looking for Abra. Then again, would he ever have any peace if he didn't?

———

Abra had dreaded the love scene all week, well aware Alec Hunting, the leading man, had a crush on her.

Franklin made jokes about it, but she could tell he didn't like it. The script called for Alec to be in love with Helena, the lead, while Abra played the friend who was secretly in love with him. The kiss was supposed to be purely platonic and was intended to bring the women in future audiences to tears. Franklin had told her a hundred times this one scene could make her career soar. If she could pull it off. Franklin had rehearsed with her for hours before he was satisfied with her performance.

The moment had come. She had spoken all her lines. Only the kiss remained, and the long, soulful look while Alec walked away. She gasped the instant Alec took her in his arms, knowing there would be trouble. The director shouted, "Cut!" but Alec didn't stop kissing her.

"Cut!"

The laughter was bad enough, but then Abra heard Franklin cursing. Something crashed. Voices rose in surprise. She almost fell when Alec was yanked away. She stumbled back, gasping. The director was shouting again. Two men grabbed hold of Franklin before he could hit Alec. Alec cursed now, too. Men held their arms, pulling them away from each other.

Exasperated, the director yelled, "Get him out of here!" The two men hauled Franklin to the exit while he shouted that he'd knock Hunting's teeth down his throat if he touched Lena again.

Alec shrugged off restraining hands and laughed. "That guy is crazy!"

"You shouldn't have kissed me like that!"

"He thinks he owns you. You should dump him and find someone with a cooler head." A makeup artist dabbed the perspiration from his face. "Good thing he didn't hit me, or I'd be suing him."

The director took his seat and shouted for them to get back on their marks for another take. "Keep it sweet and chaste this time, Hunting, or I'll be punching you myself for wasting film!"

This time Abra botched the scene. Alec clearly thought it was his kiss that had shaken her. He flashed the famous smile that had women swooning and writing him love letters by the thousands. "Don't worry. I'll keep it friendly." She was too distracted to offer a rebuke, worried about Franklin outside, pacing, fuming. It took five takes to get the scene right. When Alec came back, she brushed past him. He caught her wrist. She jerked free. The director called Alec over and they had words. Alec stormed off the set.

Helena gave a dramatic sigh. "Men! Can't live with them and can't live without them." She winked. "Don't worry about it, Lena. It's become a cliché for the leading man to fall for the leading lady."

"Are you in love with him?"

"Me? Are you kidding? I meant you."

"You can have him."

Helena laughed. "No thanks. I'm good and married."

"Married?"

"Shhhh. The studio wants to keep it hush-hush. It ruins the fantasy for male fans, but it keeps me safe from callow coyotes like Alec Hunting."

Franklin was waiting in her dressing room, taut as a tiger ready to spring. "Did they make you do the scene again?"

"Yes." She didn't tell him how many times. His expression told her he already knew. "He treats Helena with respect."

"He's not in love with Helena."

"He's not in love with me either, Franklin, and Helena's married. That's the difference. Maybe if we told him we were married, he wouldn't think he could take any liberties."

Franklin's expression altered. "You want to get married?"

She sat. Did she? She looked in the mirror and fussed with her hair.

He put his hands on her shoulders. "You're trembling."

"You almost punched him!"

His fingers tightened. "I would have, if they hadn't stopped me." He gentled, kneading the tense muscles in her neck. "Maybe you're right. Maybe we should get married. Then nobody would think they could step over the line."

"Are you serious?" She met his eyes in the mirror and saw he was. He'd already made up his mind.

"The call sheet doesn't have you scheduled until Friday." He was back to business. "That gives us three days. We can drive up to Vegas, have a private ceremony in a wedding chapel, and be back in time for the shoot on Friday."

"How romantic." She shrugged his hands off and stood. She wanted to scream. She wanted to cry. But Lena Scott wouldn't do either.

"It was your idea, Lena. How long have we been living together? More than two years. Why not make it legal?"

"What a beautiful proposal." She turned her back on him.

He spun her around, hands firm at her waist. "You already know I love you." He didn't ask if she loved him. If they did get married, would he be less jealous, less suspicious, less possessive? She asked if he was sure. He said he was and kissed her.

They returned to the apartment. Franklin packed for her, two outfits, nothing suitable for a wedding. She kept hoping he would change his mind. He noticed her silence. "We'll have a honeymoon later."

On the drive to Las Vegas, he said things would be even better between them once they were married. Maybe he did want to build a life and not just a career with her.

Neon signs announced wedding chapels. Franklin chose one that reminded her of a miniature Haven Community Church, except for the blaring lights instead of a cross on the steeple. The proprietor had a rack of black tuxedos and white wedding gowns from which to choose: some plain, some with lace and pearls, some tiered confections. Abra felt like wearing black, but picked white satin. The proprietor's wife insisted she wear a veil and handed her a small bouquet of silk flowers, probably used a hundred times before by a hundred other brides who'd come for a quickie wedding. Franklin stood at the altar looking handsome in a rented tux. His eyes shone when she took her place beside him. Maybe everything would be all right. When he smiled, she put her hand in his, and smiled back.

"You're so beautiful. We should have done this a long time ago."

The ceremony lasted only a few minutes. Franklin slid a simple gold band on her finger. Did the chapel have a tray of those for sale, too? They signed papers and received their marriage certificate. Elated, Franklin took her to a casino for their wedding dinner. He ordered champagne. The sound of slot machines and bells announcing winners assaulted Abra's senses. She told Franklin she wanted to go upstairs. She wanted silence. Franklin thought she wanted sex. She played her role as Lena Scott. Maybe too well.

"You don't know how much I love you, Lena. Tell me you love me."

"I love you, Franklin." In truth, she said it to calm him. She made it sound like she meant it. She wanted to. She said it again because he didn't believe her. She kept saying it because she wanted so desperately for it to be true.

Joshua got up early and made coffee. He hadn't slept much. He'd started dreaming about Abra again, vivid dreams that haunted him.

Dad came in the back door from his morning walk. "You're up early."

"Rough night." He rubbed his face.

Dad poured himself a cup of coffee and took a seat at the table. Joshua stood. "What do you say I cook some bacon, scramble some eggs?"

"Sit down, Son."

Joshua eased back into his seat. "Something wrong?"

Dad looked at him over the rim. "Michael told me Dave offered to find you a job last summer."

"Yeah. I've been praying about it."

"It wouldn't hurt to call him. If a job turns up, you'll have an answer."

———

When Franklin finally slept, Abra slipped from his embrace and closed herself in the bathroom. She stood under the stream of hot water and scrubbed herself. Numb, she put her palms against the tile and let the water pound her flesh. Words welled up, unbidden, sharp and clear. *"Oh! precious is the flow that makes me white as snow . . ."* She could hear Mitzi. *"It'll all come back to you someday. Take my word for it."*

All those old hymns haunted her.

Tears came. She knew if she let go and started sobbing, Franklin would hear. He would come in and want to know what was wrong. What could she say? That she had married him because she didn't have the courage to say no?

Hymn lyrics stuck like burrs in her mind. She couldn't shake them. *"Nothing but the blood of Jesus. . . ."* She pressed her hands over her ears and begged. "Leave me alone." But she couldn't shut out what was inside her head.

Sometimes she wanted to go back. But it was too late. Dylan had called Haven a dead-end town with nothing to offer. She had to think of it that way, too, or spend the rest of her life in regret.

Abra shut off the shower and dried off.

Lena got back into bed with Franklin.

———

1958

By the time Dave called with a lead on a job, Joshua had all but forgotten the possibility. "I'm sorry it took so long. These things can be unpredictable. But if you're still interested, I have a job lined up for you with a production company. It may only last a couple of months, but it'll give you a foot in the door."

Joshua wondered if he'd want to stay away from Haven any longer than that. The prospect of living in a big city had never appealed to him. Two months should give him time enough to find Abra. He wasn't sure what he'd do when he did. But this was the open door he'd been praying for, and he was ready to walk through it. Luckily Jack Wooding's crew had just finished one tract and had some time off before starting the next. It wouldn't be a problem to get away for a while.

"Don't worry about finding a place right away. We have plenty of room. You can live with us. How fast can you get here?"

"The time it takes to pack a suitcase and drive down."

Exhausted and hungry, Joshua arrived at Dave and Kathy's house late in the afternoon the next day. He met their two children—David Junior, called DJ; and Cassie, short for Cassandra, named after Kathy's mother. Dave showed Joshua downstairs to their guest suite with private bath. At a glance, Joshua knew it had more square footage than Dad's entire house.

Dave looked smug. "What do you think?"

"You may have to kick me out."

He laughed. "I'll fire up the grill and get the steaks on."

Joshua took a quick shower and changed into a fresh short-sleeved cotton shirt before going upstairs and out through the French doors to the deck overlooking the San Fernando Valley. In less than twenty-four hours, he'd decided to come south, packed, and made the five-hundred-mile trip. His truck had overheated when coming over the Grapevine, and he'd needed to pull off for a while. Other than that, he'd only stopped a few times for gas and food. The smell of barbecuing steak made his stomach growl.

Kathy had set fine china, crystal glasses, and silverware on the glass table with an umbrella. The napkins on each plate were folded like tulips. Kathy asked Joshua what he'd like to drink—bourbon, Scotch, gin and tonic? "Or fresh lemonade." Joshua asked for lemonade. Dave asked for another Scotch on the rocks. Kathy's expression told Joshua she thought Dave had already had enough.

Joshua watched Dave at the grill. "Smells great."

Dave gave a sardonic smile. "Never thought you'd see me cooking anything, did you?"

"Oh, I don't know. You managed hot dogs and marshmallows over a campfire. What do you have there? Half a steer?"

"I figured you'd be hungry, and porterhouse steaks are the best. How do you like your meat? My wife likes hers still mooing." Joshua told him medium. The steaks sizzled as Dave speared them with a long fork and turned them over. "I've got some bad news." Dave took Kathy's steak away from the heat. "About the job."

"I've been fired before I've been hired?"

"The shoot's been postponed. I told you the business was unpredictable." A muscle jerked in his cheek. "There may be something else. Kathy's father wants to do some remodeling."

Joshua could see the furrow growing in Dave's brow. "And?"

"He's a tough man to please. A perfectionist. It's probably a waste of time to talk to him."

"A waste of time?"

Dave looked annoyed. "I'm not saying you're not a good carpenter." He uttered a short, foul word under his breath and then rushed on. "You'll understand when you see the house. It's not like anything you've worked on in Haven."

"Are you worried that my feelings will be hurt, or that I'll botch a job for your father-in-law?" Joshua laughed. "Don't worry. If the job's beyond my abilities, I'll tell him."

Kathy came back from breaking up a squabble between their two children. Joshua told her the lemonade was the best he'd ever tasted.

"David planted the trees right after we bought the house." She pointed out the orange, lime, and lemon trees growing along the fence beyond the swimming pool, where the two children now splashed and played.

Dave still looked worried. "Have you ever done cabinetry and finish work?"

"I built my dad's pulpit and the altar, renovated the choir loft, and did the front doors of the church." He gave Dave an amused smile. "Not that you ever saw them. I don't think I've ever seen you in church."

"And you won't. It's a waste of Sundays. Kathy's been talking about it since our visit to Haven." He gave a snort. "Did you plant that idea in her head?"

"Not that I know of." Joshua lifted his glass of lemonade. "Maybe God is working on her in hope of getting to you."

"Yeah. That'll be the day." His smile grew derisive. "What would God want with me?"

"Don't ask me. Ask Him."

"Always the evangelist." There was no sting in Dave's tone this time. "I'm a lost cause."

Dave had always been stubborn and bullheaded. Now he was driven and ambitious besides. Joshua knew God could use those traits for a good purpose, just as he'd turned Saul of Tarsus from persecutor and killer of Christians into a man who spread the gospel throughout the Roman world.

Now, with television and airplanes, this new guy, Billy Graham, might reach even more of the far corners of the earth.

"DJ! Cassie!" Kathy called. "Time for dinner." The children clambered from the pool, grabbed towels, and raced to the table. Dave looked exasperated at their squabbling. Kathy noticed and admonished them to settle down. "We have company. Behave!"

Joshua asked if he could say grace. Dave looked irritated, the children curious, but Kathy quickly said, "Please do."

Joshua told a brief story of one of Dave's exploits when they were boys. The children wanted to hear more. Dave told them to be quiet and eat. They could go back in the pool when they finished. Kathy said if they went in too soon, they might get stomach cramps and drown. "With us right here?" Dave countered, annoyed. DJ and Cassie squabbled again. "Knock it off!" Dave thundered. Cassie started to cry. Dave muttered something and got up. He grabbed his empty glass and headed for the house.

Kathy looked embarrassed and worried. "He's not always like this." She shooed the children onto the lawn, then headed for the house. DJ did a cannonball into the pool while Cassie stood on her towel, calling out, "Mommy, DJ is in the pool!" Dave came back outside, another drink in his hand, Kathy on his heels. Exasperated, she went to talk with DJ. He balked, but obeyed.

Dave closed the barbecue without cleaning the grill. He wanted to talk about business. Kathy joined them again and Dave stopped talking. She wanted to hear about Haven and what they'd done as boys. Joshua told her about Dave's most spectacular plays on the football field.

Dave's silence stretched taut. Kathy glanced at him in concern. "I think I'll let you two talk." She rose and called for the children to come inside.

As soon as they were gone, Dave opened up again. "You never really know who your friends are in this town. You never know what anyone is really thinking. Friends can turn into enemies overnight in this business." The sun went down and he was just getting wound up.

Joshua let him talk for a long time before asking, "You sure this is where you want to be?"

"I'm locked in, Josh. It's a little late to change my mind."

"Change course."

"Easy for you to say. You're single. You don't have a wife who grew up with a silver spoon in her mouth. Her father is the one who opened the doors. He's the one that loaned us the down payment for this house. He'd want to string me up if I quit."

Kathy opened the doors. "DJ and Cassie want a story, David."

"You read to them! I've got to scrape the grill and clean up out here." He got up and headed for the barbecue, as though to prove his point.

"The barbecue can wait, David." Kathy sounded annoyed.

"No, it can't. It'll be dark soon."

"It's already dark, and the kids need to get to bed so they'll be willing to get up tomorrow for—"

"Who's stopping you? You're the mom. Take care of it!"

Joshua rose. "Mind if I tell them a story?"

"Good luck with that," Dave muttered, scraping the grill. "All they ever do is fight over which book they want. I'm too tired to deal with them."

Kathy warned Joshua the children were keyed up and might not settle down for him. She ordered them to sit and behave so Daddy's friend could tell them a story. DJ bounced on the edge of the couch. Cassie pushed him. He shoved her. Kathy made them sit on swivel rockers. DJ rocked; Cassie turned in a circle. Joshua took the challenge. He sat on the sofa and started talking. It took two minutes for the fidgeting to stop and five more to get DJ and Cassie on the sofa with him. Joshua leaned back, an arm around each of them, still talking.

When Dave came in through the French doors, he looked surprised. Kathy was sitting in one of the swivel rockers and listening. Cassie was asleep, curled up against Joshua's side with her thumb in her mouth, but DJ was wide-awake, listening. Dave took a seat, looking more perplexed than relieved. When Joshua finished, Kathy stood and scooped up Cassie in her arms and told DJ to head for bed. DJ followed and then stopped in the doorway. "Are you going to be here tomorrow morning?"

"Yep." Joshua smiled. "Your mom and dad said I could stay until I can find a place of my own."

"I don't think I'd like to spend three days inside a whale."

Joshua grinned. "Me either."

"You said it was true."

"It is. I have another true story to tell you about a boy who killed a giant with a sling and a stone."

Dave looked half-amused, half-annoyed, as DJ trundled off to bed. "Bible stories. I should've guessed."

Joshua laughed. "Would you like to hear one? I could tell you about Gideon and the Midianites. He felt persecuted and outnumbered, too. Actually, come to think of it, he was, but then again—"

"Spare me."

Kathy returned from tucking in the children. "You'd make a wonderful father, Joshua."

Dave gave her a narrow-eyed look. "Beware, Josh. Anytime a woman meets a bachelor, no matter how content he is with his life, she won't be happy until she sees him roped and branded." His tone wasn't light.

Kathy stiffened. "I've been told married men live longer than bachelors."

"Unless they work for their father-in-law."

Kathy's mouth opened in hurt surprise.

Swift regret filled Dave's expression before he shut down. He got up. "I'm going to bed." Joshua stood and thanked them both for dinner and the use of their guest room. Dave waved it off and turned to his wife, who remained in her chair, head down. "I have to get to the office early." His tone was quiet, bland. "You'd better write out directions so Josh can find your father's house."

"I'll give him the Thomas map. That way you'll know I didn't mislead him."

Dave didn't say anything as he headed for the hallway. He stopped and looked back at Joshua. "Be there a little before ten. If you're even one minute late, you might as well turn around and come on home."

"That's not fair, Dave." Kathy looked close to tears. "You talk as though my father is unreasonable."

"Try working for him."

"Maybe if you'd try to understand what he's going through . . ."

"Good night!" Dave disappeared down the hall.

Kathy glanced at Joshua. "He's been waiting for you to come. He said you're the only friend he trusts." She looked crushed. "And he's wrong about my father. My mom died two years ago and . . ." Her expression beseeched him. "I hope you'll make up your own mind when you meet him tomorrow."

"I'm looking forward to meeting him."

Joshua sat on the edge of the double bed in the guest room, head bowed. He'd always known the job was a secondary reason for coming south. He'd really come to find Abra. Now it seemed he had four more reasons for being here.

Abra wasn't the only lamb lost in the wilderness.

———————

Abra came out into the sunshine, Franklin at her side, talking. She was too tired to pay attention. The day had gone well, the dance sequences all finished. Ben Hastings, the star of *Ladies and Gents*, was a professional hoofer and a perfectionist. He had taught her to tap-dance on set, drilling her harder than Franklin ever had in acting. She knew the steps so well, she danced them in her sleep. Today had been the last and most difficult and evocative dance he'd choreographed, and she'd kept up with him right to the last step.

The director called, "Cut!" and came out of his seat, he was so excited. "That was better than Fred Astaire and Ginger Rogers!" Ben grabbed and hugged her tight and called her a trouper. She should have felt triumphant. Instead, she'd felt relief it was over, finally over. She'd fought tears, desperate to escape. She wanted to get out of the studio and breathe fresh air. She wanted to be away from the lights and the cameras that followed her every move. How many little mistakes would show up on the big screen? What would the critics say?

What would the audience feel? She felt like a fraud, always playing a part, always being someone other than herself. The problem was she didn't know herself anymore, what she wanted, where she belonged. She became whatever persona Franklin wanted, what the script and director demanded.

What had become of Abra?

Franklin's hand tightened at her elbow. Perhaps he sensed she wasn't really listening. He always wanted her undivided attention. "I'm sending you to the salon for a pedicure." He never asked, and she didn't have the strength or courage to tell him she wanted to go back to the apartment and sleep for a week. "We're going to a party tonight. Billy Wilder will be there. Rumor has it he's going to do a courtroom drama. I want you polished and ready." She wondered if she could stand—let alone walk—in a pair of heels after the day she'd had. Franklin kissed her cheek and opened the back door of the limo. "You did well today. I'm proud of you."

"Proud enough to give me an evening off?"

"Don't be cute."

The driver slid into the front seat and gave her a quick smile and greeting before starting the Cadillac. When he asked her a question, she answered politely, then asked him to turn on the radio. He took the hint. She didn't want to talk. Unfortunately, the station he chose was playing "The Great Pretender" by the Platters. Sighing, she closed her eyes and rested her head against the seat. Would there ever be a time when she didn't have to pretend? Was there anything in her life right now that was real?

She still felt queasy whenever a camera started to roll, knowing the director was watching every move she made, every expression on her face, listening to every word and nuance she spoke, always looking for a flaw, a mistake that would mean more rehearsing and another take, and then another.

Franklin was keeping his word. He was getting her bigger and better parts. He'd warned her from the start that it would be hard work. She learned her lines. She knew her marks. She listened and did exactly what the director told her to do. She found it easier to play the parts in a movie than to be Lena Scott. She had to remember to play that part no matter where she was, especially in the apartment when only Franklin's eyes were on her. Whenever Abra slipped through, Franklin gave her that look. *You're not that girl anymore. You're Lena Scott now. Don't forget.* How long before the role became natural and she, Abra, ceased to exist? And would it matter to anyone if she did?

Abra relaxed as soon as she entered Murray's. It was the one place Franklin let her go by herself. And there was something peaceful about these rooms, something beyond the hair dying, the manicures, the pedicures. "You're looking beautiful, Miss Scott." The receptionist beamed a smile. "I'll let Mary Ellen know you've arrived."

Afraid if she sat she wouldn't be able to get up, Abra stood until Mary Ellen came up front. Her brown eyes were as warm and bright as a puppy's. She showed Abra to a quiet, private room. The lights were low and classical music played softly. Abra moaned as she sank into the comfortable chair. Her thigh and calf muscles ached. How long before they cramped? Bending over, she bit her lip as she tried to work off one pump.

"Rest back, Miss Scott. I'll do that for you." Mary Ellen knelt and slipped the shoe off Abra's foot. "Oh!" She gasped at what she saw. "What have you been doing?" Her tone was full of sympathy.

"Tap-dancing." She sucked in her breath as Mary Ellen carefully removed the other shoe. Her heels throbbed and burned with pain. The tape Franklin had wrapped around her toes that morning had bunched and was tinged pink with blood.

Mary Ellen carefully cut away the tape, murmuring in sympathy when she peeled it back and exposed raw skin where blisters had burst. "A nice long soak to start." She prepared a basin with some salts. "It's going to burn a little in the beginning, but it will disinfect and soothe, too." Abra gasped as she slipped her feet one at a time into the water. "I'm so sorry, Lena." Mary Ellen looked distressed.

"It's fine." After a moment, the pain subsided and Abra relaxed with a sigh.

Mary Ellen sat in front of her, hands folded, looking troubled. "Will you have to do more dancing?"

"Not for this movie, and not if Franklin manages to get me into a courtroom drama." Billy Wilder was no fool. He would take one look at her and know she wasn't the caliber of actress he would want in one of his movies. She could hope, anyway. *Ladies and Gents* was no *Singin' in the Rain*. She had her doubts it would be a hit, but Franklin said nothing succeeded in Hollywood like repetition.

"My husband and I haven't been to the movies in a while." Mary Ellen knelt on a cushion and began to gently knead Abra's aching calves. "Our neighbors sold us their television set before they moved. They were worried it would get broken and be a complete loss. We watch *The Ed Sullivan Show* and *Cheyenne*. I love Perry Como's show. My husband stays up for *Gunsmoke*, but I'm usually too tired. And we watch the news every evening after dinner."

"I've been told television is the future." Not the future Franklin envisioned for Lena Scott.

"I love movies, but it's so easy to turn on the television and it's such a constant flow of entertainment. The advertisements are annoying, but I suppose they have to run them to pay for the shows."

Franklin said every home in America would have a television in their living room soon. The networks had to mass-produce shows. They came up with new material every week, week after week. Working on a movie set was hard enough. She had met television actors who worked six days a week, starting at six in the morning, sometimes not leaving the set until ten at night. They had studio contracts and spent up to seven years living like indentured servants.

They might become rich and famous, but were more likely to be canceled and released, or locked down and waiting to be cast in a situation comedy or have a part in Dick Powell's *Zane Grey Theater.*

The movie industry was hot. Some studios designed posters before writing a script. All they had to have was a good idea to get financial backing. She'd met a dozen girls in the last few months who could sing and dance circles around her, and yet they ended up giving a half-hour private lap show in some studio exec's office. At least Franklin had saved her from that. But things could change quickly if she didn't hold up her side of the bargain and play her part. Every time she was awake in the night and stared out the bank of plate-glass windows in the silent living room, she saw Hollywood was one long boulevard of broken dreams.

Mary Ellen lifted Abra's foot carefully from the water. She used small, sharp scissors to cut away the torn skin. "I hope I'm not hurting you."

"I'm fine."

"You say that a lot."

"Do I?"

Hands still, Mary Ellen raised her head. "Are you?"

Abra looked into her eyes and knew she could be honest. "I don't know what I am anymore."

Mary Ellen's expression softened. "Well, the Lord knows who you are and what He meant you to be."

Abra had become used to the way Mary Ellen always managed to bring God into every conversation, as though He were another person in the room she wanted to include. Like Mitzi, Mary Ellen centered her life around Jesus. She talked about Him the way she would a beloved father, a good friend she trusted, someone she wanted to share. Talking about God made Abra uncomfortable. Talking about Jesus reminded her of Joshua and Pastor Zeke and Peter and Priscilla and Mitzi, and it filled her with homesickness.

She might be a rising screen star, but she was lonely. The pain in her feet was minuscule compared to the pain in her heart. She didn't think she could bear more today, so she wrapped herself in a protective armor of disdain. "The way He wanted you to be a manicurist, I suppose." She heard the derisive tone of her voice and felt ashamed.

Mary Ellen met her eyes with a smile. "For now."

Words came unbidden. "I wish I knew what He wanted from me."

"Oh, that's easy enough. He wants you to love Him."

"Well, then, I don't know what He wants me to do."

"Ask Him."

Abra let out a breathy, mocking laugh. "He might send me to Africa."

"I suppose He could, but if He did, you'd end up happy you'd gone." She gently applied salve to Abra's foot. "A missionary came to visit last Sunday. I wish you'd been there to hear her." Mary Ellen had invited Abra to church a dozen times at least, never giving up hope. "She grew up in our church. She said her mother dragged her to a Sunday night service to hear a missionary from Africa. On the way home, she told her mother there were two things she would never, ever be: a nurse or a missionary in Africa. Take a guess what God did?" She laughed. "He made her a nurse and sent her to Africa. And she said she's never been happier or more fulfilled. She's been out in the bush country managing a hospital for twenty-five years and plans to stay until God takes her home."

"Then, I guess He never intended me to be an actress."

"Why do you say that?"

"Because I hate being someone else all the time. I hate pretending everything is wonderful and I'm happy. I hate—" Her voice broke. She bit her lip and shook her head. When she could breathe again, she spoke. "Pay no attention to me. I'm just having a bad day."

"Is that all it is?" Mary Ellen waited.

Abra leaned back and closed her eyes, hoping that would end

the conversation. Mary Ellen finished with the salve and wrapped a warm towel around Abra's right foot before she lifted, dried, and began working gently on Abra's left. They didn't speak. Feet mended and wrapped in warm towels, Mary Ellen massaged Abra's sore calves again. She hummed another familiar hymn that made tears prick behind Abra's lids. She could have sat at the piano and played the Fanny Crosby hymn straight through without a mistake. It had been one of Mitzi's favorites, along with dozens of others, added to the hymns of Isaac Watts and Charles Wesley. Melodies and words ran through her mind.

"Jesus is tenderly calling you home . . ."

Abra tried to shut out the memories by making a mental list of her sins. There was no going back and undoing the past. She'd have to carry the guilt forever. The weight of it pulled her down deeper into the shadows where she lived. She wanted to curl up in a dark corner where God couldn't see her. She only had to look at where her life had begun to know God had never loved her. She'd always been a castaway, an outsider, an interloper. She remembered Pastor Zeke standing at the gate in the dark of night and felt the same wrenching pain she had felt as she watched him walk away.

She raised her hand and pressed it hard against her chest.

Mary Ellen's hands stilled. "I didn't mean to hurt you."

"I'm fine." Abra winced. There was the lie again, so quick to her lips. She fought tears. *I'm fine?* "It's nothing you've said or done, Mary Ellen."

"Then what is it, Lena? How can I help you? Please. Let me help you."

Abra shook her head and looked away.

The truth was, she hated being Lena Scott. But she didn't know where to find Abra anymore.

CHAPTER 13

The serpent deceived me.
EVE'S EXCUSE

ZEKE STOPPED BY for a trim at Hair Today Gone Tomorrow on the corner of the square. Javier Estrada's barbershop was slow on Monday mornings, and Zeke would have the opportunity for immediate service and plenty of time to talk baseball. Javier kept up with players and stats. Next, Zeke stopped in at the Vassa Bakery for a loaf of Swedish rye and a short visit with Klaus and Anna Johnson. They had a passel of children who'd all worked in the bakery at one time or another, but who were now scattered north and south, establishing family businesses of their own.

It was a nice morning for sitting in the square. People always stopped by to chat or just said hello in passing. Zeke liked to be out among the people. He ate a piece of fresh rye bread, enjoying the sunlight that shone through the redwood and maple trees, splashes of light moving like dancers on the sidewalk. It had been a busy week. Mitzi had wanted a ride, and he'd taken her with him to visit several families outside of town. She knew how to make people laugh, even when they were determined not to crack so much as a smile. He'd had a memorial service on Friday and a wedding on Saturday. He'd gone home right after church on Sunday, changed into more casual wear before heading out for dinner at the MacPhersons'. He'd been at Bessie's at six thirty this morning. Susan served him at the counter, but hardly spoke. He'd stop in later and see if she felt more like talking.

As though his thoughts had tapped her on the shoulder, he heard the distant jangle of the old bell over Bessie's front door. Susan came out and crossed the street. She'd cut her hair. The new pageboy suited her. She was heading straight for him like a pigeon to its roost, and she looked decidedly grim.

"I'm on break, Zeke, so I've only got a few minutes to talk with you."

"Sit. Please." He'd been preaching a series on the book of Romans. She was sure to have a question that would challenge him. He frowned when she remained standing, glancing around nervously. "I don't think Bessie will fire you if you're out here for a few minutes."

"Bessie would love it if I stayed out here with you all day." She sat, leaving plenty of room between them on the bench.

She looked around again. The square was empty. Everyone was at work. "Bessie said Joshua left town." Why the worried expression? "Did you two have a fight or something? I mean, I know it's none of my business, but . . ."

Ah. "Joshua was offered a job in Southern California."

"That's a long way from home, Zeke."

"There was an opportunity he couldn't pass up."

Susan smoothed her skirt over her knees. She seemed upset about something, and Zeke knew it had little to do with Joshua's departure. "What's on your mind, Susan?"

She let out a sharp breath as though she'd been holding it a long time. "People have been asking if I knew anything, as though I should know what was going on in your home. I keep telling them I don't know any more than anyone else, but they . . ." She pressed her lips together. He could see emotions flitting across her face.

"Persist."

"Yes." She frowned and returned to her first question. "You two are so close. Why would Joshua want to go to Southern California? It's a world away from Haven."

"There's a time for all things, Susan. Just because he's gone now doesn't mean he'll be gone forever."

"It doesn't bother you that he's so far away?"

"We're still in touch." Joshua had called to let him know he'd arrived safely and to ask for prayer for Dave and Kathy. He didn't offer specifics, but God would know what they needed.

Susan relaxed a little. "It's nice out here, in the fresh air." She folded her hands, but didn't lean back. She still sat on the edge of the bench. Zeke knew she had something else on her mind. She sighed, eyes fixed on her hands. "I've been here long enough. I think I should go."

Zeke had the feeling she didn't mean back to Bessie's. "What's troubling you, Susan?"

She cleared her throat. "People are speculating." Her knuckles whitened. "About us."

Was she just beginning to realize that? "And that bothers you."

Susan blushed. "Yes. It does."

He felt a sharp jab in his chest. He wasn't quite sure how to apologize. He'd felt drawn to her from the beginning, wanted to be her friend.

She bit her lip, worrying it before she spoke. "Cole Thurman said people see you come into the café almost every day and know you're coming in to see me."

The implication had an unsavory quality about it. Understandable, considering the source. "I didn't know you knew Cole Thurman."

"He comes in now and then and asks me out. I always say no. He thinks I'll change my mind. That'll be the day hell freezes over." She grimaced. "I've known men like him all my life and want nothing to do with him." She looked at Zeke. "I couldn't care less about him, but I am concerned about you."

"Me?" Zeke raised his brows in surprise.

"People think there's something going on between us." She blushed as she said it, clearly appalled at the idea.

"I enjoy your company. You make me think."

"What about your reputation? You being a pastor and all."

"We ain't misbehavin', Susan."

"This isn't a joke, Zeke."

He saw her eyes awash with tears and knew he couldn't take this lightly. "Don't worry about it."

"You can't have people thinking you're interested in someone like me."

"Someone like you?" It saddened him to hear her say it. "Why shouldn't I be interested?" More than interested, for that matter?

She shook her head. "You know what I mean."

"I know exactly what you mean, and it grieves me that you think so little of yourself when I think very highly of you."

She studied his face for a moment. "That's not the point, and you know it." She started to stand.

He put his hand over hers so she wouldn't leave. "It is precisely the point. Listen to me, Susan." His hand tightened as he leaned toward her. "You and I are good friends. I am who I am. People know me or they don't. And they know you, too."

She sighed. "How can you be that naive?"

"We can live to please people, or we can live to please God." He gave her a reproving smile. "Bessie wouldn't be too happy if she knew you were out here trying to talk me out of coming in so often. I'm one of her best customers."

She gave a soft laugh. "She'd skin me alive, but not for the reasons you think. She'd be convinced I was breaking your heart."

Zeke squeezed her hand lightly and lifted his away.

Her expression softened. "You're the only real friend I've ever had, Zeke."

Zeke thought of Marianne and wondered what she would make of this relationship. "You say that like you're saying good-bye."

"I've been thinking about moving on."

Zeke felt a pang of disappointment. "Any place in particular?"

"I've been here longer than anywhere else." Susan gave a half-hearted shrug.

She looked away, but not before he saw the glimmering moisture in her green eyes. Zeke didn't want her sacrificing God's blessings because of him. "I think you'd better stay. If you leave town, people will start speculating about me and Mitzi."

She frowned. "Mitzi?"

"Well, yes. I spend a lot of time with her, too. She even gave me a car. Now why would she do that unless there was something a little unsavory going on? And where do we go on those long drives?"

Susan laughed. "Don't be ridiculous!"

He realized he'd never heard her laugh before. He wanted to hear it again. "Oh, I don't know. Even Hodge might start worrying. A younger man after his mother." Zeke put his arm on the back of the bench and grew serious. "Don't use me as an excuse to leave Haven. You can run, Susan, but you can't hide from God."

She looked startled, then pensive. "I came to Haven to find peace, Zeke." She shook her head. "Considering everything I've done, I don't think that's possible."

He knew what she really meant. She wasn't yet able to receive God's grace. She still felt like she had to earn it. "Give God time to work, Susan. His love never fails."

She let out a shuddering sigh. She stood. "I'd better get back to work." She gave a bleak laugh and glanced around uneasily. Others had come into the square while they'd been talking. Neither of them had noticed. "I came out here to warn you about what people think is happening between us, and I've probably given people more cause to gossip."

Susan took a few steps away and then turned. "Oh." She gave him a sad smile, her expression full of realization. "Joshua has gone to find Abra, hasn't he?"

"If God allows, he'll bring her home."

―――――――

Joshua found his way to Harold Cushing's house on Mulholland Drive and arrived a few minutes early. The mansion sat perched on thick concrete pylons suspended over the hillside with panoramic views of the San Fernando Valley. If the day had been clear, Joshua knew he would have been able to see all the way to the Pacific coast.

A maid in uniform ushered him into the living room while she went to tell Mr. Cushing he'd arrived. He used the time to make note of furnishings, mementos, style, and color, as well as the spectacular view. He had a feel for Harold Cushing long before the man finally entered the room, and it didn't agree with Dave's evaluation.

"Freeman?" Cushing's voice was low and deep, like a radio announcer's. He did not apologize for the wait. Had he hoped Joshua would grow impatient and walk out the door? He made a brief self-introduction, shook Joshua's hand, and said, "This way," before leading Joshua down a wide hall, talking as he walked, listing what he wanted: lateral files, a wall of bookcases, a desk with a credenza, storage and display cabinets. "I want organization and easy access." His tone was clipped, no time to waste.

Joshua glanced left and right, taking in as much as he could. He'd admired the oil paintings of windjammers, brigs, and schooners in the living room. He'd noticed *Captain Caution* by Kenneth Roberts, open facedown, on a side table. "Do you sail, Mr. Cushing?"

He gave a short laugh. "Used to dream about it. Never had time. Had I been born a few centuries ago, maybe. We live in an age of airplanes."

For some. Most people rode the bus.

Cushing opened a door at the west end of the house. "This is it. Take a look around. I'll give you until the end of the week to come up with plans. I have another contractor in mind, but Dave thinks you might be the right man for the job." He didn't bother to hide his opinion. "You're going to have to convince me."

Joshua liked his frankness. "I appreciate the opportunity."

Cushing stepped out into the hall again. "Take whatever time you need. Maria will show you out. Friday morning, ten o'clock." He left.

Joshua looked around, took measurements, and smiled. He stopped at an art store on the way back to Dave and Kathy's. He had to ring the doorbell.

Kathy answered, wearing a sarong over her bathing suit. "I forgot to give you a key, didn't I?" She closed the door behind him. "David just got home. Put on a suit and join us at the pool."

Joshua came out with a beach towel over his shoulder. "How was the meeting?"

"Went better than I expected." Dave sat on a chaise lounge, a drink in his hand. "How'd it go with Kathy's father?"

"I'll know a few minutes after ten on Friday." Joshua tossed the towel on a vacant chaise lounge and dove into the pool. The cool water gave a refreshing shock after the long, hot drive back. DJ wanted to play ball. Joshua made it a threesome with Cassie. He taught them how to play Marco Polo and was "it" for the first round. Once they understood the game, Joshua returned to the chaise lounge and the lemonade Kathy had set out for him. He drank half of it while rubbing his chest dry. "Wow, does that taste good."

Dave launched into business politics, deals, and personalities. DJ kept peering up at him from the pool, wanting Daddy to come play. Preoccupied, Dave barely noticed him. Joshua finished the lemonade and got up. "How about a game of keep-away? You team up with DJ. Cassie! You're on my team." He didn't listen to hear Dave's excuses, just tossed a sneering laugh over his shoulder. "Chicken!" He dove into the pool, knowing Dave wouldn't let that insult pass. It had worked a hundred times when they were boys.

It took less than ten seconds for Dave to join them. He and DJ won the first match; Joshua and Cassie, the second. Joshua suggested a change of partners. The children were all smiles and whoops of delight. Kathy sat up on her chaise lounge and watched for a while, and then went into the house to fix dinner.

They ate outside again. Dave looked tired; Kathy, relaxed, happy. The children ate quickly and wanted to swim some more.

"How did you two meet?" Joshua asked.

"In college," Kathy answered, casting Dave a smiling look. "I was on the cheerleading squad. We were practicing a pyramid formation and I lost my footing and came crashing down, taking half the team with me. Knocked the wind right out of me. Dave got to me first. He knelt down and asked if I was okay. I'd had a crush on him all season, and there I lay, gasping like a fish out of water, unable to breathe, let alone say anything witty." She laughed. "And that's the moment he decided to ask me for a date."

"The words just sort of jumped out. I felt like a total idiot."

"I managed to gasp a yes before he changed his mind." She smiled at Dave. "I'd say two broken ribs were worth it."

"The ambulance arrived. I figured she'd been in shock and would forget all about it."

"When he didn't call me, I hobbled back to the next practice and sat on the bench. I stared at him all through his workout on the field."

"Coach wanted to know why I couldn't throw a decent pass. He told me to take a walk."

Kathy smiled smugly. "So he came over and sat on the bench with me. He took off his helmet and just sat there, turning it in his hands. I had to ask him if it was his habit to ask a girl out and then leave her hanging."

Dave grinned. "She can be forward."

Kathy was unrepentant. "I was tired of waiting, and I knew what I wanted."

"A football player." He said it with disdain.

That made her angry. "You are such an idiot sometimes."

"I'm no Rhodes Scholar."

"I didn't want a Rhodes Scholar. I wanted one particular guy who happened to play football." When he didn't say anything, she shoved her patio chair back and got up. Grabbing his empty dinner plate, she stacked it on her own and reached for Joshua's. "You know something, David? Maybe you do have more brawn than brains!" She headed for the house.

Dave watched her go. Joshua waited a few seconds. "Are you just going to sit there?"

Dave did exactly that. A few minutes later, he suggested they lob a football back and forth on the lawn. Joshua noticed DJ watching, and made a gentle toss. DJ fumbled it, but managed to hold on. Dave looked surprised and told DJ to throw it to him. The ball came end over end rather than in a spiral. Joshua held up his hands. "Play with DJ. Looks to me like you have another football player in the family."

Joshua took a walk that evening. He prayed as he followed the uphill climb of Amanda Drive and around Laurelcrest and back. The porch light was on and he let himself in with the key Kathy had given him.

When he came upstairs the next morning, he was surprised to

find Kathy already in the kitchen, dressed for the day and making coffee. "Wow. You're up early."

"I'm always up before five," she told him. "It's the only time David and I have alone."

Things must not have gone well this morning. "Mind if I ask you a few questions about your father?"

"What do you want to know?" She poured him a cup of coffee.

"You said he's been going through a hard time. Do you mind talking about that?"

They sat at the kitchen nook table overlooking the backyard while she told him about her mother's diagnosis of pancreatic cancer. It had moved like a wildfire through her body, leaving both Kathy and her father in shock when she died. "I'm coming to terms with it, but he just works harder and harder. I wouldn't be surprised to get a call that my father's died of a heart attack. He's loved my mother all his life. They grew up together. They were high school sweethearts."

Sounded like Dad and Mom. Joshua remembered the long months when neither he nor Dad slept. Losing Mom had been bad enough, but Dad had made the most difficult decision of his life at the same time. He'd let go of Abra. Joshua wondered what would have happened if he hadn't.

"Mom helped put Dad through college." Kathy went on, her hands wrapped around her coffee mug. "They lost their first child, my older brother. He died of a heart defect at eighteen months. I never met him. I came seven years later. Dad was in real estate. We lived in the Valley until I was in my teens. When they bought the place up on Mulholland, I was already in a private school, so it didn't matter. Mom wanted it, so he bought it."

"It's a big house."

"Small when compared to most up there, but Mom had fun turning it into Daddy's castle on the hill. I started college and they went to Europe. She came back with all kinds of ideas. You saw the results.

She finished every room in the house but the one on the west corner. That was going to be Daddy's office. It's a good sign he's finally doing something with it. Mom would have had something creative in mind, something that would suit him. She knew him so well." She looked wistful. "Now, he's all about time management. I'm sure he said he wants something 'simple and functional.'"

"You said real estate. How did he get into the movie business?"

"Mom and Dad loved movies. We went all the time. Working for a studio, he knows a lot of people and sometimes invests in productions. He told me the other day he's putting some money into a production based on a Tennessee Williams play, if they can get all the details pulled together and the star they want." Dave came into the kitchen. She rose and poured coffee for him.

Joshua spent the day doing sketches. When he had what he wanted, he spent the next two days on scale drawings. He also started looking through the newspapers for an apartment to rent. Dave noticed him circling addresses. "Don't get in a rush. Get to know the area before you start looking at apartments. Location is everything."

Friday morning, he put his preliminary drawings into a folder and drove up Mulholland Drive. He arrived early, but another truck was already parked in front of the house—a white Ford fully equipped and with a logo reading *Matthias Construction*. Maria led Joshua down the hall. Cushing seemed surprised to see him. "I didn't think you'd be back. You didn't have much to say for yourself when we met."

"I was listening." He looked at his watch. "It's 9:50." He extended a hand to Cushing's guest, who grinned at him and introduced himself as Charlie Jessup. He had a firm handshake and looked Joshua in the eye with an air of warmth and confidence. Joshua stepped back. "I'll wait my turn."

Cushing looked embarrassed and annoyed because of it. "Charlie's done work for me before."

Jessup laughed. "I'm not afraid of competition, Harold. Let the man show his plan before you throw him out."

Joshua gestured toward Jessup's sketches. "Mind if I take a look?" Jessup handed them over. The drawings were excellent; the plan, functional and organized, exactly what Harold Cushing had said he wanted. "Nice work."

"Thanks. Now, let's see yours."

"Fine!" Looking annoyed, Cushing intercepted the file before Jessup got his hand on it. "I'll take a look." His tone implied that whatever Joshua might have come up with would be inferior to Charlie Jessup's proposal. His expression changed when he saw the drawings. "You didn't listen." He sounded uncertain.

"Change the windows, cut out those shrubs, put in lawn, and you'll have the view to go with the design."

Charlie Jessup stepped alongside Cushing, tilting his head to get a look. "A sea captain's cabin!" He laughed. "Wow! Let me see these!"

Cushing thrust the drawings into Jessup's hands and glared at Joshua. "Not what I asked for."

"No. I acted on a hunch."

Cushing might not be interested, but Jessup took the file and looked over the drawings. "Can you do this?"

"If I had six months."

Jessup cocked his head and studied Harold Cushing. "You're kind of quiet."

Cushing looked unsettled. "That's the sort of madness Cassandra wanted."

"You bragged about her ideas."

Cushing ignored him and glared at Joshua. "I gave you clear instructions. Why did you come up with that design? Did Kathy put you up to it?"

Kathy? "No. Actually, your ship paintings and the Kenneth

Roberts book in the living room gave me the idea. And the room faces the ocean and the setting sun."

Charlie Jessup looked enamored. "What's your estimate?" He seemed interested even if Harold Cushing wasn't.

"I don't have one."

"Well, there you go." Cushing gave a dismissive laugh.

Jessup handed the drawings back to Joshua. "It's a better idea than mine." When Cushing glanced at him, he grinned. "And you like it."

"I'm not made out of money."

"What're you saving it for? The man's an artist, and he needs a job." He looked at Joshua. "Make a guess."

"Depends on materials, deadline, cost of other men coming in to do electrical work." He named a sum. "Could be less."

"Or more," Cushing said.

"I could run some numbers." Joshua shrugged and looked at Charlie Jessup. "A contractor would know better than a carpenter about all those kinds of details."

Jessup grinned broadly. "Yes, he would."

Cushing looked between them. "And if you worked together, how soon could you finish?"

Joshua was more surprised than he expected to get the job. With two men on board, he and Charlie figured it would take eight to ten weeks. It seemed like a major miracle that a man who didn't know Joshua from Adam had just made him a partner on a significant job.

Jessup offered to draw up a contract for Joshua, but Joshua followed his instincts. "No need. I trust you."

Cushing watched, scowling. "You're not a businessman, are you? Never do anything without getting it on paper first."

"A man is only as good as his word, Mr. Cushing."

"Not in my book."

"In mine, a man's yes means yes, and no means no." Joshua had noticed the simple gold cross Jessup wore around his neck. He wondered about the name Matthias. A relative? Or did it have to do with the lottery after Jesus' crucifixion and resurrection? They'd needed a man to replace Judas as the twelfth disciple. God chose Matthias.

———————

Abra stood in front of her full-length mirror, staring at herself, wondering. The first night with Dylan, and the long week on the road with him, she hadn't had the presence of mind to worry about getting pregnant. Lilith, Dylan, and their doctor made sure she had what she needed to protect herself.

Franklin had never left it her sole responsibility. She had thought him considerate, until she broached the subject of children soon after they got married in Las Vegas.

He gave a dark laugh. "Two is more than enough heartache for a lifetime."

He might as well have slammed a door in her face and locked it. "Why? Because you don't see them as often as you'd like?"

"Because my wife uses them as a weapon against me."

His wife? "I'm your wife now, Franklin. We'll be a family."

He drew back from her, frowning. "Why are you talking about children now?" He had been in the mood to make love. Clearly, the subject upset him enough to put that idea out of his head.

"I was just wondering. That's all." She propped her head up on her hand and studied him. "We're married, Franklin. It's something we should talk about. Isn't it?"

His eyes darkened. "You're barely twenty-one, Lena. You have years ahead of you." He pushed the sheet off and got up.

She felt the cold air. "Don't you mean *we* have years ahead of *us?*"

"Same thing."

She crossed her arms behind her head. "I'd like to have children someday."

He gave her a cold smile. "It's not something to joke about, Lena."

Lena. The name grated on her nerves. She pushed herself up. "I'm not joking."

"Then we'll talk about it. Someday. Not now. Not this week or next month or this year."

She stood and grabbed her robe. "That sounds more like *never.*"

"I didn't say *never.*" He sounded irritated. "But let's give ourselves a year, at least, preferably two, to enjoy each other. I want you all to myself for a while." He went into the bathroom. She heard the shower go on.

Abra gave him six more months before she decided it would never happen unless Lena Scott made him lose his head at the right time of the month. She knew when he was most susceptible to Lena's charms and poured a little extra Scotch into his drinks on those afternoons.

He'd change his mind once she was pregnant. He loved his children. She could tell by the tone of his voice when he tried to talk with them, the hurt when they cut the conversations short. This child would love him back. They could be a family. They could have a real home, instead of this airless apartment.

She ran her hand lovingly over her abdomen. She was two months along. She'd hoped, but still been surprised at how quickly she got pregnant. She'd gained two pounds in the last month. Her breasts felt tender. She was so tired sometimes, she just wanted to sleep. Weren't those positive signs?

Everything would change now. Franklin would be happy, too, seeing how happy she was. She only had to tell him and have him make a doctor's appointment to verify what she already knew. Her heart jumped when the apartment door opened and she heard Franklin's voice. "Lena! Where are you?"

Abra threw on her robe and stepped into her slippers. The last two months had been hectic. They'd been to dinners at LaRue on Sunset Strip and Ciro's, met celebrities at Cafe Trocadero, attended premieres at Grauman's Chinese, the Egyptian, and the Carthay Circle, giant klieg lights crisscrossing the sky, women in shimmering satin and sequins, men in tuxedos, shiny black limos, red carpets, and lobby posters. She met Gail Russell and Guy Madison, exchanged pleasantries with Lana Turner and Ronald Reagan. They'd been out late last night, at another Hollywood party where he'd shown her off and introduced her to another producer. Abra hoped the time would come when she didn't have to listen to Franklin sing her praises to men who looked her over like a prime piece of meat.

"I've got good news." He came into the bedroom. "You got the part!" He lifted her and spun her around. "I feel like celebrating." He set her down and started to open her robe.

A quick stab of fear gripped her. She turned and stepped away. "Which part?"

"*The* part." He came up behind her, his arms at her waist. Her heart knocked like a jackhammer. "The one we've been talking about for weeks. You finish this movie, and we're all set." He kept talking as he slipped his hands inside her robe. This was their big chance. A dramatic role this time, a movie based on a Tennessee Williams play.

Her heart fell. Hadn't Franklin listened to her at all? She'd told him she couldn't do it. She didn't have the acting chops. He said she had him, and that's all she needed. He'd teach her how to play the part. She knew what that meant. He'd hammer and chisel her into the role.

Franklin let go of her and stripped off his suit jacket. He yanked his tie loose. Her fear grew as he unbuttoned his shirt. "Why are you just standing there?" He laughed. "You should be dancing!"

"I can't do it, Franklin."

"You *will* do it!" He caught her by the shoulders, his eyes glowing. "And you'll do it better than anyone else!" He cupped her face. "You don't know what you're capable of, Lena. Not yet. The whole world is going to know you before I'm done." He kissed her forehead, her nose, her mouth. "The money is all lined up, the production team ready; it's all a go! This will establish you on the A-list. All they need is your pretty signature on the contract."

His hands traveled down her back. "This is what I've been waiting for. It's all coming together faster than I dreamed. It's as though the hand of Providence is on our side."

She shuddered, doubting God had anything to do with this. Franklin frowned. "What's wrong?" He looked down over her body. "You've put on a few pounds."

Abra felt a shock of cold go through her body. "Franklin . . ." She had to tell him.

"Forget about it. You can diet tomorrow." Franklin gave her no time to draw her breath. "I love you so much." He covered her mouth again. Raking his fingers into her hair, he drew back to look at her. "I can't get enough of you." He wasn't seeing Abra at all, but Lena Scott, his own creation.

She wanted to weep. He didn't even know Abra existed anymore.

Like Galatea, she remained silent as Pygmalion worshiped her.

Abra told Franklin the news the morning after the postproduction party for *Lorelei*. His face went white. He held his glass of Scotch half-suspended between the counter and his mouth as he turned to stare at her as though he didn't understand. "What do you mean, pregnant?"

He said the word as though she'd just told him she had terminal cancer. Abra swallowed hard, heart pounding. She hadn't expected him to look so devastated. "I'll need to see a doctor to know for sure, but it's been over two months since . . ."

The news was sinking in fast, like a toxic chemical into a white sandy beach. "This isn't happening."

"It is happening."

"No. It can't be. We've been too careful." He downed his Scotch in one gulp.

"Not always." She saw the narrowing coldness in his eyes, and rushed on. "Sometimes you were in too much of a hurry." She watched the memory sink in.

Franklin swore and threw his glass against the wall. "Not after all my work!"

She flinched, but her own anger rose. All *his* work? How nice that he'd forgotten the pounding and hammering and chiseling she'd taken: the blistered and bloodied feet while learning to dance, the exhausting hours of running her lines with him, feeling exposed as a fraud every time the cameras rolled.

Three years of her life had gone into becoming the woman of his dreams. Three years of doing hard time in this godforsaken prison. Every minute of every hour planned by her master.

His eyes darkened. "You planned this, didn't you, Abra?"

It was the first time she'd heard her name on his lips since the morning after he brought her to this apartment. It felt like a punch in the gut. His tone was glacial with suspicion, accusation. She knew exactly what he was thinking. Lena would never betray him. Abra had.

"I've done everything you asked since the night you brought me here, Franklin. I've worked hard to be what you want. I handed my life over to you." Tears blurred her vision. "If you love me so much, why do you see this as a problem?"

He studied her face, his expression shuttered. "You should've told me sooner."

"I wanted to wait until I was sure." She stepped forward, a hand out. "I—"

"Be quiet and let me think." He stood abruptly and stepped away.

"What do you have to think about?" It was a done deal. There was no turning back. Or so she thought, until she saw the look in his eyes.

"You still have a movie to make. You can't have a baby."

She blinked. "I'm going to have a baby."

"No, you're not. You're under contract."

Whose contract did he mean?

He paced, one hand at the back of his neck. "It's not the first time this has happened. I'll make a few calls. Find a good doctor."

"We have a doctor."

"Not the kind we need."

She felt a chill at the way he said it. What was going through his mind? "The schedule can be altered."

"And cost the studio tens of thousands of dollars? Have you look like a prima donna? The other deal I'm working on would go right down the drain."

"It wouldn't be that big a change. They could shoot all my scenes in a few weeks, and then I could take whatever time off I need to have the baby."

"You're not having a baby, Lena."

Why wouldn't he listen to reason? "You can't undo what's been done. It's our baby, Franklin." Her stomach quivered. "Yours and mine."

He erupted, face reddening as he shouted at her. "I told you I didn't want more children! I told you how—"

"*I'm* your wife now. It won't be that way!"

He wasn't listening. He continued to pace, muttering under his breath. "Why do women always betray the ones who love them?"

The trembling started again, deep inside. "I haven't betrayed you, Franklin. You said we'd talk about having children."

"You talked." He glared at her. "I said we'd *wait!*" He came at her, teeth bared, eyes wild. "You're not ruining everything I've worked so hard to accomplish."

She backed away from him and knocked over a stool. He stopped. He clenched and unclenched his fists as he went to the windows. He looked down Hollywood Boulevard. "If not for me, you'd be out there working the street like a hundred other girls. And you know it! You owe me!"

She pulled on Lena, grasping the role tightly as she went to him. She spread her hands on his back, rubbing gently, hoping to soothe him. "Everything will be fine. You'll see. There will just be three of us, instead of two."

He stepped away from her and went back to the bar, pouring himself another Scotch. "Do you want to end up like Pamela Hudson? Three movies, a promising career, then step down off the pedestal to get married and have a baby. Who remembers her now? You're on your way up, Lena. We have to keep the momentum going. Audiences are fickle! A year off and you'll be forgotten."

Her resolve slipped a notch. "I don't care." She turned away, staring out the windows, seeing nothing.

Franklin came to her. He turned her to face him. He touched her brow with gentle fingers. "I do care, Lena. I care enough for both of us. I need to make a few calls. Sort things out." He tipped her chin, but didn't kiss her. "You look tired. Why don't you go to bed?"

She awakened some time later and heard Franklin talking in the office. She got up and went down the hall. He held the receiver to his ear while he bent and wrote notes on a pad. He said a brief thanks and hung up.

Good. Franklin must have called the director. The sooner he knew the situation, the sooner he could make up a new schedule, rearrange scenes to shoot. "Is everything all right?"

"It's all taken care of. You don't have to worry about a thing. You're doing your most important scene on Thursday. We'll see the doctor on Friday."

Relieved, Abra came into his office and wrapped her arms around his waist, hugging herself against him. "Thank you." Her voice came out choked and hoarse with relief. "I was so scared, Franklin. Everything is going to be so much better now. I just know it is."

He rubbed her back. "Everything will be fine. Trust me." His thumb stroked her temple. "You won't have to be back on set until Tuesday next week."

On the way to the set the next morning, Franklin told her not to mention the pregnancy, not to anyone. She didn't understand why not. He'd told the director. Why should they keep it secret? Franklin stared at the road ahead. "No director wants needless distractions on the set. Keep this quiet." He gave her a hard look. "Keep your focus."

The makeup artist dabbed foundation. "You're looking much better today, Lena."

"I'm feeling better, too." She wanted to blurt out the news, but there were always spies who wanted to profit on tidbits of information. One phone call, and the press would be at the door wanting a story on Lena Scott's pregnancy. The production would be disrupted.

Franklin waited outside the door. He seemed even more protective than usual. "Do the scene the way we did it this morning, and you'll be great." Tense, she stood on her mark, the lines racing through her head. Every scene was one less she would have to do, one closer to the end of Lena Scott's last movie.

The next few days went quickly. Franklin watched the dailies with the director. She hated watching herself on-screen and spent the time resting in her dressing room. Friday morning, Franklin was edgy and preoccupied. He drove in silence, his hands tight on the wheel. Sweat beaded his brow. She slept. She awakened when he turned off the highway. How long had they been driving?

"We're almost there." He reached over and ran his knuckles along the curve of her cheek. "They said it wouldn't be too bad. You'll feel cramping for a couple of hours. Then it will all be over."

It will all be over? She froze, panic bubbling up inside her. "What are you talking about?"

"The abortion."

When he said he'd taken care of everything, she thought he meant the difficult conversation with the director, not killing their child.

"No." Her voice quavered. "It's wrong."

"Who's to say what's right and wrong? Right now, this is right for you. It's the best we can do under the circumstances."

"I don't want an abortion!"

"Do you think I don't know why you planned this? I know I've pushed you hard, Lena. Maybe too hard. We'll take more time off between movies after this is over."

"It's against the law!"

"It's done all the time!" He let out a sharp breath. "I won't tell you how much this little mistake is costing me." He looked angry now, determined. "I didn't want just anyone doing it. I wanted the best."

"The best?"

"A doctor, not a backroom butcher."

Abra started to cry. "I won't do it! I won't!"

"I've been thinking. Once your career is established, then you can take time off to have a baby. We could hire a nanny. You'd have to work with a trainer for a few months to get back in shape, but it can be done."

"Aren't you listening to me?"

"You listen!" His fingers turned white as he tightened his grip on the wheel. Did he wish it was her neck? "You're nowhere near ready to be a mother. You don't know the first thing about children." He turned onto a country road toward the hills. He glanced at a sheet of notes and turned down a long driveway.

He parked in front of a small house. He shoved his door open quickly and came around to the passenger side. Seeing no escape, Abra stopped resisting. Franklin didn't let go of her arm. "I'll stay with you every minute. I promise."

A woman answered the door. Abra didn't look up. Franklin said something about the lupines being particularly beautiful this year, and they were invited in.

"I have to be careful, you know." The woman sounded annoyed, not apologetic. "The Catholics would love to see me put in jail."

"We're not Catholic."

"Do you have the money?"

Franklin pulled out his wallet and extracted two crisp hundred-dollar bills.

The woman took the cash and folded it into her pocket, then stepped back. "I have everything ready. This way."

Franklin took Abra by the arm again. "You're going to be fine. I promise." Abra kept her head down as they followed the woman into the house, down a hall, and into a back room with white walls, a table with stirrups, and drawn shades.

"This isn't what I was expecting." Franklin sounded worried.

"I have everything I need."

"Is there going to be a lot of pain?"

"Not as much as childbirth, and it'll be over soon. Have her take off everything below the waist and then get her up on the table."

Abra felt frozen in fear as Franklin undressed her. He kept talking, his voice tense. "You're going to be fine. It'll all be over in a few minutes. Then we'll forget this ever happened." He scooped her up in his arms and placed her gently on the table. He helped lift her feet into the stirrups. Her legs shook. "Easy." He leaned down, resting his forehead on the inner curve of her shoulder. "I'm sorry," he whispered. "I wish there was an easier way."

Clenching her teeth, she whimpered.

Franklin stroked her forehead with icy fingers. "It'll be over soon." It was.

The woman straightened and stripped off rubber gloves. She washed her hands in the basin. "It should be all over by tomorrow morning."

Franklin straightened, his face going white. "What do you mean, *tomorrow*? You said it would be over soon."

"My part is. The saline solution takes time to work on the fetus." The woman opened the door.

"Where are you going?" Franklin sounded alarmed. He went after her.

"Franklin!" Abra tried to grasp hold of his arm. He said he wouldn't leave her. Abra could hear them arguing. He cursed loudly. A door opened and closed. Abra managed to sit up and get off the table. Her body shook so violently she had trouble putting her clothes on.

Franklin came back into the room, face livid, until he saw her. He slipped his arm quickly around her waist, supporting her on the way to the car. "We can't stay here. We'll check into a motel, down by the beach. Everything is going to be all right. It'll be okay."

All through the night, Franklin sat beside her and held her hand. When the pain grew and grew, he put his hand over her mouth. "Shhh. Don't scream. Please, Lena. Someone will hear and call the police." He left her long enough to roll a washcloth so she had something to bite down on other than his hand. "I'm sorry, Lena." He cried. "I'm so sorry. I love you, Lena. I love you so much. I'll make it right again. I swear."

"How are you going to do that, Franklin?" Keening, Abra clenched the bedcovers, twisting them as the pain became unrelenting, while he stood helpless, watching.

It was all over before the sun came up. Franklin wrapped everything in a towel and went out to the beach. It was a long time before he came back, his face ashen, his fingernails full of sand.

He bundled Abra in one of the motel blankets and carried her out to the car before checking out. When he reached for her hand, she jerked away, staring out the window, seeing nothing.

Neither spoke a word on the long drive back to Los Angeles.

CHAPTER 14

"What a fool I was," said he, "not to tear my heart out on the day
when I resolved to avenge myself!"

ALEXANDRE DUMAS

JOSHUA CLOSED THE PHONE BOOTH DOOR and broke a roll of quarters open on the counter. He dialed Dad's number. Between work, spending time with Dave's family, and taking his evening prayer walks, he hadn't had time to write home. Dad would want to hear how things were going. Leaning against the glass wall, Joshua looked out at Hollywood Boulevard while he waited for his father to answer.

He watched people walk by, some looking upbeat and successful, others hungry-eyed, a few downtrodden. An attractive girl in a short skirt and fitted top stood across the street, a large purse slung over her shoulder. She flirted with men as they passed by. Joshua thought of Abra, thankful she had had a measure of success and wasn't on the streets trying to make a living.

Dad's voice came on the line.

"Hey, Dad. How're things up in Haven?"

"It's been a busy week. Dinner with Gil and Sadie. Mitzi's in the hospital and has the nurses in hysterics."

"Anything serious?"

"Trouble with her lungs. She promised Hodge she'd give up smoking. He thought she already had."

"How's Susan?" He meant it to be a leading question.

"Susan and Bessie are just fine," Dad responded in a deadpan tone, and then chuckled. "They both said to say hello. How's the project going?"

"We'll be done by the end of the week. Harold has Kathy helping him put together an open house to celebrate the completion. Charlie wants me to join his company. He's got a couple of projects coming up. He wants me to head up a renovation project in Pacific Palisades."

"You like working with him, don't you?"

"Yeah. I do." The operator prompted him to put in more coins. "Hold on. . . . Yeah, Charlie's honest, works as hard as anyone he hires, wants everything as perfect as we can make it. He's a good man—and a brother. We've had some deep conversations." He hesitated, waiting for a comment from Dad. Silence. "You still there?"

"I'm listening. Have you made a decision?"

"I'm not sure I want to stay another six months, and that's what it'll take to complete the project he wants me on." He watched the girl across the street negotiating with a businessman. "I had lunch today with Dave at Chuck's Hofbrau on Hollywood Boulevard. Good food, but it lacks Bessie's homey touch."

"What's on your mind, Son?"

"There are a lot of beautiful young women down here, Dad."

"All with big dreams of becoming movie stars, I imagine." His father sounded weary.

They were both silent. The man in the suit hailed a taxi. The girl got in with him.

"I'm still looking for her. I called the studio connected with her last picture and got nowhere. I went by there, but they wouldn't give me the time of day, let alone tell me how to get in touch with her. A hundred other guys must say they knew her when."

"Have you talked to Dave about it?"

"No. Every time I'm ready to, something else comes up. Dave has a lot on his mind. I've written to the film companies that produced the films she was in. I hoped at least one would forward the letter. Then she'd know how to get in touch with me. It's been a couple of months and no response."

"She may get a lot of fan mail."

"And she may not be the one reading what she gets. I keep hoping whoever does open one of those letters will pass it along to her. Charlie said the quickest way to track down an actress is through her agent, but the studios weren't forthcoming with that information." He gave a bleak laugh. "I must've sounded like a crazy fan."

"So, what do you plan to do?"

"I don't know, Dad. I'm still praying about it."

Joshua looked into the faces of the young women passing by, knowing Abra wouldn't be strolling casually down a street where she might be recognized. She'd only had a few roles, but she'd managed to make Lena Scott a rising star. Maybe this was the life she wanted. Maybe Lena Scott didn't want to be reminded of Haven and the people who loved Abra Matthews.

Maybe it was time to stop looking.

"I think you know what God wants, Son."

The answer God had given Joshua wasn't the one he wanted to hear.

Let go.

———

The bridge to Haven stood before Abra. She walked onto it and stopped a few feet in. Leaning over the railing, she looked down into the darkness. Someone called out to her from the other side. "Come across. Now. While you can."

Was it Joshua? She took a few steps toward him and stopped, the sound of the rapids rising. A mist came up from beneath her, surrounding her in fog so dense she couldn't see the end of the bridge.

She called out, "Are you still there?" Her voice came back, an echo.

"I'm here." Not Joshua, but Pastor Zeke's voice.

She stepped back, not wanting to face him, and heard footsteps coming toward her. Her heart slowed its frantic beat when she heard a man singing, but then it quickened in fear when the sound changed from a sweet melody to discordant mockery.

Dylan came out of the fog. She felt paralyzed as he walked slowly toward her. Her heart beat faster the closer he came, until he stopped right in front of her. His dark eyes glittered hot as he smiled his bright-white smile. "Where are you going to run now, little girl?"

Abra awakened abruptly, heart pounding, body drenched in perspiration. She sat up in bed, trembling. It took a few moments for her body to relax and her heart rate and breathing to slow.

The apartment was so quiet. Had Franklin finally left her alone? He hadn't gone out in days, staying close, watching her like a hawk. What did he think she'd do? Commit suicide? Not that she hadn't thought about it. But she was too much a coward to execute herself. Better this prison with Franklin holding the keys. Better this hell than the one in the next world where she'd burn for all eternity.

She wasn't making it easy for him. She wanted Franklin to suffer, too. She wanted him to know what his dream had cost her.

Forgive. The word stroked her mind like an unwelcome brush of gentle, healing fingers on her brow. She raked her fingers into her hair, holding her head, wanting to press it out. Forgive? Neither of them deserved it.

Maybe she could have forgiven Franklin if he had called her Abra instead of Lena when he cried and begged for forgiveness. When they'd made it home from the horror, he'd called one of the most expensive restaurants in Hollywood and ordered a meal delivered, along with champagne, no expenses spared. He'd popped the cork and said they'd start fresh. As if she'd ever forget.

She'd been too sick to eat or drink. While she sat silent, Franklin talked as though she had been a willing participant, as though a small problem had been dealt with and now they could move forward. She wondered if he'd lost his mind somewhere along the drive back.

Abra thrust Lena aside that night and took center stage. "If you think *anything* will *ever* be the same, you're crazy!" He'd stared at her as though she were some alien being who had taken possession of his lover. She went to the pastel bedroom and locked the door.

Over the next few days, Franklin ordered so many flowers, the apartment felt like a funeral home.

Now, famished, Abra pulled on a robe and quietly opened her door. She felt light-headed from not eating for days. She leaned against the wall until the black and yellow spots before her eyes receded. Dread filled her when she saw Franklin sprawled on the couch, pale and unshaven.

Surprised, he pushed himself into a sitting position. His blue eyes lit with hope. "You're up." He looked disheveled, but alert, watchful, cautious. Maybe he was afraid she'd go crazy right along with him. Trying to ignore him, Abra went into the kitchen and opened the refrigerator. Bottles of red and white wine and cartons of take-out food filled the shelves. "Mexican, Chinese, Italian—take your pick." Franklin had followed her. He stood with hands shoved into his pockets, watching her closely, assessing.

She opened a carton of congealed Chinese noodles and lost her appetite. She opened the cabinet under the sink and threw it into the trash.

"You have to eat something, Lena." Franklin looked worse than she felt. "You've lost weight."

"Isn't that what you wanted?" She felt a twinge of guilt, seeing her thrust had struck hard and sunk deep. He had dark patches under his eyes. How long since he'd slept? How much had he been drinking since she locked herself away? She didn't want to care. They both deserved to suffer. She went to the bar and poured herself a shot glass of Scotch.

"Do you remember what happened last time you drank on an empty stomach?" His tone was cool, dry, testing.

"Yes. But what does it matter?" She swallowed the Scotch in one gulp. Grimacing at him, she poured another. "I've always wondered how you can stand to drink this stuff." She downed that as well.

"It relaxes me."

The Scotch pooled like hot lava in her empty stomach. "I don't want to relax. I want to forget." She lifted the bottle to her lips.

Franklin crossed the room in three steps and yanked the bottle from her hand. "Enough!"

Abra flinched. "Are you worried there won't be enough left for you?" She'd go back to her room if he wasn't blocking her way. She pushed trembling fingers through her matted hair. Her head pounded a hard drumbeat. Lack of food? Nightmares repeating, awakening her in a cold sweat?

The piano stood silent in the corner of the room, beckoning. She'd always been able to lose herself in music. She could close her eyes and play and pretend she was back in Mitzi's living room. What would Mitzi think of her now? Abra went to the bank of windows and stared out at the street below. Cars passed by in both directions; people walked along. The world continued to tick.

She felt shattered inside, broken beyond repair.

Franklin came and stood right behind her. She could feel his pain, his yearning. He'd said he was sorry. And she knew he was sincere. He was deeply sorry Lena wasn't acting the way he wanted anymore. She'd understood that night that he'd never wanted Lena

Scott to have a child. It spoiled the image in his mind of his perfect lover.

His hands gripped her waist. "Lena." He sounded so wounded.

Unable to stand his touch, she jerked away and put a few feet between them. They might live together in the same apartment, but a yawning chasm separated them. "Don't say anything, Franklin. Nothing you can say is going to make any difference." It was too late for either of them to be sorry, too late to undo what had been done.

"You just need a little time to forget."

Forget? Her guilt grew heavier every day. She was worse than her mother. Abra covered her face. At least her mother gave her a chance for survival.

"Lena . . ."

Why did I let Franklin walk me in that door? Why didn't I run or fight? I just went like a sheep to the slaughter.

Franklin grasped her wrist and pulled her around. She thought for a moment he meant to pull her into his arms and soothe her. Instead, he held her wrists in an iron grip, staring in disgust at her hands. "You've chewed your nails to the quick."

Of course, Lena would never do such a thing. Abra yanked free. If she'd had fingernails left, she would have clawed his face.

His expression changed. "I'm sorry. I spoke too harshly."

Abra squeezed her eyes shut. She didn't want to see his pain. It had been his decision, hadn't it? So Lena could keep dancing to his tune. *What have I done? Oh, what have I done?* She wrapped her arms around herself, breathing shallowly through the pain. What would Pastor Zeke think? And Joshua? *Oh, Joshua, if you could see me now.* A mocking tune played in her head. She'd burned the bridge to Haven long ago.

What did it matter? Joshua was probably married by now, to some nice girl who'd saved herself for her husband. And Pastor Zeke had a church full of parishioners and most of the town that loved him and called him friend. Neither would miss her. Would they even know

Abra Matthews had become Lena Scott? She couldn't imagine either of them wasting time on the five lousy movies she'd made.

That old life in Haven seemed a halcyon dream now. She'd been such a fool. She'd turned her back on everyone just so she could be with Dylan. She'd awakened from that rosy dream in San Francisco, but still clung to him, hoping. When she moved in with Franklin, she'd signed her life away. She hadn't realized he saw her as clay in his hands. He put her on a pedestal and began to reshape and remold her. He thought he was God.

Her stomach cramped with hunger. She hadn't the willpower to starve herself. She found a box of cereal and week-old yogurt. The food tasted like sawdust mixed with sour cream. She swallowed bitterness and guilt.

Franklin poured himself a drink. Then another. After the third, he stopped looking sorry. "I did what I thought best for you."

"Best? You buried our baby in the sand."

He slammed the bottle on the counter. "It wasn't a baby!"

"Only because you didn't want her." The same way Abra's mother hadn't wanted her.

Exasperated, Franklin came to the table. He yanked her chair around and knelt on one knee in front of her. "It wasn't a *her*. It wasn't a *him*. It was *nothing*."

She leaned forward, her face close to his. "Just like *I'm* nothing! And *you're* nothing! We're *both* less than nothing now, aren't we? And damned besides!" Franklin straightened and stepped away from her, his hand clenching into a fist. "Go ahead. Do what you want to do to me." She lifted her chin, waiting, half-hoping for the blow. "Hit me if you think it'll change the truth. Beat it out of me."

His hand loosened and hung limp at his side. "I know you're punishing me. I know I said there'd be no pain, Lena. I saw how you suffered." His eyes filled with tears. "I didn't know it would be like that." He looked wild with pain. "I swear I didn't know!"

Abra covered her face with her hands. "Just leave me alone, Franklin. Please. Just leave me alone." She gulped down sobs, swallowing the agony until it felt like a hard ball of poison in the pit of her stomach. She heard him leave the room. She thought he'd give her peace, but he came back.

"I have something for you." Franklin shook out two pills from a prescription bottle. He went to the bar to fill a glass of water. He came back and presented the water and pills like an offering. "The doctor said these will make you feel better. It's just a mild barbiturate."

She looked up at Franklin. How far would he go to get Lena back? She didn't trust him or his doctor. "I don't care what it is. I'm not taking it."

His eyes narrowed. "This has got to stop, Lena." It was his agent's voice, the manager trying to grab and control again. "I'm trying to help you."

She knew better. She looked pointedly across the room. "And your concern has nothing to do with the script on the coffee table." Her tone reeked of sarcasm. She went over and picked up *The Gypsy and the General* and flung it at him. "That's what I think of it." Did he really expect her to be interested? She wanted to rip the pages in pieces and throw them in his face. "I've done enough acting for a lifetime, Franklin. I'm done." She held her hand out. "If you want me to take pills, give me the whole bottle."

He sank onto a barstool, staring at her. "You're not the woman I thought you were."

"Surprise, surprise." Maybe he was finally beginning to understand.

"We can't go on like this. You have to put it behind you."

She saw the raw look in his eyes, the confusion. He'd always been the sculptor, the worker in clay, the puppet master, pulling the strings. Now the marble statue had cracked, the clay dried and crumbled. The marionette had come to life and loathed him because he wasn't sorry about what they'd done. He was grieving the loss of his great love, Lena Scott.

"How do I put it behind me, Franklin?" Every decision she'd made in the last five years had brought disaster, each worse than the last. Everything she thought she wanted tasted like ashes in her mouth.

"Don't you understand how much you're loved? Did you even read any of the letters I brought you?"

He'd shoved dozens under her door.

"Why should I read letters from strangers who don't even know Lena Scott? Or that Lena Scott is Abra Matthews! They only love that fake image on a screen. Just like you! Everyone's in love with a figment of your imagination!"

He stood, face livid. "Stop saying that!" He held his head as though in more pain than she.

"It's true." She'd made five movies and played five parts: a one-minute walk away that made men long to see the whole body beneath the white blouse and tight pencil skirt, a passionate wife to a zombie lover, an ingenue in love with her best friend's fiancé, a dancing role that had left her unable to walk for weeks, and a mermaid who ultimately pulled the man she loved over the side and down into the depths.

Franklin had done that to her. Pulled her over and down, down, down into the deep, dark world of make-believe.

A flood tide of sorrow washed over her and she felt herself drowning in it. "I'm sorry, Franklin. I'm sorry. I can't pretend anymore." How much of her life had she spent doing just that? She no longer knew who she was.

Franklin took her by the shoulders, his eyes adoring. "You've never pretended with me. I know you better than you know yourself." His fingers dug into her. "I've poured my heart and soul into you!"

Her body went cold at his touch.

His hands cupped her face, his eyes worshiping. "A thousand men want you, but you gave yourself to me. You love me. I've kept every promise I've ever made to you. Haven't I?"

That was the awful truth. He had.

She had just never stopped to count the cost.

———————

Harold Cushing's open house had been going for an hour when Dave nudged Joshua. "I'd better warn you, Kathy is playing matchmaker again."

It wasn't the first time Kathy had tried to fix him up with a friend. Joshua had hoped she'd understood when he told her he wasn't looking for a girlfriend.

Dave nodded toward Kathy, coming outside with a slender, diminutive, and very attractive brunette. "That's Merit Hayes, one of Kathy's college friends. She's a studio lawyer. Don't let her size fool you. She might look like a minnow, but she's a shark." People mingled, talking and laughing as the catering staff served hors d'oeuvres and replenished drinks. Merit looked like she had come straight from an office in her white silk blouse, black pencil skirt, and shiny black patent-leather pumps. She looked annoyed while Kathy talked and nodded toward Dave and Joshua.

Thankfully, Harold Cushing called Joshua over. Harold introduced him to a middle-aged couple. "Chet works for Walt Disney. He's impressed with what you've done to my office."

"Walt is always looking for men with imagination." Chet went on to boast of how Disneyland was bringing in money faster than a harvester bringing in the sheaves. The mind behind the amusement park wasn't idle, but caught up in ideas of how to expand. Chet laughed. "The irony is Walt got fired once because his boss said he had no imagination. Families are flocking to Disneyland, and it doesn't look like the crowds are going to die down anytime soon."

Someone tapped Joshua on the shoulder, and he turned to find

Kathy standing behind him, Merit Hayes in tow. "Sorry to interrupt, Dad, but I wanted Joshua to meet an old friend of mine. Merit Hayes, this is David's best friend, Joshua Freeman."

Joshua gave the appropriate smile and polite response as he held out his hand. Merit had a small, delicate hand with long, red fingernails, and a grip like a prizefighter. Her eyes turned cool with wry humor. "I should warn you, she's trying to set us up."

Joshua chuckled. "I know."

Merit raised her brows. "Are you a coconspirator?"

"Sorry, but no, not that it isn't a pleasure to meet you, Miss Hayes."

Kathy blushed. "Okay." She raised her hands in defeat. "Okay. I've done my best. Have fun."

Merit winced. "Awkward, I must say."

"Kathy has the best of intentions."

She eyed his can of Coke and took a martini from a passing tray, startling the server, who looked ready to protest. "She's naive." She plucked the olive from the drink and ate it. "If I wanted a man, I'd find him myself."

"Dave said you're a studio lawyer."

"Guilty as charged. He's had to deal with me before." She laughed. "He never gets what he wants." A waiter offered dainty sandwiches. She took two. "I take that back. He did get Kathy." She shrugged and gave him a catlike stare as she ate. He knew she was waiting for him to comment. When he didn't, she nodded toward the house. "I saw Harold's new office. Impressive work."

"I didn't do it by myself."

"You came up with the concept and did half the work—the finish half, I was told. It was all part of Kathy's glowing recommendation. So I have to wonder. Why does a man with your obvious talents now do part-time work on a back studio lot?"

He smiled and sipped his Coke. "Maybe I came down here to be discovered."

"Meaning it's none of my business." She plucked a canapé from another tray. "You managed to get your foot in the door without joining the union. Nice that you have such good connections." She lifted her glass to Dave and Kathy watching them. "Look at them over there, Kathy with such hope, Dave wishing I'd take off on my broom." She laughed, enjoying herself.

She looked at Joshua. "Kathy told me you're a churchgoing man." She sniffed. "And you've got them going, too. She calls you the real deal; did you know that?" She made a wry face. "Odd that I think I like you." She popped the canapé into her mouth and wagged her finger as she chewed and swallowed. "Not that I want to give you the wrong idea. I'm not saying I want to go out with you."

He grinned. "Have I asked?"

She looked surprised. "I should be insulted."

"But you're not."

She leaned closer and whispered. "Maybe we can pretend we're attracted to each other. It might serve to distract my dear friend from further matchmaking attempts on my behalf. She has no idea how hopeless that is." She took his arm and batted her lashes. "I'll be nice. I promise. Let's mingle."

Merit Hayes knew everyone and, like Dave, loved to talk business. People kept coming, and she zeroed in on specific people. Joshua listened, answering questions only when asked. She patted his arm. "I like a man who doesn't talk more than necessary." She steered him toward a couple who had arrived late—an older, portly man with shrewd eyes and a beautiful, much-younger woman who looked vaguely familiar. Merit greeted them both warmly, the two women exchanging air kisses on each cheek before Merit introduced Joshua to Terrence Irving and his wife, Pamela.

Joshua told them it was a pleasure. Pamela kept looking at him, and when he frowned, she sighed. "My star fades already."

Her husband slipped an arm around her waist and drew her a little closer. "You shine with more beauty and light than ever."

Merit made a soft choking sound, and Joshua noticed the laughter in her eyes. He wondered why until she apologized to Pamela and her husband. "You'll have to excuse my friend here. He comes from a small town in northern California that probably doesn't even have a theater. Joshua, this is Pamela Hudson."

Joshua remembered now, though he'd only seen one movie in which she starred. He could probably dredge up the story line, given the opportunity.

"Pamela gave up acting to marry me." Terrence Irving smiled at his lovely wife. "And then she gave me the added blessing of two beautiful daughters."

Merit took the cue and asked about their darling little ones, and if the couple planned to have more. Pamela looked piqued, but Terrence said they both wanted more. Others joined them. Merit slipped her hand through Joshua's arm and drew him away. "Well, that was a complete disaster! Did you see the look on her face?" She looked at him, laughing. "How could anyone not know Pamela Hudson?"

"We don't inhabit the same circles."

"Where are you from? The moon?" She shook her head. "I'm being a witch. I know. The booze is going to my head. I've had a long, hard week."

"Then I suggest we eat." He steered her toward the elaborate buffet.

She took a plate, handed it to him, and moved ahead with one of her own. "Pamela has been in all the Hollywood newspaper columns."

"I get my news from other sources."

"Well then, I'll tell you the story. Pamela came out of nowhere and burst on the scene like a nova." She picked through the salads and vegetable dishes. "She had a high-powered, brilliant agent who literally built her career. Franklin Moss. Have you ever heard of him?

He's a bit too intense at times, but he knows talent when he sees it, even if it appears in a diner on Sunset Boulevard. Or so the story goes. The Hollywood dream." Her tone dripped cynicism. "I was the lawyer on one of Pamela's movies, and I can tell you, that man knew how to fight for his client. Franklin Moss is shrewd, ambitious, and a tough negotiator. Unfortunately, he lost his head and had an affair with Pamela—always a bad idea between business partners. She's one ambitious honey. She left Moss's little love nest and jumped into the sack with Terrence. Lucky for her, Terrence has lawyers who can find a loophole in any contract. Every newspaper across the country ran the scandal. Everyone expected to see her star shining in the next Irving movie. I think Pamela banked on that. Instead, her career came to a screeching halt." She gave a dark laugh. "From the way Terrence talked, he's going to keep Pamela pregnant and tending babies at home."

"Maybe it's what she wants."

Merit looked skeptical. "Even if she did, she's got a hard road ahead. Terrence Irving has always loved beautiful women. The leopard might want an heir, but I doubt he'll change his spots. There you have it. A Hollywood marriage made in heaven."

"Things aren't always what they seem."

"Spoken by a naive romantic. Sorry to disillusion you, but Pamela Hudsons are a dime a dozen in Tinseltown, buddy boy. Franklin Moss lost his head and his job at the agency when he lost her. His wife left him, got full custody of their children, and moved to the big house in Malibu. He disappeared for over a year. I guess he went off to lick his wounds or whatever men do when they come to their senses." She told the chef she wanted a nice thick piece of rare prime rib. "He's back now. Franklin, I mean. And giving me another massive headache." She held out her plate for the slab of juicy meat. "He's created another Venus and wants an Olympian price for her." She took a roll and three pats of butter. "I hate negotiating with the man. Unlike Pamela over there, this girl actually has talent and she follows directions. It's unusual to find a triple threat that doesn't have an ego the size of Texas."

"Triple threat?"

Merit explained that meant the girl could act, dance, and sing. "She stole every scene in her last movie. Some drivel about unrequited love." Her derisive tone changed to briskness. "Giant steps forward from her first speaking role as a zombie. This girl has the potential to become a real star, one who lasts."

Joshua's pulse shot up. "A zombie?"

Merit laughed. "You heard me. You didn't recognize Pamela Hudson, so you've undoubtedly never heard of Lena Scott. But take my word for it. If our production company gets her, you'll see her everywhere."

———

Joshua found a telephone number, but no address for the Franklin Moss Talent Agency in the yellow pages. He tried phoning on his lunch hour. A dispassionate woman answered and said Joshua could leave a message. She hung up before he finished. He called back. The woman sighed. "You have the wrong agency, mister. Franklin Moss isn't handling anyone named Abra Matthews."

Joshua wanted to hit himself in the forehead. "Abra Matthews is Lena Scott, and I'm an old friend."

"O . . . kay. Give me your contact information and I'll pass it along to Mr. Moss. I can't promise he'll call you back."

"Can you give me the office address?"

"Sorry. I don't have that information. Billing does, but they can't talk to you. Anything else?"

Joshua called Kathy and asked for Merit Hayes's phone number. Kathy sounded unduly happy. Merit wasn't. "I thought you and I had an understanding."

"I'm calling for information, not a date. Can you give me Franklin Moss's telephone number and address?"

"Let me guess." She gave a cynical laugh. "You don't know Pamela Hudson, but you'd like to meet Lena Scott." She asked if he had a pencil and paper. "If he won't let studio execs close, I doubt he'll give you the time of day." She gave him the same number listed in the yellow pages. He told her he had that number and had hit a wall. "It's what I've got. No surprise I can get through, but a fan can't."

"What was his wife's name? Didn't you say she was in Malibu?"

"You are a determined man, aren't you? Shirley, I think. Or Cheryl. Maybe Charlene. Something with a *shhhh*."

He found a listing for Cheryl Moss and dialed. A boy answered and said his mom wasn't home. When Joshua asked when she might return, he laughed and said she'd gone to the Valley shopping with his sister and he didn't expect to see them until late. Joshua said he'd call back tomorrow. He'd used up his hour lunch break and went back to work. It was hard to concentrate.

Dave grinned when Joshua came upstairs from showering and changing after work. He handed him a letter marked *RETURN TO SENDER* in big block letters. "I didn't know you were a fan."

The production company address was crossed out and the letter forwarded to Franklin Moss, with a Hollywood Boulevard address also crossed off. The letter had been opened and taped shut again.

Let go, Joshua. She doesn't belong to you.

It was time to listen. Joshua crumpled the letter and dropped it into the wastebasket.

Dave and Kathy were watching him. Kathy was grave. "You look like you just lost your best friend."

"I lost her a long time ago." He told them who Lena Scott was.

Dave gave a soft whistle and said he never would have guessed. Then he told Joshua the last thing he ever wanted to hear. "Rumor is, she's married to her agent."

Joshua released his breath slowly.

Kathy went back to peeling potatoes. "You had a couple of calls today." She nodded toward the end of the counter. "Charlie Jessup wants to talk with you."

Joshua glanced through the messages. Three job offers. He wanted to go home. "Mind if I use the phone?" He called Jack Wooding, who said he had a full crew. He sure wished he'd known sooner Joshua might be coming home. He'd be glad to let him know as soon as he had an opening.

Joshua rubbed the back of his neck and bowed his head. *Lord, are You telling me to stay in Southern California?*

God seemed to be giving him mixed messages.

———

Abra awakened, groggy from drinking too much. Franklin was talking. Was someone in the apartment?

His office door was open. He must be on the phone. She could tell by his tone that he was talking to his son. Something about an Impala and why didn't he ask his mother? She heard him yank open a drawer and peered in. Franklin had the telephone receiver locked between his ear and shoulder as he read the combination and worked the dial on the safe. He cranked the handle and opened the iron door, wheeled his chair back, and tucked the paper into the drawer. Before he wheeled back, she saw money stacked on a shelf inside the safe, and files just below. She withdrew silently.

Everything she needed to leave him was within reach, but she couldn't get to it as long as Franklin stuck so close to home. He was never gone for more than half an hour, and then just to pick up a few groceries and come right back.

The only way to be free from him was to play Lena Scott for one more day.

Abra arose early, showered, and took the time to shampoo and dry her hair. She dressed in fitted black capris and a green sweater that accentuated her eyes. She had lost weight and the clothes were a little loose, but she couldn't worry about that now. She took special care with her makeup. Lena always wore more of it than Abra liked. She brushed her hair and left it loose about her shoulders.

The door to the master bedroom was open. Franklin was still asleep, his bed a shambles, blankets kicked aside, half on the floor, half on the bed. He never slept well after talking to his children or his ex-wife. He stirred.

She hurried quietly to the living room. She had a role to play, and it had better be worthy of an Academy Award. What would Lena do when Franklin came into the room? What would Lena say? She wouldn't confront him for withholding her money. She wouldn't threaten him with divorce or breach of contract. Lena would tantalize him with hope. She would be cunning, wise enough not to rouse his suspicions.

Abra realized she was chewing her nails and stopped herself.

She'd always been able to set her clock by Franklin's routine. He got up at five, used the bathroom, and then did a hundred sit-ups and fifty push-ups. He shaved and took a ten-minute shower. He always set his clothing out the night before—dark suit, white shirt, colorful Italian silk tie . . . the uniform of a successful businessman. He kept his wallet, gold cuff links, and watch in a pewter tray on his dresser. At seven thirty sharp, he came down the hall, set his leather briefcase in the entryway, collected *Daily Variety* and two newspapers from just outside the apartment door, and went into the kitchen to fix himself breakfast: three boiled eggs, two pieces of toast. If his bathroom scale had said anything more than 185, he'd have yogurt and bran. He read fast and scanned everything, his eyes quick to spot any mention of Lena Scott.

Things had changed in the last two weeks.

She heard him in the hall. "Lena?" He must have seen the open door. "Lena!"

"I'm in the living room, Franklin." Grabbing the script for *The Gypsy and the General*, she seated herself on the couch, back against the armrest, legs stretched out. She folded pages back, pretending to read.

He came into the living room disheveled and shaken, a look of panic on his face. He let out a sharp breath and struggled to regain control. "I thought . . ." He shook his head, as though to remove the fear from his troubled mind. "You're feeling better?"

"I feel rested." The lie came easily, without a twinge of guilt. In a few hours, she would be out of this prison and away from him.

"That's good." His pajama bottoms hung on his hips. He'd lost weight, too. "You're reading the script."

She lifted one shoulder. Lena wouldn't sound too eager. "I've read everything else in the apartment. Only thing left to read." Lena would do what? Her mind went blank.

Franklin opened the front door and scooped up the newspapers. He pulled the rubber band from one while looking at her. "What do you think of it?"

It took a second before she realized he was asking her opinion of the script. "So-so."

"So-so?" He looked annoyed. "It's written by one of the best screenwriters in Hollywood. An Oscar winner."

"I didn't say I didn't like it, Franklin. I'm only ten pages into it. I'll let you know what I think of it this evening."

His expression changed. "You're going to love it." The stress of the last weeks showed around his eyes.

"It'll take me all day to read through this and think about the role they want me to play."

He went into the kitchen and put three eggs in a pot and turned on the tap. He took bread and butter from the refrigerator. "I see you've had breakfast."

She had run water into a bowl and left it with a spoon in the sink so he would think she had. "I'll clean up later, Franklin." He liked everything neat and tidy. It had always bothered him whenever she left dishes in the sink. His irritation over a little thing would make him less suspicious about the possible big things she could do to thwart him. She folded back another page of the script, though she hadn't read even a single line of dialogue and never would.

Newspaper pages rustled while eggs bounced in boiling water. The toaster popped. She heard the scrape of knife against toast. She could feel him watching her while he ate. "You want to go out to lunch?"

She looked at him over the back of the couch. "Do you want me to read the script or not?" Lena would ask if he wanted to play house instead. Abra didn't. He surprised her by smiling. She'd only offered a little hope, but he'd grabbed on.

Franklin cleared and washed his dishes. "I'm going to take a shower and get dressed." She pretended to be too absorbed in the script to listen. "I think I'll give Merit Hayes a call. See if I can't set up a lunch for tomorrow. Or is that too soon?"

She sighed and laid the script on her lap. "I suppose, Franklin. Maybe you're right. The sooner I get back to work, the sooner . . ." She couldn't say the rest.

"I love you, you know." Franklin looked at her, but didn't approach. "I have from the first minute I saw you."

Just like Pamela Hudson. He didn't know either one of them. A molten rage welled up between the cracks of her facade. She kept her eyes locked on the script, brushing away angry tears, hoping he'd think them tears of regret for time wasted.

"We've been through a hard time, Lena."

She knew what he'd want Lena to say. "You've been very patient with me, Franklin. I don't know how you've put up with me." She kept her tone soft, apologetic. When she felt in control of her inner turmoil, she lifted her head. He wanted her. If he touched her now, Lena would slip away and Abra would be exposed. She lowered her eyes. "Maybe we can talk tonight. After I finish this." She lifted the script lightly and didn't raise her head again.

She heard him make a telephone call in his office. Setting up an appointment. Good.

Half an hour later, Franklin came back into the living room dressed in a dark suit. He had his briefcase. "Will you be all right if I'm gone for a few hours?"

She gave him a wry smile and spoke in the sultry voice he liked. "I think I can manage."

He smiled back. "Can I bring you anything?"

"We could use something other than leftover takeout."

"We'll go to dinner." He came over and leaned down. She presented her cheek. He ran a finger down her jawline and tipped her chin. His mouth was firm and cool. He looked into her eyes. "I'll take good care of you."

Dylan had said the same thing.

"I'll be back soon." He picked up his briefcase and left the apartment.

Abra hoped she'd never see his face again.

She waited a full minute before darting to the windows. She waited again until she saw him get into the car Howard had brought around. As soon as Franklin drove away, Abra went into his office. Franklin's calendar was spread open on his desk. He had missed an appointment yesterday with Michael Dawson, his ex-wife's lawyer. He'd made a note to meet Merit Hayes at nine thirty this morning. She pulled open the small pen drawer and found the worn slip with the combination. She spun the dial right, left, right, and left again. The safe lock clicked on her first try. Exultant, she cranked the handle and the heavy door swung wide.

Heart pounding, she took visual inventory. She didn't know he had a gun. He'd put it on the top shelf, beside the money. She set the gun on the desk and took out sixteen neatly bundled stacks of hundred-dollar bills, a thousand dollars in each. Sixteen thousand dollars! If he had that much in the apartment, how much had he put in the bank?

How long had it been since she'd had any money of her own? She'd never seen a paycheck. When she asked, Franklin gave her what she needed. As to the rest, he said he'd invested it so she'd get a good return. He always held the purse strings. Seething, she stacked the money on Franklin's desk calendar. She thought about taking it all, but her conscience held her back. Franklin had paid for her beauty treatments, manicures, pedicures, weekly hairstyling appointments, and clothing. He'd paid for the portfolio of professional pictures. He'd picked up all the tabs for taxis and limos and dinners delivered from various fine restaurants. During all the time she'd lived with him, she'd never paid for anything.

How much would she need to start life over?

She put eight thousand dollars back into his safe and kept the rest. It was a community property state, wasn't it? She pulled out the files, scattering them until she found the two copies of the contract Franklin had given her to sign the night he brought her here.

Franklin had kept his promise.

The betraying thought weakened her resolve. She reminded herself he hadn't done it for her. He'd done everything possible to obliterate Abra Matthews's existence so he could create Lena Scott, the woman of his dreams. She tore up her copy of the contract. She ripped Franklin's copy in half. She ripped it again and kept on until postage stamp–size pieces fluttered about the floor. She found the Las Vegas wedding certificate and tore it in half, then rummaged through the safe in search of the ring. When she couldn't find it, she jumped up and ran into the bedroom and found it on the pewter tray where he kept his wallet. She set the ring on top of the pieces of the wedding certificate.

Franklin had a set of Hermès luggage. She grabbed a piece she could easily carry. He could always buy himself another with the money he'd made off of her. She'd take only a few outfits. With eight thousand dollars in her pockets, she could pick out her own clothing. She tossed the suitcase on her bed and pulled open the closet, taking out a few favorite dresses, Hepburn slacks, a couple of blouses, and undergarments. She stuffed the money into a shoulder bag, grabbed the suitcase, and headed down the hall. She was at the front door when the desire for a little revenge gripped her. Dumping the suitcase, she went back into his office and grabbed a notepad.

A small, quiet voice inside her head told her not to do it. Anger spoke louder. Why shouldn't she, after what Franklin had put her through? She yanked open the top drawer and took out one of his fine Montblanc fountain pens.

I hate you! I never loved you. I just pretended. Don't bother looking for Lena Scott. She's dead!

She tore the page off the notepad, slapped it on the desk, and tossed the pen on top of it. Storming back to the entry hall, she grabbed the suitcase and went out the door.

The doorman was surprised to see her coming out of the elevator. "Miss Scott! You're feeling better."

"Better than I have in a long, long time, Howard." Maybe Franklin had told everyone she had pneumonia or a lingering flu or tonsillitis.

He noticed the suitcase in her hand and frowned. "Mr. Moss didn't leave me any word about you taking a trip." He looked undecided. "Do you need a cab?"

"No, thank you." She didn't have a destination yet. She'd take a little walk and then decide.

Howard looked worried now. "Are you sure, Miss Scott?"

When he made no move to open the door, she did. She hadn't been outside for two weeks. Or was it three? She couldn't remember. She filled her lungs with air. It tasted of exhaust. Howard had followed her. "Why don't you come back inside and wait in the lobby, Miss Scott? It'll only take me a minute to get you a cab. You shouldn't just go walking around by yourself."

Howard would have the name of the cab company and driver, and Franklin would be on the telephone faster than Superman could change his clothes. "Thanks, but I need to walk." The sun was shining, but it was autumn cool. A fissure of nervous tension shot through her when the door closed behind her. She glanced back. Howard was already on the telephone. Franklin's answering service always knew how to reach him. Howard would want Mr. Moss to know Lena had just gone out the door carrying a suitcase, and what should he do about it?

She crossed the street without looking. A car honked and screeched to a stop. She blinked in surprise and then looked both ways before continuing to the other side.

"Miss Scott!" Howard had come out of the apartment house. "Mr. Moss wants you to wait for him. He's on his way back." When he started across the street, Abra fled. "Miss Scott! Wait!"

When the suitcase hindered her speed, she dropped it and bolted down Highland, the shoulder bag holding Franklin's money clutched under her arm. She ran around the corner onto Sunset Boulevard, almost colliding with two businessmen deep in conversation on their way to the crosswalk. They both stared after her. Slowing to a fast walk, she wove her way through the pedestrians. A few stopped to stare. When one said her name, she darted between two parked cars, waving at a cab. It pulled up in front of her. She yanked the door open and flung herself into the backseat.

"Go." She gasped for breath. "Go! Go!"

The cabdriver stepped on the gas. He drove two blocks before he glanced in his rearview mirror. "Where do you want to go?"

She had no idea. "Away. I don't care." She turned and looked out the back window. She didn't see Howard. She felt hysterical laughter welling up as she imagined the portly and dignified doorman trying to outrun a cab. She let out a shaky breath, her fingers digging into the edge of the seat.

"Don't know where you're going?"

Abra looked at the cabbie in the rearview mirror. Her whole body was trembling, her skin moist with cold perspiration. She tried to calm herself. Where did she want to go? *Where? Think, Abra! Think!* "Somewhere I can rest."

"Everybody goes to the beach."

"Fine. Take me to the beach."

"Lots of beaches in Southern California. Which one you want?"

She had money to burn. She gave him a radiant Lena smile. "The best."

CHAPTER 15

I can never escape from your Spirit!
I can never get away from your presence!
If I go up to heaven, you are there;
if I go down to the grave, you are there.

PSALM 139:7-8

JOSHUA DROVE FORTY MILES northeast into the Sierra Pelona Valley and arrived in Agua Dulce, where work was scheduled to start on the Soledad Ranch main street. With no job waiting for him at home, he'd decided to take one more temporary job before heading back.

He checked into a motel on the edge of town and ate at the small diner next door, where he saw a Help Wanted sign taped to the front window. The food was good, plentiful, and cheap. More workers arrived and took up more of the small rooms in the single-story, L-shaped motel. Others towed Airstream trailers and set up camp near the construction site.

No one questioned why the production company had decided against renting Gene Autry's Melody Ranch twenty miles closer to Los Angeles in the Santa Clarita Valley. The television hit *Gunsmoke* was in residence there. Besides, some said, their movie didn't call for an entire Western town complete with mercantile store, Victorian mansion, and Spanish adobe hacienda; just a saloon, a church, and a couple of houses, best built in proximity to old-time bandito Tiburcio Vásquez's hideout, Vasquez Rocks. Numerous scenes would be filmed there, including battles between the cowboy hero and sidekicks and rampaging Indians, mostly played by Hispanic extras who knew how to ride a horse.

It was hot and dry. Dust filtered under the door and covered the side tables and quilted bedspread. Stains spotted the rug. The bathroom light fixture flickered, but the Agua Dulce water, true to its name, was clear and sweet.

Joshua settled in and got up early for work. He took an apple, bread and cheese, and a jug of water for lunch. At the end of the day he returned dust-covered, drenched in sweat, and famished like everyone else. Most headed for the bar down the street; Joshua chose the diner next door. He ordered the special—meat loaf and mashed potatoes with string beans and homemade apple pie for dessert.

Clarice Rumsfeld, the proprietress, reminded him of Bessie: well-fed, friendly, and a talker. Never idle, she wiped the yellow Formica counter and polished the chrome edge while he ate. She frequently replenished his tall glass of iced tea.

Other men came in later, hungry after cooling down with ice-cold beer. Clarice picked up the pace, delivering plastic-coated menus to the red-and-white oilcloth-covered tables and calling out orders to her husband, Rudy, back in the inferno of a kitchen. She looked hard-pressed. The Rumsfelds could use another good worker like Susan Wells.

Thinking of Bessie and Susan made Joshua homesick. He'd be glad when this job wrapped up and he'd be free to return to Haven.

It was dark when Abra awakened. She heard strange sounds and felt a moment of panic until she remembered she wasn't in Franklin's apartment anymore, but in a bungalow across the street from the Pacific Ocean.

The cabdriver had delivered her to the Miramar Hotel in Santa Monica, regaling her all the way with tales of how Senator John P. Jones had built the original Santa Monica mansion for his wife Georgina, and how razor blade mogul King Gillette had bought the property from him. For a short time, the building had been used as a boys' military academy, and eventually the estate was sold to Gilbert Stevenson, who had grand plans of turning it into a hotel. Twenty years ago, the mansion had been torn down, leaving only the present six-story brick building and bungalows. Greta Garbo had stayed there. Betty Grable was discovered by an MGM executive while singing in the hotel bar. The Miramar was a favorite getaway for Cary Grant. Abra figured the tourists must love this cabbie. He was full of information and all too eager to share everything he knew.

The cabdriver had recognized her, much to her dismay, as had the hotel clerk. But Abra had asked them not to tell anyone where she was. She paid cash for three nights in a bungalow, enough time to decide where to go and what to do next. She wandered through shops and picked up a wardrobe of casual clothes Franklin would hate. She picked out a one-piece black bathing suit and a green-and-turquoise sarong Dylan would have detested. She bought sandals and sunglasses, a beach towel, tanning lotion, and four candy bars. How long since she had eaten a Mars bar or Snickers? Franklin wouldn't allow her to eat chocolate for fear her flawless skin would break out. She bought a suitcase and shoved all the merchandise inside before returning to the bungalow, which turned out to be a mini paradise. She'd dumped the suitcase and sprawled, exhausted, on the king-size bed.

Relieved to remember she was safe, she dozed again, troubled by dreams of Franklin crying. He accused her of betraying him. An empty bottle of Scotch lay on a red rug.

Abra heard voices and realized it was morning. Frightened, she got up and peered between the curtains. It was only a waiter delivering breakfast to another bungalow. How long since she had eaten? Gathering her courage, she called room service and ordered a pot of coffee, scrambled eggs, bacon, and pancakes with extra syrup. The last time she'd had pancakes, Priscilla had fixed them.

A wave of homesickness swept over her. She thought of Peter in the living room watching the news while Priscilla fixed dinner in the kitchen. She wondered if Penny had ended up going to Mills College. She would have graduated by now if she did. Abra remembered sitting in Pastor Zeke's office. She couldn't remember anything he'd said, but she remembered how he'd looked. Heartsick, worried. About her, she realized now. Was Joshua still in Haven? Was he married, or still living with Pastor Zeke? One of the last times she'd seen him, they'd had a fight in the street outside the Swan Theater. She remembered how she used to sit in Mitzi's kitchen, sipping Ovaltine and waving to Carla Martin, keeping an eye on her mother-in-law from next door.

Abra put her forearm over her eyes and gulped down tears. *I want to go home.* She pushed the pain down again. She didn't have a home. Especially not in Haven.

She got up and opened her new suitcase, laying out her purchases on the bed. She stood back, hands on her hips, satisfied. Lena Scott wouldn't be caught dead in jeans and a T-shirt. She wouldn't wear simple cotton pajamas or underwear.

Someone tapped on the door. Lena would be aghast at being caught in the rumpled clothes she'd slept in. She wouldn't be seen by anyone until she was wearing makeup and her hair was brushed and coiffed. Abra answered the door.

The waiter was friendly and courteous and said, "Miss Scott," as though she could be "Miss Smith."

Abra drank coffee and ate her fill of eggs, bacon, and pancakes. She felt queasy after the heavy meal. Franklin had carefully monitored her diet, pushing vegetables and grains, chicken and fish, purified water and tea, no coffee. When her stomach settled, she put on her new bathing suit and tucked a hundred-dollar bill into the bodice. Surf and sand would make her feel better. Wrapped in the new sarong, she went out to walk on the beach. She shivered in the cold morning air. Rather than go back to the bungalow, she ran on wet sand to warm up, enjoying it far more than the usual five-mile run on a treadmill under the watchful eye of Franklin's hired trainer.

Young men and women came out to enjoy themselves. Abra felt lonely watching them, half-hoping someone would recognize her and want to talk, half-afraid they might. She sat on a bench and watched teenage girls in skimpier suits than hers spread hot-pink and yellow beach towels before lathering their bodies with lotion. The air was scented with Coppertone. They all reminded her piercingly of Penny and Charlotte, Pamela and Michelle, and lounging on the banks of Riverfront Park.

Franklin haunted her. *"We have to take advantage of your day in the sun, Lena."*

He hadn't meant sunlight, but press coverage. He'd always hoped for a headline. How ironic, considering she'd started her life as a headline story in the Haven *Chronicle*, after Reverend Ezekiel Freeman had found an abandoned baby under the bridge.

More and more people came to the beach. Most stretched out on towels, soaking up the sun. Abra loved the warmth on her shoulders and back, the salt breeze in her face.

She had come to the right place: Santa Monica, named for the devout mother of St. Augustine, who prayed for years for her wayward, feckless son until he finally repented and became a saint himself. Abra thought of her own life and what a mess she'd made of it.

Did her mother ever wonder what happened to her?

Did Pastor Zeke, or Joshua, or Peter and Priscilla?

Hungry, she broke another of Franklin's cardinal rules and bought a hot dog, french fries, and a Coke from a concession stand. She could almost hear him yelling. Just thinking about him made her angry. She intended to waste time judiciously and break every rule in his book. She bought an ice cream sandwich on the Santa Monica Pier and rode the carousel four times. It took that many rides before she snagged the brass ring, and then she was too sick to go on the free ride. She gave the ring to a little redheaded girl in pigtails. Had she ever looked that innocent?

Free and finally out from under Franklin's thumb, she didn't know what to do. She wanted to get farther away than Santa Monica. But where? She wished she could get a car and just start driving. She'd go all the way across the country to the Atlantic Ocean if she knew how to drive. Now that she thought about it, she didn't even have any form of identification. The only legal document in the safe with a name on it was that marriage certificate, and it said Lena Scott, not Abra Matthews. Was the marriage even legal?

Lena Scott didn't exist anymore. Neither did Abra Matthews, it seemed.

She wanted to talk to someone, but the only person who came to mind was her manicurist, Mary Ellen, and she'd have to call Murray and ask for her number. And if she called Murray, he might call Franklin. Her mind went round and round.

Call home.

What home?

Sunset splashed red, orange, and yellow across the western horizon. On the way back to the hotel, she bought a hamburger, fries, and a chocolate shake, and couldn't stop thinking about Joshua. Her eyes burned and her throat closed up so much, she threw away most of the meal.

She spent her time wandering the beach, trying to decide what to do and where to go. She had thought it would feel good to be alone. To be Abra again, invisible. Instead, she felt vulnerable and scared when people looked at her, a flicker of recognition lighting their eyes. Franklin said fans had ripped clothing off Elvis Presley's back and tried to grab hunks of hair. *"Sometimes their devotion is dangerous. They want a piece of you. That's why I have to protect you."*

Franklin hadn't wanted a piece of her; he'd wanted everything. He'd wanted her mind, body, and soul to belong to him. He had been her biggest fan—and more dangerous than everyone else combined. He would share her on a movie screen, but in real life, she belonged to him and he wouldn't share, not even with a baby.

Sleep came fitfully. She heard a soft tap and found a newspaper just outside her door. A partial headline caught her attention. Heart in her throat, she brought it inside and unfolded it on the coffee table.

AGENT FOUND DEAD, STAR MISSING

Franklin Moss, well-known star builder, was found dead in his apartment . . . apparent suicide . . . His mistress, rising star Lena Scott, is missing . . . The doorman of the apartment house said Miss Scott left the premises soon after Franklin Moss departed that morning. "She was carrying a suitcase, but dumped it on the sidewalk across the street and ran when I called out to her."

Franklin Moss has been estranged from his wife since his affair with Pamela Hudson, now married to director Terrence Irving. Close friends say Moss was a perfectionist, great at his job, but often suffered deep depression. Mrs. Moss filed for divorce when the story of his affair with Pamela Hudson reached the press, and then withdrew the petition in hope of reconciliation.

Neighbors of Moss report overhearing loud arguments

between Moss and Lena Scott, who have been living together for three years. The doorman hadn't seen her for several weeks. "Mr. Moss said she wasn't feeling well."

Dropping the newspaper, Abra fled into the bathroom and threw up.

"Be careful he doesn't pull you over with him," Pamela Hudson had said.

Abra had escaped, but had she pushed him over the edge? *I hate you!* she'd written. She remembered the gun she'd left on the desk. Abra heard an awful sound, like an animal dying, and realized it was coming from her.

Joshua stepped around the counter and picked up the freshly brewed pot of coffee, delivering five mugs to the new customers taking stools.

"Well, ain't you a handy man to have around!" Clarice grinned as she stacked plates of meat loaf and mashed potatoes up her arm.

"Figured you could use a little help."

"I'm thankful for the packed house, but I need more hands. Only happens when a movie company comes to film something at the Rocks." She whisked past him and delivered the meals. Rudy hit the bell again and she called out, "All right, all right, I'm coming; I'm coming!" Shaking her head, she bumped past Joshua. "I'd hire you if I didn't know you already had a better-paying job. But I sure could use someone around here. Not enough local girls interested." The sound of men's voices filled the place. By seven, the place was emptying fast. Four a.m. start-up time came mighty early.

Joshua lingered, in no hurry to go back to his hot, dusty motel room. Rudy came out of the kitchen and sank onto a stool at the counter a couple down from Joshua. Clarice poured him a tall glass of water. He chugged it. "I feel like a horse rode hard and put away wet." He took a cloth from his apron pocket and wiped his perspiring face.

"Well, enjoy it while it lasts, you old coot, 'cause six weeks and the crew will hightail it out of town, and we'll be right back wondering why we ever thought we could make money on this place."

"I'm getting too old for this."

"I'm no spring chicken myself. I should share my tips with this gentleman. He poured coffee and bused tables."

"My pleasure, Clarice." Joshua smiled at Rudy. "You serve a good, hearty meal."

"He learned to cook in the Army," Clarice volunteered. "World War II."

Rudy snorted. "You won't get anything fancy, but I can fill you up."

"Only thing he refuses to cook is Spam, and I love the stuff."

"You didn't have to live on it for four years."

Joshua laughed and said he'd felt the same way after Korea. They shared experiences while Clarice cleaned the counter and took another plastic bin of dirty dishes into the kitchen. Rudy looked around. "Where's the newspaper?"

"Hold your horses!" She pulled it out from under the counter. Rudy separated the sections, found the sports, and left the front page on the counter.

A headline caught Joshua's eye. *Agent Found Dead, Star Missing.* His heart took a fillip. "Mind if I take a look?"

"Help yourself." Rudy rattled the paper as he turned it inside out. "You can have the sports page as soon as I finish it."

Joshua read the cover story and dug for his wallet. "Can I have change for the telephone?" He pulled a few dollars out.

Clarice handed him nickels, dimes, and quarters. "Something wrong, Joshua?"

"Just need to call home." He went outside to the phone booth and closed himself inside. The heat was stifling as he dialed. The phone rang once, twice, three times before Dad answered. He gave Dad the news.

"You think she might come back to Haven?"

"Maybe. Keep an eye out for her. I don't know, Dad." Joshua sighed. "It'll be now or never."

"What are you going to do?"

He'd already given his word. "Stay here and finish the job."

———

Someone knocked on the door. "LAPD, Miss Scott. Please open the door."

As she did so, she expected to be arrested and hauled away in handcuffs. The officer looked at her face and the open newspaper and said they just wanted to ask some questions. It felt like an interrogation, despite Officer Brooks's gentle manner and Officer Gelderman's offer of a glass of water from the bathroom.

Her hand shook so hard, water sloshed over her wrist. "I didn't know he'd kill himself! I just wanted to get away from him. I couldn't breathe anymore. Did he take pills? He kept sedatives in his pocket."

"Sedatives?"

"He said they were barbiturates. He said the doctor prescribed them for me."

"Did you know he had a handgun?"

She stared at him. "No. Don't tell me he used the gun. Don't tell me." She covered her ears and rocked back and forth.

The two officers waited and then asked if she knew anything about the papers torn up and left strewn around. She told them it was the contract between her and Franklin and the wedding certificate from a chapel, which probably wasn't worth the paper it had been printed on since she'd read that he wasn't divorced from his first wife after all. She'd also left the ring he'd never let her wear and a note. She could tell they'd read it.

Did they blame her for his death? Even if they didn't, she knew it was her fault. She'd never considered what Franklin might do if Lena Scott left him. Abra just wanted to get away.

Officer Brooks spoke in a soothing tone. The other officer called the front desk and asked in hushed tones if the hotel had a doctor on call. They didn't want to leave her alone. A bubble of laughter rose before she regained control. Maybe they were afraid she might kill herself, too. Another headline. Wouldn't Franklin be happy? No, he wouldn't be happy. He wouldn't feel anything ever again. Because of her.

She scarcely heard what Officer Brooks was saying about no question of guilt. "You're not a suspect, Miss Scott. We confirmed what time you checked in here." He put a hand over hers and squeezed gently. "Try to calm down. You're not to blame. We just needed to ask a few questions and have the information on record." He went on to explain.

"The doorman heard a shot fired an hour after Franklin Moss returned to his apartment. He called the police and opened the apartment when they arrived, finding Franklin in the living room, dead."

Had his blood splattered his precious paintings of Pygmalion and Galatea? She clutched her hands together, her fingers as cold as ice. "How did you find me?"

"We received several calls from people who recognized you."

It could have been the cabdriver who gave his word, or the teenage girl looking for movie stars on the palisades, or a staff member in the hotel eager to protect the reputation of the Miramar. If the police hadn't come to her door, would she have called them? Or would she have run away like she always did?

A doctor came. Officer Brooks spoke to him quietly before he and his partner left. Dr. Schaeffer suggested a few days in the hospital. When she refused, he gave her a pill and spoke comforting banalities until she wanted to scream at him to shut up; he didn't know what he was talking about—she wasn't Lena Scott; she wasn't anybody. The shaking stopped and he took her pulse. "It's still fast."

She assured him she was fine now. She gave an Academy Award performance. How many had she given over her lifetime? No one had ever been able to guess what she was really thinking or feeling.

I see you. I know.

"I'll be all right. Thank you for coming." She saw him to the door.

He hesitated. "I'll check on you in a couple of hours."

The front desk called and asked if she wanted to make a statement. Reporters waited in the lobby. She asked how many reporters and the lady said three, but more were expected. Abra said she wasn't ready to talk about it and hung up.

Guilt gnawed at her. It didn't matter anymore what Franklin had done to her or why she'd run away. She'd sent him over the edge. If only she'd left a simple note of gratitude and apology. She couldn't be Lena Scott anymore. She couldn't be his Galatea. Maybe then he'd still be alive.

She awakened at every sound. She dreamed of Haven and Pastor Zeke and Joshua. She stood in front of the congregation. Everyone she'd ever known in Haven sat in the pews, looking at her, waiting for her confession.

Franklin sat in the front row. "It would have been better for everyone if you'd died under the bridge."

She woke, sobbing.

Other words came like a whisper from the past. *If you go to the bottom of the ocean or climb the tallest mountain, there is nowhere that I will not find you.*

Someone tapped softly on the door. "It's me, baby."

Dylan!

She opened the door a crack. He gave her his bright-white smile and told her to take the chain off; he'd just come to help her out.

When she did as he asked, he stepped inside quickly as though she might change her mind.

He closed the door and took her in his arms, all sympathy and pretense. "I'm so sorry, baby." He drew back, cupping her face and kissing her. She felt nothing but the hard press of his lips against hers. His hands moved, digging into her flesh. She'd forgotten how rough he could be, but she hadn't forgotten how he'd handed her over to Franklin Moss.

She pulled away. How had he found her? One of his many spies, most likely, or one of Lilith's. That wretched woman was probably already at work on a column about her and Franklin. What was Dylan doing here?

"Ah." He read her face so easily. "You haven't forgiven me." He came close again. "I tried to put you out of my head, baby, but here I am."

Abra brushed his hand away and put distance between them. "You dumped me, remember? You practically shoved me into Franklin's car."

"Go ahead and blame me. I have broad shoulders." He didn't look the least bit remorseful. In fact, he looked amused. "The truth is, I set you up with Franklin. I was looking out for you, baby. And you've done pretty well for yourself, with his help, of course. A star on the rise. Just like Pamela Hudson." His soft laugh grated her nerves. "I should've warned you the guy was crazy as a loon."

She could see the malicious gleam in his eye. "Franklin was a good man, Dylan."

"Really?" His dark eyes flared. "Don't expect me to mourn. He despised me and my mother, but he didn't mind swilling our champagne and playing polite to get his protégé's name in her column. I don't know why he came around that first time after Pamela took off, but I knew what kept him coming back. *You.* He couldn't take his eyes off of you." He gave a cold laugh. "I knew he'd become obsessed.

I also knew he'd have his hands full with you." He grinned. "A little birdie told me Franklin took you to Vegas and put a ring on your finger. You fell for that sham wedding, didn't you?"

"What little birdie?"

"Oh, baby. I have friends everywhere. You know that. I have one or two right here in this hotel. I got a telephone call two minutes after you stepped inside the Miramar. And you paid cash." He raised a brow. "You're paid up for one more night."

She blushed. "It's money I earned, Dylan."

"Oh, I'm sure you did." His smile was filled with provocation. "That's why you ran away. That's why you dumped your suitcase on Hollywood Boulevard and took off like a scalded cat with a pack of dogs on your heels. How much did you take out of his safe?" He tilted his head, eyes unblinking as they surveyed her face. "You're looking pale, baby. Conscience troubling you again?"

She could feel a headache coming on. He'd always loved baiting her. "Why are you here, Dylan?"

Dylan's expression softened. He sat on the sofa and patted the seat beside him. "I have a proposition for you." When she didn't sit beside him, he leaned back, watching her with those dark, glistening eyes. She wondered how much he'd paid for his Italian loafers. "I want to be your manager."

"What?"

"Don't look so surprised. I have more contacts in the industry than Franklin ever did. And I know how to get what I want out of them."

Blackmail. Abra remembered how he and Lilith worked, collecting stories and secrets, twisting facts, making innuendos. *You scratch my back and I'll scratch yours.*

"Don't look so down in the dumps, baby. We can turn this whole scandal around and make it work for you. There's a script making the rounds, about a woman with a secret past who marries a wealthy man, then takes a lover."

"I'm not interested."

"They're still looking for backers, but with you on board, the sky would be the limit. It's the perfect role for you, baby."

"No, Dylan. I'm not going to act anymore."

He stood, all masculine beauty and grace, eyes like black pits. He'd never been able to sit for long. "Sure you will. What else can you do? Go to work as a carhop? You've already been discovered. Listen to me. Reporters are going to be all over you the minute you show your beautiful face in the lobby. Weep. Wail. Cry your eyes out. Tell them all how sorry you are Franklin Moss blew his head off over you."

She turned away. "You don't listen any better than Franklin."

"You gave yourself to me, remember? You sold yourself to him." He came up behind her and turned her around to face him. "I want you back." He ran his hands up and down her arms. His touch gave her chills. She could tell by the look in his eyes he thought she was aroused. "Oh, baby, it's been too long." When he leaned down, she ducked under his arm and fled into the bathroom. When she locked the door, he laughed. "Are we back to that again?"

She sat on the edge of the tub, holding her throbbing head. "Go away, Dylan."

"You don't mean that, baby." He kept talking as he moved around the bungalow. Was he pacing like a lion, waiting to pounce?

He drummed his fingers on the door. "Come on, baby. We'll make a great team."

She flashed back to the first night in San Francisco, and the second, and all the months of misery that followed. She knew better than to say a flat no. "I need some time to think, Dylan."

"Let me hold you. I'll make you forget Franklin Moss." He gave a throaty laugh. "You know I can." When she didn't respond, he moved away from the door. She heard him opening drawers. What was he doing? He came back. "I'll give you time, baby. Tonight. I'll be back in the morning to pick you up."

She heard the door open and close. Had he really gone? She waited another five minutes before she opened the bathroom door and came out. Dylan sat on the end of the bed. He'd taken off his jacket. That sultry smile that once melted her insides now turned her cold. "I thought you left." Her heart pounded when he got up and walked toward her.

"I'll go when you say yes." He touched her hair, stretching out one strand, rubbing it between his fingers. Was he thinking about making her a blonde? "You wanted to be free of him, and who could blame you? The guy was nuts." He took his hands away and spread them. "If you don't want me to touch you, I won't. We'll keep it strictly business between us. As to what happened between you and Moss, we can tell the press anything we want."

"I won't lie, Dylan."

"Oh, baby, you've been lying for as long as I've known you. Now you have scruples? Don't make me laugh."

How he'd always loved twisting the knife.

"Don't you get it, Abra? No one cares what the truth is. People just want a good story—the juicier, the better. Franklin took you pretty far; I'll give him that. I can take you all the way to the top."

She'd give him the answer he wanted if it would get him out of the bungalow. "Give me the night to sleep on it. Alone. Then we can start talking about your plans tomorrow."

He looked surprised at her capitulation. "Good. I'll bring the contract in the morning." He shrugged into his jacket and cocked his head. "Eight o'clock too early for you?"

She glanced at the clock on the bedside table. "It's after midnight, Dylan. Let's make it nine."

When he walked toward her, she lifted a hand. "Strictly business."

He raised his hands in surrender. "Okay." He went to the door and opened it. "Sleep tight, baby. See you in the morning." His smile was smug. "I don't think you'll go anywhere without me."

The moment Dylan went out the door, Abra fastened the chain. It didn't occur to her until he was gone what he had been looking for. She got down on her hands and knees and pulled the shoulder bag out from under the bed. The money was gone.

She sank to the floor. No wonder Dylan had left with such confidence, his expression so mocking. What now? Stay and let him take over where Franklin had left off? Or follow Franklin's example? She rose and went into the bathroom. Digging through her toiletries, Abra found the package of Gillette razor blades. She unwrapped one and held it over the blue-green veins in her wrist. Her hand trembled. How deep would she have to cut to make sure she bled to death? Tears blurred her eyes.

Shaking violently, Abra looked at herself in the mirror and saw a girl with big green eyes, ashen cheeks, and a mass of wavy black hair. She'd missed her regular hair appointment with Murray. Franklin wouldn't be happy to see red roots showing. Uttering a cry, Abra grabbed a handful of black hair and sawed through it. Keening, scalp stinging, she kept at it until a pile of severed black locks lay around her bare feet on the white marble floor.

Cursing Dylan, she held her head. *Think, Abra. Think!* Each time she'd left the room, she'd always taken a hundred-dollar bill with her. She ran back to the bed, flung her suitcase on it, and went through all her clothing, digging through every pocket. She found enough to buy a bus ticket somewhere and have a few meals, if she didn't order steak.

Run, Abra.

This time she listened to the quiet voice.

She threw her things back into the new suitcase and closed it. Heart thumping wildly, she opened the door and peered out. It was late enough for everyone to be in bed. She wove around the bungalows and snuck away in the dark shadows of the giant Moreton Bay fig tree.

Few cars traveled the road this time of night. The surf crashed along the beach as she ran down the sidewalk. A taxi drew up to the curb, but she didn't want to use any of her remaining cash to pay for a cab ride. Several inebriated young men came out of a club. She hid behind a shuttered hot dog stand. They came closer as another cab came toward her. Changing her mind, she waved it down and asked how much it would cost to get to the Greyhound bus station. She couldn't afford to linger. Sliding in, she looked out the back window, wondering if she'd see Dylan's Corvette following.

A few passengers waited to board buses at the station. She asked where the next bus was going. "Bakersfield." She bought a ticket just as the bus pulled in. She found a seat in the last row and hunched down so no one would see her. She didn't look out the window until her bus pulled onto the main street. No cars followed.

Abra ached after an hour on the bus. It had stopped half a dozen times before climbing the grade and descending into a high valley. Feeling sick, she got off the bus in Saugus and went inside a café to use the bathroom. When she came out, she didn't see the bus outside the windows. She ran outside and down to the corner, but it was too far away to run fast enough to catch up.

"Miss?"

In despair, Abra turned. The waitress from the small diner set Abra's suitcase down. "The driver left it for you."

"What am I going to do now?"

"Catch the next bus, I guess." The girl shrugged and went back inside.

A bleached blonde in a short skirt and low-necked blouse came outside. "You going any place in particular, honey?"

Abra shrugged. "I was heading for Bakersfield."

"Bakersfield! Never been there. Nice suitcase. Must have cost a bundle."

Abra felt the woman studying her and kept her face averted. With her hair all hacked off, surely she no longer looked like Lena Scott.

"You look like a rich girl running away from home." The woman sounded sympathetic and curious.

"I'm not rich. And I don't have a home."

"No one in Bakersfield?"

"No one anywhere."

"Well, then, I can give you a ride, if you don't mind ending up in Vegas by way of Mojave."

Las Vegas was as good as anywhere else, maybe better. Abra looked at her. "Where's Mojave?"

"Out thataway." She pointed northeast. "Past Palmdale and Lancaster. I'm going to see a boyfriend stationed at Edwards Air Force Base before going on. You're a pretty girl, even with that mop of hair. You wouldn't have any problem finding yourself a lift with a trucker."

Abra thanked her. She couldn't stay in Saugus. She didn't have enough money left to pay for a night in even a cheap motel. The woman led her to an old car with cracked leather seats. A pillow and blankets were rolled and tossed on the floor of the backseat. "Excuse the mess." The woman got in, tied a red scarf around her hair, and started the engine. Abra dumped her suitcase in the backseat and slipped into the front.

The woman pulled away from the curb and drove down the street, following the same route the bus had taken, and then headed east. The woman talked about car problems and horses. She'd worked from the time she was a kid on a ranch in the Central Valley. "Couldn't wait to get away from the smell of cow manure." She'd had hard luck for the past two years, but things were looking up now.

"You didn't eat, did you?" The woman glanced at her. "I should've let you eat something before we took off. What do you say we stop for a bite in the next town?"

Abra still felt queasy from riding the bus. She hadn't eaten anything since finding out Franklin had killed himself. She glanced at her watch. Less than twenty-four hours since her life had once again been turned upside down and inside out. She looked out at the desert and felt barren inside.

The woman parked in front of a diner next to a run-down motel. The town didn't look more than a few blocks long. "Some coffee and eggs, and we'll be on our way." A bell above the door rang as they entered, reminding Abra of Bessie's Corner Café back in Haven and the booths with red vinyl seats. How many times had she and Joshua sat in one? He'd buy her a chocolate shake and fries, and they'd talk and talk. Her throat closed at the memory.

The woman slipped into a booth by the front windows. She took a menu from the stand holding salt and pepper shakers, plastic bottles of ketchup and mustard, and a glass sugar dispenser. "You should eat hearty. You still have a ways to go." She handed the menu across to Abra. "Order me a Danish and coffee. I forgot something in the car."

The waitress looked like she had entered her twilight years, but her hazel eyes had a youthful spark. "What can I get you, dearie?"

"Scrambled eggs, toast, and orange juice, and a Danish and coffee for my friend."

Her brows rose slightly. "You mean the friend who's driving away?"

"What?" Abra turned and saw the woman backing the car out of the parking space in front of the café. Sliding quickly out of the booth, Abra raced outside. With a screech of tires, the woman changed gears and the car shot down Main Street. "Wait! You have my suitcase!" The woman honked twice and waved as she drove away. Mouth agape, Abra stared until the car was out of sight. Turning, she came back up the steps and sank onto the bench outside the diner.

You can run, but you can't hide from Me.

Abra hunched over, covered her face, and wept.

The waitress came outside and crouched next to her. "You look like you could use a real friend."

Abra took the napkin the waitress held out and thanked her. Blowing her nose, she mumbled, "God hates me." He'd hunt her down and torment her until she died. And then He'd send her straight to hell.

"Why don't you come on back inside out of the heat and eat your breakfast?"

Abra felt a surge of panic. "My purse!"

"It's in the booth, right where you left it."

Shoulders drooping, Abra followed the lady inside and slid into the booth again. Rummaging through the shoulder bag, she lost hope. "I'm sorry." She shook her head. "I can't eat this."

"Something wrong with it?"

"Nothing. It looks delicious." Her stomach growled loudly, and heat filled her already sunburned face. "I just don't have enough money to pay for it."

"Well, you eat up, sweetie. It's on the house." The waitress headed for the counter and then retraced her steps. "If you need a job, we sure could use some help around here. I can even give you a uniform and apron."

"I don't have any place to stay."

"Bea Taddish runs the motel next door, and she's a good friend of ours. She's got one room left and was just saying this morning how she could use another hand cleaning the rooms. There's a work crew in town. The men are all out by early in the morning, but they like things nice and tidy when they come back. You could work the breakfast rush here, make up rooms for Bea, and have time for a nap before you come on back to help with the suppertime crowd." She let her gaze move around the empty diner. "You wouldn't know it by looking at the place now, but we're full up when the crew is hungry." She looked at Abra. "What do you say?"

"Yes! Please! Thank you!"

The lady chuckled. "Good. Funny how things work out." She took a few steps away and looked back. "What's your name, by the way?"

Abra almost said Lena Scott, then remembered the note she'd left for Franklin. Lena Scott was dead—and not worth resurrecting. Abra Matthews had disappeared a long time ago. Who was she going to be now?

"Abby Jones." It was as good a name as any and one she'd easily remember.

"Nice to meet you, Abby. I'm Clarice." They shook hands.

"Can I ask you something?" Her voice came out small and child-like.

"Sure, sweetie. What do you want to know?"

Abra looked out the window at the small town that sat in the middle of high desert wilderness. "Where am I?"

"You're in Agua Dulce."

CHAPTER 16

Hope springs eternal in the human breast:
Man never is, but always to be blest:
The soul, uneasy and confined from home,
Rests and expatiates in a life to come.

ALEXANDER POPE

JOSHUA WIPED SWEAT from his brow before nailing down another wooden shingle on the roof of the movie-set hotel. Hammers pounded up and down the make-believe street as other shell buildings were framed. Everything would look authentic from the outside, but inside was another story. He secured the rest of the shingles and called for another bundle to be brought up.

The sun beat down on his back. He'd tucked a damp cloth under his baseball cap to keep his neck from burning. The air was still and stifling. He pulled a canteen of water from his tool belt and gulped half the contents. Dumping a little in his hand, he wiped his face and then went back to work. No one wanted to work any longer than necessary in the blistering heat. They'd started at four and would call it quits by two.

"Hey, Freeman! Slow down a little, would you? You're making the rest of us look bad." The man standing next to Joshua's ladder was only half-joking.

"Just doing my job, McGillicuddy."

"Well, do it slower. We're ahead of schedule. We're not in a race."

"Just trying to please the Boss."

"I haven't heard Herman complaining. Have you?"

"I wasn't talking about Herman."

"Yeah, yeah. That Jesus stuff again." McGillicuddy laughed. "Does God pay you?"

"Yep. Herman just signs the checks."

"Seems to me God could have given you a better job than out here in this inferno pounding nails into a roof that'll be torn down as soon as the movie is in the can." Shaking his head, McGillicuddy crossed the dusty street and climbed up the ladder to the roof of the set bordello.

Joshua called after him. "I've been wondering about that, too."

An hour later, the crew came down, stowed tools, and headed back into town. McGillicuddy pulled his new GMC truck up beside Joshua's and shouted through the open window. "What do you say to a couple of beers at Flanagan's?"

"I'd say thanks. I'll see you there after a cold shower and change of clothes."

He joined the men at the bar and ordered a Coke. They teased him, but quickly resumed talk of work, sports, women, and politics. A small television had been set up at the end of the bar so they could watch wrestling matches. They picked favorites and shouted as though they were ringside and the opponents could hear them. Herman left his stool and took a booth, waving Joshua over. "You're welcome to join me for dinner, unless you haven't had enough of those yokels yet."

Joshua slid into the booth. "They're a good crew."

"I've been watching you, Freeman. Good finish carpenters are hard to come by." He sipped his beer. "Why are you out here and not working with Charlie Jessup?"

"I didn't know you knew him."

The waitress came over and took their orders. Herman leaned back and looked at Joshua. "Charlie is a friend. He has a lot of respect for you, even on short acquaintance. That's saying something."

"Thanks for telling me."

"So answer my question. Why here and not high-end projects in Beverly Hills?"

"It's only a short-term commitment, and then I'm going home."

"Where's home?"

"Haven."

"Never heard of it."

"You could say God shoved me here."

"Whatever your reasons, you sure put your all into it."

"Rule number one in my book." He didn't tell him his book was the Bible.

"You make my job easier." He jerked his head toward the men at the bar. "They've been watching you. A few grumble, but most have picked up the pace."

Joshua smiled slightly. "Are you telling me I'll be out of a job sooner than expected?"

"Maybe, but I have another ready to go. If you change your mind about Haven, let me know. You're the top man on my long list. I need a good foreman. What do you say to that?"

"Unless God tells me otherwise, I'm going home."

It was early when Joshua returned to the motel, but after a full day working in the desert, he was ready to turn in. He stripped off his clothes, fell into bed, and was asleep as soon as his head hit the pillow. He dreamed of Abra sitting at the piano in the front of the church, sunlight streaming through the side window and making her red hair like flame. He sat in the choir loft, arms resting on the railing, watching her. He didn't recognize the poignant hymn. Someone patted his knee, startling him. Mitzi grinned, looking spry, radiant, and smug. "Didn't I tell you she'd never forget?" She took his hand and squeezed. "It's time, Joshua."

He awakened in darkness and heard a woman crying. Was he still dreaming? It took a moment to remember he was in a motel in Agua Dulce. He'd slid the windows open before hitting the sack, but the room was still stifling. Crickets chirped. He went into the bathroom and splashed water on his face. When he came back into the bedroom, the woman was still crying on the other side of the wall. The sobs pierced his heart. Someone pounded on the far wall. "Shut up, will you? I need some sleep!" The occupant in room 13 fell silent.

Wincing, Joshua debated knocking on the woman's door and asking if she needed to talk. He could imagine what she might think if a man she'd never met made such an offer. She must have come in late. She'd probably be back on the road to wherever she was going in the morning. Joshua put his hand against the wall and sent up a quick prayer. *Lord, You know what's wrong and how to fix it. Help her find Your peace.*

———

Abra hugged her pillow, gulping down sobs, trying not to make another sound. The Gideon Bible she'd been reading lay open on the bed. If she'd needed any more confirmation of how much God hated her—and why—she'd found it. *"A proud look, a lying tongue, and hands that shed innocent blood, an heart that deviseth wicked imaginations, feet that be swift in running to mischief, a false witness that speaketh lies, and he that soweth discord among brethren."* The words broke through the walls she'd built around herself and brought them tumbling down.

She tried to find excuses for the decisions she had made, but she couldn't justify anything she'd done, not against the standard God laid out. She couldn't escape condemnation. She was guilty.

Her conscience rose, and the pain immobilized her. She couldn't run anymore.

How far back had this descent begun? When had she begun strangling her conscience? She thought it had started with Dylan. She tried to tell herself she hadn't known what he was, but she had. And she now realized with abject misery that Dylan had been right—he had merely fanned the flame already burning inside her. Running away with Dylan had been the culmination of her rebellion, and she'd been scrambling every day since by her own wits and determination to make something good out of so much bad.

Hadn't she been trying to prove she was worth something when she went off with Franklin Moss? She'd wanted to get back at Dylan, make him sorry he was throwing her away. She'd entered a relationship with a man twice her age, ready to do whatever he wanted, so she could get what she wanted. And what was that? To be *somebody*? Instead, she'd allowed herself to be made into somebody else.

She wanted so badly to blame Franklin for that, but she was culpable. She had helped him create Lena Scott; she'd followed his every command, allowed him to guide her, even to his bed. Her protests had been weak and petty, mostly made in silence, while bitterness and resentment grew. She'd been the hypocrite, not Franklin, and it had led her down that dark hallway to that woman waiting with surgical gloves. She could have balked. She could have said no. Instead, she went through with it and blamed him for everything. Why? Because down deep, she'd still wanted to be . . . What? What did she want to be?

Loved.

Franklin's dream had been her dream in the beginning. It had become their shared nightmare. She could see now the countless times people had tried warning her—Pamela Hudson, Murray, even Lilith and Dylan. She'd made a grab for the brass ring, and now she was riding the merry-go-round.

"You can talk to me," Murray had said, and she hadn't taken him up on it. Mary Ellen had talked about God and she'd closed her ears. Franklin was always the excuse.

She felt overcome with shame now over her cruelty to him. She'd wanted revenge for what she thought he'd done to her. And she knew where he was most vulnerable, where her words would cut deepest. Lena, his dream, his undoing.

"Vengeance is mine; I will repay, saith the Lord."

Now she understood why. She'd never meant to hurt Franklin so deeply he'd give up life. She'd only wanted him to cut her free, let her go.

Or had she? Her conscience writhed. *Be honest, for once in your life, Abra. Or don't you even know the truth anymore?*

Sweat broke out; her heart pounded.

She remembered how broken Franklin had looked over those last weeks. He'd been crumbling. That last day, she'd offered him a tiny bit of hope and he'd grasped at it. And then, what had she done with the last bit of time allotted to her in that prison he'd built for both of them?

She cried until the tears no longer came. *I'm sorry, God. I'm so sorry for what I've done and the people I've hurt. I don't want to be this way anymore. Have mercy . . .*

She stifled that plea. How dare she cry out to God now and ask for mercy? She'd never cried out to Him in praise. She'd never thanked Him for anything, not since Pastor Zeke had taken her to Peter and Priscilla's and left her there. In fact, she'd hated God and blamed Him for everything that went wrong in her life.

Her own stubborn pride had brought her here. That night she met Dylan on the bridge and let him rip Marianne's necklace off and throw it away, she'd set her course, told herself she wanted to be free, and made herself a captive, instead.

Another of Mitzi's hymns came to her. *"Make me a captive, Lord, and then I shall be free."* She hadn't understood then. She didn't understand now. All she knew was she had gone as far as she could go on her own strength. She'd tried everything to feel whole and now felt like Humpty Dumpty.

You can have it, God. I'm so tired of the fight. Do whatever You want. Burn me to ash. Turn me to a pillar of salt. Wash me away in a flood. I don't want to hurt anymore. I don't want to hurt anyone else. I just want . . . I don't even know. Exhausted, Abra relaxed and rested her head against the pillow.

She slept deeply for the first time in days and dreamed of clear sparkling water and the bridge to Haven.

———

Joshua awakened early and stretched. The motel room walls were thin enough that he could hear the squeak of the mattress in room 13. He reached for his clock and turned on the light. Three in the morning. He turned off the alarm and got up. He sat in the worn chintz chair near the front windows and opened his Bible to the place where he'd left off the morning before.

Pipes thumped as the shower went on next door. He'd finished his reading before they thumped again as they were shut off. When the door opened and closed, Joshua pulled the curtain aside enough to get a peek at the woman who'd cried as though the world had crashed down upon her last night. It was still dark out, but the dim light from the motel sign revealed that she had dark hair that looked like it had been hacked off with hedge trimmers. The white-collared dress and apron showed she was thin, but had curves. He felt the slightest stir of something inside him. Joshua rose and watched the young woman walk away. She had shapely calves.

The lights came on inside the diner. The girl opened the door and went inside. Joshua smiled and let the drape fall closed. Clarice had help. One prayer answered. He thought of Susan Wells and wondered how things were going for Dad.

Time for him to get moving. Joshua shaved, showered, and dressed for work. Men's voices rose and fell as hungry crew members walked past his door, heading for the diner. Joshua joined McGillicuddy, Chet Branson, and Javier Hernandez. The bell jangled and they slid into a booth by the front windows and talked about the coming day's work. The young woman was nowhere in sight. She was probably around the corner, handling tables in the larger dining area.

"Well, well, well. There's a new girl in town." McGillicuddy jerked his head. "Pretty, but get a load of that hair."

The girl was collecting breakfast platters from the cook's counter. When she turned, Joshua felt like the air was sucked from his lungs. Abra!

His heart picked up speed, racing faster as she passed right by him on her way to deliver meals to the men in a booth farther down. She looked pale and placid until she turned and saw him. She froze in shock for an instant and then lowered her eyes quickly, face flaming red, then losing all color as she walked by him. He had to clench his fist to keep from reaching out and grabbing her wrist. He turned his head, wondering if she'd go back to the cook's counter or run for the door. He tensed, ready to go after her if she ran.

Someone called out from the booth where she'd delivered the meals. "Hey, miss! Can we have more coffee over here?"

Abra looked blank, then confused. She blushed again. "Sorry." She hurried for the coffeepot.

McGillicuddy waved his menu as she came by again. "We're ready to order when you've got a spare minute, miss."

"I'll be right with you, sir." She hurried down the line.

McGillicuddy leaned his forearms on the table and looked hard at Joshua. "Quit staring, Freeman. You're making her nervous."

Joshua knew he was right. His pulse hadn't slowed since he recognized her. What had she seen in his face to make her look so scared?

He forced himself to look at the menu. It took willpower not to look up when she passed by again to deposit the coffeepot back on the burner on the other side of the counter. She came to their booth. He didn't think his heart could pound any harder. She was wearing tan leather sandals. They looked brand-new. He recognized those toes. He noticed her legs again. She stood a foot away.

After five years of wondering where she was, he could reach out and touch her right now. And he wanted to do just that. He would have caught hold, lifted, and swung her around if he hadn't seen that look on her face. He was pretty sure he'd put it there. *Get a grip, Joshua!*

"What can I get for you gentlemen?" The words were right, but her tone was filled with nervous tension. What was she doing here in Agua Dulce? It made no sense. He raised his head and looked at her. She avoided looking back at him as she held a notepad and pencil ready. "And you . . . sir?" She was trembling. She blinked, eyes glassy, moist. Was she ready to cry again?

"She's talking to you, Freeman." McGillicuddy kicked him under the table. "What do you want for breakfast?"

Joshua picked a random number from the menu just as the cook hit the bell. Abra flinched and dropped her pencil. Squatting, she retrieved it quickly, almost banging her head on the table as she straightened. She jotted the number on the pad and bolted.

"What the heck is wrong with you?" McGillicuddy scowled.

"Nothing."

"You should see your face."

"What?" Joshua snarled, praying Abra wouldn't drop any plates or spill hot coffee on anyone. Anyone watching could see her tension, her quick, jerky movements. She knew him. Why was she so afraid?

He tried to take it in. Abra was the girl in room 13. She'd been the one crying last night, the one broken and sobbing. Was she grieving Franklin Moss's death? Had she loved him that much? Pain pierced Joshua's heart. He knew what loss felt like. He'd felt it when he saw the way she looked at Dylan Stark. He'd felt it when she disappeared. He'd felt shades of it over the last five years. He thought he had his emotions under control. What a laugh!

What kind of joke are You playing on me, Lord? You told me to let her go, and I did. And now, here she is, smack-dab in the middle of nowhere, the last place I ever expected to run into her. Clearly I'm the last person she ever hoped to see. Do You know how that feels? Of course He did.

Joshua tried to relax and listen to what McGillicuddy and the others were saying. His ears seemed tuned to Abra's footsteps. He'd act normal when she came back. Problem was, he couldn't remember what normal felt like.

She clutched four mugs by their handles and set them on the table, filling each and handing them out carefully. He thanked her, but she was already moving away, pouring coffee for occupants in the next booth, and then going back to get another freshly brewed pot. She didn't look into his eyes, even when she delivered his breakfast. When she leaned down, he saw the pulse beating in her throat. It matched his.

Say something, Joshua! He couldn't find words. When she left, he felt bereft, until he looked down at the bowl of oatmeal. Ugh!

Javier grinned from his place by the window. "Don't you like oatmeal, Freeman?"

"It's great. Would you mind sharing your maple syrup?"

McGillicuddy laughed as he cut a piece of juicy breakfast steak. "Never figured a good Christian boy like you losing your head over a girl like that."

A girl like that? Heat flooded Joshua's system. He had to clench his jaw so he wouldn't say something stupid.

Chet Branson scraped strawberry jam onto his sourdough toast. "A little thin, but she sure has curves in all the right places. She looks nervous. First day on the job, and she draws a bunch of goons like us."

Javier Hernandez had drenched his pancakes in maple syrup while watching Abra. "That's the worst hairstyle I've ever seen. Why would a pretty girl do that to herself?"

Joshua checked the menu for the cost of his meal. He dug out his wallet and left enough to cover the cost, plus a good tip, then gathered his silverware, bowl of mush, and mug of coffee and stood. "Nothing personal. But if you gentlemen will excuse me, I think I'll sit at the counter."

McGillicuddy laughed. "Careful, Freeman. She might spill coffee in your lap."

Joshua took a stool next to the break in the counter, closest to the coffeemaker. Clarice delivered several breakfasts and looked from him to the three men in the window booth. "Trouble?"

"Not at all." He watched Abra pick up two more breakfasts from the cook's counter.

Clarice looked at Abra and back at him. "Oh. I see." She smiled and came closer, lowering her voice. "Her name's Abby Jones. Some thieving woman in a Cadillac gave her a ride from Saugus and then took off with her suitcase in the backseat yesterday." Abra went past without looking at them. "Poor girl doesn't have a dime to her name. But she's an answer to my prayers. She's working here and at the motel to pay her way. Not sure what she'll do when you all head out and we won't need her anymore."

Joshua had a few ideas about that, but he didn't want to get ahead of himself. His list of questions kept growing. Abra came back and reached for a coffeepot. Clarice stepped over, said something in a low voice, took the second coffeepot, and headed out. Abra wilted a little. She approached him like a lamb facing a hungry lion ready to tear into her. She refilled his mug. He leaned forward, willing her to look at him. "Hello, Abra."

"Hello, Joshua." Her hand shook enough to spill coffee on the counter. She uttered a tortured sigh as the rivulet of brown ran over the edge onto his work pants. "I'm sorry. I don't know why I'm so clumsy . . ." She looked around and grabbed for a rag, then didn't know what to do with it.

Joshua took it and dropped it on the spilled coffee. "It's all right." He brushed drops of scalding hot coffee from his jeans. "No harm done."

She lifted his mug and cleaned up the spilled coffee. "How'd you find me?" She stared at him with wide, pale-green eyes.

"I didn't. I've been here for a week working on a movie set just outside town."

"Oh." Her cheeks flushed pink, a look of disgust on her face. "Pretty conceited of me, isn't it? To think you'd come all this way to look for me."

He frowned slightly, wishing he knew what was going on inside her head. "I would have come all this way to look for you, if I'd known you were here. I went after you the night you left with Dylan. I came south three months ago, thinking I might make another attempt at finding you."

He didn't want to make her cry again, and she looked perilously close.

"I've been living with Dave Upton. Remember him?"

She swallowed convulsively. "You used to ride bikes together."

"Yep." He pushed the bowl of oatmeal aside and crossed his arms on the counter. "He's married now and has two kids." Someone called for more coffee. He wanted to turn and yell, "Give us a minute, would you?" But he knew she had a job and he was keeping her from doing it. She slipped away. Clarice shook her head at him. Frowning, he sipped coffee.

Rudy slapped the bell again, and Abra came to fetch the plates and head out from behind the counter to serve customers. She returned for the coffeepot. Men ate quickly, paid their tabs, and left. Joshua managed to get the oatmeal down. He needed to have something in his stomach for the day ahead. The place was clearing out quickly.

He didn't have to wonder if she was avoiding him. She kept moving around the diner, overly attentive to the remaining customers. As much as he wanted to stay and corner her, he had responsibilities.

Clarice bused the counter, wiping it down and setting out new paper place mats and silverware. "More coffee?" He said no thank you and dug for his wallet until Clarice reminded him he'd left money to cover the meal and a tip at the booth.

"Don't take this wrong, Joshua." She took a quick glance at Abra busing tables, and gave him a steady look. "That girl needs a friend, not a boyfriend, if you take my meaning."

"I do. You don't have to worry."

"I'd better not." She set the coffeepot into the machine behind her and faced him. "Plenty of others in here this morning who looked like they have ideas about her, and in her circumstance that could be a temptation and a problem all in one."

He didn't pretend not to understand. He'd seen too many women in Korea turn to prostitution to survive. Clarice went out to clear a booth as Abra headed back with a tray of dirty dishes and glasses. Joshua stood where she couldn't get by him. She didn't raise her head. "I'm on duty, Joshua."

"I know. I'll make it quick. This can't be a coincidence, Abra. God orchestrated this meeting."

She gave a bleak laugh. "I doubt God wants anything to do with me."

"Then how do you explain you and me ending up in the same one-horse town on the edge of nowhere at the same time? God put me here a week ahead of you. I think He's trying to tell you something. I heard you crying last night."

She lifted her head, lips apart, mortified. Maybe he shouldn't have told her that.

"And don't give me that look. I wasn't the one telling you to shut up." He could see the brokenness now in the way she stood, the way her gaze flickered away. The dishes rattled. Time to leave her alone. "Are you still going to be here when I get off work?" *Oh, God, please. Don't let her run away again.*

She looked up at him then, eyes glassy with tears. "Where could I go that God wouldn't find me?" Her voice broke.

Joshua wanted to dump the tray, pull her close, and hold her tight, but they were standing in a diner. And Clarice gave them a worried look. It wasn't the right time or place. "Good."

She bowed her head. "Please move."

Joshua gave her room to get around him. He gave her a last look before he went out the door. *Lord, let her know how much You love her.*

———

Abra bused the remaining tables, headed back to the motel, and spent the rest of the morning making up beds, cleaning toilets, and vacuuming worn rugs. Her mind churned with a chorus of voices. *You don't have to listen to Joshua, you know. He probably wants to remind you of how many people you hurt back in Haven. He probably wants to find out what happened with Dylan so he can say he told you so.* Half a dozen men had hinted they wanted to "get to know" her. She could pick any one and attach herself long enough to get away.

Like a leech, a parasite attached to its unsuspecting host?

Another Franklin?

The fact that she had even considered it filled her with self-loathing.

Joshua. What was she going to say when he came back?

She'd thought about him so many times since she'd left Haven. She couldn't believe it when she saw him sitting there in that booth, staring at her like she was a ghost. Or a zombie. She gave a mirthless laugh. Did he even know about all that? It was hardly the kind of movie he'd ever pay to see.

Five years and she'd never called anyone back home. What must he think of her? Whatever he had to say, she owed it to him to listen.

Wiping sweat from her forehead, Abra went on scrubbing the bathroom floor. She couldn't think more than a day ahead. When she finished her shift tonight at the diner, she'd have to wash the uniform and apron in the motel sink. With the desert heat, her clothes would be dry enough to iron by morning.

I have a job and food to eat and a place to sleep. That's enough right now. Thank You, God, for the roof over my head. It's more than I deserve. She took freshly laundered towels from a delivery bag and stacked them on the storage room shelves.

She finished making up the motel rooms by two, and went to the five-and-dime. She'd made enough in tips this morning to buy a package of cheap underwear, a toothbrush, toothpaste, and a hairbrush. She showered and tried to nap before the evening shift at the diner, but her mind wouldn't rest.

Pulling the Gideon Bible out of her nightstand, she went to the list of topics in back. She spent the next two hours looking up Scriptures. She remembered many that she and Penny had memorized for Sunday school classes when they were little girls. Pastor Zeke had preached on some. Joshua and Mitzi had often spoken in words like these.

She'd lived in darkness for so long, but now, somewhere deep inside her, light flickered.

Clarice told her there wouldn't be as many customers for the supper shift. "Most head for the bar and grill. We have steaks, too, but we don't serve alcohol. Rudy's got a thing about it. Means less business, but he's adamant. The special tonight is pot roast, mashed potatoes, and carrots. Fresh apple, peach, and cherry pie."

"Is there anything I can do right now?"

"Marry the mustard." Clarice's eyes lit with amusement at Abra's expression, and she explained. "Mix the fresh in with what's left in the dispensers."

Every time the bell over the door jangled, Abra's heart jumped.

She swooped on customers and offered them quick service in order to keep from thinking about Joshua. Maybe he'd changed his mind about coming back. Maybe he had gone down to the bar and grill. Did he drink now? He never had before. She thought of Franklin pouring Scotch, getting drunk almost every night because it was the only way he could sleep.

Everyone else had begun to leave when Joshua came in the door. His hair was wet and he was wearing clean jeans and a lightweight, short-sleeved blue-checked shirt tucked in at the waist.

He had changed in five years. He was broader, more muscular, his dark hair cropped short. He chatted briefly with Clarice and took a table in Abra's serving area.

She knew she couldn't avoid him forever. She didn't know what she expected, but certainly not the look that met hers when she gave him a menu. He smiled the same smile he always had. "I'm glad you stayed." He'd always been confident. From the time he was a boy, he knew who he was. It didn't matter what he did as long as he did his best at whatever God had set before him. He liked people. He'd always been warm, friendly, interested in everyone and everything going on around him.

"Nowhere else to go." What chance was there that they could ever be friends again, let alone anything more? She needed to remind herself. "I've burned all my bridges."

"Do you really think so?"

Hope hurt. Better not to let it grow.

"I know what I want." He handed the menu back without looking at it.

She felt an odd sensation in the pit of her stomach and took her pad and pencil from her apron pocket. She kept her tone neutral. "What can I get you?" Joshua ordered the special. She brought him water and iced tea, then left him alone until his dinner was ready.

She set the plate in front of him. "Enjoy your dinner." She refilled his glass of iced tea once, kept busy and at a distance until he finished. She delivered his check and cleared his plate. He paid at the register and handed her a folded bill as a tip. A dollar was far too much. She tucked it in her apron pocket without looking at it.

"I'm not leaving, Abra."

He looked at her like nothing had changed between them. But everything had. She wasn't the same girl he'd known in Haven. She'd been naive, innocent, troubled, full of angst, so eager to rebel, to break free. Joshua had watched over her as an infant, played with her when she was a toddler, taken her under his wing when she was a teen, and tried to make her listen to reason when she'd wanted nothing more than to throw herself at a devil who'd end up using her, abusing her, and throwing her away.

How could Joshua have that tender look in his eyes, as though he still cared the same way he always had? "It'd be best if you did leave, Joshua."

He tilted his head, trying to study her face. "Why?"

She straightened her shoulders and met his gaze. "Because I've done things you couldn't even imagine since I left Haven."

"I was in a war, Abra. Remember?" He spoke gently. "I've seen plenty." His fingers brushed her arm, and she felt her skin tingle, but not the way it had when Dylan touched her. "Let's talk when you finish your shift."

She swallowed hard. "I wouldn't know what to say."

"Then we'll start with silence."

She didn't want to start crying again. If she confessed, he'd leave her alone. Was that what she wanted? She knew the answer, but knew the truth mattered more.

"What are you thinking?" He spoke so gently.

"What I should tell you." She pushed a shaking hand through her cropped hair. "For once in my life, I want to be honest." She saw his quick, questioning frown and pushed her hands into her apron pockets. It took an effort to stand still while he waited. "After I tell you everything, Joshua, then you can decide if you still want to be my friend or not."

"Nothing you can say will change my feelings for you."

He would be kind enough to say such a thing. "I won't hold you to any promise. I have another hour. . . ."

"I'll be outside on the bench waiting for you."

She had the feeling he thought she might go out a back door and disappear into the night. Yesterday, she might have done just that. She washed, dried, and put away dishes. She cleaned the floor and put chairs up in the open seating area while Clarice wiped down the booth seats.

Clarice took up her bucket of soapy water. "Everything is tidy as a pin, Abby." She nodded toward the front windows. "Is Joshua waiting for you or just watching cars go by?"

"He's waiting for me."

"He's a nice young man. Leave your apron on the counter. I'll give you a fresh one in the morning." Clarice smiled. "Enjoy your evening."

Joshua stood when Abra came outside. She looked across the street. "We can sit over there on that bench."

"Have you seen Vasquez Rocks?"

"No, but I—"

"My truck is at the motel. It won't be dark for another hour. And we'll have a full moon."

"I don't have hiking shoes or—"

"It doesn't matter. Come on."

She walked beside him without speaking. She recognized the truck, though it had a fresh coat of shiny orange paint. It looked newly washed. Joshua opened the door for her. She watched him walk around the front and slide into the driver's seat. He grinned as he started the engine. "Bet you're surprised to see this old clunker."

"You put a lot of time into fixing it up." She touched the old leather, supple from Joshua's tending. He backed up and headed down the road. She smiled, remembering all the rides she'd had in this old hunk of junk. "You were going to teach me to drive."

"You never learned?"

"Never had a lesson."

He pulled off the road, turned off the engine. "No better time than the present."

"What?" When Joshua got out, she called to him. "Are you kidding?"

He opened her door. "Don't be chicken." He took her place in the passenger seat as she went around to the driver's side. Flustered, she tried to concentrate as he gave her step-by-step instructions. It all sounded easy.

"Lesson number one." He sounded amused. "Turn on the engine."

She followed his patient prompting, ground the gears as she worked the clutch. The truck lurched forward and died.

She tried again, palms sweaty, jaw clenched, trying to remember everything at once.

"Relax, Abra. You're gripping the steering wheel like you're in the ocean clinging to a life preserver."

She grumbled. "Relax, he says."

"You're catching on." He put his arm on the back of the seat.

"I'm murdering your truck!"

"She'll rise again. Start her up."

"We're going to end up in a ditch, Joshua."

"Try giving it more gas."

"*More* gas?"

"Only if you want to get to Vasquez Rocks before Christmas."

She laughed and pressed her foot down harder.

"That's better, but try to stay on the *right* side of the road."

"I am on the right!"

"A little more right. Right of the white lines."

"Oh, God, help," she prayed aloud. "There's a car coming!"

"You're doing fine. Hear the gravel? That means you need to be a little more to the left."

Why did he have to sound so calm?

One arm still on the seat behind her, he stretched out the other, pointing. "The turn into the park is just ahead. See it?"

"Yes!" She sped up and made the left turn. Gravel pinged beneath the truck. They bounced violently on the dirt road. She jammed on the brakes and the wheels skidded a few feet. Joshua braced himself with a hand on the dash before the truck came to a complete stop. She let out her breath in relief.

Joshua gave her shoulder a pat. "Well done." He shoved his door open and got out. Raising his hands in the air, he yelled, *"I'm alive! Thank You, Jesus!"*

She laughed again. "Oh, shut up! What did you expect? It was my first lesson!"

How long since she had laughed—really laughed—and not just pretended? The relief of it made her burst into tears. She ducked her head so he wouldn't see, wiped her cheeks quickly, and got out of the truck. As she came around, she heard a strange sound.

"Watch out!" Joshua had the snake's head under the heel of his boot before she knew what was happening. The snake thrashed and wound coils around his ankle. Joshua twisted his heel and the snake went limp. "They aren't usually right out in the open."

She stood back, shuddering. "Is it dead?"

"Yep." Joshua used the toe of his boot to toss it into the nearby brush. "A pity it didn't stay where it belonged." He headed for the rock formations.

She followed halfheartedly, eyes darting around. "Maybe we should go back to town. There might be more snakes."

He looked over his shoulder. "There are always snakes in this world, Abra. We'll keep our eyes wide open." He held out his hand.

His hand was warm and strong. It always had been. When they came to an outcropping of smooth stone, he swept her up in his arms, setting her feet on the rock. Bracing his hands on it, he lifted himself up while she was still trying to get her breath. He took her hand again as they walked up the tilted, stacked layers. They stood together, not close enough to the edge to be dangerous, yet close enough that it still took her breath away. If she'd had any lingering thoughts of suicide, this would be a good place to accomplish the goal.

"Quite a view, isn't it?" Joshua sat, resting his forearms on raised knees.

Wrapping her uniform skirt around her legs, Abra sat carefully, near enough to talk, but not so near she wouldn't be able to see his face. She stretched out her legs, covering her knees with her skirt. The stone felt hot beneath her.

His mouth tilted in a wistful smile. "Remember how we used to climb the hills on the other side of the bridge so we could look over Haven?"

"Yes." Memories came rushing back. She'd been able to tell Joshua anything in those days. Could she do the same now?

Joshua didn't say anything more. He looked out over the land, but she sensed he wasn't as relaxed as he looked. She waited, not wanting to ruin the moment, but each second increased her inner agitation. Should she confess? Shouldn't she? Her breath came out tremulous. Everything or nothing, and nothing meant they couldn't be the friends they had been.

She bowed her head. "You were right about Dylan." She could feel him looking at her, and started slowly, stopping and starting again when she caught herself in an excuse. She told him about meeting Dylan on the bridge, the ride to San Francisco, that night in the fancy hotel, the next night in a club.

Joshua looked away, and she saw the muscle clenching in his jaw.

Haltingly, she told him about the party in Santa Cruz, Kent Fullerton, driving around California, Dylan shoplifting and drinking.

She told him about Lilith Stark, living in the cottage, attending the parties, feeling important among all those movie stars, hearing the gossip, seeing the constant competitiveness.

Franklin, her savior. Franklin, the sculptor. Pygmalion and Galatea. She'd used him. He'd used her. He'd married her, but hadn't really, as it turned out. Their baby had become the sacrifice on the altar of Lena Scott's rising star. She'd hated and blamed Franklin for that, before she realized she was equally at fault. She'd hurt him in a thousand ways and then, in the end, stolen what she thought belonged to her and left a note that put a gun to his head. Literally.

"That's all of it. My life in a nutshell."

Joshua stared out over the desert.

Her hands kept pleating and unpleating the blue uniform Clarice had given her.

"I know you must despise me now, Joshua." She didn't blame him. She hated herself.

"No." He turned his head and looked at her. "I don't despise you."

She was afraid to hope that possible. "How can you not?"

"I've always loved you, Abra. You know that. What you don't get is my love has never been dependent on you being perfect." He gave a soft, humorless laugh. "God knows we're both human."

"What have you ever done that you have to apologize for?"

"I thought of a hundred ways to track down Dylan and kill him."

"It's not the same thing as murdering someone." She thought of her child.

"God doesn't see things the same way we do, Abra. The human heart is deceitful and full of all kinds of evil. I'm no exception."

She remembered what he'd said to her that night after they'd been to the Swan Theater. *"Guard your heart. It affects everything you do in this life."*

Or had it been Mitzi? She couldn't remember anymore. "I can't think of anything good I've ever done for anyone." Even being a "good girl" for Peter and Priscilla had been tainted with self-interest and pride.

"We're all a mess, Abra. You're not alone."

She bowed her head and didn't say anything.

"Ready to go back?"

The sun had set while she talked, and the sky was losing light. She knew he had to get up early. "I think so."

Joshua straightened and held out his hand. She put her hand in his and allowed him to pull her up. When she stumbled, he caught her by the waist, steadying her. "Do you feel any better now that you've confessed?"

She knew she'd hurt him deeply. "I've been such a fool, Joshua."

He didn't deny it. "No one sees with eyes half-shut, Abra. Your eyes are open now."

So was her heart. She looked at him and realized she had never really seen him before, not in the way she saw him now. Something flickered in his eyes and then disappeared. He took her by the hand as they walked down the slanting rock formation. He let go and jumped to the ground, then reached up. She leaned forward so he could grasp her waist. She put her hands on his shoulders as he lifted her down. His manner toward her hadn't changed—foster brother, companion, her closest friend. But tonight something shifted inside her, as if the very rocks beneath her feet had moved.

They walked in silence to the truck. Joshua jingled his keys, capturing her attention. "You need more practice." He tossed the keys so she had to react quickly, then grinned. "Good catch."

She stood, undecided. "Are you sure? I might wreck your truck."

"I doubt it." He went around to the passenger side and got in.

Excited, she slipped into the driver's seat and put the keys in the ignition. She frowned as she looked out through the windshield. The moon shone brightly, but she still worried. "It's dark, Joshua."

He leaned over, his shoulder firm against hers as he reached beneath the wheel, almost brushing her knees, and pulled a knob. As he drew back, she looked into his hazel eyes and felt her heart give a little flip. He smiled. "There's always light when you need it."

CHAPTER 17

The eyes of the Lord search the whole earth
in order to strengthen those whose hearts
are fully committed to him.

2 CHRONICLES 16:9

JOSHUA COULDN'T SLEEP after he saw Abra to her room. He waited until she closed the door before he unlocked his own. He gave her plenty of time to settle for the night before he went out again. He headed down the street to the all-night Chevron station and closed himself into the telephone booth. Dad would be in bed, but Joshua didn't think he'd mind having his sleep interrupted.

"She's here, Dad. In Agua Dulce."

The groggy voice came awake. "Have you talked with her?"

"I gave her a driving lesson on the way out to Vasquez Rocks. We talked. Actually, she talked. I listened."

"Is she ready to come home?"

"I don't know. I don't think so. Not yet, anyway." Joshua rubbed the back of his neck. "Start praying, Dad."

"I've never stopped. I'll call Peter and Priscilla."

"Better wait."

"They've been waiting a long time for any news, Joshua."

"Okay. But don't get their hopes up."

Abra shivered in the cold morning air until Clarice unlocked the door of the diner and let her in. "Well, you look better this morning." She smiled broadly. "I take it you had a good time with Joshua."

"Yes. I did." Abra took chairs down and put out napkins and silverware while Clarice got out the Farmer Brothers coffee and got four pots brewing. Rudy already had bacon going, the scent drifting into the diner. He and Clarice talked through the open window between the counter and kitchen. The work crew would start coming in soon. She had just laid out the last few bundles of silverware when the bell jangled and Joshua walked in. She smiled at him. "Good morning."

"Good morning to you, too." He sounded well-rested, in good humor.

"Well, aren't you both cheerful!" Clarice chuckled as she looked from one to the other. "So where did you take her, Joshua? There aren't any movie theaters around here."

"We went out to Vasquez Rocks. We used to hike together back home."

Clarice's eyes popped open. "You know each other!"

Abra went behind the counter. "We grew up together."

"We lost touch." Joshua sat on a stool.

Abra set a mug in front of him and filled it with fresh coffee. She felt oddly shy with him now. "Thank you for my driving lesson yesterday. And for listening."

"Would you like to have another driving lesson this afternoon?" He lifted his mug and looked at her over the rim. "You need more practice using a clutch."

"And the gas and the brakes and the steering." She kept her tone light, trying to ignore the flutters in her stomach. She set the pot back on the burner.

"You have a lot to learn. And we still have a lot to talk about."

She thought of Haven and all the people she had known there. Some had meant more to her than others. One, in particular, but she didn't dare mention Pastor Zeke. "How are Peter and Priscilla?"

He lowered his mug. "Call them and ask."

She winced. "I doubt they'd want to hear from me."

"You're wrong. Peter went looking for you. Priscilla's been in and out of Dad's office ever since you left. They love you."

The guilt came back like a steamroller. She blinked back tears. "I know the address. I'll write."

His eyes narrowed. "You wrote once before. You left notes to everyone. Remember? Except me. Why was that?"

She couldn't speak for a moment. "What would you like to order for breakfast?"

"I'm not attacking you." Joshua set the mug on the counter and held it with both hands.

Wasn't he? It felt like it. "When you go back to Haven, tell everyone you saw me. Tell them everything I told you. That should make them all happy never to see me again." The instant the first insulting word flew out of her mouth, she knew she'd regret every one that followed. She drew in a shaky breath, waiting for him to retaliate.

Joshua leaned back and looked at her, eyes darkening in anger. He didn't speak.

She lowered her eyes, ashamed. "What would you like for breakfast?"

"Surprise me."

She turned away.

"Wait a minute." He called her back. "I don't want oatmeal." He grabbed a menu and gave it a quick once-over. "Steak—medium rare—three eggs, hash browns, sourdough toast, orange juice, and keep the coffee coming."

At least she hadn't made him lose his appetite.

The bell over the door jangled, announcing the arrival of more customers. Abra welcomed the distraction. She took orders and filled water glasses and coffee cups. When Rudy rang the bell, she collected and delivered Joshua's breakfast and refilled his mug with coffee, then went back to work.

Joshua ate, paid his bill, and left without another look at her. She tried not to feel abandoned. She wanted him to leave, didn't she?

Her shift done, she returned to the hotel and stocked the cart with fresh sheets, towels, boxes of tissue, and small bottles of shampoo. She worked quickly and efficiently until she came to room 12.

Except for the Bible and notebook on the birch coffee table, Joshua's room was the same as all the others. He had a double bed with a quilted boomerang-patterned bedspread, two pale birch side tables with space-age lamps, a Scandinavian fabric and wood chair in the corner with a hanging lamp for reading. His toiletries bag was open: Barbasol shaving cream and his razor, a wood-handled brush, Old Spice deodorant. His toothbrush and Colgate toothpaste stood in a glass.

Abra stripped the bed and gathered the used towels into her laundry bag. She whipped open the fresh sheets, tucking them in with hospital corners. She plumped pillows with fresh cases and smoothed over and tucked in the bedspread. She scrubbed the blue linoleum bathroom floor, the toilet and shower, polished the mirror and fixtures before dusting the furniture and lamps and vacuuming the beige rug. She looked around to make certain everything was just right before closing the door.

She'd already made her own bed, but she exchanged her damp towel with a fresh one before moving on to do a thorough cleaning of the last seven rooms. Stowing the work cart, she went back to rest up for the evening shift at the diner. She slept for an hour and awakened feeling hot and sticky. She'd been dreaming about Penny. Stepping into the shower, she let the lukewarm water cool her overheated skin. She kept thinking about Priscilla and Peter and Mitzi and all the others who had been kind to her.

And Pastor Zeke.

She hadn't allowed herself to think about him for so long, and now she felt such an intense longing to talk with him. Of all the people she'd ever known, she'd hurt him the most. Mama Marianne had told her how he'd saved Abra's life. *"He found you and tucked you inside his shirt to keep you warm . . ."* She vaguely remembered him singing to her and holding her in the night. She'd always felt warm and safe with him. She'd felt loved. Until he gave her away.

Her world came apart when Marianne died and Pastor Zeke abandoned her. *"You need a family, Abra. You'll have a mommy and daddy and a sister."* Everything changed that last day when he went out the door. She never felt a part of any family after that.

Abra covered her face as the water soothed her. Had everything been tainted by hurt and anger? For weeks after, Pastor Zeke had come back to check on her and she'd hoped he'd take her home. Then he stopped coming. After that, Peter took the family to a different church. She never understood why, only that it was somehow her fault.

Pastor Zeke didn't come to visit after that, but sometimes she'd awaken and sit in the window, waiting. She'd see him come around the corner in the wee hours of the morning. He'd stop at the gate and bow his head.

"We love you, Abra." How many times had Priscilla said those words? *"We want you to be our daughter, too."*

But Penny had said things, too, things that might be closer to the truth. *"They only adopted you because I said I wanted a sister. I can tell them anytime I want that I've changed my mind."*

Abra had waited for that day to come. She'd never let them get too close. She was afraid if she did, they'd give her away, too. She thought they were just saying nice words, but didn't really mean them. She saw how they loved Penny. She knew the difference.

Now she wondered. Was that their fault or hers?

She hadn't let anyone get close until Dylan, and what a disaster that had been. She thought of poor Franklin and put her head against the tile wall. Maybe if she'd been honest. Maybe if she had stayed Abra instead of being so willing to become someone else.

Turning off the water, she stood shivering. *God, I don't know what to do or where to turn. How do I move ahead with my life if all I can do is look back?*

———————

Every time Joshua was with Abra, he felt the struggle going on inside her. They went out every day together after she finished her shift. She must have had a hundred questions about people back home, but she didn't ask one. She talked less and less. Ten days had passed already and the work was going more quickly than anyone had expected. The movie town would be finished soon, and he'd be out of a job. So would Abra. What then? Would she board a bus and disappear into the night again? He had to remind himself she didn't belong to him. It wasn't his business what she decided to do with her life.

God, she's in Your hands. She's always been in Your hands.

They haunted Vasquez Rocks. She had tennis shoes and jeans and T-shirts now.

"Thanks for teaching me to drive." Abra clasped her arms around her knees and stared at the gold-streaked pale-blue horizon.

Was that comment a prelude to saying good-bye?

She kept her eyes on the horizon. "How long before you finish work here?"

So she was thinking about it, too. "Three weeks, maybe less."

"And then?"

"I'm going home."

He saw the glistening of tears, though she widened her eyes before giving him a wistful smile. "I thought you would." She didn't say anything for a moment. "Clarice has already given me fair warning. So has Bea. Business will be back to normal, which means they won't need extra help."

They hadn't talked about the future. He hadn't put any pressure on her about going home, but he felt the moment at hand. "What do you want to do, Abra?"

"I've saved some money." Her mouth curved in a grim smile. "The men have been nice about leaving me good tips. I have enough to buy a bus ticket to Las Vegas and pay for a few nights in a motel. I can find a steady job there."

"What kind of job?" He wanted to bite his tongue. The question came out all wrong.

"Don't worry. Not that kind of job. I've prostituted myself before. I won't do it again."

Wounded people made a lot of promises they couldn't keep. Joshua decided not to let the question go. "What do you want to do, Abra?" He said it slowly, deliberately, looking straight at her.

She rested her chin on her knees and closed her eyes before speaking. "I know what I should do, Joshua. I just don't know if I have the courage."

"It might take less than you think."

"And hurt more than I can bear."

"I'd be right beside you."

Her mouth trembled and she pressed her lips together tightly. She shook her head.

Joshua knew she wanted him to let it go, but he couldn't. "Which is it, Abra? Fear or pride?"

"Both, I guess." She faced him, eyes bright with tears. "You know who I dread seeing most? Your father."

"Why?"

"He sees things in black-and-white."

He knew what she meant. Life didn't hold any gray areas for Dad. Right and wrong. Good and bad. Life and death. Serving God or serving something else. But she had missed the most important thing about him.

"He sees through eyes of grace, Abra." He hadn't talked to Dad since he let him know Abra was here in Agua Dulce, but he knew he was praying. He imagined Peter and Priscilla praying, too, and Mitzi, and so many others hoping for an end to the heartache. "You'll never have any peace unless you face them."

"By *them*, you mean everyone: Peter and Priscilla, Penny, Mitzi." She looked away and he saw her swallow before she spoke in a hoarse voice. "Pastor Zeke."

He turned to her. "Come home with me."

"I can't." She stood, her raw expression piercing him. She took a step back, wrapping her arms around herself. "Let's go back. It's getting cold."

Joshua let her drive back to the motel. She removed the keys from the ignition and put them in his hand. The lightest brush of her fingers stirred his senses. She looked at him, her expression a mixture of sadness and longing. "I love you, Joshua."

He brushed his knuckles down her cheek. "I know you do." But not the way he wanted. "I love you, too." More than he had. Her skin felt warm and velvet soft. She moved under his touch, like a kitten wanting to be stroked, and his heart rolled into a fast beat. Heat spread and sank. He took his hand away. He opened the truck door and got out, drawing in a deep breath of cool night air.

Abra got out and closed the driver's side door carefully. He met her on the walkway between rooms. She stood still and looked up at him, searching, pensive. "Abra." He put his arms around her, half-expecting her to pull away. Instead, she buried her face in his shoulder. His pulse quickened when she stepped closer, pressing her body full against him. He doubted she knew how he felt about her, how he'd felt when he came home from Korea and saw her standing on her front porch. When she slipped her arms around his waist, he felt on fire. He wanted to lift her head and kiss her. He wanted to lose himself in her. How easy that would be. *Oh, Lord, help.*

Joshua put his hands on her shoulders and put a few inches between them, hoping she didn't notice his heightened breathing. He took the room key from her hand, unlocked the door, and pushed it open. Stepping back, he forced a casual smile. "I'll see you at the diner in the morning." He wondered at the defeated look before she turned away from him and went inside.

Joshua went into his room and tossed the truck keys on the coffee table. He took out his wallet and set it on the side table, and stretched out on his bed. Las Vegas! His breathing was still shallow and his heart hadn't stopped pounding. He wished the motel had a pool so he could cool off and swim laps. A run would help, but it was dark.

Men's voices came from outside. He heard McGillicuddy, Chet, and Javier. They must have gone to the bar because they didn't sound like they were feeling any pain. Doors opened, closed. Silence. Minutes passed. His heart kept racing. A truck went by, heading out for the Mojave, a night run.

He had to be up early tomorrow. He needed to get some sleep. He untied and took off his work boots, then stripped off his socks. He unbuttoned and yanked off his shirt, flinging it with needless violence into the chair.

Restless, he went into the bathroom and washed his face with cold water. He brushed his teeth. He paced the room, unbuckling his belt. Leather whistled against denim as he pulled it from the loops and tossed it on the bed.

He didn't know he was waiting until he heard the tap on his door. His pulse rocketed. He knew who was there and what could happen.

He opened the door a few inches. Abra stood under the dying light, looking broken and vulnerable. "You shouldn't be here, Abra. People might see you and get the wrong idea about us."

She looked at his bare chest and bare feet, her gaze flitting away in embarrassment. Still, that one brief look had its impact. "I don't care, Joshua."

"I do." She'd seen him without a shirt before, but he felt the awareness between them. It shook him. His hand tightened on the door.

"Can I come in? Just for a few minutes."

Temptation wrapped its arms around him and whispered in his ear. He fought against it. "We can talk tomorrow."

"I don't want to talk, Joshua." She looked at him with pleading eyes. "I want you to hold me."

He let out his breath sharply and went hot all over.

Her eyes widened. "I didn't mean *that.*" She bit her lip. "I mean the way you used to hold me. When I was a kid and . . ."

He saw the sheen of tears in her eyes and curbed the instinct to pull her inside his room and enfold her in his arms. "We're not children anymore, Abra."

"Nobody cares what we do."

"God cares. *I* care."

She sighed softly. "You've been like a brother to me."

She was lying to herself as well as to him. "But I'm not your brother, am I?"

He saw her eyes flicker, fill with self-recrimination, and then clear. Her face softened. "Wouldn't it be nice if we could go back to the way things were?"

"In some ways." He wanted to keep moving forward. At least the tension between them had eased. He could breathe a little easier. "Try to get some sleep."

She stepped back with a smile, relaxed now. "It's nice to know you're on the other side of the wall."

Joshua didn't close his door until she'd gone back into her room. Stretching out on the bed again, he put his arms behind his head, listening to the soft squeak of her mattress.

Someday, God willing, there would be no walls between them.

The buildings lining Main Street of movie town looked weather-worn, the street dusty and unpaved. The crew had gone on to earn gold elsewhere, making it a ghost town on the cusp of rediscovery. Abra walked ahead of Joshua. She stepped up onto the boardwalk and pushed through the swinging doors of the saloon.

The bar had a brass rail and an ornate mirror mounted on the wall. She started up the stairs. Joshua came through the doors. "Careful. The railing above is breakaway."

She looked over and gave a breathless laugh. "It won't be a star that makes the fall. It'll be a stunt double." She tried a door. It didn't open.

"It's all for show. Nothing but air on the other side."

"Impressive work. A brand-new ghost town." She came downstairs. She looked around. All it needed were props and actors to make it feel real. "Franklin wanted me to audition for this movie. I'd have played the part of a dance hall girl with a heart of gold. He said it would be the next step to making me a star." She ran her hands over the bar and came away dusty. "He had such dreams for Lena."

"I imagine you could go back to Hollywood."

"Why?"

"Sounds like you miss it."

Did she? She had enjoyed wearing beautiful clothes, having heads turn when she walked into a restaurant or party, but the price had been too high. She had to lose herself. It had always felt like an alien environment to her, one where she could never be comfortable. Whenever the cameras rolled, she felt like a fraud, just waiting for a director to ask what she thought she was doing on the set. She had watched other actresses work, admiring their skill and the love they had for the work. She had tried to fit in, but she hated standing in front of cameras with those lenses like eyes that could see into her very soul.

"I tried to be Lena Scott, but Abra Matthews kept fighting to get out."

"Did you make any friends?"

"I can think of two who might have become friends, but I didn't let them get close enough." It seemed to be a pattern in her life. Joshua didn't press. They went back outside and walked along the boardwalk.

She felt the tension grow between them. "Now that the town is finished, you'll be leaving soon."

"I paid my bill at the motel. I'm leaving tomorrow morning."

The news took her breath away. "So soon?"

He gave her a wry look. "Not all that soon, Abra."

"No. I guess not." He'd been warning her for days the job was coming to an end, and so was his time with her in Agua Dulce.

"Have you decided what you're going to do?" His tone was gentle now, interested, but not pressing. He was a good actor, too.

Two pickup trucks towing trailers had driven past the diner this morning. The film company would arrive soon, bringing props and costumes. A catering service would be handling meals. Bea's motel had been fine for a few carpenters, but better accommodations had been arranged for the actors. Bea said she could have the room until the end of the week, and then Abra would have to start paying.

Had she done as Franklin wanted, Abra might have been the star of *Desert Rose*, living in a fancy trailer between takes in that saloon Joshua had built. Instead, she had three simple, decent dresses, a pair of sandals and white tennis shoes, and a zippered tote bag. Her last paycheck and the tips from the diner would be enough for a bus ticket, meals, and a couple of days in a cheap motel in Las Vegas.

"I'll figure it out, Joshua." She touched his arm. She owed him so much. "I'm not your problem."

She'd run away from home to find home. She'd traveled with a devil who led her to dry water holes and a barren wasteland filled with desert beasts of prey. *Stop at the crossroads and look around,* a soft voice whispered. *Ask for the old, godly way, and walk in it. Travel its path, and you will find rest for your soul.*

She'd heard the same message in Haven and had said, "No, that's not the road I want." Now she knew the road she had thought would lead to freedom had only led to despair.

Her mind told her what had been wrong could never be made right. What had been missing could never be recovered. But her heart hoped.

She could make a good living on her own. All she had to do was resurrect Lena Scott and find some enterprising club owner willing to hire her to play piano in his bar. Lilith Stark had taught her how scandal could be good for business. Newspaper reporters would come flocking. Dylan would come knocking.

Lena Scott or Abra Matthews? Which do you want to be?

Live a lie or live in the truth. It all came down to that.

She couldn't pretend God wasn't interested in her anymore. Who but God could have put Joshua in Agua Dulce and then brought her to him? *"I once was lost but now am found, was blind but now I see. . . ."* The hymns kept coming back, quatrains singing inside her head. Whose prayers had God been answering? Hers or Joshua's?

Pastor Zeke, Priscilla, Peter, and Mitzi had all talked about God's mercy. She'd never really listened. Maybe it was time to seek Him. She wanted to come out of the shadows into the open and let God burn away all the bad in her, the selfishness, the conceit, the pride. But it was a frightening prospect. God might send her somewhere else she didn't want to go. *I wonder if God will send me to Africa.* She hadn't realized she'd spoken the words aloud until Joshua looked at her.

"Africa? Why would He do that?"

She shrugged, embarrassed. "Isn't that where God sends people who give their lives to Him?"

He stopped, his eyes filling with a sudden brightness. "Is that what you want? To give your life to God?"

She didn't want to give him false hope. "I don't know, Joshua." She kept walking. "I still have—" she tried to think of the right word—"reservations."

"Even people with rock-solid faith struggle at times, Abra."

"You never did."

He gave a short laugh. "Are you kidding? I've had a monumental battle with Him for quite a while now."

"You?"

"Yeah. Me. He let me have my way long enough to know it wouldn't work. But I exhausted myself in trying."

"When was that?"

He gave her a droll look. "When I went looking for you the first time. And the second." He lifted his head, a muscle tightening in his jaw. "And now, when I'm going to leave you behind."

Again, that hard thrust to her heart. She slipped her arm through his and put her head against his shoulder. "I'm sorry. I've been a trial to you. I'll go back to Haven someday. I just don't think I'm ready right now." She'd write first, test the waters, and see if Peter and Priscilla wanted to see her. Then, maybe . . .

I have not given you a spirit of fear and timidity.

She could scarcely remember a time in her life when she hadn't been afraid.

Joshua slowed. "You'll never get things right until you go back to where they went wrong."

She removed her arm from his. Go back. Take the blame. Face the shame. She would have to be Abra Matthews, with all her flaws and frailties, all her failures, her history laid bare. She would be held accountable for the suffering she'd caused others. She had always felt exposed in front of cameras. In Haven, there would be no place to hide. Everyone knew her story: the unwanted baby abandoned under the bridge, then passed from one family to another.

I knit you together in your mother's womb. You are mine.

She felt a quickening inside her, and it frightened her. It would be easier and less painful to ride a bus to Las Vegas. She could become Lena Scott again, a girl no one ever really knew, least of all poor Franklin. *Make up a new life as you go.* An enticing thought.

At what cost, Abra?

She had never counted the cost before. Joshua said God had a plan for her life. Maybe she should wait for that instead of going her own way. All the plans she'd made for herself up to now had led to devastation.

Words tumbled through her mind—long-forgotten words she'd heard or read. *"I can never escape from your Spirit! I can never get away from your presence!"* The writer hadn't wanted to get away. He'd wanted to get close. *"As the deer longs for streams of water, so I long for you, O God."*

Where was she most likely to find Him? Anywhere. Everywhere.

Another hymn melody came, lyrics slipping through her mind. *"Come, ye disconsolate, where'er ye languish, come to the mercy seat, fervently kneel. Here bring your wounded hearts, here tell your anguish: Earth has no sorrow that heaven cannot heal."*

She blinked and let out a soft breath. Why did all those old hymns Mitzi had taught her come back so clearly now? They tormented her with promises that felt just out of reach, just beyond her grasping fingertips.

"Ready to go back?"

Abra glanced up and saw the shadows beneath Joshua's eyes. He hadn't been sleeping well either, and he would need to get a good night's sleep before the long drive north to Haven. He didn't ask if she wanted to drive. She would've said no if he had.

The air had turned cool, the North Star appearing in the heavens. He didn't take her hand as they walked back to the truck. She wished it were a more companionable silence.

"I won't say good-bye, Joshua."

When he didn't respond, she wondered if he'd heard her.

"I'll write to you. I promise."

He drove, eyes straight ahead, unspeaking. He didn't look angry or sad. He looked resolved.

A few lights were still on inside the diner. Clarice and Rudy sat in a booth, talking. She knew they had a decision to make, too. Would they close down or try to keep the place going one more year?

Joshua made a wide turn and aimed the truck at the parking space in front of his room. He set the parking brake, turned off the engine, and removed the keys. He didn't move and the silence pressed down on her.

She felt the heat of tears building, but held them back. Would he try one last time to talk her into going home? Did he think her a fool? Hadn't she always been just that?

She didn't know he was holding his breath until he exhaled sharply. "Well, I guess this is it."

It sounded like the end. "I guess it is."

He turned to her then. "It's your life, Abra." He took her hand and pressed it against his cheek before he turned and kissed her palm. "I wish you nothing but the best." He let her go and opened the truck door.

Shaken, Abra got out quickly. She stood, arms crossed against the cold, looking at him from across the orange hood, confused by the sensations his kiss had wrought. He kept walking. "Will I see you in the morning before you leave?" She stepped onto the walkway. Moths fluttered around the light.

Joshua unlocked his door and pushed it open. "Depends on what time you get up." He went in without looking back. The door made a sharp click as it closed behind him.

Abra stood for a while, staring at that closed door, getting a taste of what life would be like if she never saw Joshua again.

After a few hours of tossing and turning, Joshua gave up trying to sleep. If he waited until morning and saw Abra again, he might end up driving her to Las Vegas. And then what? Stay? Keep tabs on her? Drive himself crazy? Better if he started the long drive home now, even if it was still an hour before dawn.

He'd refilled the tank and checked the oil before taking Abra out to see the movie town. He'd wanted her to understand the job was done and he was leaving. He'd hoped—prayed—she would change her mind and come home with him. If she had, he was ready to roll. Well, she hadn't.

Let go, Joshua. He'd done it before. He'd do it again, no matter how much it hurt. For however long it took.

Joshua showered, dressed, stuffed the last of his things into his duffel bag, and zipped it. He put his wallet in his pocket and picked up his keys. Dumping his duffel bag in the back, he yanked open the driver's side door.

"Joshua?" Abra stood on the walkway, holding the handles of her tote bag with both hands. "Can I hitch a ride?"

"Depends. Where do you want to go?"

"Home."

CHAPTER 18

So he returned home to his father.
And while he was still a long way off,
his father saw him coming.

THE STORY OF THE PRODIGAL SON

IT WAS LATE that night before they left the main highway and headed by country roads across rolling hills and ranchlands, past sloughs and into high hills, vineyards, and apple orchards. Abra closed her eyes. "It smells like home." Cooling earth, growing crops, grass, and clean air.

They had driven all day and through the evening, with occasional stops for meals and coffee. They had been slowed by an accident around suppertime. Joshua was bone tired. Had he been alone, he would have pulled off the road to sleep for a couple of hours, but with Abra beside him, he kept going. Her fear increased hourly. It did no good to tell her she wouldn't be led to a public scaffold.

They reached the turnoff to Haven in the wee hours of morning, the full moon reflecting off the river, the trusses of the bridge to Haven rising ahead.

"Stop," Abra breathed, then louder in a tone of panic. "Stop!"

Adrenaline poured into his system and Joshua jammed on the brakes, skidding. "What?"

"He's there."

A man stood by the railing in the middle of the bridge.

Joshua relaxed. "It's my dad. He must be on his morning prayer walk." His father stepped off the walkway into the open beneath the canopy of trusses. He looked straight at them. Joshua lifted his foot off the brake and the truck rolled forward.

Abra drew in her breath. "Wait."

"He's seen us, Abra."

"I know." She pushed her door open and slowly got out of the truck.

Joshua got out and came around to take her hand. "It's going to be all right. Trust me." They hadn't gone more than a few feet onto the bridge when Dad met them. Joshua let go of her.

"Abra." Eyes glistening, Dad cupped Abra's face. "You're home." He kissed her forehead before enfolding her in his arms. Joshua heard Dad's muffled voice. All the tension went out of Abra and she wept.

Knowing they needed this time alone, Joshua headed back to the truck. He got into the driver's seat and rested his forearms on the steering wheel, watching the two people he loved most in the world. Dad released Abra and the two stood close. Abra was talking fast, looking up at him, then down. Dad was leaning toward her so their foreheads almost touched. Dad made no attempt to stop the stream of words that came out of broken pride. When she stopped talking, he ran his hand over her hair and said something to her. Abra stepped forward and clung to him.

Joshua started the truck and pulled up alongside them. "It's been a long night, Dad."

Dad put his arm around Abra's shoulders and kept her at his side. "Thanks for bringing her home, Son." He looked twenty years younger.

Abra's face was awash with tears and relief as she mouthed, *Thank you.*

"Do you two want a ride back to the house?"

"We're going to take a walk."

Joshua knew where Dad would take her, and that he couldn't interfere. "See you later, then." He drove across the bridge, glancing in the rearview mirror before he turned right. Dad and Abra were walking hand in hand.

Abra felt weak with relief as she fell into step with Pastor Zeke. She'd poured out her confession and seen no condemnation in his eyes. When he ran his hand over her hair, she remembered how he'd done the same thing when she was a little girl. She felt overwhelmed with emotions, not the least of which was the question, if he'd loved her so much all this time, why couldn't he have found a way to keep her? She was afraid to ask the real question that had tormented her since the day he left her in Peter and Priscilla's care.

They walked in companionable silence, her hand engulfed in his, until she realized where he was taking her. Maple Avenue. She pulled away and stopped. "They won't want to see me."

"Oh, but they do."

"It's too early." She meant too soon.

He was at the corner and could see down the street. "The light's on in the kitchen." He held out his hand.

Abra surrendered. Her heart knocked when they reached the white picket fence. Pastor Zeke opened the gate and waited for her to enter. Fighting tears of panic, she took a deep breath and followed his lead. He walked with her up the stairs, but let her ring the doorbell.

Priscilla, in bathrobe and slippers, opened the door. She looked from Pastor Zeke to her. "Abra?" she barely whispered, aghast. Then her face flooded with relief. "Abra!" She was on the front porch in one step, reaching out, then withdrawing. Flustered, she burst into tears and ran back into the house. She stood at the bottom of the stairs and cried out, "Peter! Come quick!"

Abra heard the sound of hurried footsteps upstairs, and then Peter came down, wearing pajamas and a hastily thrown-on robe. He looked ten years older. The lines of worry smoothed and he uttered a choked "Thank God."

"I'm sorry for the things I said and didn't say. I . . ."

Peter marched forward and hugged her so hard she could hardly breathe, let alone speak. He pressed his chin onto the top of her head and withdrew, but didn't let go. He held her firmly by the arms, his head down, his eyes capturing hers. "It's about time." Abra saw anger and pain, relief and love. He let go of her and held out his hand to Pastor Zeke. "Thank you for bringing her home."

"It wasn't me."

"Come on in. We can all talk in the living room."

"I'd better get home." Pastor Zeke stepped back, leaving her again. "I have a full workday ahead of me." He lifted his hand, stepped out the front door, and closed it behind him.

Priscilla wiped away happy tears. "You look so tired, Abra."

"We drove straight through."

Priscilla lifted her hand to touch Abra's cheek and then lowered it. Abra remembered all the times she'd withdrawn from Priscilla and the hurt she'd seen in her eyes. She stepped closer and took Priscilla's hand and put it against her cheek, then closed her eyes.

Priscilla's breath came in a soft catch, and she put her arms around Abra. "I'm so glad to see you," she said hoarsely. Peter said something and Priscilla interrupted. "Later, Peter. She needs to rest."

The upstairs bedroom looked exactly as she'd left it. Priscilla pulled the covers back. Sighing, Abra stretched out, half-asleep before her head touched the pillow. Priscilla tucked her in. "We've been praying constantly since Pastor Zeke told us you were in Agua Dulce with Joshua."

"Have you?"

With a faint frown, Priscilla smoothed Abra's hair back from her forehead. "We've been praying since the night you left." She fingered a clump of Abra's hair.

"I know it looks awful. I cut it off with a razor blade."

"A razor blade?"

"I'm so sorry for everything, Priscilla. Mom. I—"

Priscilla put trembling fingertips over Abra's lips. "We love you, Abra. Get some sleep. We'll talk later." Priscilla leaned down and kissed her the way she'd always kissed Penny. "You're home now. You're safe."

Exhausted, Abra relaxed. She didn't even hear the door close behind Priscilla.

———

Birds sang outside the open window. Eyes still closed, Abra listened. *"Joys are flowing like a river since the Comforter has come . . ."* Stretching, she got up, feeling stiff and groggy. How long had she slept? The sun was well up. She went to the window and looked out at the backyard with pristine mowed lawn encircled by roses, delphiniums, and foxgloves, rising from beds of sweet white alyssum and lamb's ears.

When she turned away from the window, she noticed presents stacked on her dresser—some in Christmas wrap and others in multiples of pastels—with a profusion of ribbons. Envelopes bearing her name were taped to each one. She opened a birthday card with a touching poem about a daughter and signed *Mom and Dad*. Tears blurred her vision as Abra touched the packages, one for every Christmas and birthday she'd missed.

Pulling open a drawer, she found some underwear. High school outfits still hung in the closet. She'd only taken what she'd bought with her savings at Dorothea Endicott's shop.

Penny's bedroom door was open, the canopy bed and French provincial furniture in place, but the walls stripped of movie posters and repainted pale green instead of pink. The room looked neat and empty. Where was Penny now? Married? Working?

Abra went into the bathroom and found laid out for her a new toothbrush, tube of Colgate toothpaste, and hairbrush on the bathroom counter. She took a shower and shampooed her hair. After drying it with a towel, she brushed it. She looked in the mirror and saw a pale, green-eyed girl with spiked and matted black hair that showed roots of red. *What a mess you are, Abra. Inside and out.*

As she came downstairs, she heard voices in the living room. She felt a fillip of worry when she heard Penny. The living room looked exactly the same. Abra stood, uncertain, in the doorway, until Peter spotted her and rose from his armchair. "Abra. Come in and sit down." Priscilla and Penny sat on the sofa.

Penny glanced up, her cornflower-blue eyes widening in shock. "You look awful!"

Abra stared, no less shocked, as Penny struggled to stand. "You look . . . pregnant!"

Penny giggled. "Well, that's an understatement if I ever heard one." She put her hand on her protruding belly. "Rob and I are expecting our first in three weeks."

"Rob?"

"Robbie Austin. Remember him?"

"Robbie Austin?" Abra couldn't believe it. They'd both grown up with him. Robbie hadn't been a football player or the most handsome guy in school. He'd been rather ordinary, and sometimes a pain in the neck. Abra had to bite her tongue before she said so. "He used to dunk you when we swam at the river."

"He said he was trying to get my attention."

"You couldn't stand him."

Penny was beaming. "He grew up." She sank onto the sofa and leaned back. Abra took the rounded swivel rocker closest to her. Penny's smile faded. Shifting, Penny tried to make herself comfortable. "I didn't think you'd come back."

Peter's face stiffened. "Penny." His tone held warning.

"Well, it's been five years, Dad! And not so much as a letter!" She gave Abra that old haughty look. "You're an actress now, aren't you? In movies." Her tone was faintly mocking.

"Lena Scott was."

"You are Lena Scott."

"Not anymore."

"We read the newspapers." Penny acknowledged the soft parental protests this time. Her gaze flickered over Abra's hair.

Abra pasted a smile on her face and pretended to fluff her damp, poorly cropped dyed-black hair. "It's my new look."

Frowning now, Penny looked straight into her eyes. "What happened to you?"

"They seem to be cutting us out of the conversation, Priss." Peter rose and nodded toward the kitchen. "Let's give the girls a chance to talk."

Abra felt no more relaxed when they were out of the room. She wondered if Penny was still the family gatekeeper, the one elected to ask the hard questions. Penny let her anger show as soon as Peter and Priscilla were out of earshot. "You have a lot of nerve coming back at all, you know that? Mom lost twenty pounds after you ran off with Dylan. Dad barely slept for weeks! All they've done over the last five years is worry about you." She stopped long enough to take a breath. "Tell me. Was Dylan the knight in shining armor you hoped he'd be?"

Abra felt every word like a well-aimed, well-deserved blow, but hurt pride still raised its ugly head. She wanted to defend herself, then wondered how she could do that without making excuses for the inexcusable or casting blame on others when she'd made her own choices. If she and Penny were ever going to be sisters—or even friends—again, she had to be honest and pray Penny could forgive her.

"I was a fool, and Dylan turned out to be worse than you could ever imagine."

Penny's lips parted, but all the heat went out of her eyes. "Where did you go that night?"

"He took me to a fancy hotel in San Francisco. I knew before the night was over, I'd made the biggest mistake of my life. But I didn't dare come home."

"Why not?"

"I was too ashamed."

"Oh, Abra." Penny looked crushed. "Mom and Dad would have walked through fire to get you back."

"I didn't know that." She'd never believed they loved her at all. She thought they'd taken her out of a sense of Christian duty, and because Penny wanted a sister.

Penny's eyes filled. "It's partly my fault. I should have warned you about Dylan. I knew he was bad news."

"No, you didn't. You were as gaga over him as I was."

"In the beginning. The first two or three times I was with him. He still stands out as the most handsome man I've ever met. But the last time I was with him . . ." She sighed. "You probably don't believe me, but when Dylan touched me, I got chills. And I don't mean the good kind." She spoke earnestly. "Sometimes the way he smiled at me gave me the feeling he wanted to hurt me, that he might even enjoy it."

"You saw him more clearly than I did."

Penny's chin wobbled, eyes welling. "I tried to tell you in the hallway at school one time. I thought I'd be able to talk to you later at home, and then I forgot all about it until the night Mom and Dad woke me up and said you were gone. They wanted to know if I knew anything, and I didn't." She swiped tears away. "Mom was frantic. She had a feeling about him, too. She was afraid you'd be found in a ditch somewhere, and I knew it'd be my fault if you were."

"None of it was your fault, Penny."

"I know I was awful to you at times, Abra. I always knew I was loved. No matter what I did, I was still their daughter. And you are, too. Only you never acted like it. You never even called them Mom and Dad. And I think it's because of things I said to you. I remember telling you the only reason Mom and Dad let you live here was because I wanted a sister. It wasn't true, Abra, but I was so jealous when Mom would spend time with you." She shook her head. "And you always did everything right. You did your homework. You did your chores and mine. You played piano as well as Mitzi. I think I went a little nuts when Kent preferred you over me."

"He ended up being your boyfriend."

"Some boyfriend." She grimaced. "All he ever talked about was you. I got over my crush in less than a month. You know what I held against you most? You filled out a swimming suit better than I did! I had the blonde hair, but you had the curves." Penny sat up straighter, shoulders back. "Of course, I don't think I have that problem anymore."

Abra smiled wryly. "Just don't put on a bikini."

Penny burst out laughing. "Oh, boy, there's a thought!"

Abra felt a softening inside her. Maybe they could be sisters after all. "You were always the prettier one, Penny. Boys always prefer blue eyes and blonde hair."

"Oh, I thought so, too, until Rob called me a stuck-up pom-pom girl with a head full of air." She gave a self-deprecatory laugh, and then studied Abra with speculation. "You know, Kent and Rob are good friends. Kent's a really nice guy, and still handsome, despite Dylan breaking his nose."

Embarrassed, Abra clenched her hands in her lap. "You heard what happened."

"Everyone heard after he came home at Christmas that year. He had to have his nose broken again and reset. It's still just a little off. He says it gives his face character. Would you like to see him?"

"Only to apologize."

"Why? You didn't break his nose. And he certainly didn't blame you." Penny grew serious. "Everybody's been praying for you—Mom and Dad, Pastor Zeke, Mitzi, Ian Brubaker, Susan Wells, me and Rob, and probably a dozen others. Even with that whole gang trying to get God's ear, I didn't think you'd ever come back to Haven. You always seemed so unhappy here."

She wouldn't have come back on her own. "Joshua brought me."

"Oh." That one word held a wealth of meaning, though Abra wasn't exactly sure what. Penny smiled slightly. "He would. He's the only one who could ever get through to you."

"Not always. He warned me about Dylan." She shook her head. "I said some terrible things to him."

"And he still went looking for you." Penny reached out and grabbed Abra's hand in a firm grip. "I'm glad you're back. Are you staying? We've got so much to talk about! I want to hear what it was like in Hollywood! I saw a picture of you with Elvis Presley!" She might be married and almost a mother, but Penny was still all girl in some ways.

She stayed all day and Abra only told the truth. It was difficult at times, and ruined some of Penny's illusions about life in Hollywood among the stars. Rob came over after work and greeted Abra with a chaste kiss on her cheek.

Priscilla had been in and out of the kitchen all afternoon. When she said dinner was ready, everyone sat at the table, and Peter held out his hands to Abra and Penny. Priscilla took Abra's other hand. Peter looked at Priscilla, his eyes moist, his voice choked. "It's the first time our family has been together in five years. Praise God." Abra bowed her head as he offered a prayer of thanksgiving.

The fear that still bubbled to the surface subsided a little. They had all welcomed her. She was a daughter, a sister, a friend. But as warm as they all were, this place still didn't feel like home.

Abra and Penny cleared dishes and continued to talk in low voices. The doorbell rang, but they paid no attention until Priscilla called Abra.

Joshua stood in the entry hall. "I just came by to drop off your tote bag." He handed it to her.

She held it at her side. "Don't you want to come in?"

"You need time alone with your family." He went out to the front porch.

Abra set the tote bag down and followed. "They wouldn't mind."

"Another time."

Abra walked down the steps with him. "Thank you for bringing me home."

"My pleasure." He went out the gate. She would have followed, but he stopped and pulled it shut, leaning forward to latch the gate behind him. She felt a tug of intense longing. The warmth in his eyes sent strange tingling sensations through her body. He seemed to be studying every square inch of her face. "I'll call you in a couple of days."

She stayed at the gate until Joshua got into his truck and headed down the street.

———

Joshua wanted to give Abra plenty of time to be a daughter and sister before he started knocking at her door. He went by to see Jack Wooding and was hired back as a foreman for the new Quail Run subdivision. By the end of the following week, Joshua picked out a lot at the end of a cul-de-sac and floor plans for a three-bedroom, two-bathroom ranch-style home in the first phase of building. He talked to the sales manager and went to the bank. With a 20 percent down payment, a full-time job, and a list of references, he was assured he would have no trouble qualifying for a VA loan. When construction started in a few weeks, he planned to check frequently on the quality of work and step in with a few upgrades he could do on his own time. The projected completion date was six months off.

Jack called him over. "Heard you bought the biggest lot in the first phase."

"Yep."

"It's a good investment."

Joshua smiled. "Yep."

Jack's mouth tipped in a knowing smile. "Thinking about putting down roots, Joshua?"

"As deep as they can go, Jack."

"You've been crazy about that girl for as long as I can remember."

"Timing is everything."

"If you ask me, you've waited long enough."

Abra had been warned that Mitzi wasn't well, but she wasn't prepared to find a nurse answering the front door and Mitzi frail and wizened and lying in a hospital bed in the living room. But Mitzi's eyes still sparkled. "Well, if it isn't our little wanderer. It's about time you came home!" She patted the bed. "Sit down right here where I can get a good look at you."

"Mitzi." Abra couldn't say anything more than that.

"Stop looking at me like that. I'm not dead yet." Mitzi took her hand and patted it. "All this folderol was Carla's idea. Of course, Hodge kowtows to her. They both wanted me in a rest home, but I said over my dead body. So this was the next best thing." She looked around Abra and introduced Frieda King. "Hodge hired her." Mitzi smirked. "I'm sure he knew ahead of time that she's a pill-pushing drill instructor."

"And you're the most cantankerous patient I've ever had." Frieda winked at Abra.

Mitzi glowered. "Would you kindly roll me up so I'm not laid out like a corpse?"

Frieda laughed. The two needled each other as Frieda cranked the handle at the end of the bed. Mitzi raised a hand when she was in a sitting position. "Whoa! That'll do it, unless you want me touching my toes and kissing my knees."

"Don't tempt me." She headed for the kitchen. "I'll fix you some tea and your guest some cocoa."

Mitzi gave Abra a stern look. "So. You took off with Romeo and ended up with King Lear." When Abra dipped her chin, Mitzi raised it, her gaze full of tenderness. "Don't worry, sweetie pie. I'm not going to beat you up about it. I think you've probably done more than enough of that on your own time. I don't want to waste mine." She gripped Abra's hand firmly. "It's a new day the Lord has made. What do you plan to do with it?"

"Finish high school, get a job, and try to rebuild the bridges I burned."

"Plenty of people willing to help with that."

"So I've discovered."

"Ah, the girl is growing up." Mitzi started coughing. She let go of Abra's hand, covering her mouth with one hand and waving at a box of tissue with the other. Abra pulled out two or three and handed them to her. Mitzi kept coughing and fighting for breath. Frieda appeared and took over, encouraging Mitzi to get the stuff out of her lungs. She braced Mitzi and rubbed her back, then took the tissues and deposited them in a covered waste bin.

Mitzi leaned back, pale and weak. "I had pneumonia. Just can't seem to bounce back."

"Takes time, Mitzi." Frieda picked up a stethoscope and put in the earpieces before listening to Mitzi's chest.

"Is there a heart in there?"

"Stop talking. I'm trying to find it." She gave Mitzi a teasing smirk. "There it is."

"Now that you know I'm alive, how about that tea?"

"In a minute."

Clearly the two women had been through this drill before. Frieda removed the stethoscope and picked up a clipboard with a pen tied to it. She jotted a few notes. "Steady improvement." She went back into the kitchen.

Abra sat on the edge of the bed again. "You look exhausted, Mitzi."

"All that coughing and breathing does take more than phlegm out of me."

Frieda delivered tea and cocoa and a plate of homemade macaroons, and said she was going to be in the kitchen for a while getting dinner started.

"She's trying to fatten me up."

"Well, please let her."

"Don't you start in on me." Mitzi picked up a macaroon. "Now, what about your music?"

Abra shrugged. "I've probably forgotten everything you ever taught me."

"I doubt that. But let's see, shall we?" She nodded toward the piano. "Play me 'In the Sweet By and By.'"

Abra winced. "Can I finish my cocoa and cookies first?" She'd always associated that hymn with Marianne Freeman's memorial service.

"Make it fast. I'm not getting any younger." Mitzi sucked macaroon crumbs off her fingers with gusto. "I'm making a list of songs I want played at my funeral."

Abra barely managed to swallow. "That's not funny!"

Mitzi chortled. "Oh, you should see your face!"

"I should dump cocoa on your head!"

"At least you don't look like you're here for a viewing. Now get your backside on that bench. It's been five long years. I want to hear you play again."

Abra set the mug aside and went to the piano. Positioning the bench, she ran her hands reverently over the keys. She started with scales to warm up, her fingers racing from one end of the keyboard to the other. She played chords and resolutions.

And then the songs came from memory, one after another. "Amazing Grace." "O the Deep, Deep Love of Jesus." "Immortal, Invisible, God Only Wise." "Holy, Holy, Holy." "All Hail the Power of Jesus' Name." One ran into another with easy transitions. Mitzi's clock chimed and Abra lifted her hands away from the keyboard.

"I knew you'd never forget, sweetie pie. I counted on it."

Abra closed the piano, running her hand across the polished wood. "Lines of hymns used to come to me at the oddest times."

"Probably when God knew you needed them most. Have you thought about writing any music of your own?"

"Me?" Abra laughed. "I wouldn't know where to begin."

Mitzi studied her. "You don't just look different. You play differently. There's more Abra coming through those nice long fingers of yours. You should play around and see what comes to you. You never know what'll happen unless you step out in faith."

Abra sat on the side of the bed. "What about you, Mitzi? Do you have some original compositions tucked away? Something you poured your heart and soul into?"

Mitzi took Abra's hand and smiled into her eyes. "Just you, sweetie pie. Just you."

———

Joshua called and asked Abra to dinner. When he pulled up, she came out the door in a pretty yellow sundress, her hair now burnished brown rather than ebony, neatly trimmed into a soft cap that framed her face. He got out of his truck, but she came down the steps and out the gate before he reached the sidewalk. "Wait a minute!"

"What for?" She opened the passenger door and slid in.

Annoyed, Joshua went around and got back into the truck. "Next time, wait until I ring the bell."

"Why?"

"Because that's what a lady does, and I want to usher you to my chariot like a gentleman."

She laughed at him. "Oh, just start the truck, Joshua. I can't wait to go to Bessie's."

Joshua turned the ignition key, but his engine was already revving. "I thought I'd take you to the new steak house out on—"

"Oh, no. Please. I haven't had a good hamburger, fries, and a chocolate shake in ages."

So much for his plans for a quiet, private dinner in a nice restaurant. Joshua hoped this wasn't an indication that Abra expected them to go back to being good buddies. He had something more than a platonic relationship in mind.

Bessie beamed when they came in the door. "Well, if you two aren't a sight for sore eyes! Susan! Look who the cat dragged in!" She seated them in a booth across from the counter and put her hands on her hips. "Do you two need a menu? Or shall I just bring out the usual?"

Abra grinned. "I don't need a menu."

Joshua shrugged in defeat.

A little frown flickered across Abra's face when Bessie left them alone. "I'm glad you called. I haven't seen you for a while."

He could have told her the number of days and hours. "Worried I'd forgotten about you?"

"When I didn't see you in church, I thought you might've changed your mind and gone back to Southern California."

Not a chance of that happening now that she was back in Haven. "You didn't see me because your family comes to the second service, and I attend the first."

"Oh."

Joshua grinned. "I dare you to say it."

"Say what?"

"You missed me."

She gave a soft laugh. "Okay. I missed you."

Joshua kept looking at her. He let his gaze roam leisurely over her face, lingering on her lips, her throat. She swallowed, and he raised his eyes, watching hers dilate. Color rose into her cheeks, and her lips parted. She looked aware, but uncertain. He smiled. "Your hair looks better."

"Pris—*Mom* took me to Snips and Clips to repair the damage I did. It's going to be a while before it's red again, but at least I look a little more like—" she shrugged—"me."

He hadn't missed the new reference to Priscilla, but he didn't want to make a big thing out of it. "What else have you been doing?"

"Peter is going to tutor me so I can pass the GED test. Dorothea Endicott hired me part-time. I start at her shop on Monday, twenty hours a week. What about you?"

"I got my old job back with Jack Wooding. He's starting a new subdivision on the northeast end of town. When the model homes are up and ready, I'll take you by to see them." He didn't mention the lot or house plans or how soon the house he wanted would be ready.

"I'd like that."

"How are you and Penny getting along?"

"We've been spending a lot of time together. She's at the house every morning. The baby's due anytime now. Penny and Rob were arguing about names last night. Paul or Patrick if it's a boy, Pauline or Paige if it's a girl." Abra's smile held no reservations. "Either way, there will be four *P*s in the pod."

"And one *A*," he reminded her.

She laughed. "I could always change my name to Pandora." Her expression changed. "I've been spending time with Mitzi."

He'd been by for a visit. "She said you're playing piano again."

"She wants me to work with Ian Brubaker. She thinks I should write my own music. I don't know about that. I wish I'd come home sooner. I've wasted so much time."

He watched the emotions flicker and be battened down, then well up again. "You had things to learn, Abra."

"Oh, Joshua, some things I wish I didn't know." She forced a smile when Bessie delivered their hamburgers and fries.

Susan brought their shakes. "It's good to have you home, Abra." Abra said it was good to be back. Joshua noticed she didn't call Haven her home. Susan looked from Abra to him. "Nice to see you, too, Joshua." Susan left them alone, but glanced their way several times.

Abra picked up the hamburger and took a bite. Her soft moan of pleasure made his pulse jump. He watched her chew, swallow, and take a sip of chocolate shake. She rolled her eyes. "I'm in heaven." She looked at his plate. "Aren't you going to eat?"

"I'm having too much fun watching you."

"Oliver's are the best. Franklin wouldn't let me eat hamburgers or french fries. Or drink sodas." She took another bite, obviously enjoying the meal. "Bad for my skin, too many calories." She relaxed again and talked, and he was getting a picture of her years in a penthouse with a man who controlled every facet of her life. "I shouldn't be telling you all this."

"Why not?"

"It bothers you."

He'd tried hard not to show how much. "Nothing you're telling me changes how I feel about you, Abra." That's as much as he would say for now, knowing it would be enough.

They lingered over their hamburgers and then sat in the square.

Abra had already shared the facts with him in her confession; now she shared feelings. He heard things between the lines, things she didn't even know to say. The hurt went way back to a time when she would've been too young to understand or even remember clearly. She needed to talk to Dad.

The clock tower bonged. Abra turned and looked up. "Midnight! I've talked your ear off and you've hardly said a word."

"I've been listening." His arm rested on the back of the bench behind her. "You know, if we stay here long enough, we can have breakfast at Bessie's. Do you have a curfew?"

"Peter—I mean, Dad—knows I'm with you. He wouldn't worry if we stayed out all night."

"Nice to know he thinks I'm safe."

She scooted closer and rested her head against his shoulder. "Thanks for listening, Joshua." She straightened abruptly. "What time do you have to be at work?"

"Seven."

"Oh! I'm so sorry." She stood, taking his hand and pulling him up. "You need to get home so you can get some sleep."

"Only if you go out with me again tomorrow night, and let me choose the place."

"If you'd like."

"We just got started in Agua Dulce." He took her by the hand. "We have a lot of catching up to do."

Ian Brubaker said the best place for Abra's lessons was at Haven Community Church because the congregation had unanimously agreed to invest in a grand piano. With Ian's connections, they had purchased a concert-quality Steinway at a bargain price. No one had objections when Ian asked Pastor Zeke and the board of elders for permission to use the instrument for Abra's lessons.

Ian proved to be as strict as ever, a hard-driving teacher who reminded her in some ways of Franklin. Franklin had been a perfectionist, and he had drilled her until lines of dialogue became confused with reality. Franklin had been lost before he found her, and he had made Lena Scott the center of his life. *And I helped destroy him, Lord. I can't say I didn't know what I was doing.*

Things had been going well until today. She couldn't concentrate, kept fumbling notes and then having trouble finding her place to start again. Frustrated, she raised her hands, fighting the urge to pound her fists on the keys. It wasn't the piano's fault she couldn't make her fingers work today.

Ian put a firm hand on her shoulder. "Enough for today. It'll take time to get you back to where you were. I'll see you on Sunday."

Abra gathered the sheets of music. Instead of walking home, she went to the church office, where Irene Farley greeted her with a hug before peeking into Pastor Zeke's office. "Go on in. I have to step out for a while."

Pastor Zeke came around his desk and embraced her. He rubbed his chin gently on the top of her head before releasing her and gesturing to a chair while he took the other, facing her. "I was going to come into the sanctuary and listen to you play. You're finished with your lesson already?"

"Yes. And a good thing you didn't listen. I couldn't seem to play anything without making a dozen mistakes." She chewed on her lower lip.

"Something on your mind?"

Something had been on her mind for a very long time, a wound that had never healed. "I have to ask you a question."

"You can ask me anything."

She had the strangest feeling he knew what she would ask. But even now that the moment had come, she wasn't sure she could get the words past the heartache, past the constriction tightening her throat. "And please," she begged, "tell me the truth this time." She saw hurt flicker in his eyes at that.

"I always have, Abra."

Had he? Maybe he didn't even realize. She raised her eyes and looked into his. "Did you blame me for Mama Marianne's death?" He looked surprised, then distressed. "Don't answer until you think about it. Please."

He leaned back, closing his eyes. He sat so long, Abra wondered if she should go. She was ready to rise when he let out a soft sigh and spoke bleakly. "Not consciously."

He looked into her eyes, hiding nothing. "Though I can see how you might have felt that way. I was so caught up in my own grief, I had trouble thinking of anyone's needs other than my own."

He leaned forward, hands loosely clasped between his knees, his gaze fixed upon her. "The greatest trial of my life had to do with you. I didn't want to give you up. Then God made it clear that's what He required of me. I was called away at all hours of the day and night, and Joshua was just a boy. I couldn't leave him responsible. Once before I had rejected God's plan, and then had to face the cost."

"You tried to explain it to me."

"Yes, but what can a child of five understand?" His eyes glistened. "I know I hurt you, but I have more to confess, Abra."

Hands clenched in her lap, Abra waited.

"When I found you and saved you, I loved you as though you were my own flesh and blood. It wasn't just Marianne who wanted to take you home and make you part of our family. I knew we shouldn't. Marianne had rheumatic fever when she was a child and it weakened her heart. Giving birth to Joshua took a great toll, and the doctor advised us against having any more children. But she'd always dreamed of having a little girl. You were the answer to all her prayers, and an unexpected gift to me, too."

He leaned back slowly, looking weary. "Had I been stronger—or less selfish—I would have stood firm. We both knew the risk, but I wanted her to be happy. Since then, I have often wished that we had given you to Peter and Priscilla in the first place."

"What do you mean, in the first place?"

"Peter and Priscilla came to the hospital right after I'd found you. They wanted to adopt you. I didn't have the heart or courage to take you from Marianne's arms."

"They wanted me?"

"Oh, yes. Right from the beginning, Abra. I didn't think about the possible ramifications of my decision until Marianne died and I faced the truth. I couldn't take proper care of you by myself. I didn't have the money to hire someone to watch over you. And I was gone so often. You were barely five and grieving for the only mother you'd ever known, and I couldn't be there for you. Peter and Priscilla were so helpful with you after Marianne died—Penny already loved you like a sister—and I knew what God wanted. It broke my heart to take you to their house and leave you there. I saw that you didn't understand. I heard how you withdrew. You weren't the same child after that. I tried to make it easier on you by coming by as often as I could. I kept hoping you would make the transition. Peter finally had to ask me to stay away. My frequent visits were only making everything worse." His mouth curved in a sad smile. "How could you bond with them if I was always around? I realized my selfishness and stayed away."

Pieces of the past came together. "That's why we went to another church."

"Yes. We all agreed that would be best." Pastor Zeke shook his head, his expression filled with regret. "Or hoped it would be. It helped Penny become more outgoing, but you closed yourself off even more. Every change seemed to do more harm than good. You strove to be perfect, to please everyone. It hurt to watch. I felt helpless. All I could do was pray. There hasn't been a day in your life when I haven't prayed for you, not once, but many times."

She felt the tight fist of her heart opening wide to him. "I saw you standing at the gate, night after night. I wanted you to come and ring the bell and take me home."

His eyes filled. "You were home, Abra. You are home." He held his hands out, palms up. "I ask for your forgiveness."

She put her hands in his. "As you have forgiven me, so I forgive you." She remembered how much he had grieved over Marianne, and knew in the years that followed, her coldness had wounded him even more. "It's true. Marianne might have lived longer had I not come into your lives?"

"No. I struggled with that thought and blamed myself until God reminded me He knows the number of hairs on our heads. He knows the days He has allotted us. Those five years you spent with us were a joy to Marianne." He kissed her right hand. "And to me." He kissed her left. "And Joshua." When he raised his head, his expression softened with an expectant smile. "God holds the future in His hands." He put her hands together between his. "Any other questions?"

She could breathe again. "Probably, but none come to me right now." When he let go of her, she stood with a deep sigh. "Thank you."

"Anytime." He put his arm around her shoulders as he walked with her. "My door is always open."

Turning, she stood on tiptoe and kissed his cheek. "I love you. Daddy."

"I have not heard those words from you in a very long time." His eyes grew moist. "I love you, too."

She opened the door and almost collided with Susan Wells, who stepped back abruptly, her eyes going wide with surprise. She stammered a quick apology. Flustered, she looked past Abra to Pastor Zeke and blushed.

Abra's brows rose slightly as she brushed off the apology, stepped around Susan, and went out the door. Susan hadn't just looked surprised. She'd looked guilty. Abra kept walking, a smile tugging at her lips.

So that's why Pastor Zeke had spent so much time at Bessie's Corner Café over the years!

Pastor Zeke and Susan. Now that she thought about it, they would make a nice couple.

CHAPTER 19

1959

Abra finished her morning shift at Dorothea's and sat on a bench in the square, soaking in the peace as early spring sunlight descended through the towering redwoods. She lifted her face and felt the caressing warmth. Rising, she walked past the bandstand and crossed the street to Bessie's. Sometimes Pastor Zeke went there for lunch, and she might be able to sit and talk with him for a while. She hadn't seen Joshua for a few days and missed him. He said he was working late on a project, but wouldn't say what it was.

Susan glanced up, looking surprised. "Nice to see you, Abra."

"And you." Abra sat at the counter instead of in a booth, wondering again if something was going on between the waitress and Pastor Zeke. Marianne had been gone a long time. Susan was a nice woman, though she'd always been something of an enigma.

Susan gave her a warm smile. "What can I get you?"

"I think I'll live dangerously and have a root beer float."

"Seems like you're usually with Joshua when you come in." Susan spoke over her shoulder as she scooped vanilla ice cream into a tall glass.

"He's my best friend."

Susan pulled a lever, and root beer hissed over the ice cream. She poked a straw into the drink and set it on the counter. "Joshua is a special guy."

"Yes."

"He loves you, you know."

"I know."

"No, I don't think you do. I've watched you two over the years I've been here. Things changed for him when he came home from Korea."

"What do you mean?"

"He's in love with you. That's what I mean. There isn't a soul in this town that doesn't know it, except you."

Abra stared at her, mouth agape. There had been moments when she wondered, hoped, but he acted with the same circumspect manner he always had. "People don't know everything."

Susan seemed to be on a mission. "I see the way he looks at you when you're not aware, and I see the way you look at him. You love him, Abra. What are you going to do about it?"

Abra felt the heat flood her cheeks. She'd never had a conversation like this with Susan—or anyone else, for that matter—and she was unprepared to answer with anything but flat truth. "He deserves someone a lot better than me."

"He wants *you*."

Someone came in and took a booth. Susan put her hands on the counter and lowered her voice, her expression almost pleading. "You have a chance for real love, Abra. Grab it! Hold on tight! Not all of us are so fortunate."

On the walk home, Abra heard the familiar rumble of Joshua's truck behind her. Her heart jumped, and everything Susan had said sounded like trumpets in her head. Turning, she smiled and stuck out her thumb.

He pulled over to the curb and shoved the passenger door open. "How could I pass up such a beautiful girl?" His gaze swept over her as she slipped into the passenger seat.

Her pulse kept climbing. The scent of healthy male sweat filled the cab.

She breathed in Joshua as Elvis Presley's "One Night" played on the radio he'd installed. *"Life without you has been too lonely too long."* How odd to realize that she'd once met the young man who had gone on to such fame and fortune. She wondered if he had been able to find what he'd been looking for amid the glitter and glamour that had proven so empty for her.

Joshua put the truck in gear. "I was going to come by after I got cleaned up. The model homes are finished. Want to take a look?"

Another place had beckoned for a long time, but she hadn't wanted to heed the call. "Can we go to Riverfront Park first?"

His brows rose in surprise. "Sure. I'll drop you off, get cleaned up, and pick you up in—"

"I'd like to go now, Joshua, if you don't mind." If she waited, she might find more excuses not to go.

"Okay." He made a U-turn at Maple Avenue and headed for the bridge. "What's going on?"

"I don't know." She rolled down the window as Joshua reached the bridge. Leaning over, she stretched her neck to see the water rippling blue and clear below. It was too early for summer visitors. No trailers in the campsites, no racing children on the banks. She listened to the *thump-thump* of the truck wheels as Joshua drove across the bridge. He downshifted and turned into Riverfront Park on the other side.

He parked so they faced the river. "Okay. We're here. What now?"

"I'm going to take a little walk by myself." She got out and walked over the grassy mound. Her feet sank into the white sand Haven brought in each year to replenish "the beach." She headed for the cement piers supporting the bridge.

Abra looked up and saw the covering of the bridge. She stepped out, so she could see the railing. She had dreamed countless times of Pastor Zeke standing up there, looking down at her. He said once he'd just had a feeling he had to come to the bridge that morning. He'd always believed God had sent him.

Why hadn't she believed that? Yes, her mother had abandoned her, but God hadn't. God had placed her in Zeke and Marianne Freeman's arms, and when Marianne went home to the Lord, and Pastor Zeke had the responsibility of a congregation of needy people, God had seen her safely to another family, with a second father and mother, and added another blessing of a feisty sister. When she ran away, God reached out through Murray and Mary Ellen. When she lost all faith and hope, He brought her to Agua Dulce and Joshua.

Abra stared up at the bridge—a canopy of protection, a road to cross, a way home—and felt overwhelmed at the love she'd been offered. *You have a chance, Abra. Grab it. Hold on tight.* Why did she see so clearly now what had been hidden from her for so long?

I have held you in the palm of My hand, and I will never let you go.

Abra felt alive and free as she fully accepted what her heart had always longed to believe and couldn't quite grasp.

She gave a soft, broken laugh of joy. "You love *me*, Lord. In spite of my stubborn and rebellious heart."

I knew you before you were born. I've counted the hairs on your head. I have written your name on the palms of My hands.

As she looked up through the trusses of the bridge and back over her life, she saw the truth. Humbled, she whispered lines from one of Mitzi's favorite hymns. "'O the deep, deep love of Jesus, vast, unmeasured, boundless, free! Rolling as a mighty ocean in its fullness over me.'"

Turning, she saw Joshua standing not far away, thumbs hooked in his pockets, relaxed, watching her, waiting. Her heart turned over and filled up with love. She called out to him. "Would you baptize me, Joshua?"

His face registered surprise. "Sure. We can talk it over with Dad."

"I don't want to wait. I want you to baptize me now."

"Here?"

What better place? What better time? "Yes!" Abra waded into the river until she stood waist-deep, the current gently pulling at her skirt.

Joshua met her there, his calloused hands cupping hers as she covered her nose and mouth. He lowered her back. "Buried with Christ . . ."

She held her breath as she went under the cool, clean water. Opening her eyes, she saw the shimmer of the cleansing stream moving over and around her, Joshua above.

His arm tightened beneath her shoulders as he lifted her. ". . . raised to the newness of life." He supported her until she had her feet firmly planted.

Wiping water from her face, Abra laughed. "Oh, Joshua, I've been a blind beggar all my life." She lifted her head. "And now I see!"

"Abra." Her name came in soft exaltation, his eyes shining as he cupped her face. "Abra." He kissed her, not as a brother or a friend, but as a man in love.

"You have a chance for real love, Abra. Grab it! Hold on tight!"

She slid her arms around Joshua's waist and lifted her head. When his arms came around her, she molded herself against him. When he kissed her this time, she kissed him back.

Pulling away, Joshua set her back a few inches. "No more." He was breathing hard, his eyes dark. "Until after you marry me." He winced in apology. "Sorry. That was the lousiest proposal in history."

"It was good enough. Yes!" She was laughing and crying at the same time. "When?"

Laughing with her, Joshua swung her up in his arms. "We'll ask Dad to open his calendar." He carried her from the river.

―――――

On the day of the wedding, Zeke stopped by to see Abra on his way to the church.

"I'll get her." Priscilla headed up the stairs. "Penny! Paige is hungry and I can't feed her. Abra, honey, Pastor Zeke is downstairs. He wants to talk to you."

Peter rolled his eyes and led Zeke into the living room. "Thank goodness we only have two daughters. I don't think Priss would survive another wedding."

"Pastor Zeke!" Abra appeared in a fuzzy pink bathrobe and slippers, her hair in curlers. "I'm sorry I'm not dressed yet."

Zeke gave her a hug. "Don't worry," he whispered against her ear. "You look beautiful." As he drew back, he took a small box from his jacket pocket. "Something old to go with something borrowed and something blue."

Abra opened the box and caught her breath. "You found it."

She looked up at him, and the pain and guilt in her expression filled him with an overwhelming tenderness. "A few days after you left."

Tears slipped down her cheeks as she touched Marianne's gold cross. "I don't deserve to have this."

"Marianne wanted you to have it. She wore it on our wedding day."

Abra stepped forward and rested her forehead against his chest. "Thank you."

―――――

Abra's heart jumped like a frightened rabbit when Joshua pulled off the road and parked in front of a small house with a partial second story in the shape of a lighthouse. Cypresses hedged the two sides and back. A small hamlet was a quarter mile down the road with a few lights on in the windows. Surf pounded just across the road and she smelled salt-sea air. Joshua got out of the truck and came around to open her door. He took a flashlight from the glove compartment before he helped her out. The misting night raised goose bumps. Wind tossed her hair. She shivered.

Their wedding had been everything she could have dreamed. It seemed like the whole town turned out for it—even Mitzi, dressed in red with a colorful scarf wrapped around her hair. She was showing her age and failing health, but she still knew how to put on the ritz. She had whispered to Abra after the ceremony, "I promised myself I wouldn't give up the ghost until I saw this wedding through."

Priscilla and Rob, with baby Paige in his arms, sat in the front row, along with Susan. Pastor Zeke must have placed her there. Dave Upton and Penny stood up with the bride and groom, and of course Pastor Zeke had performed the ceremony. He reminded everyone that marriage had been ordained by God in the Garden of Eden between the first man and woman, confirmed by Jesus' first miracle in Cana, and declared by divine inspiration by the apostle Paul: "When a man and woman come together in marriage, they become one in flesh and spirit. Wives, submit to your husbands' leadership in the same way you submit to the Lord. Husbands, love your wives as Christ Jesus also loved the church and gave Himself for it. So you ought to love your wives as you love your own bodies. Again, I say to you, love your wife as a part of yourself. And wives, see to it that you respect your husband, reverencing, praising, and honoring him."

Joshua hadn't told her where he was taking her for their honeymoon. He'd simply told her to pack jeans and sneakers. He hadn't let her see the inside of the house he'd built either. He wanted to surprise her. She wasn't sure she could handle much more excitement.

Joshua took her hand and led the way, unlocking the front door and flicking on the light just inside. The living room looked cozy and comfortable with its simple furnishings. Before she could take a step inside, Joshua swept her up in his arms and carried her over the threshold. He kissed her before he set her down. "Home sweet home, for the next seven days." She tensed when his hands slid down her back and rested on her hips. A slight frown flickered before he stepped away. "Bedroom and bathroom through that door, light switch on the right. I'll get the fire going and then bring in your suitcase." Everything had been prepared. All he had to do was strike a match.

Her stomach tightened with tension.

An open door revealed steps, but she went through the small bedroom to use the bathroom first, wondering why the double bed had been stripped of all but the bottom sheet. The bathroom had plenty of freshly laundered towels, a claw-foot tub with a shower, and a pedestal sink. The mirrored medicine cabinet held a toothbrush, toothpaste, men's deodorant, shaving cream, and a razor. When she came into the bedroom again, she noticed a couple pairs of Levi's and cotton shirts hanging in the closet. Abra checked the bureau and a trunk under the window. The front door opened and closed. "We don't have any blankets, Joshua." And it was cold and she was growing colder.

Joshua came into the bedroom and put her suitcase on the trunk. "We're not going to sleep in here." It was the way he said it that made her pulse quicken. He stepped back. "Someone put a basket in the truck. Let's see what's inside." He went into the living room, where the fire crackled and a single lamp cast a golden glow.

"That's Priscilla's picnic basket."

Joshua set it on the rug in front of the fireplace. She knelt and opened it. Chicken salad sandwiches, grapes, Brie, crackers, a bottle of champagne, two crystal glasses, and a couple of candles with holders.

"Nice. Everything we need for a romantic supper."

The room was already growing comfortably warm. Abra kicked off her shoes and sat, feeling overdressed in her green suit. She stretched out her legs. Neither had eaten more than a couple of canapés and the bites of wedding cake they fed to one another.

The last three months were a blur of wedding preparations, showers, visiting Mitzi, working with Ian Brubaker, and spending half a day five days a week at Dorothea's. Abra had seen less of Joshua after they set the date than before.

Yesterday, Penny had brought baby Paige and a bassinet over and announced she was spending the night. Penny fussed over her baby while she talked about her wedding and honeymoon. Abra had felt an aching sadness and regret as she watched her sister cover herself modestly and nurse Paige.

"Rob knew more than I did, not that he was vastly experienced, mind you. He and his father had *the talk* the night before the bachelor party." She laughed. "Rob said he'd never seen his father blush and told him he already knew about the birds and the bees." She laid sweet Paige on her lap, sound asleep, tiny bow mouth still moving, and readjusted her clothing. "Mom gave me the talk, too." As she lifted Paige to her shoulder, she looked at Abra and stopped laughing. "What's wrong?"

Abra shrugged. "At least Mom will be spared that embarrassment. I know more than enough about the facts of life." She looked away, tears running down her cheeks. "I threw it all away, Penny. I can't give Joshua the gift you gave Rob. I'm not a virgin. I'm not innocent."

Penny's eyes filled with sympathy. "Joshua doesn't hold your past against you. It's all part of who you've become now." She held out Paige, unwittingly causing more pain. "Here, Auntie Abra, hold your niece." She touched Abra's knee. "It won't be like it was with Dylan or a man old enough to be your father. Joshua is . . . well, Joshua."

Abra held the baby close, looking into her sweet face, another sorrow. She didn't even know if she could have another child after what she'd done. Why would God allow it? Joshua knew everything, but she should have raised that question, given him a chance to consider the other gift he might never have.

Joshua brushed his knuckles lightly against her cheek, startling her out of her reverie. "It's just you and me now, Abra."

She knew what he meant. *Don't let Dylan or Franklin into the house. Don't invite them on the honeymoon.* She didn't want them here any more than he did. Joshua's eyes were so tender, she was afraid she'd let him down. She was afraid when it came to the final moment, she'd go cold.

Yes, she felt stirred by him as she never had before, but could she surrender, and what might that mean? She already felt the tension growing inside her body, the niggling fear she wouldn't be enough. She felt the instinctive desire to protect herself.

Stop worrying. Stop, stop, stop. She wanted to remember one kiss in the river, not the thousand kisses that had brought disillusionment.

Joshua wasn't like Dylan or Franklin. He hadn't even touched her during the past three months. When she'd asked why, he'd told her it was because he wanted her too much, and he wanted all things to happen properly and in God's time. He'd joked about the number of cold showers he was taking. His commitment to purity before marriage made her grieve that she had no purity to offer him. She'd tempted two men, and brought out the worst in both. She didn't want to tempt Joshua.

The fire crackled. The surf pounded.

"Do you want to talk about what you're thinking?" Joshua watched the shifting expressions on Abra's face and wanted to draw her back to the present and to him. She'd been pensive in the weeks before the wedding, but this was something else. Honeymoon jitters? He had butterflies in his stomach, too. He wished that was all it was, but he knew her too well. He brushed a strand of hair away from her cheek and tucked it behind her ear. "This is a night for love, Abra, not regrets."

"I'm sorry. I'm trying."

He put his arm around her shoulders and rocked her gently against him, kissing the top of her head. "Don't try so hard. It's going to be good between us."

Dad had years of counseling experience behind him, and they had talked about what Abra might feel after what she'd been through. She'd been abused and used, never loved. It was understandable she'd shut down, retreat inside herself. Dad talked about what a honeymoon was meant to be. Tonight wouldn't be just about their sexual union; it would be about finding ways for Joshua to show his bride how much he cherished her, that she could trust him completely, that he intended to restore her and lift her up and love her.

It would be a night of patience as well as passion—if he could hold his desire in check long enough. He'd laughed a little when admitting that to Dad, and Dad told him to bring God into the midst of everything, to ask for self-control. Joshua had fasted and prayed that his physical needs wouldn't win out over his desire to give Abra whatever time she needed. Now he breathed in the unique scent of her, and his head swam.

Oh, Lord, I'm walking in a minefield. Help me reach my wounded bride. Help me bring a healing touch.

He took his arm from her, remembering she'd barely eaten at the wedding reception. "God bless Priscilla for thinking of this." Joshua smeared Brie on a cracker and held it out to her. "I planned our meals through the end of the week, but I didn't think about tonight. We didn't get much of a chance to eat, did we?" He smiled into her eyes. She broke his heart. He didn't like seeing that look in her eyes, nor thinking about who and what had put it there.

She nibbled at the cracker and set it on the side table. Joshua took the cue and set the basket aside. They'd eat later. "We've known each other all our lives, Abra. But this is new territory, isn't it?"

"Yes." Her voice caught softly and he felt her increasing tension.

"Do you trust me?"

She looked at him, studying his face. "Yes." She took a shaky breath. "How did you ever find this place?"

He knew delaying the inevitable wasn't going to make things any easier for her. "Jack told me about it. He and Reka come out a couple times a year." He stood and held out his hands. Hers were cold. "The owner is an architect. He lives in San Francisco and doesn't get up here very often. So he rents the place out. There's a nice stretch of beach right across the street. You'll see it in the morning. We can take a walk whenever we want."

He drew her close, felt her body trembling. "It's okay, Abra." He spoke gently, his lips against her hair. "We're going to take our time tonight." Her heightened breathing against his throat aroused him. He brushed a few curls back from her temple. "We're in no hurry." This wasn't going to be a drag race down a backcountry road, but the Indianapolis 500.

"Oh, Joshua." Her tone implied she knew better than he what to expect of this night.

He lifted her chin. "I love you." He kissed her the way he'd longed to do for weeks. She tasted like heaven, and he savored her. "I cherish you." He took his time and felt her body relaxing, growing warm. She moved closer, and desire rose in him like a fire. He drew back a little, banking it. She gave a soft sigh, eyes closed. He unbuttoned her wool jacket and smoothed it back off her shoulders, then sucked in his breath sharply when she tried to unbuckle his belt. "No." He captured her hands and drew them up over his shoulders. If she started touching him below the waist, it would all be over. "I want us to get to know each other."

"We already know each other, Joshua."

"I know your mind and heart, Abra. I want to know your body, what you need, what pleases you." Her eyes flickered with surprise and grew moist. "I want to undress you. Are you ready for me to do that?"

Abra gathered her courage and nodded because she couldn't trust her voice to answer. Her skin burned under his fingers' touch. He removed each layer, like layers of wrapping paper hiding a precious gift marked *Fragile: Handle with care.* He removed everything but his mother's cross necklace, and then looked at her in wonder. When his gentle hands moved down over her, she shivered.

"Are you cold?"

"No." Was that throaty voice hers? Abra felt a sense of wonder, an inner assurance.

Cast all your fears away, beloved. Everything was going to be different with Joshua.

"You're so beautiful." His hands moved over her body. "So soft."

She drew in her breath as currents of warmth and sensation swept through her. When he smiled at her, she smiled at him. He took her hands and put them flat against his chest. She could feel the strong, fast beat of his heart. "Your turn."

Following his lead, she took her time. He trembled, too. When he stood naked, she ran her hand over the scar on his side. Leaning in, she kissed it. Michelangelo's *David* could not compare to her husband.

When they both stood face-to-face, like Adam and Eve in the Garden of Eden, she felt no shame, but only a sweet, urgent expectation opening like a flower inside her. He was so perfect, so strong, so beautiful, and she loved him so much her heart ached.

She caught her breath at his strength when he swept her up in his arms as though she weighed nothing and carried her into the bedroom. She reminded herself how well she knew him. This was the boy she'd played with, the teen who'd teased her, the friend who'd driven her around town and treated her to hamburgers, fries, and chocolate milk shakes. This was Joshua, the man she loved. Joshua, the husband who was about to become her lover. He placed her on the bed.

She touched his face as he leaned down over her, loving the planes, the light stubble of beard, his lips slightly parted, the warmth and sweetness of his breath. She gave a soft laugh and then gasped as he stretched out beside her—rough against smooth; hard muscle against soft curves. She felt herself retreat, and knew he felt it, too.

"What do you need, Abra? What do you want?" He spoke gently, his eyes tender. "Tell me."

"I don't know." She'd never been asked before, and she didn't know what it would take for her to shed the niggling fear that kept trying to ruin this. "Joshua." She said his name to remind herself. "Oh, Joshua, I'm sorry."

He put his fingertips against her lips and smiled tenderly. "We'll figure it out."

And miraculously, he did. The coldness melted, and her body filled with voluptuous sensations. When Joshua finally slipped his hand beneath her head and drew her into the marital embrace, she was ready. A symphony began inside her when she looked into his eyes so tender and pleasure-saturated, as she touched his face.

The surf pounded. She heard drums beating, the tempo quickening. The tension went deep, stretched taut, and then raised her up higher and higher until harmonious chords broke into exaltation. Suspended, she felt the exquisite resolution, the drifting like a leaf fluttering downward softly back and forth until it rested, spent, on earth.

Joshua shifted his weight. "And God came up with this idea." He gave a throaty laugh, nuzzling her neck as he rolled over, holding her on top of him. His hands ran down her back in a sweeping caress. "How do you feel?"

Abra sighed and rested her head against her husband's chest. "Born again." Languorous and drowsy, she tucked herself close. "I think I could sleep for a week now."

"Then it's time we went to bed." Joshua rose and took her by the hand. He led her up the stairs to the observatory, where he'd made a bed of sheets and blankets.

"I wondered how we'd stay warm."

"Did you? Look up."

Nestled in each other's arms, they slept beneath the canopy of stars.

Zeke waited a few days before he dropped by Joshua and Abra's home to see how they were doing. He heard the faint sounds of someone who knew how to play a piano very well. Mitzi had surprised Abra with the gift of her piano, delivered and tuned while the newlyweds were on their honeymoon. Sounded like Abra was already putting it to good use.

"Dad!" Joshua opened the front door. "Come on in. You haven't been over since we got back from our honeymoon."

"I wanted to give you a little time alone."

Abra came to hug him.

"I heard you playing. A piece I haven't heard before."

"Just something I've been working on." She asked him to sit and make himself comfortable. He took one end of the sofa, Joshua the other, while Abra perched on the arm beside her husband. His son looked happy and relaxed, Abra radiant. Zeke had never doubted Joshua and Abra would do well together. As they talked of ordinary things, he watched their interaction—a brush of fingers, a quick glance, an adoring look. They had used their honeymoon wisely. The faint shadow of doubt had left Abra's eyes. They were clear now, sparkling, full of joy. She knew she was loved and could now love fully in return. The promise of what could be was being fulfilled.

"I brought you something." He handed the gift to Abra and watched her unwrap Marianne's Bible. Would she remember she had returned it to him with instructions to save it for Joshua's wife?

Abra held it against her chest and smiled at him through shimmering tears of gratitude. "I'll cherish it." He saw she remembered everything, especially that her sins had been put as far away from her as the east is from the west.

CHAPTER 20

Nearer, still nearer, close to Thy heart,
Draw me, my Savior, so precious Thou art;
Fold me, O fold me close to Thy breast,
Shelter me safe in that "Haven of Rest."

LEILA MORRIS

JOSHUA AWAKENED when Abra moaned. She moved restlessly beneath the covers, as though in a struggle. She talked, but not distinctly enough for him to understand. He moved closer, touching her bare shoulder. "Abra." She startled awake, panting. He rubbed her arm. "You were having a bad dream, honey." Her breathing slowed and then she started to cry.

"Tell me." He stroked her hair.

She gulped. "I almost saw her face."

When she curled on her side, Joshua curved his body around hers in comfort. He rubbed the top of her head with his chin. "Whose face?"

"My mother's." She shuddered a sigh.

Joshua felt her breathing ease. He was tired, but if she wanted to talk, he'd listen.

"I used to dream about the bridge and I'd be lying on the gravel, helpless and cold. I could see Dad up on the walkway, looking down at me, but I couldn't cry out."

Joshua drew her closer. "He found you and brought you home." He'd loved her the first time he saw her. He shifted his body, giving her room, and propped his head up on his hand. "Dad didn't want to give you up."

"I know."

"We wouldn't be married now if he hadn't."

"I know." She turned onto her side and ran her fingers through the hair on his chest. "I'm glad he gave me to Peter and Priscilla."

"Mom and Dad."

"Yes." He heard the smile in her voice. "Mom and Dad."

―――――――

Abra woke up early without much memory of the nightmare and no desire to think about it. She'd gone to Dr. Rubenstein a week ago for a pregnancy test. Maybe it was keeping a secret from Joshua that made the nightmare come back. She hadn't mentioned anything because she didn't want to get Joshua's hopes up. She had taken the life of her first child, and she wasn't sure whether God would give her a second chance.

She slipped out of bed carefully, not wanting to awaken Joshua. She went into the bathroom, closed the door quietly, and turned on the shower. God had forgiven her. So had Joshua and so many others. Someday she'd meet her child in heaven. She wasn't going to think about the past. She wasn't going to wonder where she'd come from.

She dried off, dressed, and brushed her hair. It had grown out to her shoulders, as red as it had ever been. She looked like herself again.

She made coffee and turned up the heater so the house would be warm when she awakened Joshua. Drawing the covers off, she admired her husband's body. He was fearfully and wonderfully made. She knelt on the edge of the bed and leaned down to kiss him.

"Time to get up." His eyes were sleep hazy. She kissed him again, lingering this time. He made a sound of pleasure and said she tasted like toothpaste. When he tried to pull her into bed, she pushed his hands away. "Ah, ah, ah . . ." She moved out of reach.

"You started it." He gave her a lazy grin and patted the mattress. "Come back to bed."

"It's Monday morning. You're going to be late for work."

Peering at the clock on the side table, he groaned.

"You can always come home for lunch." Laughing, she headed for the kitchen. "I'll have breakfast on the table by the time you're ready."

They prayed and ate together. He asked what she planned to do with her day. She'd be practicing piano and working on the music she was trying to write. Ian Brubaker would be over later in the afternoon to advise her. Other than that, she had plenty to do in the house and garden.

Joshua gave her a lingering kiss at the door to the garage. "I'll see you at noon."

Abra spent an hour reading Marianne's Bible, then cleaned the kitchen, made the bed, started a load of wash. She debated going outside, afraid she wouldn't be able to hear the telephone or get to it in time. But she had work to do in the garden. She had just opened the glass door when the telephone rang. She ran for it, catching it before the second ring.

"Have you been sitting by the telephone for the last week?" Dr. Rubenstein chuckled.

"Yes or no?"

"The rabbit test said yes. You're pregnant. I'm handing you over to Colleen. She'll set up an appointment for you to come in for a complete checkup. We'll figure out the due date."

"Thank you! Thank you!"

He laughed. "Don't thank me. Thank Joshua." Colleen came on the line and asked if she'd like to come in on Wednesday.

Abra danced around the living room. "Thank You, Jesus. Thank You, Jesus!" She wanted to call Joshua and tell him to come home right now, but thought better of it. She didn't want to tell him the news over the telephone, and he'd think something was wrong if she said she needed him right away. It was ten thirty. She could wait an hour and a half. Couldn't she?

The doorbell rang.

Door-to-door salesmen had been coming by all week. She'd already turned down a vacuum, a selection of Fuller brushes, and Avon cosmetics. She opened the door and gave a start of surprise.

"Susan!" She'd never come by for a visit. "It's nice to see you." Remembering her manners, Abra pushed the screen door open. "Come in, please."

Susan hesitated for a second before crossing the threshold. "I hope I'm not catching you at a bad time."

"It's a perfect time, actually." The joy over the baby just kept bubbling up inside her. A baby! She was going to have a baby! "Can I get you something to drink? Coffee, iced tea?"

"Nothing for me, thank you."

Abra turned in the kitchen doorway and came back. "Are you sure? It's no bother."

She saw the discomfort now, and felt an odd sense of impending doom. "Please. Sit. Be comfortable."

Susan sat on the edge of the sofa. She was trembling.

Abra couldn't imagine why the woman was so nervous. They'd talked many times when she was a high school girl hanging out at the diner. In fact, Susan had helped her make up her mind about Joshua. A thought popped into Abra's head. "Did you come to talk about Dad? Everyone knows how much time he spends with you." No wonder she was nervous. Rumors were rampant. She hoped she could put Susan at ease.

"Everyone has the wrong idea about us." Susan shook her head.

"He's been the best and only real friend I've ever had." She swallowed hard, looking at Abra, and then looking away. "He wanted me to come, but I don't know if I can do this."

"Do what?" Abra leaned closer. Susan became more ashen with every second that passed. Her mouth trembled and her hands clasped so tightly, her knuckles turned white.

Susan shifted on the sofa so she was facing Abra. From the expression on her face, she might have been facing a firing squad. "I'm your mother."

A chill spread over Abra's body. "What?" She couldn't have heard right.

"I'm your mother." Susan repeated it in a matter-of-fact tone, though her eyes betrayed fear. Bowing her head, she rushed on. "There's no excuse for what I did to you."

Abra stood and retreated, heart pounding hard. Her mother? All her life, she had wondered about the woman who had given birth to her under the bridge and left her to die.

But you didn't die, did you? the still, small voice whispered inside her.

Abra put a shaking hand to her forehead, trying to think. Susan Wells? She'd always liked her. How could she have done such a thing?

Do not judge others . . .

Abra clenched her fists. How dare she come into this house? *Why today, of all days? I was so happy . . .* She stopped, remembering why.

The standard you use in judging is the standard by which you will be judged.

The telephone rang.

Susan jerked at the sound. "I'm sorry, Abra. I'm so very, very sorry." She put her hands on the edge of the sofa and started to rise. "That's all I came to say."

"It's not enough!" Abra looked at the telephone and then at Susan. "You're not leaving. You're staying right there." She pointed at the sofa as the telephone rang again and again, demanding to be answered. "You came and you're not going until you tell me *why!*"

The telephone kept ringing.

"You can't drop an atomic bomb on me and then just walk out the door! I won't let you!"

Susan sank, shoulders hunched. When the telephone finally stopped, the room echoed silence.

Minutes passed. Abra clenched her fists and fought not to cry. When she finally had reasonable control, she spoke, her voice constricted with hurt. "Just tell me *why?*"

Susan didn't raise her head. "I've asked myself that question a million times. Anger. Fear. Shame." Her hands clutched her knees. "Guilt."

"And you thought leaving a newborn baby under a bridge would make things better?" As soon as the words came out, Abra felt a sharp pang of guilt and heard the whisper in her mind again. What right had she to judge? Hadn't she done worse? She put shaking hands to her head.

"I'm sorry, Abra. I shouldn't have come."

"Maybe you shouldn't have, but it's too late now. Isn't it?" Abra felt like she was choking. She heard the screech of tires down the street. She glared at Susan through tear-filled eyes. "Why did you have to bring up the past?" She thought of Franklin and all his arguments against having a baby. She thought of riding through the night with him. She remembered the woman waiting in the back room of a shack in the coastal hills. She choked on a sob, and the look on Susan's face mirrored what she felt.

The front door opened.

Joshua hurried in, worried something had happened to Abra. He'd had a bad feeling all morning and called home, but she didn't answer the phone. He saw her standing in the living room, distraught, and knew something was wrong. He didn't even notice that there was someone else in the room until he had reached Abra's side.

"Susan?" He looked from her to Abra again. "What's going on?"

Abra pointed an accusing finger. "She's my mother." She wrapped her arms around herself.

Blushing, shaking, Susan stood. "I'm sorry." All the color receded. "I'll go. This was a mistake."

Abra took a step toward her and spoke in a fury of hurt. "You mean *I* was a mistake."

"No." Tears welled and spilled down Susan's pale cheeks. "No!"

Joshua could feel the enemy in the room with them right now, and the enemy wasn't Susan Wells. He saw Abra's pain and anger, her confusion, and he saw Susan's fear and misery. She was clearly ready to run, and if she did, Joshua knew she'd never look back. She'd just keep running, alone, into the wilderness.

"Please sit down, Susan." Joshua gestured a welcome. Lips parting, Abra stared at him. He went to her and put his arm around her. "Let's talk this over. Please." He could feel Abra shaking. Shock or fury? Her body felt cold. He rubbed her arms and spoke gently. "You've been dreaming about her again. Remember? You need to find out what happened."

Abra leaned into Joshua for support and let him do the talking. He asked Susan to tell them everything.

Susan's voice was soft, broken. "I was seventeen and thought I knew everything. My parents warned me about the young man I was seeing, but I wouldn't listen. When I got pregnant, he wouldn't have anything to do with me. I'd been such a fool. I managed to hide my pregnancy until the end. And then the pains started. I was so scared and ashamed. I didn't know what to do. I took the keys to my father's car and just started to drive. I didn't know where I was going. I just wanted to get away, far away. I passed the turnoff to the coast and then thought about turning around and going back. I thought maybe I could drive off a cliff into the ocean and no one would ever know what happened to me or what I'd done. But the pains were so bad by then. I pulled off the main road. I saw Riverfront Park and stopped. It was so dark . . .

"I can remember it like it was yesterday. I can still hear the crickets in the grass. There was a full moon. I didn't know what to do, but I had to get out of the car. My contractions were coming faster and faster. I thought maybe I could find shelter, someplace hidden. I tried the ladies' room, but it was locked. I wished I had stopped sooner, checked into a motel, but it was too late.

"I was so afraid that someone would hear me. And I'd felt such hope when I found out I was expecting you. My boyfriend had said he loved me. He'd said if I really loved him, I'd give myself to him, and I did—heart, mind, body, and soul. Then when I told him I was pregnant, he didn't even believe the child was his. If I gave myself to him, I'd probably given myself to others. He said, 'Why should I believe you? It's your problem, not mine.' He dropped me off at my parents' house and never came back. I was such a fool.

"Somehow, I managed to reach the shadows beneath the bridge. I knew no one would see me there. The sound of the river would muffle my groans, and there would be water to wash with when it was all done. When you were born, you were so quiet, I thought you were dead. And to be honest, I thought it was for the best. You lay there, so pale and perfect on a dark blanket of earth. It was too dark to see whether you were a boy or girl. I pulled off my sweater and laid it over you. I didn't know where I was going to go, but I had to get out of there. I knew I would never be free of guilt and regret. I never deserve to be. I was planning to find some place to kill myself. But in the end, I didn't even have the courage to do that."

Abra bent over, putting her hands over her head, not wanting to hear any more. Joshua told Susan to go on. When Abra looked up at him, she saw he understood. She had told him everything, hadn't she? She had confessed the worst of what she'd done back in Agua Dulce, and he still loved her. Susan's words sounded like her own.

Seventeen . . . thought I knew everything . . . Everyone warned me . . . I was a fool. Like mother, like daughter. Abra wept. Her nose ran. Joshua got up and came back with two handkerchiefs, one for her and one for Susan, who sat sobbing a few feet away.

"It's going to be all right." He was talking to both of them.

Was it?

Gulping down tears, Abra looked at Susan and saw her own anguish mirrored there. "Who was my father?"

Susan clutched the handkerchief in both hands. "No one you should ever know." Susan lifted her head and looked at Abra sadly. "He was handsome, charismatic, and spoiled. He came from a wealthy family and thought he owned the world. I wasn't the first or last girl he used and threw away."

"That's why you warned me about Dylan."

"I tried." Susan's eyes were full of regret. "I knew what that boy was the minute he walked in the diner."

"And I wouldn't listen." She studied Susan's face and searched for similarities. "Do I look like my father?"

"Not at all." Susan's voice turned wistful. "You look like my mother, actually. She had red hair. But you have my hands." She held hers out so Abra could see the long fingers, the shape of her nails.

Abra leaned back against Joshua, taking comfort in his solid support, his warmth. She looked into Susan's eyes and felt her pain. Twenty-three years of it. "Did you go home after that night?"

"After a few days in a cheap motel. I never told my parents what I'd done, but they knew something had happened. I wasn't the same after that night. I did finally try to commit suicide, but my mother found me. I went back to school, but I couldn't concentrate. I got a job as a waitress down at Fisherman's Wharf."

"I was a waitress in Agua Dulce."

Susan smiled faintly. "I know. Zeke told me."

They looked at each other, really looked. She'd always wondered who her mother was. She understood now why Susan had paid such attention to her when she came into Bessie's, why she sought her out and spoke to her, why she'd been so adamant about grabbing love and hanging on to it.

"I cried all day after you were born. I knew I had to go back, but I saw a newspaper the next morning outside the motel. The headline said a pastor found an abandoned baby in Riverfront Park. I thanked God you survived. You were in good hands. I knew you'd be all right. I thought I could forget."

"But you couldn't." Abra knew how that felt.

"No. I couldn't."

Joshua filled the silence. "Can we meet your parents?"

"They've both passed on. An automobile accident. I moved around a lot after that. I have pictures of them, if you'd like to have them."

"Please."

"I'll make sure you get them." Susan's eyes remained full of pain. "I couldn't stop thinking about you and wondering. That's why I came back to Haven, to find out what happened to you. You hear everything at Bessie's." She glanced at Joshua. "I heard all about Marianne Freeman. She must have been a wonderful lady." She turned her focus back to Abra. "Peter and Priscilla had adopted you. They wanted you from the beginning. Bessie talks a lot—kindly, of course. She knows about everybody." She gave a faint, sad smile. "Well, almost everybody. She doesn't know about me." She focused on Abra. "You spent a lot of time there. When you ran away with that boy, I kept praying you'd come back."

So much made sense now. "You always seemed interested in what I had to say."

"I was. Very interested."

"Dad knew, didn't he?" Joshua sounded certain.

Susan's smile was pained and self-deprecating. "I told him a few years ago, but he already knew." She flexed her fingers. "Maybe it was my hands that gave me away. Zeke said God just opened his eyes."

Abra's eyes filled. She knew what he meant. She looked at her mother and saw herself.

Susan sighed. "I know it's too much to ask you to forgive me, but I thought you had the right to know." She stood. "Thanks for hearing me out." She headed for the front door.

Abra stood quickly. She felt the tears welling again. "I know it wasn't easy for you to come here, Susan."

She paused. "I never thought I would, but Zeke wouldn't give up." She opened the door. "I'll be leaving soon."

It seemed a shock to meet her mother and then know this might be the last time she ever saw her. Abra felt Joshua's hands gentle on her shoulders. "Where will you go?"

Susan shrugged. "Someplace where I can start over."

Abra thought of the night Joshua had brought her back to Haven. Dad had been standing on the bridge. It almost seemed as though he'd been waiting there the entire time she'd been gone. When she got out of the truck, he met her more than halfway and embraced her. He forgave her before she'd even confessed. He'd never stopped loving her. She thought of Joshua and how long he'd waited for her to grow up, how much he'd forgiven. Everyone in town knew Dad loved Susan. They just didn't realize how much.

Susan seemed so lost. She went out the door.

Abra heard God's whisper. The choice was hers. It always had been. She went outside. "Susan, wait." She stepped away from Joshua, praying God would give her the words. She caught up with Susan halfway to the sidewalk. When Susan turned, Abra took her hands. "I do forgive you."

"Thank you." She gave Abra's hands a gentle squeeze.

"Don't go."

Susan's shoulders drooped. "I have to."

"But you've already started over. You don't have to do it again."

Susan stood for a moment, considering her words, and then slipped her hands from Abra's. "I'm glad I got to know you. You are a remarkable young woman." Her eyes filled with tears. "Good-bye, Abra." She went around her old Chevy and got into the driver's seat.

Abra looked back at Joshua beseechingly. He shook his head, but came out to stand beside her. Abra kept hoping, but Susan drove away without a backward glance. "At least I know."

Joshua stood behind her, arms around her waist. He rubbed his chin on the top of her head.

Abra felt the weight of the past lift, the chaff fluttering away. Joshua knew everything about her. He'd known the wrath that had dwelled in her from infancy, the willfulness, the self-righteousness. And he loved her anyway. What happened to change her? *"God lives in you now,"* Dad had said when they told him Joshua had baptized her at Riverfront Park. *"You've become His temple."* Without her even realizing what was happening, the Holy Spirit had begun the work of transformation. How else could a lifetime of hate be washed away by forgiveness in the space of a few minutes?

She let out her breath. "God will never cease to amaze me."

Joshua let her go and turned to head back inside. "I'd better call Jack and let him know the house didn't burn down and you're not in the hospital."

Hospital.

Dr. Rubenstein.

The baby!

"Joshua. When you're off the phone, I have something to tell you."

Zeke knew by the sound of Joshua's excited voice what news he had to impart. "So I'm going to be a grandpa."

"Yes, sir. In five or six months. We'll know more on Wednesday after we see Dr. Rubenstein." Zeke heard Abra saying something in the background. Joshua laughed. "Abra is already talking about repainting one of the other bedrooms. Green or peach, something that will go with a boy or girl. She'll probably want to go out and look for a bassinet tomorrow."

"It's good to be prepared."

"Speaking of being prepared, Susan Wells came over. I guess you know why."

Thank God. "She told Abra she's her mother."

"Yes, she did." His tone changed. "I had this odd feeling something was wrong all morning and called. When Abra didn't answer, I came home and there they were in the living room, and I could feel the devil ready to have a field day. It wasn't my battle to fight, but I prayed."

"How did Abra take the news?"

"She was in shock and ready to explode at first, and then she cried through most of what Susan said. I don't think either of them expected Abra to forgive her, but that's what happened."

"Thank God." Zeke felt joy well up inside him. Forgiveness was evidence of a life surrendered to God.

"Amen. Too bad Susan is leaving town."

"Is that what she said?"

"Abra tried to talk her out of it. I don't know how far she got with that."

"Time will tell."

After hanging up the telephone, Zeke got his jacket and cap from the hook and walked downtown to Bessie's. When he came around the corner, he looked through the window. Bessie stood behind the counter. The bell jangled as he walked in and she glanced up.

When he looked toward the kitchen doors, she shook her head. "If you're looking for Susan, she's not here. She came in a little while ago and quit. Just like that. You could've knocked me over with a feather. I thought she liked it here." She took an envelope out of her pocket. "She left this for you."

Heart sinking, Zeke opened it and read the brief letter. Folding it, he put it back into the envelope and tucked it in his shirt pocket.

"What'd she say?"

"'Thank you.'" All her other words were for his eyes only.

———

The old hoot owl in the backyard pine tree awakened Zeke. It wasn't yet three, but he got up anyway. After dressing quickly in the dark, he put on his jacket and St. Louis Cardinals cap and set out. He'd dreamed about Susan last night. They'd been sitting in Bessie's Corner Café again, talking about the Lord as they always did, when Marianne came through the door. She smiled and joined them at the counter. Zeke fell silent and let the two women talk. Marianne had always known when to speak and what to say when someone was hurting, though he couldn't remember any of her words now that he was awake.

And Susan was still gone. It had been a month and no word or sight of her. *She's out there in the wilderness, Lord. She's in danger again and hurting.*

Zeke felt the response inside his heart, God whispering quiet words of comfort. Susan wasn't lost; she was on her own journey. When Abra left, Joshua suffered horribly, and Zeke had told his son to let go and trust in the Lord. Now Zeke had to take his own advice. God knew where Susan was and what it would take before she would be able to surrender, to give up her life, and to experience the resurrection power Jesus offered. Susan could run to the ends of the earth and still never be out of the sight or loving care of God. Nor would she be out of the reach of Zeke's prayers. Each one he offered would bring Susan before the throne of the omniscient, omnipresent, omnipotent God. The Lord would have His way with her, whether it was in Haven or Timbuktu. How many years might pass before she understood that?

Still, Zeke's heart ached. The enemy had a stronghold in Susan.

Hands tucked in his jacket pockets, Zeke strolled along his street past the homes of friends and neighbors. It had been years since Joshua mowed lawns for the Weirs and McKennas.

As Zeke wound his way through the neighborhoods, he prayed. Penny, Rob, and Paige were doing well. Another baby was on the way. He chuckled. Would the child be a Paul or Pauline this time?

He kept walking and giving thanks for answered prayers.

Dutch and Marjorie were opening their home for a Wednesday evening Bible study.

Gil and Sadie MacPherson came into town to attend it and spread the word that Dutch was a pretty good teacher.

Mitzi had bounced back after a long bout of pneumonia and was now ensconced at the Shady Glen residential care facility, much to Hodge and Carla's relief. Mitzi had bucked them in the beginning. She said she didn't like feeling as though she had one foot in the grave and the other on a banana peel. She was making waves as well as friends. She had announced on arrival that if anyone thought she was going to play bingo or put puzzles together for the rest of her life, they had better think again. They had a piano and she was going to play it. The staff didn't mind one bit. "They like ragtime in the morning and hymns in the evening. Like reveille and taps," Mitzi quipped. "Get us old fogies up and moving in the morning and then ready to meet our Maker before bed at night."

Zeke passed by Good Samaritan Hospital and prayed for the staff and patients. Dr. Rubenstein, nearing retirement, had taken his nephew Hiram as a partner. The young man was fresh from residency at Johns Hopkins and gifted enough to choose where he would practice. Zeke remembered how Doc shook his head when he told him about it. "I tried to talk him out of it, but he says he wants to be here." Hiram Cohen wanted to follow in his favorite uncle's footsteps and be a small-town GP. "My sister had loftier ambitions for him, but the boy has a mind of his own. She says she'll forgive me if I can find him a nice Jewish wife."

The police station lights were on. Jim Helgerson came through the door. Zeke stopped. "You're on duty awfully early, Jim."

"Comes with being a small-town chief of police letting his deputy go on vacation. Got a call and caught a young hooligan painting graffiti on the back of the train station. He's none too happy in lockup, but it might make him come to his senses. His parents are at their wits' end. I'm going to swing by Eddie's and see if he's still up to taking on a new project."

Zeke smiled. "Eddie never says no."

Heading back into the center of town, Zeke passed Brady Studebaker's sign shop. Sally and Brady were expecting their first child. Haven seemed to be having a population explosion. Penny and Rob's, Sally and Brady's, and Joshua and Abra's children would be growing up together.

The lights were already on in the Corner Café. Bessie and Oliver sat in a front booth, sharing a cup of coffee and talking before their day started. The Help Wanted sign was still taped in the window. They hadn't yet found anyone to replace Susan.

Feeling a nudge, Zeke headed for the bridge into Haven. When sorrow came in crashing waves, the peace of the river soothed his troubled heart. There was something about listening to the movement of living water.

He stopped in the middle of the bridge and leaned his forearms on the railing, listening to the ripple below. He remembered the night he found Abra, and grieved for the mother on the run again. Clasping his hands loosely, he bowed his head and prayed. *Bring her home, Lord.*

All in good time.

He could almost hear Marianne singing a beautiful hymn that had come out of great loss. Closing his eyes, he spoke the words softly. "'It is well with my soul.'" Somehow, saying the words aloud brought peace. He lifted his head and listened again. He wasn't alone.

Over the years, Zeke had witnessed many miracles. He knew he could expect more. Other words came, unwritten, but straight from his heart. He straightened as he sang them now for his Lord. A song of hope, a song of thanksgiving for all that had happened and was yet to come. His voice moved across the water and rose like the first hint of dawn on the horizon.

Words of love for his people, his children, the flock God had given him to shepherd. Oh, how he loved them. They made him laugh. They made him weep. They made his heart swell with love and break in grief. Ah, but he wanted nothing more than to be what Jesus called him to be—a bond servant for the living God, a spokesman for the Good News. He spread his hands as though over his flock in blessing and let his voice rise with the words God gave him. And as he obeyed the impulse, the darkness receded.

A light came on inside a house overlooking the river, then another, and another.

As Zeke fell silent and his arms lowered to his sides again, he renewed his promise. *I will sing over them with thanksgiving every day of my life, Lord. In Your strength, I will love them with all my heart and soul. Always.*

As will I.

Heart full, Zeke tucked his hands into his jacket pockets. He stood a moment longer, savoring the assurance that all was well. Then he crossed the bridge into Haven, ready for whatever the new day would bring.

A NOTE FROM THE AUTHOR

DEAR READERS,

The inspiration for *Bridge to Haven* came from Ezekiel 16, where God speaks of His chosen people as an unwanted newborn whom He cared for, watched over, and eventually chose as His bride, despite their rejection of Him. The story spoke profoundly to me, one who grew up in a Christian home and then abandoned what I had been taught. I set off on my own way, squandering the gifts God had given me. That quest brought its own consequences of pain and regret, but the repercussions eventually brought me to my knees, where I surrendered to the Lord who loved me through it all.

I have struggled in writing this book. I wanted Pastor Zeke to reflect the character of God, but I came to realize no man, not even a fictional one, can do that. Only Jesus, God incarnate, is a true representation. Zeke needed to be a loving father, fully human with strengths and weaknesses, faults and failures. The same was true of Joshua, the son, who strives to be like Jesus. Abra is like so many of us: wounded, confused, pursuing happiness by chasing after things that never truly satisfy. Few of my friends came to faith easily. I myself struggled and fought against the Lord, believing that to surrender would be to admit defeat. It took a long time for me to open my fist. But when I finally did, He was waiting for me, and He took my hand. He has never let go, and I've been in love with Him ever since.

My prayer is that the story of Zeke, Joshua, and Abra will draw you into a closer relationship with the God who sent His only Son, Jesus, to die for you so that you might live forever in Him. Our dreams of happiness are fulfilled only in Him.

May you step out in faith and cross the bridge to the haven of rest God provides.

Francine Rivers

DISCUSSION GUIDE

1. The bridge to Haven figures prominently in the story: Abra is born—and abandoned—under the bridge. Pastor Zeke finds her there. Abra crosses over the bridge to leave, and later to return. Joshua brings her as far as the bridge, and Zeke is waiting for her there, but Abra has to decide to cross the bridge herself. Eventually she is baptized under the bridge. Discuss the symbolism of the bridge to Haven. Who—or what—is the bridge? What are some bridges in your own life? Are you eager or reluctant to cross them? Why?

2. Pastor Zeke gives in to Marianne's pleas to take the infant Abra home, even though he knows it's dangerous. Do you think he made the right choice? Why or why not? Do you believe it's important to distinguish between God's leading and our own desires? If you do think it's important, what are some ways we can do so?

3. Peter and Priscilla Matthews want to adopt Abra from the start. Why do you think they are prepared to love this abandoned baby? In what ways do they show their love for Abra, both as a child and as a rebellious young woman? What mistakes do they make? Is there someone in your life who causes you the kind of heartache Abra caused her adoptive family? How have you have coped with that relationship?

4. After Peter and Priscilla adopt Abra, she watches Zeke from her bedroom window and prays that God will give her back to him. Convinced that God has refused to answer her prayer, she turns her back on Him for many years. How and when is her prayer eventually answered? What prayers or dreams in your life have seemed to go unfulfilled, maybe for years, before finally becoming reality? What prayers or dreams are you still waiting to see fulfilled?

5. Mitzi is a stable force in Abra's life, a loving friend who is always honest with her. Did you have a mentor like that when you were growing up, or do you have one now? If so, what is the most important thing your mentor taught you? Is there someone in your life—a child or a young adult—for whom you can be a godly mentor? What would that involve?

6. Joshua, a man of peace, is deeply scarred by his experiences in the Korean War. Today we would call his condition PTSD. How does his emotional state affect him when he returns home? How does it impact his relationship with his father? With Abra? Is there someone in your life who struggles with PTSD? What are some of the ways we can help people in this situation?

7. As soon as he meets Dylan Stark, Joshua sees him for what he is. But he isn't able to persuade Abra to stay away from him. Could Joshua—or Zeke or Priscilla or Peter—have done something different that would have been more effective? Have you ever seen a loved one heading down a path you didn't agree with? How did you handle it?

8. Part of Abra's reluctance to return home, even once she realizes that running away was a mistake, is her fear of what people will say. Do you think her fears are founded? Has there been a time in your life when you struggled to make the right choice for fear

of how other people would react? How did you handle it? What advice would you give to a young person in Abra's situation?

9. As a teenager, Abra tells Joshua, "I can't remember a time when I haven't felt like I wasn't enough." Why do you think she feels this way, when she is surrounded by people like Pastor Zeke, Joshua, Mitzi, and the Matthews family—all people who love her? What is missing? Have you ever felt this way? How have you tried to fill that need in your own life?

10. After Abra runs away, Joshua feels the need to pursue her. But Zeke repeatedly tells him that maybe the best thing he can do is let go of her. Did you agree with Zeke's advice? Have you ever had to let go of someone or something—like a dream? What was the result? How do you know when it's time to keep pursuing something or time to let go?

11. Franklin Moss asks Abra what she wants, and she says she wants to be "somebody." What do you think she means? Why does she feel that way? What kinds of things does she think will help her achieve her goal? What do these things really end up giving— or costing—her? In what ways have you, or someone you love, chased after things you think will satisfy you? In what ways were those things fulfilling? In what ways did they leave you empty and wounded?

12. Is Abra to blame for Franklin's suicide? If she had not left the note for him, do you think things would have turned out differently? Are there things you have wished you could take back after you saw the effect they had on someone else?

13. As Joshua points out, it seems providential that both he and Abra end up in Agua Dulce at the same time. Can you point to an instance in your life like that—something that was so

coincidental you couldn't help but see the hand of God at work? Why is it easier to see God's hand in our lives in retrospect than to trust that He's leading us in any given moment?

14. When Abra reads the Gideon Bible in her motel room at Agua Dulce, she seems able to focus only on the verses that confirm her guilt and sin. If you could sit down and talk with her at that moment, what would you tell her?

15. When Joshua brings Abra home to Haven, Zeke is praying on the bridge, almost as if he is waiting for her. How did that scene make you feel? Have you ever experienced a similar situation, either in Abra's or Zeke's position?

16. Joshua is the only man who has ever loved and desired Abra as God intends for a man to love and desire a woman. What are some examples that show how his love is different from the ways Dylan and Franklin felt about her? Are there people in your life who love you in a godly way? Are you able to love others like this?

17. What do you imagine will happen to Susan Wells after the conclusion of the story? Do you think her life will be different when she starts over somewhere else? Should she have stayed in Haven? Why or why not?

18. Each of the main characters in the book has a unique struggle: Zeke has to give Abra away; Joshua has to let Abra go; and Abra has to decide whether to return. Which character do you most identify with? Why?

ABOUT THE AUTHOR

New York Times bestselling author Francine Rivers began her literary career at the University of Nevada, Reno, where she graduated with a bachelor of arts degree in English and journalism. From 1976 to 1985, she had a successful writing career in the general market, and her books were highly acclaimed by readers and reviewers. Although raised in a religious home, Francine did not truly encounter Christ until later in life, when she was already a wife, a mother of three, and an established romance novelist.

Shortly after becoming a born-again Christian in 1986, Francine wrote *Redeeming Love* as her statement of faith. First published by Bantam Books and then rereleased by Multnomah Publishers in the mid-1990s, this retelling of the biblical story of Gomer and Hosea, set during the time of the California Gold Rush, is now considered by many to be a classic work of Christian fiction. *Redeeming Love* continues to be one of CBA's top-selling titles, and it has held a spot on the Christian bestseller list for more than a decade.

Since *Redeeming Love*, Francine has published numerous novels with Christian themes—all bestsellers—and she has continued to win both industry acclaim and reader loyalty around the globe. Her Christian novels have been awarded or nominated for numerous honors, including the RITA Award, the Christy Award, the ECPA Gold Medallion, and the Holt Medallion in Honor of Outstanding Literary Talent. In 1997, after winning her third RITA Award for inspirational fiction, Francine was inducted into the Romance Writers of America Hall of Fame. Francine's novels have been translated into more than twenty different languages, and she enjoys bestseller status in many foreign countries, including Germany, the Netherlands, and South Africa.

Francine and her husband, Rick, live in northern California and enjoy time spent with their three grown children and taking every opportunity to spoil their grandchildren. Francine uses her writing to draw closer to the Lord, and she desires that through her work she might worship and praise Jesus for all He has done and is doing in her life.

Visit her website at www.francinerivers.com.

Books by beloved author
Francine Rivers

The Mark of the Lion series
(available individually or in a collection)
- *A Voice in the Wind*
- *An Echo in the Darkness*
- *As Sure as the Dawn*

A Lineage of Grace series
(available individually or in an anthology)
- *Unveiled*
- *Unashamed*
- *Unshaken*
- *Unspoken*
- *Unafraid*

Sons of Encouragement series
(available individually or in an anthology)
- *The Priest*
- *The Warrior*
- *The Prince*
- *The Prophet*
- *The Scribe*

Marta's Legacy series
(available individually or in a collection)
- *Her Mother's Hope*
- *Her Daughter's Dream*

Stand-Alone Titles
- *Bridge to Haven*
- *Redeeming Love*
- *The Atonement Child*
- *The Scarlet Thread*
- *The Last Sin Eater*
- *Leota's Garden*
- *And the Shofar Blew*
- *The Shoe Box* (a Christmas novella)

Children's Titles
- *Bible Stories for Growing Kids*
  (coauthored with Shannon
  Rivers Coibion)

www.francinerivers.com

CP0098

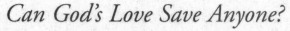
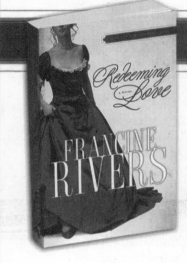

Check out Francine's website and
blog at www.francinerivers.com,
and visit her on Facebook at
www.facebook.com/FrancineRivers.